Carbon II
Redemption

Written by:
Carrie Yonge

Cover Art & Design: Caitlin Hartigan

Editors: Carrie Yonge, Ellen Reynolds

ISBN: 978-0-578-12715-6

"Those who sow in tears shall reap in joy."
Psalm 126: 5

Introduction

There is part of Elise in all of us. In this book, we find she is not as perfect as our beloved heroines and figures of lore. A little selfish, a bit cowardly, wholly needy and dependent, forgetful and weak. I encourage you to not despise these characteristics in her. Instead, as you read this story, permit yourself to see where her weaknesses are not so different from your own. May we have courage to face those things in us that are unpleasant, unpresentable, and undesirable, but which must be faced to be overcome. And may we take heart that there is indeed redemption.

Prologue

This was the moment FBI Agent Alan Stewart had been waiting for, and yet it took him completely by surprise. Sequestered in a cramped room at headquarters, he was looking over the shoulders of two tech guys to monitor the myriad of screens on the wall. Each one was a live feed from his agents on the ground in Colorado, where a massive blast had just blinded two of the cameras.

"What the…" he whispered under his breath in shock. But as suddenly as the night vision cameras went dark, each one cut off to static.

"Talk to me, guys. What's going on?"

The tech team worked furiously on their keyboards, too engrossed in their work to pay attention.

"We lost it!" one yelled tersely at the other. "What happened?"

"I don't know, all signals are gone. I've got nothing!"

Stewart cursed under his breath and used his radio. "Echo, India, Romeo, respond. Come in. Does anybody read me?"

But static was the only answer. He grabbed his satellite phone and dialed each number with no success.

"Sir," one of the men was looking at him. "We lost all communication, and it's not on this end. The equipment was either destroyed, or there was an EMP burst of some kind."

"Get me eyes in the sky now. We need to see down there." Stewart's expression remained calm, and he could feel the pressure shift into detached focus.

"Yes, sir," the man turned back to his computer. "The next satellite will be in position in fourteen minutes, but it's CIA."

Without hesitation, Stewart grabbed the secure landline off the wall. Whatever was going on down there, every minute was costing them response time. He only hoped his team had been adequately prepared. And that they weren't in that structure when it blew.

Chapter 1

Thu-dum, thu-dum, thu-dum.

Drumbeats sounded steadily, loudly inside her head. Elise exhaled slowly to minimize the movement of breathing.

It was pounding. Incessantly.

She reached and slipped the washcloth off of her forehead and into the steaming bath water. Once it was satisfactorily warm again, she replaced it, keeping her ears under water through the whole process.

Thu-dum, thu-dum, thu-dum.

The water muffled her heartbeats, a gracious relief to the angry force behind her skull. She had been lying like this nearly twenty minutes. The hot water was a temporary comfort from the coldness that had coiled up inside her body, but it was growing cool again as the heat escaped.

"Sweetheart, are you done in there?" Mrs. Allen's voice rang out from behind the closed door.

Elise cringed. Any input, sound or image, exacerbated the pain. She squeezed her eyes shut and pulled the washcloth over her whole face for a moment.

"Elise? Are you okay?"

"Mm-hm," she managed to groan in response.

"Just checking, sweetie. The fire's burning nice and hot, and I brought some extra blankets here for you."

Elise gave no response, and there was a pause before footsteps echoed down the hallway as Mrs. Allen left.

* * * *

The days blended together, and she had no concept of how much time had passed, or how many days she had spent unconscious. And because of the wracking pain, it really made no difference.

She had vague recollections of being in bed, of Mr. and Mrs. Allen introducing themselves, a farmhand they called Jesse, and the same deputy from Rayford's. But they were all overshadowed by the constant agony in her body. Whatever the passage of time was, the pain had gradually worn into heavy fatigue and sluggishness. A dull headache remained, but Elise was only grateful it was bearable.

She could see from her bed that it was day behind the heavy drapes pulled over the window. Voices rose up from somewhere beneath her, and suddenly she was overtaken by the desire to not be alone. Wincing with the effort, she slid out from under the pile of warm blankets Mrs. Allen had provided. They had also given her thick pajamas and a bathrobe that was lying on the dresser. Shrugging it on, she shuffled down the hallway blinking in the light.

Her insides felt like they had become a permanent winter, and she leaned heavily against the wooden railing as she trudged her way down. She had not been very alert during her stay, but still managed to ascertain a basic layout of this house. A homely mountain cabin, it had several bedrooms on the second story and the basic house on the lower floor.

The voices were coming from the snug little dining room, but they all fell silent as she stumbled in.

"Elise!" Mr. Allen jumped up to greet her. "Here," he pulled another chair around the table and guided her into it. "How are you feeling?"

She yawned inadvertently and hugged her bathrobe tight. She nodded and mumbled, "Good."

Mrs. Allen got up and gave her a hug. "We're glad to see you up. Let me get you something warm to drink. Would you like some tea or coffee?"

Elise fought to focus on the woman's face. She was so tired. "Tea is fine, thanks."

"Of course," Mrs. Allen instantly disappeared into the kitchen, humming a little tune.

Staring at the wooden table, Elise felt she should say something more, but the effort of coming up with and processing words was far too great.

"Ruth!" Mr. Allen called into the kitchen. "Can you get me some more coffee while you're in there?"

"Patience, dear. After I fix Elise's tea, I'll refill your mug." Her voice rang out from the other room. "If you're in a hurry, you can come get it yourself, you know."

"Who said anything about a hurry?"

Mrs. Allen didn't respond but continued humming. If Elise had not been so exhausted, the silence would have been awkward. But in her present state, she was content to sit in a daze, not thinking of anything at all.

Soon a steaming mug appeared in front of her. "There you are, sweetie." With a purposeful look at her husband, Mrs. Allen collected his mug off the table. "Shane, would you like another cup also?"

"Thanks, but I'm good."

Elise had not noticed the third person sitting there, and even now she could only afford a brief glance to confirm the deputy's presence. A reminder that she didn't know how she got here, much less why she was here. But as her ability to think and reason was just now returning, she was afraid it would be impossible to follow or make sense of any explanation. And so her questions hadn't yet been voiced. Give it time, the Allens had recommended.

"The weather is beautiful outside today. I'd be glad to take you on a little walk, it might help clear your head." Mr. Allen was regarding her kindly. "We don't have to go far. It's pretty warm too."

That did sound better than sitting in here doing nothing. Even in her fatigued condition, it was boring to sit in the same room forever.

She took a sip of her tea, allowing the warmth to spread through her chest. "Okay. Thanks."

"Let her finish her tea first," Mrs. Allen was returning with a brimming cup of coffee.

"Of course. Take your time."

Suddenly the door burst open, and after a bout of boot stomping, Jesse appeared in the doorway. "Hey, look who's up!"

Elise offered a half-smile; it was the best she could muster. Jesse seemed to be in his late twenties, maybe early thirties. With shaggy blonde hair and a classic cowboy hat, he looked every part of the farmhand title he claimed.

"Shane, can you give me a hand out here? We've got some fences that could really use repair and with this perfect weather, we can't waste a day like this."

The deputy shrugged, "Sure. Thanks for breakfast, Mrs. Allen."

"Of course."

"We should only be a few hours," Jesse added as the two headed outside.

Mr. Allen set his mug down after a swallow, "Okay. I might join you guys in a little bit. You workin' by the south side?"

"Yep," Jesse called over his shoulder.

Elise took another sip of her tea as Mrs. Allen took a seat across from her. The older woman looked at her with concern, "Do you feel up to eating something yet?"

It had been really hard to keep any food down, but it did seem like the nausea was lessening. "Maybe something small."

Soon she found herself with several small packets of crackers in her pockets, and a promise from Mrs. Allen to make chicken soup for dinner.

Her tea mug empty, Mr. Allen helped her don a heavy winter jacket and some wool socks and boots. "It might be warm today, but this is still Montana and we can't risk you getting the chills again."

She had to lean heavily on his arm to make it off the front porch. A breeze of crisp air blew over her face, and despite the exertion the bright daylight was refreshing. She found each step easier until she could walk – albeit a little wobbly – without Mr. Allen's support.

"How do you like it out here?" he asked.

"It's beautiful." Tears came to Elise's eyes unbidden. Feeling so weak left her emotions beyond her control. She felt silly, but maybe it was for the better anyway. "Is there somewhere I can just sit out here?"

"Mmm. I know just the place."

They turned around and headed back toward the house, and to her surprise he helped her into his truck. The house overlooked a wide prairie, but Mr. Allen headed the opposite direction, past the large barn in the back and onto a road that didn't appear to see much use.

The tears that had stopped in Elise's throat stayed there, and the silent drive began to melt the numbness and indifference.

In fifteen minutes they reached a clearing with a smaller barn and Mr. Allen parked next to the aging structure. "The view is beautiful here," he commented as he cut the motor.

True enough, the old wooden building faced a meadow of tall prairie grass swaying gracefully in the breeze. A stream was running somewhere nearby, and the proud mountains in the distance seemed to continue on forever, crisscrossing each other in alternating shades of green. Beautiful, but untouched. Surely he didn't mean to leave her here alone.

He helped her out of the truck in silence, leaving her to lean against the tailgate as he unlocked the barn's heavy wooden doors. After sliding each out of the way in turn, he motioned for her to join him at the entrance. "There's a fridge and a pantry inside if you need anything. Be sure to keep everything under the bear cover."

Bears? She would be an easy snack in her current defenselessness. But when she stumbled across to peer inside, she understood. The tears came back, and she couldn't stop one from sliding down her cheek.

"Elise," Mr. Allen took hold of her shoulders and tilted her chin to look into her eyes. "You have every right to cry. Don't be ashamed. Just let it out."

With a final gentle pat on her cheek, he walked back to his truck. The diesel engine rumbled to life and she listened to it become a distant echo as he drove away.

For many moments Elise couldn't find any words to say. She slid down against the front of the barn and stared at the lovely wilderness. Tears continued to stream down her face, and she simply sat, overwhelmed. No specific memories came back, but the emotions all returned. They made no sense, but she was far too tired to fight.

"I am glad to see you feeling better, Elise."

But she couldn't speak. Ducking her head between her legs, she allowed the sobs to come. The fear, the anger, the hurt and confusion flowed out as her chest heaved in contractions. Her cries were swallowed by the valley before them, and she didn't have the strength to cry for long.

She closed her eyes, enjoying the feel of fresh air against her face, the breath filling her lungs. Leaning against the old wood, she relished the feeling of freedom. And safety.

Mr. Allen was right. Being out here was just what she needed. But she still couldn't think to say anything coherent, and it wasn't for lack of things to say. Just the opposite; there was simply too much to even consider speaking. She didn't know where to start.

She was growing hungry, and retrieving one of the crackers from her pocket, she fully appreciated each bite. Finally a simple question came to mind. "How long has it been?"

"Five days."

Elise exhaled slowly. She had lost all concept of time, but that seemed to fit. Remembering what happened at Rayford's and what had happened in the days before was still a little fuzzy, but she was fine with it that way. Right now she felt relieved and comfortable. The last thing she wanted was to spend too much time focusing on why.

"If you are cold, you may sit inside."

"Thanks, Carbon. But this is fine."

Leaning her head back to take in the gorgeous blue sky, Elise sat and simply rested in the peaceful quiet.

Chapter 2

"Good morning, Alan."

Agent Stewart glanced up from his desk as a short, balding man near sixty walked in and offered his hand. He blinked in surprise, "Richardson?"

The shorter man didn't smile. "The one and only."

"Come in, please sit down." Stewart jumped up and offered a chair.

"Don't patronize me. I'm not that old." Richardson scowled.

Acquiescing with a polite smile, Stewart asked, "What can I do for you?"

"Well, it seems to be the other way around." Procuring a folded letter from his coat pocket, Richardson carefully unfolded the paper and set it on Stewart's desk. "See for yourself."

Eyeing his old boss, Stewart reached for the paper, already suspicious of what it said. He skimmed it enough to confirm his guess. There was no way he could pretend to be pleased.

"Yeah," the older man said gruffly. "I didn't expect you to jump with joy."

Stewart's eyes flashed in anger.

"Look. I want this to be as painless as possible. You get everyone together; I want a meeting in the conference room in thirty minutes. And I mean everybody." With a final severe glance, Richardson headed out the door, letting it bang loudly after him.

Stewart slammed a fist onto his desk and fought the urge to rip the letter into a million tiny pieces. He and Richardson had never gotten along well in the first place, and few people were as happy as Stewart to hear of his retirement from the Bureau five years ago.

Five years before that, they had worked the original Mathis case together, when Stewart had only been in the Bureau for a short time. Richardson had been the senior agent in charge of the investigation, and apparently the Bureau thought he had more to offer because they just brought him back.

* * * *

The following day Elise felt much worse. Jesse – who apparently knew quite a bit about medicine – said she had caught some sort of cold or virus while her body's immune system was so weak. Give it a week or so, and she should be feeling better.

In between sleeping, coughing, and sneezing, Mrs. Allen brought her the promised chicken soup and endless cups of tea. Her lungs hurt the worst, and staying vertical for very long was impossible.

She had relocated herself from her bedroom to the couch in the living room. It was nice to have people around, and if she was going to be sick, it was nicer to have them feeling sorry for you. Also, as her ability to think and remember was returning, this provided a way to eavesdrop on any conversations taking place in the dining room or the den.

This time, however, like most times, she couldn't help sliding into sleep, the others' low voices drowned out by the sound of dreams.

* * * *

Retired FBI Agent Donald Richardson sat motionless at the head of the glossy new conference table. He was in his element here, like the proud captain of a gallant ship. These agents were all competent people, but they were about to get a rude awakening. He might be short, but he was well-known for extracting every ounce of effort from his team. They hated him for it, but it didn't matter. It worked.

As the twelve-member group shuffled in, their lack of enthusiasm for the change in leadership was apparent. Stewart came in last, tight-lipped and stiff. The tall strawberry blond man had proved to be a bright student under Richardson's guidance, but by no means a happy man. And of course Richardson would never let his approval show.

Nothing but his eyes moved as the seasoned agent surveyed his wary group. Most were in their thirties and forties, a few fresh faces in their late twenties. What they lacked under Stewart was not good leadership or smarts, but direction. Something Richardson had plenty of.

Samuel Mathis had escaped him once. He was not going to let it happen again.

"Good afternoon."

The group sat still, watching him with unhappy expressions.

"My name is Don Richardson. For those of you who don't know, I worked the original Mathis case along with Alan here, and I have been chosen to lead this investigation again. Now, I have read all of your team's reports as well as each of your personnel files, so introductions and 'catching up' won't be necessary. Any questions?"

They exchanged glances with one another, but remained silent.

"Good. You guys are quick. I can use that." He clapped his hands together loudly, startling some of them, "Now. We have several leads that deserve closer attention. First, our missing deputy from Iowa. Dr. Rayford has positively ID'd him, but I want something concrete. I want every sentence of his life from the past year scrutinized, and if that isn't enough, go back farther. Find his car. There has to be a connection somewhere.

"Second, give up searching for this Carbon. The name hasn't shown up yet, and we don't have anything solid to go on. All we have is Elise's description – which came through Deputy Lawson and may not be trustworthy – and a phone call to Agent Stewart. We can't waste time. We have Rayford's interview, and he has been cooperative with all our questioning so far. You have transcripts of his account. Keep in mind he may not have been entirely truthful, but as all we have to go on right now, we are going to assume the major parts of his story are valid and move from there.

"Thirdly, the scene of the explosion has been thoroughly analyzed, but it may take months to clear the rubble. Much of it may not ever be accessible, or it is simply too expensive to dig out safely. So look for answers elsewhere. Circumstantial evidence, people. Let's use our heads.

"Finally, we need to step up efforts to find this car. There has to be a reason Carbon or Mathis or whoever is doing the running around did not dump it after all kinds of law enforcement were looking for them. If they have this many resources, obtaining a new vehicle should not be a problem. So why take the risk?

"I have assigned new groups, and given you your assignments. I want a written report from each group tomorrow. Dismissed."

* * * *

Deputy Shane Lawson honestly wasn't sure how he felt about this whole setup. Or how to react to it. His face was finally becoming less puffy, though the broken nose remained tender. The farmhand, Jesse, was easy to get along with and very friendly, but there was something these three weren't telling him.

It had only taken him two days to return to some degree of normalcy, and he had to admit the Allens were nothing but hospitable and kind. But that didn't explain who they were or what was going on. When he asked questions, they just smiled sweetly and told him to wait until Elise was ready to hear the whole story as well. Which was rather irritating.

He had no clues other than the bare bones explanation Carbon had given him about Elise's father Samuel Mathis, some sort of genetic experiment, and another scientist named Rayford who was bad. And he really needed no convincing there. He would count himself blessed to never meet that man again.

The Allens and Jesse vehemently reassured him that he was safe here, and that they were friends of Elise who could help her get well and find her father. They were nice enough, but he still had no real information and didn't know what to believe. So his tentative goals right now were to survive, not go to prison, keep the girl safe - she at least seemed as innocent and uninformed as himself - and hopefully manage to keep the car as a fair replacement of his Mustang.

On the third day they all sat around the fire and discussed his options. Jesse was mostly silent, but the Allens apologized profusely over and over again for dragging him into all this mess. They were likewise adamant in their thankfulness for his help. Mrs. Allen was nearly in tears, saying he had no idea how much it meant and that without him, Elise might be dead right now, or worse. He wondered about the worse part, but they refused to elaborate, so he assumed it meant becoming some type of experiment or something.

Mr. Allen – or Frank, as he insisted on being called – was down-to-earth practical. "Son," he had said, looking straight into Lawson's eyes. "I'm not going to sugarcoat things. Your life as Shane Lawson is history. If you leave now, I guarantee you'll live the rest of your life behind bars. Or you might have a very short life. No matter what you think you can explain, Rayford holds you responsible for stealing Elise from him, destroying his compound and shooting his hand. He is not a man to let that go."

Apparently Carbon had explained their adventures in painstaking detail to the three while he and Elise were out of commission.

"As I see it, you have three options. One, you can go back and either die early or die in prison, which I would not recommend."

Mrs. Allen had agreed, vehemently shaking her head over this option.

"Two, you can stay and start a new life here. We'll keep you fed and warm for as long as you need. After saving Elise's life, we owe it to you. Now, we don't want to steal your life away, so the third option is to fix you a new identity and send you off somewhere, maybe out of country, to keep a low profile and live like you want. But I'm warning you. Rayford will not give up, and you will probably spend the rest of your life watching your back and looking over your shoulder."

When the man had finished speaking, he sat back and stared at Lawson hard in the face. None of the options sounded particularly appealing, so he asked for some time to think about it. They seemed relieved, and welcomed him in as a son in the meantime.

"You take as much time as you need." Mr. Allen had nodded his approval of Lawson's choice. "Everything we have is yours for now, so just make yourself comfortable. We only ask that you be careful about going to public places for a while. After that last encounter, the FBI has been hunting you like you wouldn't believe."

Great. What was he, public enemy number one now? All for helping one girl escape a mad scientist.

To pass the time, he had offered to help out on the ranch. Getting out and doing physical labor had proved therapeutic for his mind, but his injured body still required that he use caution for any heavy lifting. He and Jesse were out repairing fences again, and the more time he spent with the man, he couldn't help but like him. But today the blonde cowboy was surprisingly silent.

The two worked without saying anything for a long time, and finally Lawson broke the silence. "What's going on? Is something wrong?"

Jesse sighed and shoved his post-hole digger into the ground. "I'm not sure."

He glanced Lawson up and down, then focused somewhere beyond the horizon and leaned against his tool. "You've helped us and Elise so much; we can't express how grateful we are." He paused, giving Lawson a meaningful look. "Really, you'll probably never know what it means to us. To me."

Lawson held his gaze steadily. These people had to be related to the girl somehow. There was no other way to explain their genuine concern.

"It's hard to keep so much information from you. Tonight if Elise is feeling up to it, how about we all sit down and talk. I mean, you might not be able to understand everything, but there are some things you should know."

Well, that sounded better than knowing nothing. He shrugged in response. "Sounds good to me."

"Someone brilliant and famous once said that wisdom is grief and knowledge leads to sorrow."

"What?"

"You know, sometimes knowledge just weaves around and is unnecessary to learn or worry about."

Lawson resisted the urge to snort. "Yeah, but when your life might depend on what you know, I would prefer to be informed."

"You have to wonder, which pieces of information are truly important? You can't know everything, and even if it was possible, are you sure you would know what to do with that information?"

"What on earth are you talking about?"

"I have no idea. Hey, if you would stop all this chit-chat and get to work, maybe we can fix this fence before dark." Jesse grinned at him innocently.

Glancing down the fence line that disappeared into the distance, Lawson only raised his eyebrows.

"Come on, pick that hammer back up. We're men. We don't need to accidentally have some sort of deep conversation out here." With a sly wink at Lawson, Jesse tossed a hammer toward his feet. Fortunately, it landed just shy of its target.

These people were strange. But picking up the hammer, Lawson thought back to the decision at hand. Regardless of Jesse's warnings, maybe it would be clearer after he was more informed.

Chapter 3

Elise was sitting upright on the couch, enjoying a round of hot cocoa with Mrs. Allen when the door creaked open.

"Come on in," the older woman beckoned.

"Hello Ruth," Mr. Allen swung in, swerving to plant a kiss on his wife's cheek. "I hope you've made some for me too."

"Dear, we were just having some girl time. You have impeccable timing."

"Why, thank you." He gave a mock bow, but then his face turned serious. "Elise, how are you feeling?"

"Better, thanks," she smiled at him. Even though her body was worse, her spirits had improved considerably since sitting outside with Carbon. Somehow it just put things in another perspective, and she couldn't explain it.

"Good enough to talk?"

She eyed him curiously.

"I mean a real talk. About what's going on and why we have the pleasure of your company right now."

"Oh." She paused. To some degree, it had been nice to not think about all that had happened. She could pretend everything was okay, and just focus on the kindness and care these people gave her. Knowing why might spoil it all.

Then again, she couldn't live her whole life not knowing. And she was feeling stronger. "Okay," she nodded solemnly.

Mr. Allen sighed, "That sure is good news. I told Shane he had to wait until you were ready, because I didn't want to explain the whole thing twice. If he had to wait any longer, he might explode." He patted her on the head. "Back to you, Ruth. If we could all have some hot chocolate for this occasion, that would be mighty nice. I'll help you fix it."

"Say no more," Mrs. Allen held up a hand. She shot Elise a sideways glance. "Whenever Frank here agrees to any sort of cooking, it's a miracle."

Mr. Allen offered a hand to help her out of her rocking chair, but she only returned the favor with a fierce glare. "Frank, I am not that old." With a final *hmph*, she sat up with surprising speed and marched into the kitchen. Mr. Allen rolled his eyes and motioned after her with his hands as if to say, "See what I have to put up with?"

Elise couldn't resist a giggle as he disappeared into the kitchen, going on about being a true gentleman. Wrapping a hand firmly around her warm mug, she gazed into the fire. Why was she so resistant to facing this?

"Well, you look better."

She turned her head to see the deputy walk in and sit on the other couch.

"Yeah," she coughed weakly and set her mug down on the table. She still had no real idea who this man was or what he was doing here.

"You were looking pretty bad there. If it wasn't for Carbon, I would have thought you were dead."

"I felt dead," she gave a slight smile. How do you ask someone politely who the heck are you?

"Look," he rubbed his hands together and looked down. "I really have no idea what's going on here. If anything, you probably know more than I do."

"What do you mean?"

"All I know is what Carbon told me, and that wasn't much."

Elise understood what it was to get information out of the car. "Then how... I mean what are... okay." She took a deep breath, grabbing hold of one solid question. "Why are you here?"

"I would like to say that's a long story, but it's actually pretty short. As you know, I drove you to meet with the FBI."

She nodded in affirmation. "Yeah, you thought I was crazy."

"Well," he didn't even try to explain his way out of that one. "Yes. At first. But then when you were kidnapped out of the prison, I was called back there to testify, as I had been the only person to talk to you."

He glanced over at her, but she kept her expression blank.

"They wanted every tiny detail, but wouldn't tell me anything about what was going on. The only thing I picked up was your father's name and that he had done something threatening national security."

So they had told him the same story. Elise felt stabs of disbelief again, worries that the accusations might be true.

"I was kind of suspicious, but it was the FBI after all, and after some time they let me go home. I had, uh, acquired a contact name for your case, however. The police sergeant in your hometown?"

The thought of home pushed aside the doubts, "Mesa Springs?"

"Yeah. I gave him a call, off the record, because something just didn't seem right. He agreed, but didn't know much. The FBI wouldn't tell him anything either. I was just going to let it go and move on, when I got an anonymous phone call about you."

"From whom?"

He looked at her evenly. "Guess."

"I have no idea."

"It sounded like a young kid, maybe thirteen or so …"

"Elise! You look amazing!" Jesse waltzed into the room, sweeping past to kiss her on the forehead. That was weird.

"Hm. Still a slight fever, though." He frowned, staring at her as if the explanation might come to him.

"Good, everybody's here." Mrs. Allen proceeded out of the kitchen, carrying a tray of steaming mugs. "Compliments of the chef."

Mr. Allen stuck his head out of the doorway and cleared his throat.

"I mean, chefs. Plural." She rolled her eyes and started handing out the goods.

Satisfied, Mr. Allen took a seat beside Lawson and accepted his own cup. Jesse plopped into a recliner, thanking Mrs. Allen for her efforts with a wink.

"Now, it is pretty hot, so you might want to wait a few minutes for the first sip," Mr. Allen instructed as his wife set the empty tray on the fireplace and sat down beside Elise.

They sat in silence a brief moment, the fire crackling quietly. Elise sank deeper into the many layers of blankets Mrs. Allen had wrapped around her, careful not to make eye contact with any of them.

"Shane and I got the whole south fence in good order," Jesse began. "Sure goes a lot faster with two instead of one."

"That's great. Thanks for your help, Shane. We appreciate it." Mrs. Allen smiled at the deputy kindly.

Lawson only nodded in response.

"Well," Mr. Allen slapped his hands on his knees. "Looks like we've got a lot of explaining to do."

Elise shivered and pulled the blanket even tighter. This is what she had wanted for so long, she was almost afraid to hear it out. Mrs. Allen gave her a hug and a sympathetic glance.

"To start, it has been over a week since you two arrived. Since then, the FBI has cracked down in their efforts to find you. Your pictures have been all over the news, as well as Carbon's make and model. That's why she's been parked in the back shed. It's best you all lay low for a while."

"How long is a while?" Lawson asked.

"I'd say at least a couple more weeks. The public doesn't hold on to stories like this for too long, so you should be okay after that."

"Now," Mr. Allen drew a deep breath. "We know most of what happened through Carbon, and that she didn't tell you very much. I have no idea," he looked meaningfully at Elise, "what Rayford told you, or how much of it is true."

She refused to meet his gaze, studying the swirling colors in her mug instead.

"What he did to you was inexcusable." Jesse's eyes burned angrily. "Absolutely inexcusable."

"We're just grateful Carbon and Shane got to you in time," Mrs. Allen said. "But before we get too deep into all the details, let's start with the basics. I believe it's time for proper introductions."

Lawson shifted awkwardly, and Jesse stared at her with the strangest expression. He actually looked as though he might cry.

Mrs. Allen was a step closer, tears falling down her withered cheeks. "Sweetheart, you are our grandbaby."

Elise had no immediate reaction. Her thoughts froze.

"Ten years ago, when this mess was getting started, your father had us take precautionary measures. Our names and former identities, completely gone. Mr. Allen here legally died of a heart attack, and I seemingly lost it, never to be heard from again. You see, we thought at first we could just ride out the storm together, as a family, and turn in Rayford for what he really was. But after your mother's death..." Mrs. Allen sniffled, covering her mouth with her hand. "I'm sorry."

"It's fine, dear," Mr. Allen came over to comfort his wife. "Your mother Nancy, she was our little girl."

At this Mrs. Allen broke into deeper sobs, pushing her face into Mr. Allen's shoulder.

Elise didn't know what to say. She didn't know what to think, or feel. She just stared at the scene and blinked. Maybe they were lying. Glancing over at Jesse, his face was just as broken, tears freely flowing down.

He came over and knelt before Elise, looking fully into her eyes. It was hard not to cry with so much open emotion staring you in the face.

"You see, Elise. She was my mother too."

She searched his face for any hint of jesting or familiarity. The newspaper article from Rayford's talked about a brother. Alex.

Something tried to flow out like a waterfall – she wasn't sure what it was – and she broke Jesse's gaze. Glancing behind him, Lawson's face was devoid of much emotion, but he did appear thoroughly shocked. His gaze met hers, as if asking if this was true, if she believed them.

"Are you telling the truth?" It was meant to come out as a demand, but when she spoke it was much more of a whisper.

Jesse continued staring at her somberly. "I would never lie to you, kiddo."

His blue eyes held nothing but concern and love, and as much as she fought it, a wet droplet escaped her eye as well. "You're Alex?"

He nodded. "Well, I was Alex. Just like you were Irene." He wiped the tear away gently. "You don't remember?"

She didn't move.

"You were pretty small then. So cute." A warm smile lit up his face.

"Here," Mr. Allen had retrieved a photo album from somewhere. "Look at these. Maybe it will help jog your memory."

He pulled out a photo and passed it to her. "This was all of us, the Christmas before. You were only five then."

She accepted the photograph cautiously, hoping their memory-jogging methods wouldn't work. In the picture was a beautiful blond woman wrapped in a tall man's arms, easily recognizable from Carbon's videos. At her feet was a petite little girl with light straight locks, grinning impishly at the camera. A gangly young boy was kneeling to her left, a huge smile stretching his face as he clutched a colorfully wrapped package. Off to the corner stood a mid-age couple, both of the Allens smiling brightly.

"Ah-hem," Lawson cleared his throat. "May I see that picture?"

Elise held it out toward him, and Jesse completed the handover. The deputy scrutinized the photo, glancing up occasionally to match faces.

Jesse gave a brief laugh. "Suspicious, no?"

"Hey," Lawson handed the photo back. "Just being careful."

"Cops usually are," Jesse said thoughtfully.

"Ex-cop," Lawson corrected.

"Sorry, man." Jesse stood up. "I really am."

"Yeah. Well, I went willingly. More or less."

Elise looked at him, eager to move off the topic of family. "What do you mean? Who was it that called you?"

He pointed out the window. "Yours truly."

"Carbon?"

His expression confirmed her guess.

"She just asked for your help, a random stranger? And you agreed?"

"Not exactly. Let's just say she convinced me."

"I only gave you the option to help, Lawson." Carbon's voice interrupted from somewhere near the fireplace.

"Speakers," Mr. Allen explained, pointing.

Jesse smiled at the car's retort, then swallowed it and attempted to look serious. "Yes. 'Fess up, Carbon. We know what you did."

"I did what was necessary."

"She always listening?" Lawson asked.

Jesse nodded with a slight roll of his eyes, but Carbon continued in her defense. "My actions were logical."

"You smashed my car." Lawson folded his arms across his chest. "And were about to leave me stranded in the desert."

"I would have alerted the authorities had you opted to stay. I never intended to harm you."

"Sure, Carbon. However you want to look at it."

Everyone nodded in agreement except Elise, who only looked back at the photograph again. "What about my dad? Where is he?"

Jesse regarded her somberly. For a moment no one spoke.

"He's not here, is he?" Despite the obvious lack of her father's presence, she couldn't help asking. But the Allens only exchanged heavy glances with Jesse. "Is he dead?" she blurted. Surely, she couldn't have come all this way for him to not be waiting somewhere.

"No," Jesse answered. "But we don't know where he is. Truth is, we lost all contact with him about a month ago, when things started closing in and people were starting to figure out who you were."

Elise scanned Jesse's face back and forth, unwilling to believe what he had told her.

"Look, sis..." he reached out toward her, but she brushed his hand off brusquely. The sickness and nausea that had been plaguing her was buried under this cascade of feelings. She couldn't distinguish one from the other, but looking around, these faces staring back at her were only making it worse.

"No," Elise rose on tottering feet, letting the layers of heavy blankets slide to the floor. "No. I don't know you people. I don't know you," she stared at Jesse, "and I don't know you either." She pointed at the Allens.

Nothing made sense. But she needed to get out. She knew every eye was watching as she headed for the door and flung it open, and it only made her angrier. What right did these people have - random, unfamiliar strangers - to call her family? They weren't family. They were gone. Just like her father.

Someone called after her, but she was already running. She had always been fast, and as her feet hit the frigid ground the shocks jarred the sensitivity out of them. The bedroom slippers had fallen off somewhere by the house.

She ran as long as she could, but her body reminded her quickly of its weakened state.

"Why...?" she moaned, collapsing to the ground in agony, a pitiful heap of wretchedness and confusion. Her lungs were too tired to cry from coughing, and she buried her face in the cold dirt without tears.

Get control of yourself, her mind reasoned. And part of her was mad that no searchlights or rescue effort came out for her. They just let her run off. Like that. Some family.

Then again, who was it that deserted her in the first place? All this time, they were here. Warm and cozy. And they decided to dump her in the foster system like an unwanted reject.

Hugging her cold body, Elise forced herself to get up and keep walking. It didn't matter where, it didn't matter how dead or alive she was when she got there.

There was no moon out tonight, and even though the stars gleamed brilliantly above, an inky black covered the ground and space around her. An owl cooed, reminding her she wasn't completely alone.

Fear tried to tangle itself in with the mess of emotions brewing, but she wouldn't have it. She was too angry.

And then it came. She was half-expecting the high pitched whine and the deep undertones and found herself equally enraged and relieved as it grew louder.

Here she didn't even have to be civil. It was just a car.

"Go away!" Elise yelled at the top of her lungs. "You're with them."

"I am with you."

"What do you want?!"

"The temperatures are below freezing, and you are not dressed to be out in this weather."

"So I catch a little frostbite. Who cares?"

"Frostbite is a highly painful experience that can result in amputation. It seems that you would care."

"Well I don't," she snapped. "And neither does anyone else. So back off."

"I will follow further behind if you request, but you are misinformed. Someone else does care for your well-being."

"Oh. And who would that be? Those people? I don't know them." Her tone was tight, hatred and anger seeping out after many years of avoiding the question. "I don't know who they are, what they are doing, or what they want with me. And I don't want to!"

With the final declaration, she couldn't help the few shudders that passed through her chest.

"There were years... my whole life," she drew choking breaths, her speech unsteady. "They sat here and did nothing. Nothing!"

She stopped walking and turned to the car that had become her shadow. She banged her fists hard on the hood. "They left me! And I don't need them now."

Her bitter proclamation receded into a silent night, only the distant wind howling through the mountain range.

"Elise. I have not left you. If I speak, will you listen?"

She wiped a tear off her frozen cheek and replaced her hand on the warm hood. The vibrations shook some of the cold out of her fingers, and as the door clicked open she had to steady herself against the fender.

Although she despised it, she really was far too weak right now. That exertion had cost her nearly every power of balance and motion.

Swallowing the next pitiful sob, she used the door as a prop and dumped her exhausted body into the cab. It was like blissful sauna, and as they pulled away she allowed the heat to work its way into all her senses.

Chapter 4

Lawson sat in the awkward silence, waiting for someone to do or say something. Elise had stormed out a full minute ago, and yet they were all just standing around, doing absolutely nothing. What was wrong with these people?

Finally, he couldn't take it. "Isn't someone going to go after her?"

Jesse continued to stare at the closed door, his sad expression never changing.

"Hello?" Lawson tried again.

Mr. Allen seemed to snap out of it partly. "No."

That wasn't much of a response. "Why not?"

Mrs. Allen deteriorated quickly into more tears, covering her face with a cloth as she disappeared up the stairs.

Releasing a heavy sigh, Jesse turned to face him. "It's better to just let her be. When she wants to talk to us, she'll come back."

"Yeah, but it's pitch black and she doesn't know where she is. Not to mention she's sick, and not thinking straight, and it's freezing out there!" Was no one else paying any attention? Surely they wouldn't go through all this and then let the girl wander off and get lost or eaten by a bear.

But Jesse just shook his head. "She's fine. Believe me. Carbon would never let anything happen to her. And right now, she's probably the best thing in the world for Elise."

Maybe he hadn't paid enough attention, but it seemed to him that Carbon was just a car. Granted, it was an amazingly cool car that had impressive aim and a propensity to smash other vehicles, but that wasn't the same as a friendly face to cheer someone up. That's what grandmothers are for. And yet the only old lady on the premise had run upstairs herself. These people had no spine.

Not that Lawson knew what to do either. But this wasn't his problem to solve.

"Look," he leaned forward and caught Jesse's eye. Whatever sadness this man had over his sister, he needed to snap out of it and focus. This was not the time to get all emotional. "I really need to know what's going on."

The fire continued to crack busily as Mr. Allen exchanged a long glance with Jesse. He turned to look at Lawson. "All right. Go ahead, Jess. Fill him in."

"Truth is, the situation with Elise is much worse than we first thought. Carbon ran a scan of Elise's system to assess exactly what Rayford had injected in her and how to counter it."

"Yeah, but you fixed it. She's doing better now."

"She feels much better, yes, but no, we didn't 'fix it'."

Lawson stared into the man's piercing blue eyes. Why did these people beat around the bush so much?

"We can't stop it," Mr. Allen inserted. "We've tried everything."

"But she seems to be okay. So just let it stay there, right? Being a little sick isn't the end of the world."

Jesse's face was broken. "I wish it was that simple. Her body cannot function like this forever. It leaves her immune system crippled, part of why she caught a cold so fast, and will ultimately kill her. We've slowed it down and masked some of the symptoms. Over the course of several months, she will be left to suffer an agonizingly slow death as her cells are literally destroyed from the inside out."

Lawson was shocked by the bluntness of the man's words. "Does she know?"

The blonde man shook his head. "Not yet. But it's not all lost. Carbon thinks she can develop a cure."

"Thinks she can? Why haven't you developed it already?"

"This is where it gets problematic. Rayford didn't infect her with a common disease. His compound was a delivery system for SynMOs, as they're called. Synthetic molecular organisms."

With an insulted glare, Lawson communicated his lack of understanding.

"Nanites," Jesse offered. "To counter them, we need access to the right materials, the right equipment, and the blueprint of these SynMOs. Only one person has all of those conveniently together right now."

That wasn't a hard guess. "Rayford."

"Precisely. Now, when you and Carbon snatched Elise from him on that road, you might have wondered why he managed to walk away with a shattered hand."

The question had crossed his mind.

"Carbon knew that we would need Rayford to reverse what he had done to Elise. Otherwise she would have put that bullet between his eyes."

He had no doubt to that. "So, how are you going to convince Rayford to help? Blackmail?"

"Oh, no. That would never work. I'm going to break into his lab and build the compound there. It's really the only facility suitable for that type of work.

He already has everything ready. When he injected Elise, he had no intention of killing her. So he planned to make it necessary to bring her back to him."

"Then your plan is insane. If he did this on purpose and is as powerful as you make him sound – which I don't doubt after seeing his setup – then he is waiting for you to make this move."

Jesse shrugged. "I'll be careful. But this is our only option."

* * * *

Carbon was silent for the first few minutes. Odd, after she had requested to speak.

"Where are we going?" Elise wanted to stop the car before it returned her to the Allens' house.

"We are going for a drive."

"I don't want to go back."

"That was a logical conclusion after you ran away."

Elise gave a slight smile through her sniffling. "So you're not going to make me go back?"

"No. Remember I will not force you to do anything. You are not my prisoner, and you are not the Allens' prisoner. They are trying to help."

She snorted. "The time for that is over."

"What do you mean?"

"I'm sixteen! My dad dropped me off in the foster system when I was six! All my life I've had no identity, no family, nothing! And all this time they were here. And my brother." The thought was so painful, she couldn't even say it out loud.

"They dumped me, Carbon." Even now she could only whisper the words. They hadn't wanted to keep her. Alex had stayed, but not her. History. Ten years, the most important in her life, alone in this miserable world.

"I am sorry, Elise."

Elise just stared out the window at blurry stars as more tears threatened. She had expected the car to try to explain her family's behavior, to rationalize it away. But Carbon remained silent.

"Would you like to drive? It might prove therapeutic."

A small smile cracked again. "Thanks, but I think I'd kill both of us if I was driving right now."

"I would not allow that."

What did she have to lose? Rubbing some of the tears from her eyes, Elise hesitantly reached for the slick steering wheel and placed her foot over the pedals. The engine slowed in pitch as Carbon handed over the controls.

She touched the gas lightly and the engine gave a more than generous response, revving loudly as Elise was pressed back into the seat. Taken by surprise, anger rose up from somewhere within her and echoed a similar cry.

Carbon's headlights illuminated the sharp curves in the road, and slaloming through the trees and rocky sides she felt powerful. When they finally reached a straight stretch, Elise put her head back and screamed. She just yelled. Out of frustration, out of the torment that had consumed her soul for so long, out of anger and hatred, out of love and hope. Apathy and terror collided somewhere in her spirit, and the resulting shockwave was nothing she could understand or control.

She slammed the accelerator pedal against the floorboards, and the car rocketed forward as the engine roared.

"What do you want with me?!" she yelled to no one in particular. "How could you do this to me? I'm your daughter! Your own child! Who could do this to their own child?!" She sobbed as she let off the gas and slammed the brake to throw the vehicle into a wide curve.

"I hate him!" she screamed. "I hate them all!"

Stomping the accelerator once more, the swath of road in Carbon's headlights blurred with her vision. Her voice dropped to a quiet whimper, "Why wasn't I enough? They didn't want me. He gave me away."

The road began a slow descent, and the car shifted into low gear. Elise stopped paying attention and buried her face against the steering wheel. It simply hurt. The pain cut deep, and her stomach felt sick, like she had swallowed a most bitter pill.

This was the crux of it all. Right here, the ugly truth. She hadn't been worth keeping to them. They just figured they would pick her up in a decade or so, and go on from there. She wanted to be angry with them, and her father. Mostly her father. Furious, in fact. But all that would surface was this horrible ache, and she clutched her stomach fiercely, tears streaming down her face.

She hated this. The crying, the weakness, the need. If she was this pitiful, how could she blame them for leaving her behind? She probably would have only slowed them down. All her life, they might have left clues. If she had searched harder to find her real family, maybe things would have turned out differently.

Wind blew across the car and Elise watched the silhouette of trees swaying in the darkness. The energy she had just expended left her feeling dizzy and nauseated.

"Carbon?" she asked weakly.

"Yes, Elise?"

"Please pull over."

They stopped on the road's narrow shoulder. Another solitary tear escaped, and Elise didn't even bother wiping it away.

"You are still ill. Your body temperature is elevated."

She didn't respond. That much was evident from her splitting headache and shivering in spite of the warm air blowing on her.

"I should take you back to the house. They will take care of you there."

"Why?" she muttered desolately. "What for?"

"So your body can heal and you can regain your strength."

"What's the point? I don't care if I feel better."

"Elise, do you remember why your father built me?"

She didn't want to, but the words were right there. "To protect me."

"I am going to do that. I will not leave you."

Elise dropped her eyes to the car's black dash, and a small smile crept up despite the bitter feelings inside.

"Please allow me to drive you back to the Allens. They will care for you, and anytime you need me I will come quickly. If you call my name, I can reach you on any phone."

"Thanks, Carbon," Elise swallowed. Her body was feeling worse, and a hot bath and cozy bed would be heavenly right now. But how could she ever face them again? They had only been helpful, and here she had run out like a spoiled brat.

And then there was the deputy. Poor guy had nothing to do with anything. He already thought she was crazy. But as another shiver went down her spine, she consented.

"Okay."

Leaning the seat back, Elise closed her eyes and brought her knees into her chest. Sometimes she just wanted the world to disappear.

* * * *

Elise staggered into the warm house half-conscious. Her headache had only worsened on the windy drive back. Part of it might have been the stress, as it took all her will power to re-enter the house she had fled an hour earlier.

Fortunately no one was waiting for her, and not a soul came into sight as she made her way up the stairs on wobbly legs. Falling into her bed, she prayed for the blissful state of unconsciousness and to forget everything she had just learned.

Chapter 5

The next morning Lawson was up with the dawn. He had not slept well, disturbed with last night's meeting and what it meant.

The Allens and Jesse had been honest, he believed that much, but they were not presenting a complete picture. Why would these people spend so much time and resources on one girl? Even if she was the nicest thing in the world, there had to be some other motivation. Guilt or family relations hardly seemed like enough.

The father had built some insanely expensive car that could be worth trillions, and yet its only purpose was to protect his estranged daughter. A daughter who had spent the last ten years without a family and was now terminally ill because of nanites that had been injected into her body. Jesse, granted he was her brother, was willing to risk life and limb to look for an elusive cure, going right into the territory of the mad scientist who had caused this problem in the first place.

Something big was missing, and Lawson had yet to decide on a course of action to find out what it was. Oddly, he had an overwhelming sense that the father, this Dr. Mathis character, would have all the answers he needed. But he wasn't sure if he wanted to meet him at all, or if it was even possible. If the FBI had been searching for ten years without success, the man was a ghost, and Lawson likely wouldn't have any better luck. And then there was the question of why the FBI wanted him in the first place. Jesse had seemed eager to avoid that topic.

The morning was brisk, and he kept up a good pace as he followed the narrow mountain road behind the house. He had seen the structure where they kept Carbon, but had not really spoken with or seen the car since the day he arrived. It was an improbable chance, but the easiest next step in his search for clues.

The walk was longer than he thought, more like a several mile hike, but eventually the old wooden barn came into view around the bend.

He tiptoed quietly around to the front of the building. Maybe Carbon was somewhere else this morning.

"Good morning, Deputy Lawson."

Guess not. Glancing inside, he saw that the car had been repainted black, and he had to say it was an improvement. "Good morning to you too, Carbon. And you can stop calling me that. I'm sure I've been formally fired by now."

"What should I call you?"

"Whatever you want, I don't care."

"Okay, Mr. Lawson."

"Uh, wait. That's a little formal. And weird."

"Why? It is common etiquette."

"It doesn't matter, I don't like it." He rubbed his hands together. How had he gotten this far off track already? "Look, I didn't come here to teach you proper greetings. I have some questions."

"More questions?"

"What's that supposed to mean? You didn't answer any of mine anyway."

"Why do you not ask the Allens or Jesse?"

Lawson growled in frustration. Why did he even try? "Look. I'm asking you. Will you answer?"

"What would you like to know?"

One thing he had picked up on was that Carbon shared most of her information with Jesse and the Allens. With this in mind, he had spent the walk out here working on phrasing questions carefully.

"Jesse said that you were unable to create a cure for Elise. How long does she have?"

"It is difficult to predict. Somewhere between two and three months until death, but only three or four weeks until we can no longer restrain the symptoms."

"He also said you had figured out a way to fix it, but you needed to get Rayford's supplies."

"I can likely synthesis a remedy from data and materials that could be gathered from Rayford, particularly what he injected into her body."

"So you're not sure?"

"I cannot be certain until I have all of the necessary information."

"Brilliant. What about these people? They really are Elise's family?"

"Yes."

"Where is her father in all of this?"

"I am unable to disclose that information."

He sighed. Here was this wall again. "Okay. Thanks anyways."

Lawson turned to leave.

"Wait, Shane."

He turned back to the car. It was odd to be called so personally by a machine, but delving into further debate about it seemed counterproductive.

"Get inside," Carbon instructed.

Last time she told him that, it hadn't turned out well. "Why?"

"I have something for you."

A present? How nice. Begrudgingly he complied, slipping into the black interior.

"Elise's father sent this for you." The screen flickered on and a word document opened.

"Wait. You talked to her father recently?"

"I am unable to disclose that information. Read the letter carefully, because I will delete it when you are finished."

This was the kind of thing that made him suspicious. Why all the secrecy? Turning to the short letter, he attempted to memorize every word.

"Mr. Shane Lawson,

I cannot thank you enough for your help in saving my daughter's life. Truly, if you had not been willing to assist, she would almost certainly be dead by now. I recognize this came to you at a great cost, and I am deeply moved and grateful for your actions.

It surprises me how helpful you have been despite how little you know. It must be difficult to discern wrong from right, and to know whom to trust. For my part, I can tell you my foremost interest is the safety of Elise, and restoring her health. I will do whatever it takes to fix that.

In the interest of all our safety, it is best I do not share too much information, but should you choose to remain, I would love to meet you someday and thank you in person. You may never understand how much this means to me.

Sincerely,

Samuel Mathis

P.S. – You should know that I also shed some tears over your Mustang, and should I have the chance in the future, I will gladly replace it!"

Lawson blinked in surprise. This is not what he was expecting. He scanned over the words again to make sure they didn't change.

"Have you finished?"

Man, the car was really in a hurry to delete this. With a last glance at the letter, he opened the door and peeled himself out of the cushy seat.

"Yeah. I'm done."

"Would you like a ride back to the house? It is a long walk."

"Nah. I need the fresh air."

The note had given him considerable information to consider and walking would give him time to think. Granted, it was not exactly the info he had been looking for, but it was something nonetheless. For starters, Carbon was in direct communication with Elise's father and he could send messages through her. Quite as obvious was the fact that Carbon was not about to reveal how she did this or willingly share these capabilities with anyone else.

The last part of the note was touching; at least the man had some sympathies for what had gone down. Lawson hoped he was good on that promise to replace his beautiful red Mustang. But despite an overall feeling of goodwill toward Dr. Mathis, there was no convincing evidence that he was as innocent as the family claimed he was.

It would be nice to believe that he was truly only concerned with his daughter's life, but why would he have left her all these years? And why wasn't he here now? If this place was safe enough for the Allens and Elise's brother, what explanation could Dr. Mathis possibly offer for not being present himself?

Lawson was immersed in his thoughts, but a crunching noise was drawing steadily closer and his instincts told him to get out of sight. He stepped off the dirt road into the thick woods and hid behind a large tree. It was probably just Jesse, but with the craziness of this whole situation, he wasn't about to take that chance.

The steps continued, and Lawson was careful not to exhale until they passed his position. From this vantage point, he couldn't see who was on the path until they were a few feet ahead. Straining all his senses, he waited for a figure to emerge.

"Ahhhhh!" A scream filled the air, punctuating the calm coolness of the morning. Lawson had been gripping the tree's trunk tightly, but the cry had caught him completely by surprise. He moved backwards too quickly, and fought for his balance a brief moment before he lost the battle and fell loudly onto the brush behind him.

"Ow," he hissed as his arm smacked into a sharp rock on the ground.

"Who's there?" A scared voice demanded from the road. Elise. This was going to be difficult to explain.

He stood with a groan, brushing the leaves off his backside. "It's Shane." He walked out of the bushes with his hands up in innocence.

The frail looking girl was standing in the middle of the path, hunting knife in hand. She looked shocked, and lowered the knife-hand slightly. "What are you doing out here?"

He shrugged. "Just taking a hike." She didn't seem convinced, staring at him suspiciously. He pointed to the knife. "What were you going to do with that?"

She glanced down as if she had forgotten she was holding it. "Um..."

"And why did you scream?"

An embarrassed look crossed her face, but she regained her composure quickly. "Why were you hiding behind a tree?"

There really was no good way to explain. "Touché. Truce?"

She gave a slight nod, her face a mixture of tense fear and amused relief. "Sorry for, uh, screaming. I didn't think anyone else was around."

"Yeah. That was surprising." Lawson had been looking for a chance to talk to Elise without the others around, and here was the ideal opportunity. "Mind if I walk with you?"

Elise shrugged. "Whatever." She slid the knife into her belt and started walking.

"You going to see Carbon?"

"Yep." She answered curtly. Why was she so unfriendly? Wasn't she the person who should be most grateful?

"I talked with her this morning."

"That's nice."

"She gave me a letter from your dad."

Elise stopped and swirled around to face him. "My dad?"

He nodded in affirmation.

"What did it say?"

Lawson rubbed his jaw thoughtfully. "Not much. He just thanked me for helping and said that his most important goal was your safety and restoring your health."

She looked at him questioningly. "Really? Wait, what do you mean? I thought Jesse already fixed whatever Rayford did."

Oops. He had presumed that she already knew. "Did Jesse say that?"

"No. But I feel better. Why? Is something else wrong?"

He hoped this wasn't going to get him in a lot of trouble. Then again, it was her body, and she had every right to know. "I think Jesse was trying to tell you last night. He said he was able to mask the effects for a while, but eventually…"

"Eventually what?"

This was not easy news to break to anyone, and Lawson hadn't the slightest idea how it should be done. "Um, you will… you won't survive."

Her jaw dropped slightly, and she swayed backwards like someone had hit her.

"Hey," he reached out to keep her from falling. "Elise?"

She steadied herself on his arm, her eyes vacant. "I need to sit down," she said weakly.

There weren't any chairs conveniently sitting nearby so he gently helped her to the soft dirt. He wanted to say something to make it sound better, but he couldn't think of anything to say. Somehow, "Well, at least you have a few more months!" didn't seem very appropriate.

"I'm sorry," he said quietly, sitting down next to her.

But Elise only continued staring off into the distance.

"Jesse did say there was a chance he could make a cure. He thinks that Rayford might already have a way to fix this."

She seemed to snap out of it a little. "And he's going to go steal it?"

"Something like that. But it is also exactly what Rayford is expecting."

Elise paused before asking, "This ... cure ... it's in his lab?"

"Uh, not the one you were in." Lawson had forgotten that Elise had missed the details of her own harrowing escape. "It, well, exploded."

She gave him a strange look. "What happened?"

"You sure you want to know?"

Upon her nod, Lawson launched into the entire story, relieved to move off the topic of death. Elise listened somberly, smiling as he recounted the part about Curly and Moe and Aunt Jemima. When he described the final escape, Elise looked sympathetic and remorseful.

"You shot Rayford's hand?"

"No, that was Carbon. That was the last I saw of him, though." He paused to let it all sink in.

"Wow. I'm sorry."

Considering that Elise was facing imminent sickness and death, his loss didn't seem so large. "It's not your fault."

"Yeah. Just seems like ..." but she trailed off.

It wasn't hard to guess what she was thinking. The same thoughts had crossed his mind. What a waste, to give up your whole career and future to save a girl who might live three more months. Sitting here, however, with her alive and well, his earlier reasoning seemed brutally harsh and cruel. Who was he to determine the value of life?

"Look, Elise. It's not all hopeless. Maybe..."

She interrupted him. "How long?"

"What?"

"How long until I ... until..." she stumbled over the words, unable to say it out loud.

"Oh. Carbon said you have a few months, but you will start feeling sick again in a few weeks."

Her face might have lost a few more shades of color, but it was already so pale, he doubted that was possible. Her stricken expression was hard to take.

"I'm sorry." He tried to think of something encouraging to say, but it proved a difficult feat. Standing to leave, he couldn't help feeling somewhat guilty. But then again, there wasn't anything he could do to make it better.

Chapter 6

Elise watched Lawson walk away in silence. She felt numb. Again. This emotional rollercoaster was exhausting.

What was the point of continuing if she was just going to suffer from sickness and then die? Why would her dad spend so much effort building Carbon and planning to save her if she only had a few painful months left to look forward to?

Closing her eyes, she leaned back to stretch out on the soft earth. All strength deserted her as she lay motionless. What was the point? This wasn't fair, after all she had been through. She didn't want to give up. Sure, she was mad at her family for leaving – furious, to be honest – but she still wanted the chance to get to know them.

She opened her eyes when she heard Carbon drive up. She sighed, "Hello, Carbon."

"Good morning, Elise. Do not be so discouraged." The black car's door clicked open. "Come, I will drive you to the house. Jesse is waiting to speak with you."

The car knew her circumstances. "Do you expect me to be normal? Just fine and dandy, like nothing's wrong?"

"Why not?"

"Because I'm going to die!" she exclaimed. It wasn't that hard to figure out.

"Who told you that?"

"Shane! You were probably listening anyway."

"It is true that your body is very sick, but there is no guarantee when you will die or what you will die from. Why are you worried?"

"Shane said that you told him I only had a few more months to live."

"Only if we do not remedy the current situation."

"Yeah, and we need Rayford's help. How likely is that?"

"I do not understand your point. There are many options to consider. Your father will not give up so easily. Be patient, and come talk to Jesse."

"For what? My father did this to me in the first place!"

"Did what?"

"The whole thing! The problem with my DNA, it's his fault anyway!" Spoken out loud, it didn't seem to make much sense. Rayford could have lied. She remembered her dad's last video message. He had warned her to check everything with Carbon.

"To what are you referring?" the car asked.

It seemed kind of silly now, but she might as well clarify it point-blank. "Rayford said that my dad used me to test a new drug or something. Is that true?"

"No."

"Then what caused this problem? Was he lying? What's wrong with my DNA?"

"I do not know what Dr. Rayford told you, but I do know where you can find the answers."

"Can't you just tell me?"

"No."

"That's stupid."

Carbon did not respond, but waited patiently, engine humming at an idle. Elise sat and fumed for a while, angry that she had to suffer this and angry that her dad couldn't be here in person to apologize and explain the whole thing. But the more she sat, the more Carbon's words struck inside. It was true, she was acting a little juvenile by despairing. She had met many kids in foster care whose parents intentionally gave them up as infants, parents that were incarcerated or considered too dangerous to care for their children, and some whose parents were dead and they would never meet them.

There was still some hope. Even though her family may have wronged her by abandoning her, they were obviously concerned enough to risk life and limb to remedy that situation. Besides, she didn't feel that sick. With Carbon's help, surely they could find a way to fix this.

"Carbon?"

"Yes, Elise?"

"Why is all this like it is? I mean, why would my dad do this?"

"Jesse is better suited to answer such broad questions. I can only remind you of what you already know. Would you like for me to replay your father's video logs?"

"Why not?" she remarked dryly.

From her sprawled position on the bare earth, Elise could only hear the audio, but her father's kind tone and encouraging reminders carried clearly through Carbon's speakers. Tears formed in her eyes as she listened to his reassuring words; warnings that she would hear all kinds of things about him and their family, wisdom to always check with Carbon. Somehow she had overlooked that part. He called her 'my little girl' and ended each message with an earnest 'I love you' and the promise that Carbon had everything she needed now.

Fighting back further tears, Elise felt ashamed she had fallen into such self-pity and despair. Here her father had poured out his love and concern right before her eyes, and she had been completely unable to see it.

Why should she give up? After all they had been through, after Shane losing his whole life and the Allens so happy to see her again, it seemed wrong to go down without a fight. But she wasn't sure how to face them after running off like that. And then there was Jesse, who had seemed so grateful she was alive, so determined to make her well, and she had only spat in his face.

"Do they hate me?" The question tumbled out of her mouth.

"To whom are you referring?"

"You know. Jesse, the Allens, Shane..." Elise paused. "I wouldn't blame them."

"That is a stupid question."

"Hey!" The car had never before used such vernacular. "Where did that come from? You're supposed to be nice!"

"Top definitions for nice include 'pleasant or agreeable in nature' and 'socially and conventionally correct'. For all practical purposes, 'nice' is preferable but relatively useless. I spoke bluntly because the answer to your question was already so obvious, I could not risk you missing my point."

Elise drew herself up to sitting position in a huff, glaring into Carbon's headlights indignantly. "I think I got it." She needed to be more careful around the car. But though she was still smarting from the rebuke, she couldn't disagree that her attitude was a little pathetic. Okay. More than a little.

"Fine, Carbon. You win. Let's go talk to Jesse."

* * * *

"Agent Stewart."

Alan Stewart cursed under his breath and tightened his grip on the cell phone. She had called while he was driving alone. But his cell phone, as every agent's, was monitored by the Bureau. And since she had called last time, they were especially keen to his phone now.

"Why are you calling?" he demanded, irritated.

"I am offering you two options. One, you immediately hang up and report our conversation. The FBI will have a record of this call, and I will cease all communications with you."

That one didn't sound so bad. "And the other one?"

"Two, I will continue talking with you. I have sensitive information that your superiors would like to keep hidden. The tap on your phone will record a separate conversation that never took place, and you will not tell anyone else what is said."

Was this lady for real? "Listen, Carbon. I don't know who you are, and I don't know what your game is, but I'm not playing. I don't need your 'help'. I will find and bring to justice anyone who has broken or bent the law, including you."

"I provided accurate intel on Rayford's mountain home."

"And I nearly lost three agents! Thanks, but no thanks."

"They were not even injured. I saw to it."

"You?" Stewart gave a derisive snort. "You shot a man, and fired at my agents with a machine gun."

"Your agents were not injured," Carbon repeated. "Richardson knew of the structure. Behind Rayford's house was a laboratory, funded in part by the government."

"Sure. Give me one reason not to hang up and report this call right now."

"The site is not being searched. Ask to investigate the scene yourself. I am monitoring you, Alan. If you operate according to the plan, I will contact you with further information. Choose wisely."

Stewart heard the click as the call ended. Gritting his teeth, he had to consciously choose not to crush the phone in his hand.

Chapter 7

When Elise pulled up to the house in Carbon, Jesse was sitting and rocking slowly on the porch. She couldn't express how much she did not want to confront him right now, brother or no.

"Why are you afraid?" Carbon inquired innocently.

"What makes you think I'm afraid?"

"Your heart rate accelerated and your breathing became shallow. And you are still sitting inside of me."

It was kind of obvious. "I just don't want to talk to him."

"Because you are worried he will be angry with you?"

Honestly, she wasn't even sure herself. She just didn't want to. Really didn't want to. She released a long exhale before forcing herself to breath normally. "Okay. I'm going."

But it was still physically difficult to open the door and step outside.

"Hey, Elise." Her brother smiled at her, but his face seemed sad.

"Hey," she mumbled, forcing heavy feet to take her up the steps to the porch. It was another effort to force her rear end into the next rocking chair over and stay there. "I'm sorry about running off last night. I was just upset and everything." She looked down at the wooden floor.

Jesse was silent, and she didn't have enough courage to look him in the face.

She meant to say it right away, but the words seemed glued inside of her. Finally she forced them out, "Thank you. For saving my life and all."

Still no word from Jesse.

"I feel much better," Elise added.

But the blonde man offered no response. She glanced up to see his blue eyes looking at her, his face an odd mixture of joy and misery.

"So, yeah," she said, uncomfortable. Was he mad at her?

"Do you believe me?" he asked quietly.

"What?"

"That we are your family. That I am your brother, and that Dad sent me."

She paused, heart racing for some unknown reason. It wasn't that hard of a question. "I guess so. Carbon says it's true."

"And you believe her?"

The big black car glinted in the sunlight. "Yeah. I believe her."

He was scrutinizing her, and she felt like he could see deep inside. Unnerved, she looked back at Carbon. "Shane said... he said that I'm still sick or something." Her voice dropped to almost a whisper as she stared at her hands, "That I have a few months to live."

Jesse shifted in his rocking chair, and Elise could've sworn there were tears in those sky colored eyes. His tone was somber, "Elise, I will not lie to you about your situation. It is very serious."

"Rayford did this to me?" She didn't really need an answer, it seemed pretty obvious.

"There is a way to fix this." He was staring at her again, and now he smiled. "Don't give up, and don't be afraid."

Gathering her resolve, she met his expression. He appeared calm, but there was an overpowering intensity to his voice.

"I don't even know you," she said softly.

"Yes, you do. You were young, but I remember you well."

She briefly allowed her mind to search for hazy memories of those eyes framed by a younger face. They came all too easily. It was a mountain. Nothing solid, but terror, loss, and pain. Not a mountain, an avalanche. Horrible emotions came pounding down, and she slammed shut the door to the memories. She gasped in pain, and tears had already formed in her eyes.

Jesse leaned forward and put a hand on her shoulder. "Further than that. We had to hide you in the foster system. Dad had no choice."

There is always a choice! Her mind screamed, but she stayed silent.

"He never forgot you, and neither did I. We have been working on nothing else but to get you back."

Elise turned her face away and tried to stop from crying. She felt the separation. It was a chasm in her soul. Ugly, dark, and empty. Her family, and she didn't belong with them.

"Elise, I came here to bring you back. That is why Dad sent me, and that is why I wanted to come myself."

She turned her face to him. It was too late to try to stop the tears, but she managed to keep her voice semi-normal, if a little tight. "You left me alone."

But the blue eyes that held her own could not have been filled with more compassion. He shook his head, "It can't have hurt you more than Dad or I. It was the hardest thing I can ever remember, harder than Mom's death."

She fought his words violently with logic. Her mind scoffed at the very idea that it could've hurt her father more. It was his fault. But as the whirlpool of emotions swirled inside, she felt near exploding. Desperately, she searched for something to cling to, to return to a semblance of peace.

Did she believe Carbon, or did she not? Did she believe him, or did she not?

"You were my buddy," Jesse smiled with the memory. "Still are, in fact. I am going to fix this, and you are never going to be left alone again."

He wrapped her up in a giant bear hug, and her tears broke their dam. All the pain inside seemed to flow out in her cries.

"Ah, Elise." Her brother held her close. "How I've missed you."

* * * *

The room was tense as Agent Stewart walked in. If this was a gamble, it was the biggest of his life. He could be charged with willfully withholding information, collaborating with a fugitive, or worse. On the bright side, this was his investigation. He wasn't required to share everything, and some protocol would demand he play along with Carbon to gather the most information. He was simply buying time.

But he seriously hoped she had kept her word and played a different conversation for listening ears. Letting him in on the content of that fake conversation would have been even better.

"Alan," Richardson stuck his head out the office door and motioned for him to come in. The man didn't look happy.

"Sir?" he responded respectfully, keeping his tone hollow.

The short man sat in his plush chair and swung it around to face the wall. "I need you to clear something up for me."

Stewart blinked, thinking how to best respond. For now, he would plead the fifth.

"You have been in charge of this case for months. And we have no new intel." Richardson turned back to him with a severe frown.

Studying the other man's expression, Stewart realized his secret was safe. "No new intel?"

"Yes. This is not good. Haven't you been managing these people?" He picked up a folder, "I've been through their personnel files. You need to utilize the skills you have."

Stewart winced inside at the criticism, struggling to keep his mouth shut against a sharp retort. "You're right. Give me a team, I want to investigate the Colorado explosion."

Richardson looked at him steadily.

Grabbing the folder, Stewart ruffled through the printouts. "Akers, Guerrez and Masters. Liz can stay and manage the team here. She knows the ropes."

"What are you looking for?"

Stewart replaced the folder and leaned both palms on the desk. He caught Richardson's sharp eye, "New intel, boss. I think that's where I'll find it."

A flicker of something crossed Richardson's stony expression, but it disappeared before Stewart could identify the reaction.

"If you insist," his old mentor raised his eyebrows in a challenge. "But if you come up empty handed, I am taking your post in this investigation. You will work for me."

To say that was a scary thought would be a gross understatement. What had he just done? "That won't happen," he returned evenly.

"I'm sure it won't," Richardson gave a half-smile. "You may go."

Stewart nodded and turned to leave.

"Oh, and Alan," Richardson added. "Agent Kerry goes with you. Masters stays here."

Stewart opened his mouth to protest, but was silenced by a hand.

"Non-negotiable."

Odd. As he closed the door, he wondered how Carbon would take the information. And if she would hold up her end of the bargain.

Chapter 8

The Allens had run into town to shop and they brought back Mexican takeout for lunch. It was a little spicy, but Elise loved it. Everyone devoured their tacos and tortilla chips eagerly, especially Shane, whom Jesse had sent out to work on a fence all day.

"Elise," Mrs. Allen grabbed a bag from the counter and rummaged through its contents. "I got you something. I know it's in here... aha!" she cried triumphantly, handing Elise a small cardboard box.

"Black?" Elise asked in surprise, accepting the hair dye.

"It was Carbon's idea, actually."

The car piped up from a speaker somewhere, "Now you will match me."

Elise laughed, "That's sweet, Carbon. Thanks."

"You are welcome."

"I'll help you put it in after lunch." Mrs. Allen smiled as well, returning to her half-eaten burrito. "Oh, and I got one for you too, Shane."

He looked surprised, then suspicious. "I don't want black hair."

"No, it's not black. Here," she handed him another box.

"What?!" he exclaimed. "Was this Carbon's choice?"

"Yes." The car accepted the responsibility without hesitation. "The change in color will significantly alter your appearance and decrease the risk of recognition. You should grow a moustache as well."

"No way," he set the box of red hair dye on the table. "I am not putting that in my hair, and I am definitely not growing a moustache."

A small giggle escaped Elise, but she quickly covered her mouth after Shane's stony expression. "You would look like..." she couldn't help laughing.

"I know. That's not happening."

Jesse seemed to be having trouble maintaining a straight face as well. "Don't worry, we'll find something else. Sorry, Carbon. I don't think you understand human sensitivity in this area."

"Red is a reasonable choice."

Mr. Allen seemed to understand Shane's reluctance. "You should get a blonde dye and make it a few shades lighter. Then people will think you and Jesse are brothers."

Running his fingers through presently dark brown hair, the ex-deputy didn't look thrilled, but agreed. "Yeah, I think I could manage that. But I'm serious about the no moustache thing."

"I think they're attractive," Mrs. Allen said. "Frank had one when we got married."

Shane just gave her a look.

"But they're not for everybody," she held up her hands in surrender.

Threat gone, he nodded and started back at his tacos.

"I know Grandma here doesn't like official business at the table," Jesse inserted with a meek smile at Mrs. Allen's instantly unpleasant glare. "But I'm just informing you guys that Carbon and I are finalizing plans, and we should meet later tonight to discuss what to do next. That's all."

She eyed him threateningly, "I'll let it slide."

"Thanks."

Elise helped with the dishes when they finished eating, and then she followed Mrs. Allen into the bathroom for a makeover. She tried not to look at the black liquid soaking into her hair, sad to see the honey blonde color disappear. But she needed no convincing that this was necessary.

"Don't worry, you'll look gorgeous," her grandmother reassured her. "I spent a few years working in a beauty salon, I promise to make it look good."

And so for the better part of an hour, Elise endured the treatment. Mrs. Allen wouldn't allow her to look at a mirror until she had finished snipping away a great deal of hair, spent a good ten minutes blowing it dry, and then finalized the new look with makeup.

"I'm afraid to look," Elise admitted when the older woman proclaimed that she was finished.

But Mrs. Allen only smiled. "I don't think you'll recognize yourself."

Predictably, the suspense was more than Elise could take, and it was only a few seconds before she peeked at her reflection.

The results took her breath away. Gone was the sandy haired high school girl, and standing in her place was an elegant looking young woman with a short but stylish cut and flattering makeup.

It surprised her that the jaw hanging open was her own.

"I told you."

"Wow."

"Now, I think I have something that you can wear."

She again followed Mrs. Allen after stealing a last look at the new her, this time arriving in a small walk-in closet.

"Here," Mrs. Allen handed her a light green button down and black slacks. "We have to complete the image. And I'll give you some jewelry after you've changed."

Fully transformed, Elise felt more than a little awkward walking downstairs. It was as if she had been stuffed into someone else's body, and she wasn't sure how to act.

Jesse was sitting on the couch, and though she tried to be as quiet as a mouse, her brother glanced up as soon as she stepped onto the wood floor. His jaw dropped even further than hers had as he stared in shock. "Elise?"

She nodded in affirmation, but he continued staring, speechless. This was really embarrassing.

"It's just me," she tried to smile and brush it off.

"Good job, Grandma!" Jesse called up the stairs. There was no response, but he collected himself and pointed to an easy chair. "Take a seat."

Elise did as she was told, trying not to think about how she looked. "So, what are your plans?"

"Rayford probably has a cure ready, and furthermore, he is expecting us to try to take it. We need to use extreme caution. I would recommend that you stay here, but given the close proximity of where Rayford found you to Elderidge, that may be riskier still. The choice is yours." He fell silent and looked at her expectantly.

"What, you mean between staying here and going with you?"

Jesse nodded. "Yes. Your choice."

The choice wasn't hard for Elise. Sitting around while someone else was risking life and limb for her would be awful, and just waiting to get sick and die was worse. "I'm coming."

"It will be dangerous," Jesse warned.

Elise gave him a skeptical glance. Who was he kidding? Wasn't the past adventure dangerous enough?

"And there can be no turning back."

Studying the seriousness in his face, she paused to consider what he was getting at. "What do you mean?"

"You can be healed, Elise. Set free from this horrible condition. Absolutely, there is no doubt to that. But this trip will not be a bed of roses." He was speaking gently, but the words sank into her stomach like lead.

Her blonde-haired brother continued, "The physical process itself can be painful, the road to complete recovery will be long, and the things you will have to deal with and learn will not be easy."

She searched his expression. Was he trying to scare her?

"You can handle it," he added with a confident nod. "I have no doubt you can face any difficulty or problem that might arise. Plus," he smiled softly. "You will never be alone."

She wasn't sure what he meant by that, but given Carbon's earlier claims, she was pretty confident it related directly to the car. "I'll survive, right? And get to see Dad?"

Jesse's smile widened, "Yeah. It's going to be great. You, me, Dad and Carbon too, of course."

"And if I don't, I'll die in a few months?"

At this, his expression darkened. "What Rayford inserted is actually changing the coding of your DNA. Your body will not function for long without some stabilization."

A chill entered her with the thought. But knowing that she couldn't grasp the full implications of his explanation, she merely blinked.

"Even if someone found a temporary fix," her brother went on, "the pain will be immense, and as more of your cells replicate, any chance of complete healing would become impossible."

Elise swallowed hard. That was a concept she could grasp. "What exactly does this 'treatment' do?" She didn't mean to be so skeptical, but it was her body after all. "And how does it work?"

But Jesse only gave a small laugh and looked at her in amusement. It was far different from Rayford's condescending gaze, filled instead with kindness. "For now, you should leave that to the scientists. I'm sure you'll know the whole story in time. Once Dad and I teach you biochemistry and genetics."

Her face turned red. It was true, there was no way she could grasp what was actually going on.

"Don't worry. When you need to know, you will know."

Now he sounded just like Carbon. The two were strikingly similar. Maybe Jesse helped design her. Elise would have to ask him about it later. First, there were more important things to deal with.

"You said it was going to be really dangerous. What...?" but she fumbled the question, not sure of what she was even trying to ask.

"The situation with Dad and Rayford, with your DNA, it's all complicated. There are things I cannot tell you now for security that you will undoubtedly find out later. Things may happen that you don't understand, that don't seem like the right thing. But remember this," he gave her a stern stare. "Always check with Carbon. She will set you straight."

Exactly what her dad had said. It made sense, she guessed.

"You said it would work, though. This 'treatment'? Even though it will... hurt?"

"Yes. I don't want you to be surprised. I am not trying to trick you, and I want you to understand what you're getting into before you jump. The decision is yours, Elise."

However hard it was, the promise of success sounded pretty good. And being able to see her dad again. Besides, she had Carbon and now her brother. How bad could it be?

She set her jaw and looked her brother squarely in the eye. "I'm in."

He studied her for a moment, his face scrutinizing her with an intensity she wasn't quite comfortable with. Squirming under his gaze, she added quietly, "For better or for worse." She didn't want him to doubt her resolve. Everyone seemed to. Carbon, her father, and now her brother.

He didn't respond right away, and to break the awkward tension she asked a direct question, "What do I need to do?"

Jesse's face broke out into a lopsided grin. "Do?" But his expression grew serious again, "Honestly, the only thing you need to do is simple, but not easy."

What was this, a riddle? "Okay." Elise waited for him to elaborate. Her patience counted down three seconds. "What is it?"

"Wait, and trust me."

That didn't sound like much doing. It also didn't sound very difficult. Wasn't her survival already in their hands? She couldn't create a cure. No, it was Carbon, her father, and Jesse who held her life, the very keys to her future.

She shrugged, "Sure."

He smiled, this time a genuine and generously wide smile. "That's my sister." Standing to leave, he paused to replace his cowboy hat on top of his mop of blonde hair. "We could leave any day now. Carbon is monitoring everything to wait for the best timing. When the moment comes, we will need to leave immediately. Grandma and Grandpa Allen already know, and they understand."

"Do I need to make preparations?"

"Nah, unless you particularly want something. Gran can pick things up at the store for you. Apart from that, enjoy yourself and rest. We've got everything under control." He winked playfully and headed for the door. "Wait and trust!" he yelled over his shoulder as he departed. "It's more important than you think!"

Elise watched him leave through the window. Wait and trust. It didn't sound so hard. Wait and trust, she ingrained the advice into her mind. Wait and trust.

* * * *

Richardson pulled his chair a little closer to the desk. None of these reports had revealed anything interesting yet. He had assigned a new team to scrutinize Dr. Mathis' past and look for any hidden leads there, and he had made the decision with great caution. Phil Masters was leading the team. Not only did he have extensive experience and a proven record, the man was quiet. He wouldn't dig deep enough to get into trouble, and he respected authority.

The desk phone rang, interrupting Richardson's thoughts. "Go ahead," he answered.

"Richardson, this is Hawkins."

Caesar Hawkins managed all of the FBI's major cases that pertained to national security. Although Richardson was far more senior, Hawkins was technically his superior. "Yes, sir. What can I do for you?"

"I'm concerned about one of your agents. I know he is a close friend of yours, and I want to be sure of where your intentions lie in this case."

Had forty years in the Bureau not proved his intentions? "Look, Hawkins, spit it out," he retorted gruffly. "And don't question my loyalty. I agreed to come back on this case as a favor. I could be enjoying the greens with friends right now."

Hawkins was careful in his response, but he was not a man easily intimidated. "Sir, your service to the Bureau has been invaluable and I thank you for the time and effort you've contributed."

"This is about Alan, isn't it?" Richardson asked. He didn't like dancing around the edge of fire.

"Correct. Has he mentioned anything suspicious to you lately?"

Stewart's odd request came to mind. "He did ask to investigate the scene in Colorado, but I wouldn't exactly call that suspicious. Why?"

"Did he go?"

"What?"

"To Colorado. Did you authorize him to go?" Hawkins' voice was strained.

Richardson hesitated. "It is still his investigation, sir. I was not in a position to stop him. What's the worry?"

"You may not repeat this to anybody or..."

"Hawkins," Richardson interrupted firmly. "I know protocol. Spit it out."

"Our tech guys picked up strange anomalies in his cell phone call history. We believe Carbon has contacted him again."

Richardson sat in silence for a moment. He had worked with Alan Stewart long enough to know that the man's only devotion lay with justice. Obsessively so. "What are you suggesting?"

"I am alerting you to the situation, Richardson. Keep an eye on your man. Don't ask him about it, just watch and wait. We don't know what conditions he's operating under."

That sounded like code for 'we think he's turned but are giving him the benefit of the doubt so we hopefully learn more information and catch him red handed'.

"You are close to Stewart. If you come up with anything, let me know."

"Yes, sir," Richardson affirmed. "Will do."

Replacing the phone in its cradle, Richardson leaned back in his chair to think. What had Stewart gotten himself into?

Chapter 9

Initially Elise's mind had resembled a lake in the morning time. Not a ripple or current disturbed her clarity or resolve, and hope walked hand in hand with peace in the serenity and calm. And it was strangely beautiful.

Ever since her conversation with Jesse, things had appeared in perspective. Yes, it might be hard, but that was no surprise, and she wouldn't be facing it alone. In most respects, this was a dream come true. She had found her family, and was about to embark upon a quest that would not only save her life, but lead her to her father.

That conversation had taken place four hours ago, but in that modest window of time, winds had arisen from somewhere and disturbed the calm, peaceful waters. Now waves of despair, fear, and regret were crashing violently, hurling themselves against her efforts to return to stillness. Instead of subsiding, the doubts only grew more forceful, demanding answers and explanations, seeking reasons and greater assurances.

It's not like she sat down and tried to shoot holes in Jesse's plan, it just kind of happened. And now the questions were dragging her under.

In reflection, watching TV probably hadn't been the greatest idea. Out of a twisted sense of curiosity, she had surfed the news channels for any stories about her. Even in such a negative situation, the fame was almost tantalizing. That was her. Her very own face on national news. Granted, the story received a grand total of three minutes of air time, but by the end she wished she hadn't watched it at all.

Not only was her yearbook photo displayed everywhere with a number to call for missing persons, but Shane's face was shown as a suspect in her kidnapping with another crime hotline number to call with info. There was also a computer rendering of Carbon, both white and black, and the photos were despairingly accurate.

It seemed like everyone was looking for them. How could they hope to cross town, much less the country, and not be caught?

And so her fragile faith had taken several more direct hits, and by the time Mrs. Allen returned from the store, Elise's face undoubtedly told the whole story.

Her grandmother read her expression in about a tenth of a second, and as Elise helped carry in groceries, she had already spilled out further details. And she had meant to keep those to herself.

To her surprise, Mrs. Allen only laughed off the fears and worries, patting Elise's cheek cheerily. "Oh, dear. You're too worked up in the future. One step at a time, one step at a time..." and so she had begun dinner preparations, singing a song about taking life 'one step at a time, never looking too far ahead, never accepting vain regrets'.

As they worked together, the annoyingly catchy tune worked its way into her head. While she refused to sing aloud out of personal dignity, she caught herself humming along not once, but twice.

Within a couple hours, the table was set with beef stroganoff, steamed green beans and freshly baked corn bread, and Elise's worried thoughts had been calmed by the menial tasks and cheerful companionship. When her brother came in, she could scarcely remember her reasons for doubting him. Of course he wouldn't lie to her. What was it he said? Wait and trust. How had she forgotten so quickly?

He kicked the dirt off his muddy boots in a loud fashion, and the ever-present cowboy hat found a temporary home on the kitchen counter.

Mrs. Allen sighed, "Jesse, what did I say about..."

But before she could finish, he snatched his hat back like lightning. Grinning sheepishly, he backed into the foyer and set it atop something out of Elise's line of vision.

Mrs. Allen watched him with a dry expression. Jesse raised his hands in surrender and apologized, "Sorry. I was just setting it there for a second. I won't do it again."

"That's what you said yesterday."

"Oh." Jesse offered no further explanation, but continued staring at the long kitchen knife in his grandmother's hand.

She raised her grey eyebrows in a challenge. "You scared?" After a slight nod of confirmation, she shook the knife in the general direction of his hat. "If I see it there one more time ... it might not be in one piece when you see it again."

"Yes, ma'am."

Another set of loud boot stomping, and a figure slammed into Jesse as he stood in the doorway, pushing him dangerously near Mrs. Allen's knife.

In an impressive gymnastic display, her brother bent backwards at the waist and spun around to safety behind the doorway, and in the suddenly vacated space, an off-balance Shane fell headlong with a surprised cry as he hit the wooden floor.

"Hey!" was his immediate response. "Ouch." Picking himself up, he clutched both his ribcage and his nose.

"Oh, dear!" Mrs. Allen scurried to the rescue. "Not the nose again! It was healing so nicely..." After some tut-tut noises and a disgusted moan that it was bleeding again, she made him sit down and hold an icepack to his face.

To Elise's surprise, Jesse had barely moved from where he was standing. Although he offered a pained expression immediately following the fall, she could see clear outlines of a grin as he leaned against the doorframe.

He cleared his throat, "Sorry, buddy. I was being held at knifepoint by my own grandmother, so if you want to blame anyone..."

Shane glanced around the room, trying to hold his nose high to minimize bleeding, and when he spotted Mrs. Allen, she was quick on the defense.

"Me? I'm in here cooking your dinner, and you try to blame this on me?"

Between the innocent and intent expression on her grandmother's face, Shane's awkward position and Jesse's wicked smile, Elise couldn't cover her mouth fast enough to avoid a small giggle.

"There," Mrs. Allen sighed in relief. "We have a witness." She winked knowingly at Elise with the clear expression that girls stick together. "It was Jesse, right?"

"Uh, yeah."

Jesse's face shifted to pure indignation, but his comment was masked by the sound of Shane's ice pack hitting the floor.

"Elise?" He stared at her, agape, a small stream of blood trickling out of his nose. It was kind of disgusting. Elise had never liked seeing blood.

"Yeah?"

Mrs. Allen was quick to retrieve the ice pack and shove it back on his face. "Don't bleed in the kitchen, dear. Elise just had her makeover, and I'd say it went pretty well."

"I'll say," he was dumbfounded. "You look like another person!"

She had forgotten about the new look, having not walked by a mirror in a few hours. Forcing a pleasant smile, she responded, "That's the idea, right?" But honestly, she was not so happy about it.

"I can't wait to see what you look like, Sheriff." Jesse's eyes were still laughing from his corner, "But instead of Mrs. Allen, I have the honor of styling your hair."

"Bring it on. I dare you." Shane gave him what was presumably a playful glare, but his dark eyes seemed pretty serious in their threats. This man was very touchy about his hair.

"Okay, boys," Mrs. Allen scolded them, handing Elise a final glass of water to set on the table. "I'll go get Frank, and you go ahead and sit down."

Jesse offered Shane assistance, which was pointedly refused with another glare. Elise couldn't help smiling to herself as she set the glass down and took her seat at the table. It felt like she was part of a real family here. But she reminded herself not to get too attached. It wasn't going to last, anyway. And the family wasn't whole because a major player was missing. But taking Jesse at his word, she would get to meet him soon enough.

* * * *

"Agent Stewart," a familiar smooth tone greeted him.

"What do you want?" he snapped into his phone.

"When you arrive on site, perform a sweep for motion detecting and monitoring devices. The area has already been cleared, but two devices were missed. I will send you exact coordinates of their locations."

"That's it? You think something can be proved by two little security devices?" All that proved was that this guy was rich and important. And they already knew that much.

"Dig past the immediate structure of the house. You will find evidences of the laboratory behind the debris. There is a stable way to dig a corridor. Special Agent Akers will be able to show you how. Good-bye."

Stewart groaned to himself, but his attention was grabbed. If one of those devices recorded anything, that would give them some account of what happened. And if there were more of them that were purposefully removed - and he wasn't ready to believe Carbon on that one just yet - then somebody was playing foul.

And if they were, he would find out.

Chapter 10

Elise sat on the porch after dinner watching a breeze blow across the field of grasses. The dizziness was beginning to come back, as were the chills and a slight headache. If she told Jesse, that would probably mean another shot, but if the pain continued escalating, the prick of the needle would cease to bother her.

As much as she was welcomed and included here, she couldn't help feeling a pang of homesickness for Mesa Springs. For the Madills, and most of all Nia. But the feeling was a familiar one, so she stuffed it someplace obscure without a second thought.

Jesse said he would be gone tomorrow, working on the details of his plan, but she was free to do whatever she wanted in the meantime.

Drawing her legs into her chest, she hugged them close and wished for nothing better than to feel better. If only the pain would just go away and she didn't have to worry about getting caught by the police or Rayford or – if she lived long enough – retrieving a cure from that evil man's clutches.

She sat in silence as the sun sank lower and lower, thinking about nothing in particular. Only the feel of the wind on her face and the coolness of the evening.

Her peaceful moments were interrupted by the screen porch door creaking open.

"Hey, Elise." Jesse let the door slam shut behind him. "Not feeling well?"

She shook her head, though the thought of lying passed through her mind.

He sighed. "I'll be right back."

True to his word, after two minutes he had returned with a syringe filled with a clear liquid. "Sorry about this, but until we get that cure, this patchwork is the best I can do."

Offering her arm, she still looked away and flinched as he slid the needle gently into her skin.

"There," he proclaimed, swabbing the area with a cotton ball. "You shouldn't need another shot for two days or so." He applied a band-aid before sitting down next to her. "You should start feeling better in a few minutes."

She only nodded again, suddenly reliving her earlier doubts and fears. What if his plan didn't work?

He grinned that wicked smile again, nudging her with his elbow. "Grandma is fixing Shane's hair up now." Laughing to himself, he stretched out and relaxed into the rocking chair. "I can't wait to see him. Who would've thought that hair could be so important to a man?"

"What's going to happen to him?" Elise asked. She had wondered the question before, but wasn't sure how to ask politely. After seeing his picture on national news, she doubted he could return to normal life.

"I don't know," Jesse answered. "It's really up to him. We offered to try to fix a new identity or send him somewhere remote if he wants."

"Oh."

"But I don't think he'll accept those offers. He's curious. He will probably come with us to Rayford's."

Elise could feel the medicine working its way into her body, relaxing her muscles and relieving the pain. As her mind cleared, she found this an opportune time to voice a particular question that had been bugging her.

"What's Dad like?"

Jesse gave her a sideways glance and smiled warmly. "The best father you could ever have."

"I guess you guys are really close?" Bidden or not, jealousy leaked into her words.

"Yeah. Yeah, we are. Ever since Mom was killed, and you..." he trailed off. "Well, he pretty much taught me everything he knows. But I'm sure there's a lot left to learn." He chuckled, "You should see Carbon's programming. It's not that simple."

"You helped build her?"

He shook his head. "Dad built her basic program long before me. But I helped build and integrate her into the car. It wasn't easy, but we had an incredible incentive." He reached over and gave her a light rub on the head.

"Ouch," she complained, annoyed but unable to resist the laughter that bubbled up. "Stop it. I'm not a dog."

Jesse desisted and smiled, but then got a far-away look. "I remember when we ran. Too clearly. The night Mom and Dad stuffed us in the van and left. They wouldn't say anything, but I could sense the fear, that the danger was real." He looked at her, "You were only five. You were screaming, but stopped when Mom let you sit on her lap." He glanced at her, "Do you remember?"

She shook her head quickly, but her body trembled as if the memory might escape the dark recesses of her mind. "No."

"I was fifteen," he continued. "You seemed to handle it well after that night, even though we lived out of motels and some piece of junk RV Dad bought. We thought we were safe. That he wouldn't find us. But ..." his voice fell to a whisper. "A few months later, we were starting to rebuild with new identities and Mom took you to the grocery store in town. I was begging to come along, but Dad made me stay home to help him work on the RV. She dropped you off after an hour, saying she would be back soon and had forgotten our clothes in the Laundromat."

"You and I were playing around in the RV park; Cowboys and Indians," he looked at her again, puzzled. "You sure you don't remember at all?"

With another shake of her head, she denied any memories. But it wasn't true. They were there, faint feelings. Dim shadows of hiding behind trees, aiming at her brother with a stick shaped like a revolver. And then there was panic. Everything obscured by darkness.

"Dad gave us to the neighbors and borrowed their car. When he returned, he wouldn't say anything. But there were tears on his face. And blood, all over him. He grabbed us and ran. We ditched the RV, buying another car with some money he had left. And we never went back. I never saw her again."

"What happened?" Elise remembered the newspaper clippings, the story that Dr. Mathis was implicated in the murder of his own wife.

"Dad told me later. He had received a call. A warning from another colleague, and then a call from Mom. He won't talk about it much, but they murdered her in front of him. Tried to get him to come out of hiding, because they wanted him alive. He tried to save her, but there was no way. Too many of them."

Jesse collected himself, "That's when he decided it was too dangerous for you. I was older, and could take care of myself, but he couldn't take losing you. Not after what happened to Mom. So he made some 'arrangements' and put you into the foster system with a brand new identity, completely untraceable."

"But you guys found me."

"Yeah, well. He made sure he knew where you were every step of the way. And that's when we hatched the ingenious plan to get you back and make things right."

Elise wasn't sure what he meant by 'make things right', but they were interrupted by the screen door opening again. Out trudged a subdued Shane Lawson. His dark brown hair had been cropped short when she first saw him, though now the sandy blonde color exaggerated how much it had grown out. Not to the same lengths as Jesse's shaggy locks, but not a clean-shaven cop either. He looked pained by the experience, but he was trying to bear it well.

"Aw, come on Shane. Is it that bad to look like me?" Jesse teased him.

The former deputy sighed. "First my car, then my life, and now..." he slowly walked to an empty chair like a martyr. "My dignity."

"Which was worse?" Jesse didn't hesitate to ask.

He did look quite different, kind of like a surfer dude. "It's not that bad," Elise offered.

"Not that bad?" He ran his fingers through a strand of the offensive locks, eying them with derision. "I look like ..."

"A surfer," she suggested. "What's wrong with surfers?"

"Well, for one, there are no oceans around for a good ways," Jesse pointed out helpfully.

Elise glared at him, "Just say you're visiting your country brother from your home in Hawaii."

"Yeah, that should work," Jesse agreed. "What do you want your name to be?"

"Shane," he answered firmly. "Just change the last name."

He sounded non-negotiable, and Jesse must have figured the man had suffered enough, so he let it slide. Instead he changed the subject. "So, are you coming with us?"

"I'm not just going to sit around here. And your dad promised me a new car. So now I have to find him."

"Good enough for me," Jesse shrugged. "I'll be glad to have you along." Her brother stood as if the matter was settled. "If you'll excuse me, I'm going to finish some calculations."

"That sounds fun," Shane remarked dryly.

Jesse smiled. "You have no idea. And if all goes well, expect to be leaving in the next few days." Shifting to a deep voice, he donned his cowboy hat and walked back into the house, "Hasta lavista, mis amigos."

Shane shook his head as the door slammed shut. "That guy..."

"He's ... special," was all Elise could think of to say. He was by all counts likeable, but a little odd.

Shane had not yet left the topic of his hair. "A surfer? Really?"

"Well," she surveyed his tanned face, brown eyes and now longish blonde hair. His nose was swollen, and distorted the image a little, but combined with his tall lean frame, he looked undeniably like a beach bum. "Yeah. Really."

He let out another sigh. "I suppose it could be worse."

"You mean like being terminally ill?"

He looked momentarily shocked at her bold words, but he recovered quickly. "No. This is worse."

She couldn't help but laugh at the seriousness of his tone. "Yeah, you're right. You might not make it." But she instantly regretted her statement as the truth of it hit home.

They were silent for a few minutes as the blue sky continued melting into shades of purple. Guilt began to claw at her for ruining this man's life. "Have you seen the news?" she asked.

"Mm-hm." His expression didn't change as he stared blankly into the expanse of earth and heavens. "Not so good."

"I'm sorry."

"Look, Elise..."

"It's Bonnie now," she corrected him, glad to have a fake name already. "You might as well practice."

"Whatever. You don't need to apologize. This is not your fault. I don't know who's to blame here, or what is really going on, but I do intend to find out." He gave her a strange look, as if deciding whether or not she could be trusted. "I'm pretty sure Rayford's a guilty party."

She nodded her agreement.

"But there are too many unanswered questions." He released a heavy sigh, "Too many."

"Tell me about it," she muttered.

"And you are willing to get to the bottom of this, no matter what the truth is?"

She wasn't sure if it was a question or a statement, but she nodded anyway. "Of course."

He looked relieved, and started to say more, but abruptly stood instead. "Well, good night. I'll see you in the morning."

"Good night," she echoed, staring back at the sunset. But now her mind was busy and cluttered, sifting through all the information she had just downloaded. The sky had turned black, but the twinkling stars removed the malevolence of the darkness. So many things to consider: even when you can't see the billions of lights, the sky is never empty.

* * * *

"Yes, Hawkins?" Richardson tried to keep his tone friendly, but he could feel the steam from the other side of the phone before he heard a response.

"Stewart found a way to bore into the collapsed building without risking further destabilization." Hawkins statement came out like a freight train, aimed to run over everything else.

"And?" Richardson was tired of playing this game.

"This is beyond reasonable risk, Richardson. We're playing with national security here."

"Aren't we always?" he returned. "Stewart's not going to find anything. We were assured that the structure completely caved in on itself, leaving no evidence behind. What are you worried about?"

Hawkins was silent for a moment.

"You're telling me there's something there." It wasn't hard to guess.

"We were waiting for the heat to back off so we could extract a package." Caesar Hawkins' voice switched from strained to blunt. "If your man finds it first, I cannot guarantee his protection."

"What package?" Richardson demanded.

"That is all. I will contact you later."

Chapter 11

There were times when Elise cursed her womanhood. She knew that women were supposed to be more moody and emotional than men, but this was just ridiculous. It must be because she was sick.

One minute she would be happy; content with life and hopeful that the future would work out just fine, and even be good. But she couldn't hold on to such thoughts. Within a few hours, she would run through more emotions than she even knew existed in the human race. Fear, anger, despair, hope, triumph, failure, chaos, peace, love, hate, disappointment, doubt, joy, agony; the list could go on forever.

Why couldn't her thoughts hold still? Just pick one! One solid instinct to hold on to, and resolve to see it through. But the next minute would come, and she no longer wanted to find what was real and cling to it. She was already mad that she hadn't figured it out yet.

For a lengthier peace, she had sought refuge in the pages of an old western novel she discovered in her dresser drawer, and by page fifty her thoughts were finally settling on the story. And it just figured when that moment of relaxation coincided with a knocking on her bedroom door.

"Elise?" Shane's voice asked from the other side.

She stifled her groan of frustration and rolled off the bed.

"Yes?" she answered, opening the door a few inches.

"Jesse said he wants to talk about plans with us. He'll be up in a few minutes."

"Oh." She tried not to look too unhappy, but was apparently unsuccessful at masking her thoughts.

"Don't want to think about it, huh?"

"No," she was instantly defensive. "I just… want to get this over with."

He sighed, "You're not the only one. But I think we're going to leave soon."

And now she was mad again. Mad at Shane for standing there talking to her, mad because she already felt guilty both for ruining his life and for not feeling grateful enough, mad because she couldn't make herself be happy and peaceful like she wanted.

"Whatcha reading?"

None of your business, her mind retorted. But she had learned to think before speaking, so she only shrugged instead. "Just something I found lying around."

"To take your mind off things?"

Why wouldn't he just go away? Why was he still talking? Did she really look like she wanted to chat right now? "I guess."

"Is it working?"

Shut up! Her mind screamed. Surely he could feel the angry vibes emanating in his direction. "Not really."

His eyes softened apologetically, "I'm sorry."

Don't be nice, her mind pleaded. Why did he have to be nice about things? Now her anger melted into a strange heap of wretchedness, of some basic need. She felt the urge to throw herself at him, just to have someone stronger to help. Goodness, what was wrong with her?

Footsteps echoed off the stairs, and Elise reluctantly opened the door the rest of the way.

"Hey, Elise!" Jesse greeted her cheerfully. Great, now she just wanted to cry in a corner. "How are you?"

Unable to speak – for she had no desire to become a sobbing, pathetic mess in front of the two men – she gave a half-hearted smile and hoped he left it at that. Which, mercifully, was exactly what he did.

"Do you mind if we discuss this in your room? I think we might need the computer."

She shook her head. For whatever reason, she had been given the only room with a functional computer. It wasn't exactly new or fast, but it worked.

They stood around the bed as Jesse laid out some large sheets of paper. "Okay. I want to show you guys the laboratory where we should find what we need."

It was easy to pay attention as her brother spoke, and she was surprised at the complexity of this building. She had figured that Rayford's main compound had been destroyed in Colorado, but compared with this, the other was child's play.

"We believe he is working with someone inside the government," Jesse was saying. "And they probably have a sizable hand in this facility. Carbon got a hold of the contractor's blueprints, but she suspects another section has been added underground or somewhere nearby. At least it gives us a starting point."

"Where is this?" Shane asked.

"Seattle."

"It's in a city?" Elise wondered out loud.

"Yeah, but not advertised as an experimental government research center," Jesse explained with a smile. "It used to house the genetic research facility for Ceeling University, as well the private IVF clinic Rayford and Dad ran together. Today it is a pharmaceutical lab."

She nodded, surveying the blueprints closer.

"Are you planning to sneak in there at night?" Shane asked. When there was no immediate response, Elise glanced up at Jesse. He was staring vacantly at the space beside her head, like he was hearing an invisible voice. An engine sounded in the distance, drawing closer. Odd, because both the Allens were already downstairs, and it did not sound like Carbon.

Jesse held up a finger in silence, listening. Elise strained her ears, and heard the clear sounds of a car door open and close. Twice. Two doors.

Wasting no time, he herded both of them beside the bed and pushed them back into a small closet. With another finger to his lips, and a serious expression that terrified her, he closed the door without a sound and the world went dark.

There came several knocks on the front door, and Mrs. Allen calling out in response. Elise involuntarily shrank backwards into the darkness and bumped into Shane. She felt his hand on her shoulder, maybe to steady himself, but more present in her mind was the icy hand of fear that had wrapped around her throat. Breathing was difficult – and she tried not to, for the sake of noise. One thing she was sure of, she never wanted to go to Rayford's again, and certainly never wanted to meet him again. Ever.

What if they had followed her?

The words were muffled, but she could hear voices rising up from below. An unfamiliar male, both of the Allens, and then Jesse joined the conversation. Her knees felt weak, and she dearly hoped they wouldn't fail her now.

This closet was not made for a person to hide in, let alone two people. But she was grateful for the warm body behind her, to not be alone.

There were a few small bouts of laughter – surely a good sign – and after ten minutes, she began to wonder if it was safe to come out. But instinct was firmly against it, and she willed her wobbly legs to stay put.

She felt Shane shift his weight, but he froze as several heavy footsteps resounded off the wooden staircase.

"There are three rooms up here," Mr. Allen's voice was saying. "And you're welcome to look through them if you want."

"What's in this one?" the same male voice asked.

"It's a bedroom. Mine."

"Open the door, please." It was more of a demand, and belonged to yet another person.

She could hear them shuffling around the room across the hall, unsure if her heart was beating at all. There wasn't much conversation, but after a few minutes the footsteps drew nearer once more.

The door into her bedroom clicked and creaked open slowly. Her muscles were already frozen, but they locked into place as two pairs of feet walked over the wooden floors.

"My wife sleeps here sometimes," Mr. Allen said wistfully from the doorway. "This used to be our daughter's room, and Ruth keeps it the same for sentimental purposes."

"What happened to your daughter?" one of the voices asked.

There was a heavy sigh. "Car accident. It was years ago, but it might as well have been yesterday."

"I'm sorry, sir. We'll try not to disturb anything."

Another pause. "Yeah. Well, I don't like to be up here much, but I'll be downstairs if you need me."

More footsteps. Stairs creaking with Mr. Allen's slow and purposeful steps.

"Hey," one of the men said in a low voice. "Look at this. Not a bad looking thing, was she?"

The other one laughed softly. "Bill. You need to focus."

"Too bad, though. That she's dead and all."

Another empty silence, then Bill's partner spoke again. "Come on. Let's just glance at the other rooms. We don't have forever, you know, and I don't think we're going to find anything here."

"Yeah," Bill was in agreement. "And I'm getting hungry. I smelled something pretty good in that kitchen. I wish my grandma would cook like that."

"She's still alive?" the other voice seemed incredulous, but their footsteps were receding out the door.

"Yep. And still cooking."

The two continued to chat, stepping through the remaining room in under a minute. Elise allowed a shallow breath, hoping they would move on soon. She felt Shane tense and move behind her, the hand that she had forgotten about on her shoulder pulling away suddenly. His whole body seemed to tremble, and she risked turning around to see what had happened.

In the dim light, his hand was against his nose, his eyes squeezed tightly shut. Elise's relief at not being discovered vaporized as she realized this familiar position. He took one shallow breath in, and she knew the next sound wouldn't be as quiet. In her terror, her mind both conceived of and executed an insane plan in the same instant.

Standing on her tiptoes, she covered his mouth with her own, pressing her face in to be sure and absorb any noise that might escape. He jerked back slightly in surprise, but her goal was achieved as she felt him relax, all danger of the sneeze having passed.

She pulled back as quietly as she could, straining her ears to hear the men's footsteps. They seemed to pause but soon resumed their course down the hallway and the staircase. A few words were exchanged between the two of them and Jesse, and in a few moments, the front door opened and closed. The sound of two car doors followed, and then an engine turning over. It was not until the noise of the car had disappeared far down the Allens' driveway that Elise released sigh of relief.

"It's safe!" Jesse called from below.

Trembling, Elise managed to push the closet door open and stumble out. Her nerves did not appreciate that close call, and she felt like the life had been literally sucked from her.

Shane stepped out behind her, and it became evident that she would have to deal with the consequences of her actions. She was too embarrassed to get an accurate reading of his expression, and even more so when she felt her face flush what was probably a bright red.

"Sorry," she apologized. "If you had sneezed..." but she trailed off, the second part of the statement both too horrible and obvious to state aloud.

"It's okay."

Working up the courage to look at him directly, she saw that he was smiling. A smile she wished she could help wipe off.

"It worked, right?"

"Yeah," she muttered, grateful when Jesse stepped into the room.

"What worked?" he asked.

"Nothing," she quickly responded. "Who was that?"

He looked troubled. "Two FBI agents. Carbon saw them drive up, and when they got near the cameras on the house, she matched their faces to Dad's list of people to avoid."

Elise felt the color drain from her face. "So they work for Rayford?"

"It's difficult to say. They were probably connected with the two who kidnapped you out of the prison."

"What did they want?" Shane asked.

"To look around. Somehow they must have narrowed their search radius. I don't know how they got this close, but this is not good. The sun will be down in a few hours, and we need to leave as soon as it's night."

Elise stared at her brother. How could they have found her?

He continued, "Elise, pack anything you need to take that can fit into a backpack. Mrs. Allen will help you. Shane, you can do the same, but I need you to help me move some stuff first."

They followed him down the stairs, and as she stepped into the kitchen, her grandmother was waiting.

"Elise!" she cried, jumping up to wrap her in a giant hug. "Oh, my baby," she repeated several times, crying softly to herself. She held Elise at arm's length and wiped away the tears. "They are not going to get you. Come on, we'll get you packed with everything you need."

* * * *

"How's the drilling coming?" Stewart asked, walking up behind Special Agent Melanie Akers. Guerrez and Kerry were off looking for the recording devices, leaving a contracted team boring into the rubble under Akers' supervision.

She glanced up from her calculations. "Excellent, actually. At first this looked impossible, like the whole mountain would collapse if we dug anywhere. But..." she wiped beads of sweat from her forehead. "Thanks to the blueprints you found, we were able to use the remaining structure of the hallway, which seems to be partially intact." She grinned, "Quite lucky."

"Mm-hm," Stewart acknowledged, his thoughts elsewhere. "Good work. Let me know when we get near the back of the building. According to these plans, you should hit solid mountain."

Akers nodded, "Yes, I saw that. What concerns me is how the mountain seems to have shifted. It's almost like a much larger space existed underneath. You sure this is the correct blueprint?"

"That's what I would like to know," Stewart smiled.

Chapter 12

Elise could hardly believe what was happening. She felt numb as Mrs. Allen helped her pick out and pack several sets of clothes, toiletries, and some snacks to take along. All three of the guys had disappeared in the white truck almost immediately, and she wondered what they were doing.

She was vaguely aware of the impending night and as the last light of the day vanished, she was torn between wishing she could stay longer and being anxious to leave. What troubled her more, however, was the growing ache in her body. Her head was sensitive to even the smallest of movements and her muscles felt weak and unsteady. Jesse had given her a shot just over a day ago, and he had said it would last for two days.

The headache was like an iron weight; try as she could to bear and ignore it, all her senses were dulled by the pain.

Mrs. Allen had worked deftly, and now they sat in silence at the kitchen table, waiting for the others to return.

* * * *

Ex-sheriff deputy Shane Lawson was ready. For what, he had no idea. But it didn't really matter. He watched dutifully as Jesse prepared and packaged an array of what he presumed were medical supplies and odd little gizmos whose purpose he couldn't begin to fathom.

There was one factor that Shane considered pretty important that was not included. "Uh, aren't we going to need weapons?"

Jesse glanced up at him. "Weapons?"

"You know, guns? Something?"

"Oh." The blonde cowboy pointed to Carbon, "Don't worry. She's got everything we need."

Nodding as if he understood, Shane had to ask, "What exactly are we expecting here? I mean, who's after us?"

"Besides the government?"

Shane nodded again.

Shaking his head, Jesse refused to be specific. "It's hard to say. By now, Rayford might have mercenaries out there looking for her."

All of this was leading him to a crucial question. "Why would they want Elise so badly?"

Heaving a sigh, Jesse paused from his work and looked him in the eye. "Her DNA is evidence of the research Dr. Rayford has wanted for so long. My dad destroyed all traces so the technology could not be developed or researched any further. The FBI knows this, and that's why they're looking for her as well. The idea of a genetic superiority, of being stronger, faster, and smarter than your enemies. There are a lot of people who would like to have that."

"All the information is in Elise's DNA? That's why they want her?"

Jesse nodded. "After Rayford added the SynMOs, he was probably betting on being able to stabilize the cells for months or even years for testing purposes."

"Oh. So could you use the same stuff? To make her live longer?"

"No. It's too dangerous. Occasionally she would feel great, and be able to exhibit whatever traits Rayford or whomever wanted – strength, intelligence, or whatever – but she would be completely dependent on artificial stabilizers in her cells and would lose conscious control of her body. In the end, the process is only extremely painful and it would kill her."

This was the information he had been asking for, and now it was finally coming. His mind fought to grasp the concepts and their implications. A sick thought occurred to him, "Elise is the only remaining evidence?"

Jesse nodded again.

He couldn't bring himself to say it out loud, but that meant there was a much easier solution. If she was dead, there would be nothing to trace back.

"What's wrong with the research?" he asked. "Why did your dad destroy it?"

"Sorry, Shane. I can't answer all your questions now."

"That's a pretty important one."

"No, not that important. What's important now," Jesse picked up the final box and set it in Carbon's open trunk, "is fixing Elise's DNA, and not letting them get her." Leaving no room for argument, he slammed the lid closed and walked to the driver's door. "Come on, surfer. It's time to finish packing."

* * * *

FBI agent John McAllister sat next to his partner, brows furrowed in concentration. "I can't shake the feeling that I've seen that girl before."

"The red-haired woman?" They had just left a cozy farmhouse with clear Irish bloodlines, and five children to boot.

"No. That picture you were looking at. With the old people, and the blonde guy."

But Bill looked blank.

"You know, the one who looked kinda like Owen Wilson?"

"Oh, yeah," the memory was dawning. "The girl who died in the accident. There were pictures all over, from a baby to high school. Yep. She was a cute thing."

"No, no. I mean, I've seen her before. I'm sure of it."

Agent William Morrison looked pensive. "Hmm. I don't know. Maybe an old friend? You ever live in Montana?"

John shook his head. He just couldn't shake the feeling. "How old were those high school photos?"

"About thirty years, if I remember. Close to my graduating class."

"How old would Nancy Mathis be if she was still alive?"

Bill stared at his partner. "Come on, buddy. She would be ..." but he trailed off, considering the ages of the parents. "What are the chances?"

But Agent McAllister was ahead of him. Slamming on the brakes, he did a u-turn in the gravel beside the road. "We need to call this in. It may be nothing, but we can't risk it. I bet if we age progress those photos it will be Mrs. Mathis' spitting image."

Bill Morrison said nothing as he dialed in to headquarters.

* * * *

"Excuse me," Carbon's voice interrupted Shane's thoughts. He, Jesse, and Mr. Allen were driving back to the house for the final packing of clothes, food, and water. So far they had been silent, Shane left to consider his newest piece of the puzzle. He didn't like where his thoughts took him, didn't like how his mind was almost ready to rationalize an innocent girl's death.

That and even worse, she was growing on him. Remembering her brief kiss – if you could call it that – brought a smile to his face. He really was about to sneeze. He had been working hard to fight the urge the whole time of being locked in that ridiculously dusty closet, his allergies growing angrier by the second.

And her move worked. Completely shocked him, actually. His body forgot the sneeze in its entirety.

She was too young, and might not live long anyway. For that matter, none of them might survive very long. Jesse seemed confident this mission would succeed, but that only made one of them. If that many people were looking for her ...

Carbon's voice drew him back. "The FBI agents' vehicle has turned around, and I have intercepted a call from Agent Morrison's phone alerting his unit. He recognized Nancy from the early photos in the room."

Jesse – or Carbon – floored it, and sent them all jostling over the rugged terrain. Already things were moving faster.

"Do what you can from here, Carbon. Call Mrs. Allen, tell her to have Elise and the supplies ready to go." Jesse's voice was calm, but his jaw visibly tightened. He glanced at Mr. Allen, the old man appearing equally stricken. "You two need to get out of here fast. The Explorer is ready to go, I finished working on it the other week."

The grey-haired rancher nodded. "Don't worry about us. I'm sure we'll be fine. What they're after is you guys."

With an odd grin, Jesse looked back at him in the rearview mirror. "You ready?"

Unable to fully return the smile, Shane offered a thumbs-up. "Ready."

The blond cowboy turned his attention to the dirt road, where the humble farmhouse was beginning to appear. "And so it begins."

Chapter 13

Elise staggered under the load of her backpack, several jugs of water, and a bag of snacks Mrs. Allen had given her.

"Here," her grandfather appeared from nowhere to relieve her of half the load. "Let me help you." They stashed some of it in Carbon's trunk and some in the backseat, and by the time they had finished, Jesse and Shane were returning with the final supplies.

Her headache had worsened, but not yet to the point that it interfered with her thoughts. She didn't want to ask for another shot, she felt like a drug addict already. Instead she resolved to bear up under the pain, at least as long as she could stand it.

"They are ten minutes away," Carbon informed them. "I created a brief diversion but they have resumed their course."

The Allens stood in front of their porch, hand in hand. The light from the house wasn't very bright, but it was enough to get by, and it was obvious that this time Mrs. Allen was not the only one with tears in her eyes. Elise hated goodbyes. She wished she could skip this part altogether.

"Good-bye Gran, Grandpa," Jesse gave them each a hug and a kiss on the cheek. "Take care of yourselves."

"Don't worry about us," Mr. Allen reminded him. "You take good care of Elise, now."

Jesse looked back at her and smiled. "You ready?"

Feeling obligated to do something, she stepped forward and gave both of her grandparents a small hug.

"Bye, sweetie," Mrs. Allen whispered. "I'm sure we'll see you again."

Unable to look back, Elise tried to blink away the tears forming in her eyes.

"Shane," Mr. Allen stepped down to give the ex-deputy's hand a good shake. "You're a good man. It was a pleasure."

He nodded and said something back, but Elise wasn't paying enough attention. She just wanted to get out of there. Carbon had opened both of her doors, so she climbed into the backseat with a final wave at her grandparents.

Trying to squelch her feelings, she sought refuge in focusing on the future. She was with her brother, and was going to find her father. This was going to work.

"All right," Jesse got in the driver seat and rearranged his cowboy hat. Shane got in the other side, and Elise heard Carbon click the door locks. This was definitely different than traveling alone.

They shot off down the driveway, and when Elise glanced back at the farmhouse, it was already a speck of light in the darkness.

"They will pass us in four minutes at this rate," Carbon provided a picture on the center console with blinking dots on an intercept course.

"What's your plan?" Shane asked.

"Don't get caught, don't die." Jesse grinned.

"Wow. A lot of careful planning there."

"You're telling me."

"Two minutes," Carbon warned.

Slowing carefully, Jesse pulled off the road down a dirt trail. "We'll wait behind some trees for them to pass. Hey, Carbon, do they have other vehicles en route?"

"Yes, but not within thirty miles." The screen zoomed out, and three other dots appeared in various places on the map.

"Great," Jesse shifted into park and rubbed his hands together in anticipation. "That makes things easier."

Carbon's lights and engine cut out, and in the eerie silence, Elise leaned flat on the back seat. Even against the stress and adrenaline, she could feel that her body was tired.

The sound of another car hummed in the distance, and she watched with dim concern as their headlights came and went, never pausing.

As the noise faded into the distance, Elise heard Carbon's engine restart. Sighing against the pain in her head, she closed her eyes and huddled into the soft leather seat.

* * * *

Stewart wiped sweaty palms on his shirt, watching the scene with growing apprehension. Carbon was right.

"Akers, what have we got here?" he called to the physicist as she helped Guerrez pull a stainless steel briefcase out of the robotic arm's grasp.

"Hard to say, boss!" she yelled back, nearly falling over as the magnet released suddenly. Shaking herself off, Special Agent Melanie Akers gathered her nonexistent dignity and marched toward him.

The hairs on the back of his neck raised, and Stewart felt his chest pounding. He shouldn't be this alarmed. Then again, maybe he should be far more concerned.

"Fingerprint and code locked, sir," she declared, setting the medium size case before him.

"Can we break it open?" he asked.

She studied the package for a moment. "I'm not sure. Given enough time and the right equipment, probably. That's a pretty high tech setup, and if we cut into it, we risk damaging or destroying what is inside."

Guerrez walked up behind her, eyeing the case suspiciously. "A whole separate section back there, and this case."

Melanie pulled her glasses off and wiped her brow. "Someone designed this place to collapse and conceal all evidence. It's miraculous we were able to dig in so far without destabilizing the mountain."

"This was meant to be retrieved," Stewart stated slowly as the thought dawned on him. Someone was planning on coming back. How convenient that police and FBI searches had been restricted.

"Boss," Guerrez lifted his eyes to the rubble. "How did you know to look here?"

Stewart grunted, but didn't respond. "Where's Liz?" he asked.

"Searching for the recording device."

Stewart nodded and reached for his phone as it buzzed on his belt. "Keep searching," he instructed them. "I want to know if anything else is back there."

As the other two returned to the rubble, Stewart turned and answered. "Agent Stewart here."

"You found something," Carbon's voice came.

He glanced around, annoyed that this lady found it so easy to monitor his every motion.

"Now you understand. The site was purposefully restricted and not searched."

Then there was the chance that the Bureau was simply ignorant, and did not suspect such an elaborate plot. But for now he played along with Carbon's story. "What now?"

"You and your team are in danger. News of your discovery has reached unfriendly ears. They will try to take the briefcase from you. I anticipate that they will be successful. I am warning you so that you may escape with your lives. This phone is too dangerous for me to contact you on again. I will provide you with another when the time comes."

"Wait," Stewart said, his mind rolling over the details. "Whose briefcase? What do we do with it?"

"Good-bye, Agent."

He knew better than to hope she would stay on the line. She could have planted the briefcase, she could be playing him. But why?

"Akers! Guerrez!" he called gruffly. "Get over here."

They paused, tossing him a questioning glance.

"Now!" he shouted. "Liz!" he called towards the trees. She should be heading back soon.

"Yes, sir?" Melanie asked sharply. Her face reflected his own concern.

"Someone else is after this briefcase. We are not going to let them have it."

Agent Kerry jogged up from the mountainside. "Boss?"

"This package," he held up the briefcase. "Is to be protected at all costs. We need to get it back to headquarters and find out what's inside."

Liz looked uncertain. "Who's after it?"

"Anyone is suspect," Stewart said definitively. "There is only one road out of here, and I suggest we split up. Guerrez, you're with Liz. Akers, with me," he motioned toward the cars. "Let's go. We don't stop for anything until the airport. I will have the plane waiting and ready."

Chapter 14

When Elise awoke, it was still dark outside. And now her head was pounding. She tried to sit up, crying out with the pain of the effort. Her limbs were on fire, and her stomach was clenched tightly.

"Elise?" Jesse's voice sounded concerned.

She felt a cool hand reach back and press against her forehead.

"Oh, my. Carbon, take over."

She didn't notice the prick in her arm this time, but she became aware of the pain slowly ebbing away, as if it was carried out by an evening tide.

Jesse's face came into focus, and he was snapping fingers in front of her eyes. "Elise? How do you feel?"

At first it felt like an iron weight held her tongue down, but she was able to speak as it lifted. "I'm okay," she slurred, fighting to speak clearly.

"What's wrong?" Shane asked groggily, as if he had just woken up as well.

Jesse bit his lip. "It looks like the process is occurring faster than we predicted. Carbon, run some scans please."

The car responded in the next minute, "Her vital signs are strong, and her breathing is deep. She is stable."

"I'm okay," Elise managed to say almost normally.

"I gave you a stronger dose, so it shouldn't wear off so fast next time." Jesse still looked apprehensive, but reached back to pat her shoulder in comfort. "Just hang in there. I should've been paying closer attention."

She nodded, grateful that the pain had receded. "Where are we?"

"Idaho. It will take another twelve hours to get to Seattle, and we can't travel during the day."

"What are we going to do?" Elise hoped they weren't just going to sit in the car. Sick or not, that was really boring.

"Relax," Jesse turned to wink at her. "We are going to relax."

"What?" Somehow she couldn't picture them just sitting somewhere, as if nothing was wrong. Glancing over, she saw Shane stir in the front seat.

Jesse followed her eyes. "Sleeping like a baby." He gave a little laugh, "We'll wake him up in a few hours. By then we should be deep into Glacier National Park. We can spend the day hiking and just relaxing. Not many people, and not much law enforcement. It will be like vacation."

"Vacation?"

"Yeah. Vacation. No one will look for us there. We'll leave Carbon hidden somewhere and explore a little."

Elise tried to reconcile the idea of just relaxing with the knowledge that she was being hunted.

"Rest and trust, remember?" Jesse reminded her with a smile. "It'll be fun."

Taking her brother at his word, Elise slid back down in her seat. As her body begged to return to sleep, at least the rest part didn't seem very difficult.

* * * *

The drive had proven uneventful, but Agent Stewart's senses were on high alert. Melanie was silent – not out of character for her – but after examining the briefcase more fully, she made an alarming observation. Government issue. Security cases like that were not even available to civilians.

And then she offered an even more troubling theory. If someone went to such great lengths to hide and secure the case, it was likely equipped with one or more homing beacons.

Stewart had Liz keep her car close so no one could triangulate which exact car the package was in, but it hardly made him feel better about their situation. He called ahead and alerted the pilots so they would waste no time in getting airborne. As they neared the airport, he hoped they had done as instructed.

Akers had already contacted airport security to say they would be driving straight in to board and take off. They were advised of the situation, and asked to report any unauthorized or suspicious activity.

So far, all had been quiet.

Stewart felt his muscles tense as they approached the outer fence of the airport. Everything appeared calm as they were waved through the security gate.

The Falcon jet was waiting on the tarmac, engines spooling up. "I'll cover you," Stewart told Melanie as they pulled up by the stairway. He drew his gun, eyes searching for anything out of the ordinary. "Get the case."

She did as instructed, and Liz and Guerrez also got out of their car with guns drawn.

An airport security man walked down the stairs. "We kept an eye on things for you," he said. "Everything's good."

"Who authorized you to board this aircraft?" Stewart demanded, his suspicion climbing. "Melanie, stop."

The man smiled, moving to draw his own weapon.

"Hold it!" Liz shouted first.

Two masked figures stepped out from behind the stairs, each bearing fully automatic rifles.

"Lower your weapons," the man on the stairs ordered calmly.

Stewart glanced around as two SUVs drove up with more armed figures in ski masks aiming heavy artillery at them.

"Look," the man on the stairs began. He had jet black hair, piercing blue eyes, and a well-muscled frame. Stewart attempted to memorize every detail. "We can do this easy or hard."

"Who do you work for?" Stewart shouted, his gun still trained on the man's chest. The real security forces should show up any time now.

"I'm only going to ask one more time," the man said with a shrug. "Drop your weapons."

Stewart didn't move, and the other agents followed his lead.

A loud bang and a surreal flash left the man holding a smoking gun. It took Stewart a second to grasp what happened as Guerrez dropped to the concrete with a sickening thud.

"Now!" the man barked the command, taking aim at Liz next.

Stewart lowered his weapon onto the ground. They had no chance.

"Thank you," the man smiled.

Striding toward them with confidence, he holstered his weapon and took the case from Melanie's grasp. "Thanks for holding on to this for me," he winked.

A soft hiss escaped the short physicist, and Stewart prayed the man would overlook the offense.

"What are you going to do with that?" he demanded.

But the man merely chuckled, sliding the briefcase into one of the SUVs. "Don't follow us." He climbed in the car and slammed the door.

Rounds of automatic weapons fire punctuated the air, and Stewart watched helplessly as both of their cars became bullet ridden shells sitting on rims.

Without further warning, the men jumped into their vehicles and sped away.

Agent Kerry let out a cry of frustration and dropped to her knees beside Guerrez. Her eyes were flashing dangerously as she felt for a pulse. "He's alive, but we need a doctor."

Stewart jumped into the plane, already on his cell phone. The pilots were tied and gagged in the back, both unconscious.

He cursed loudly. *"I anticipate they will be successful,"* Carbon had said. Either she was responsible, or she was their only link to truth in this case. Stewart wasn't sure which option he preferred.

Chapter 15

When she awoke the following morning, the guys were already gone. Stretching out in the seat, she looked out into the soupy wilderness. The trees were wrapped in tendrils of thick white fog though a few beams of sunlight were beginning to break through.

"Good morning, Elise."

She kept staring out the window. Inside and out, all she could see was melancholy. "Morning Carbon."

Sitting in silence for a few minutes, she finally asked, "Where did Jesse and Shane go?"

"They left to cover tracks, but continued on to go for a walk when you were still sleeping. I recommended that they not wake you."

She was undeniably miffed at being left behind, but the solitude was just as well. Remaining inside the car, however, was not okay.

Sliding over the center console, she cautiously opened the door. The stillness outside made her edgy and she tried not to make a sound. As she walked out into the white fog, the ground and scenery gradually became clearer, if only for twenty feet or so.

Figuring there wasn't much plumbing out here, she took an early bathroom break behind some trees and thick brushes. Exploring a little further, she found a small clearing with a large boulder that might as well have been made to sit on. She sat in the quiet, trying to gather her thoughts. Actually it was more like a clearing job. Trying to see through the fog. Quite metaphorical, she observed cynically.

"Elise?"

She jerked around to find her brother standing by the clearing's edge. How did he sneak up like that?

"Hey," she responded weakly. She wanted to be positive, but she couldn't fake it. Her mind was troubled.

Jesse was silent a moment. "Mind if I sit down?"

Shaking her head, she scooted over to the right.

"What's on your mind?" he asked, turning concerned blue eyes on her.

"I just..." but she didn't really want to finish, the stone in her heart heavy enough already.

"Come on, sis. It's better to get it out. Don't be ashamed, whatever you feel. But don't suffer with it alone."

She sighed, turning her gaze to the soft forest floor. "I don't want to do this."

He said nothing.

"I mean, it's just too much. It's not worth it."

"What's not worth it?" he asked softly.

She didn't want to say it out loud, but the thought had been invading her mind and plaguing her heart. "I can't do it. I'm not…" It sounded cheesy put to words like that. "You guys are risking everything. I can't, I mean, I'm…" her voice dropped to a whisper. "I'm not worth it."

Her statement was swallowed by the silent forest, the words drifting across the open space. If anyone was killed on her account, she didn't think she could live with it. She liked being treated special by the Allens and everyone, but who was she kidding? When it came right down to it, she was just an ordinary girl who was never quite good enough. This Irene Mathis person seemed like someone else entirely.

Jesse got up from the rock, and she thought he might leave. Who would want to just hear out all her complaints anyway? Here, stuck in self-pity, she couldn't even be grateful for what her brother had offered.

But he only walked a few feet away and turned back to look at her. "I asked you to trust me, remember?"

She nodded, not meeting his eyes.

"Dr. Rayford would like you to believe that you are not worth it. That the most you could hope for is to offer your body to science and die quietly. To him, that's truly all you are worth." He was silent for a moment. "When I said this would be hard, I meant it. Not just physically, but emotionally. Things may happen that don't make sense to you at all right now. You can only see so much from where you are. Perspective can make all the difference.

"That's where the trust thing comes in. Dad and I have thought long and hard about the costs and risks and possible scenarios, and while it's not even possible to tell you all that's involved and going on, you can choose to cling to what you do know. You'll always have Carbon to check that with. But for now," he bent down on one knee and forced her to look at him. "Remember who you are. You are a beloved daughter and sister, and you are worth it. Whether you feel it now or not, you are worth it."

He stood and gave her a gentle hug. "When you're ready, we're going to go for a little hike and discuss plans. Take as much time as you need."

* * * *

"Clear!" Agent McAllister shouted to his partner.

Special Agent Bill Morrison appeared behind him, gun drawn. With their flashlights, they quickly reached the conclusion that this shack was every bit as vacant as the house.

McAllister cursed and holstered his gun. "I can't believe it. Where would they go?"

"Easy, buddy." Morrison did likewise, but continued looking around. "They had to leave in a hurry, so I'm sure they left evidence behind. Forensics is sure to turn up something. They're already beginning to sweep the house."

His partner exhaled slowly, "I hope you're right."

"Come on. Late or not, this is the best lead we've had so far. Let's get back to the house. We don't want to mess up any evidence out here."

With a shrug, Agent McAllister backed out of the shed. Morrison was right. They just needed to collect their thoughts and look at the clues. It was a miracle they had found this place at all.

* * * *

It was a while before Elise was ready to move from her rock. She was comfortable here, alone in the quiet solitude of nature. She thought of what Jesse said, even believed it to a great degree, but couldn't quite shake the feelings of sadness and loss.

As much as she wanted to stay in the silence and enjoy the peace of the moment, something deeper pulled at her. Curiosity, fear, or maybe need. It didn't really matter why, and as she took in a final breath of the cool mountain air, she tried applying Jesse's advice and holding on to good thoughts. The image of her dad on the video tearfully saying he loved her and missed her, her grandparents' kindness, the fact that she had found her brother, Carbon's unwavering support...

With a sigh she retrieved her cell phone from her pocket and flipped it open indecisively. An automatic line to a car that would defend her against anything. By some counts, she could be considered lucky. It just didn't feel that way.

Lonely she was. Alone, she was not.

Swallowing the pain, Elise stood and headed back for Carbon. It was time to move on.

Chapter 16

When Stewart marched into Richardson's office early the next day, he had spent most of the night practicing control and keeping his emotions far away. This was business. He would deal with his anger later, after he had gotten to the bottom of this and figured out who to blame.

But his efforts weren't working well. He was furious.

Deliberately led astray. By whom, he didn't know. But he had fair suspicions that Richardson knew more than he was letting on. He had worked under the man long enough to read into his subtle hints, or even the lack of hints.

Instinct said this was much bigger than anyone was permitted to think. And he wasn't sure how much deeper he could go without meeting serious resistance.

"Sit down," his former boss greeted him without looking up. "And shut up."

Control, Stewart reminded himself. He forgot how easily this man could push his buttons.

"If you don't watch yourself, you're going to be thrown out of this investigation. First, you abandoned the site of the dig without the slightest attention to protocol, you push a flight to emergency clearance, and then you allow masked criminals to intercept whatever package you found. Stewart, we have a serious problem here. You had not informed anyone yet as to the discovery of your mystery briefcase, and yet someone was so far ahead as to be waiting for you at the airport. You know what this means, right?"

Of course he knew. Stewart fought to keep his mouth shut as his face burned with anger.

"We have a mole. Now I would hate to suspect that you or any of your team was involved, but you have to understand the position I'm in here. You were the one pushing to go to Colorado. You were the one who pushed to dig in the rubble. You made the decisions of how to proceed and when to leave. You chose not to call for backup and call in the discovery of the case until after it was stolen." Richardson paused for a breath, eyes boring into the younger man. "It was your responsibility. Now, I know you. I have given you the benefit of the doubt, but for now, your duties are suspended until further investigation. You may go."

Stewart sat for a moment, too shocked to respond. His recovery didn't take long. Control. "Sir, I've led this investigation for years. I know more about this case than..."

"Alan," Richardson looked up at him. "You're not hearing me." His tone was tight, but there was something in his manner that made Stewart pause. "You're off this investigation for now. Take a break. We can handle things around here, and you need to sort yourself out until you can come back and approach things calmly."

Stewart stared back, trying to make sense of it all.

"Give me your badge and your gun," Richardson motioned to the table, standing up by his desk. "Now. This is a vacation without any work. No side investigating for the team."

Furious, Stewart knew he had no choice but to comply. Sliding his gun from its holster, he set it on the table next to his identification and FBI badge. "You're making a mistake," he hissed at Richardson. Yes, it was supposed to come out calmly. No, it did not work.

"I've been around the block, kid," Richardson used a hand to steer him out of the office. "I can assure you I know what I'm doing. If I change my mind, I know how to reach you."

"You will alert me immediately if something happens," Stewart commanded.

"You are ordered to rest, agent." Richardson finished pushing him out the door without smiling. Stewart gave him a fuming glare, ignoring the stares from his colleagues. Something else was on his mind as he marched out of the building, however. The old man was on to something. He had slipped a piece of paper into Stewart's pocket as he pushed him out the door. Which could only mean one thing. There was heat on Richardson, and he was acting for show.

Still maintaining a livid expression, Stewart's mind began jumping at the implications. This was not going to be a vacation after all.

* * * *

The rain speckled a crystal blue lake in a dance of tiny droplets, the soft pitter-patter on leaves and ground providing the orchestral accompaniment. They had been hiking a narrow trail when the clouds turned grey, but were fortunately near a small area beneath a rocky outcropping.

Tired from the walk, Elise was content to sit against the hard stone and stretch her legs out a little. There hadn't been much discussion of plans so far, but through listening to conversation between Shane and Jesse as they walked, she had learned small pieces of each man's past.

Jesse talked about living with Dad as a kid and being taught all sorts of survival practices. What to eat in the wild, physical defense, how to build shelter, etc. Other than that, he had eaten, breathed, and slept science while growing up, eventually studying microbiology and genetics. Computer science was his favorite subject, and after this discussion Elise had concluded that her brother was the most gigantic nerd she had ever met, and a genius like Einstein. She felt a little ashamed that the ingenuity gene had skipped her.

Shane Lawson was not the same success story, and while he wasn't particularly forthcoming with information, Jesse was able to pry out the major points of his life. Born in Nevada, he had disappointed his parents early by dropping out of high school to work on cars and waste money, as he put it. He had later earned his GED to attend the police academy, and moved to Iowa because there was a job offer, and it was a safe distance from his family.

It then fell to Elise to share part of her own life, which she was reluctant to do, but she briefly recounted some of the foster homes she could remember. Due to Jesse's questioning, she was also forced to discuss school and friends, but then she had been saved by the rain.

Now sitting under the rocky overhang with Jesse in the middle – Elise had made a point to avoid being close to Shane after being stuck with him in the closet – she was fairly confident her brother would begin telling them his plan. Which he promptly did.

"Sometime early tomorrow morning we should reach Seattle, and we will again hide Carbon before daylight. An old colleague of Dad's works in town, and we need to pay him a visit."

Surely he didn't mean Rayford. "Who?" Elise asked.

"Dr. Juan Batiste. He's Cuban, actually emigrated to America just after the Bay of Pigs. Was a kid then." Jesse paused with a thoughtful expression. Talk about extraneous information.

Shane blinked, "And we're visiting him why…?"

"Dr. Batiste works in the same building as Rayford. He was a close friend of Dad's, and is probably still loyal to him. Records indicate he never believed the charges against Dad and that he has adamantly defended Dad's reputation."

"Probably?" Shane was incredulous. "What if he's changed his mind?"

But Jesse only shrugged, "He hasn't. And Carbon will prepare him." He checked his watch. "She's already contacted him."

Elise wasn't sure what she thought of that, but if Carbon gave it the all clear, it was most likely safe. "So he's going to help us?"

"Yep. He'll have information and some supplies that we're going to need. One compound in particular."

"And you're sure he'll have it?" Shane asked again, skepticism evident on his face.

Jesse looked at him calmly. "Absolutely. Dad left it in his safekeeping."

They took a moment of silence to digest this information before Jesse spoke again. "Now," he clapped his hands on his knees and stood up. "I have a question for each of you."

He turned to Shane first. "When Carbon called you, and moreover after she had destroyed your car, why did you choose to go with her?"

The silence seemed to swallow his question as it bounced around in time. No one spoke, and Shane dropped Jesse's gaze. "I don't know. It seemed like the only real option."

"But why?" The blonde man's blue eyes held attention to his question. "Why? What were you looking for?"

Shane twisted uncomfortably under his piercing gaze, relaxing only when Jesse looked at Elise instead. Who knew that one shaggy cowboy could command such authority? But as her brother regarded her kindly, she somewhat understood why. In his face, his mannerisms, it was obvious that he actually cared what happened to them. And that he was willing to confront difficulties and feelings that were unpleasant to face, not to mention risk his own life to try to save hers.

Yes, he was her brother. But family ties did not dictate going to such great lengths. His emotional honesty and openness was powerful, but more than a little uncomfortable. Elise found herself squirming under his gaze also, unable to meet his eyes. It was weird. In this modern day and age, people could spend their whole lives avoiding such underlying questions and emotions. Face to face with the question of why, Elise didn't even know where to begin. Could it be that she didn't even know herself?

"Why, Elise?" Jesse pointed the question at her now. "Irene?" he echoed. "Who are you really?"

His earlier words ran through her mind. "You are a beloved daughter and sister, and you are worth it." But she couldn't make her mouth repeat the statement out loud. Something deep down cried out against it, arguing that it wasn't true.

"I don't know," she whispered, realizing for once that she did not, in fact, know who she was, what she was doing, or why she was doing it. Survival? There had to be more.

Jesse smiled gently. "What happens next will test your resolve and point these questions out clearly. Be prepared."

He held a hand out past the rocky roof. "Hey, I think it stopped raining. Let's move on."

Humming a little tune, he picked up his pack and started off toward the trail. Elise risked a sideways glance at Shane as she got up, and found him watching Jesse walk off with a pensive expression. Shrugging on her own backpack, Elise followed in step behind her brother. Whatever this was, it was not boring.

Chapter 17

"Dr. Summers," Dr. Geoffrey Rayford bowed graciously and took her hand. "It's a pleasure."

Returning the handshake, the older woman forced a smile. "It's been a while."

"Yes. Yes, indeed."

He looked at her for a minute, and she could feel him judging her inside and out. From her flat grey hair and skin that grew more lines every day down to hidden doubts and insecurities about her life's work. Fear too. Fear about this meeting.

Straightening stiffly, she glared at him and huffed in indignation. "Geoffrey Rayford, you have not changed a bit."

The handsome gentleman only laughed, "You're too kind, Kay. You always have been."

Dr. Rayford was by all accounts in high spirits, a little odd for a man who had just lost a hand. She glanced at the white bandage and felt an involuntary shudder go through her body. Only a stub would remain.

"'Tis a flesh wound!" Rayford declared with a smile. "I was lucky to walk away."

Dr. Summers said nothing, pushing aside fears that she would pay a similar price for her involvement in this project.

Rayford glanced around at the stone pillars guarding the entrance to what used to be an in vitro fertilization clinic, operating in conjunction with the nearby Ceeling University. "This place brings back many memories." His blue eyes glazed over with sadness. "Mostly good ones. Some that ..." he trailed off wistfully.

Dr. Kay Summers was struggling with a different emotional reaction. She had left this project hoping never to come back, her life in jeopardy should she ever mention it at all. Behind her. She had pushed it all behind her. And now it was coming back.

"It's been a hard few weeks, Kay. Years. But things are coming together. Let me show you what we know, and what we have planned." He offered a broad smile. "I think you'll be impressed."

* * * *

Maybe it was the inky night outside, the nonstop drizzle against the windshield, or simple fatigue, but Elise couldn't see the next few days in an optimistic light.

Jesse's questions had terrified her.

Not initially, because he had seemed so resolved, so determined and set that she leaned on his confidence to ignore the probing questions at hand.

Who was she? Really? Was she actually Irene Mathis, daughter of an ingenious scientist and a member of a caring, compassionate family that had been torn apart by deception and lies, but would be reunited in the future? Because her father passionately wanted her safe in his arms?

Or was she simply Elise Perry, scientific experiment and unwanted foster child who would not live to see her seventeenth birthday?

The raindrops fell harder against Carbon's smooth surfaces, and the usually calming noise frightened her tonight. She almost missed the drive alone to Montana; the car hardly spoke with the other three inside unless someone asked her a direct question.

From the occasional snoring and the even breathing from the front seat, it was pretty safe to assume the two men were asleep. Shane had seemed irritated all day, and Elise wondered if it was just the stress, or if Jesse's questions were eating him up as well.

Sighing, she readjusted herself in the back seat, never quite reaching an adequate level of comfort. As she leaned her forehead against the cold glass, she wished Carbon would say something encouraging. Or just anything at all.

But the car remained silent, and with a heavy sigh, Elise tucked further into her soft blanket and wished for peaceful thoughts.

* * * *

Suspended FBI Agent Alan Stewart sat at a corner booth in an empty diner, hands folding and unfolding a creased piece of paper.

Richardson's note was pointed, but posed more questions than it answered. After eating, he would burn the memo.

MUCH BIGGER FISH. RECOMMEND FISHING ELSEWHERE.

The two of them used to enjoy fishing together, so the analogy wasn't hard to grasp. First, he couldn't go to anyone in the Bureau about this. Secondly, for Richardson to be so cryptic, it was safe to assume Stewart's life was in grave danger. If he continued investigating, he would probably end up in a morgue. Fortunately Guerrez had been wearing a bullet proof vest, but the man's injuries were still severe enough to put him out of commission for a while.

Richardson was right that there was a mole. And he had to know it wasn't Stewart. The only people who knew of the briefcase discovery were the hired help digging in the rubble, his three agents on the ground, and Carbon.

He couldn't be sure, but he did not think Carbon would go to the trouble to help him find it, warn him, and then have the package stolen herself. If she was that resourceful, she would've found a way to dig it out on her own and just take it. No, she was trying to get a message to him.

Which meant he needed another cell phone, one she could contact. He considered going back to his apartment, but considered it too risky. If someone already wanted him out of the picture, the best bet was to disappear.

Besides, he had the feeling that Carbon would find a way to reach him when she needed to.

Now he was left with the suspicion that one of his team was the mole. The contractors could have been posted to watch, but he doubted the Bureau would trust civilians with that much. Then there was the troubling insistence that he take Liz along. And her disappearance while they discovered the package. She had been looking for the recording device, supposedly. But what if she had found it and made sure it didn't fall into their hands?

Stewart sighed and slid his hands down his face. He had worked with Agent Kerry for years and always found her to be straight-up honest and trustworthy. To rethink his trust in her would shake his faith in other decisions as well.

The next step, he considered, was getting out of town.

That left the last piece of advice Richardson had given him.

Seattle. The old man had recommended fishing in Seattle.

* * * *

Shane Lawson was mad. Flat-out angry. At first he gave a half-hearted attempt not to let his annoyance show, but those efforts had been thrown to the wind a few miles back. Problem was, everyone else seemed to be asleep, which left his fury in a frustrating cycle of going absolutely nowhere.

The more he sat in silence, the more he stewed over the facts.

Fact #1: He had voluntarily joined a mission with a man he barely knew to save a girl he barely knew, with full knowledge that the FBI and other government agencies were against them.

Fact #2: He had no other realistic options, and felt obligated to at least ensure Elise's safety, as she appeared innocent of any crimes her father may have committed.

Fact #3: The reason he presently had no options is that he had already become a wanted fugitive, and ticked off a powerful and ruthless man who wanted him dead or worse, based on nothing but instinct and a high-tech car.

Fact #4: The leader of this expedition, Jesse, seemed like a nice guy but was also perfectly content to march into the enemy's territory without as much as the slightest game plan.

Fact #5: It increasingly appeared to him that within the next few days he would either be dead, or in jail. He really didn't want to go to jail, but then again, neither did he want to be dead.

Fact #6: He had no real idea what was going on. Nada. And Jesse wasn't talking.

Surely his life would be for something. As it stood, his family would probably remember him as the trouble child who died in his life of crime, and the government considered him a threat to national security. And for what?

Jesse's words irritated him further. "What are you looking for? Why?" He mimicked the man's tone in his head. What, was he some kind of psychiatrist? Maybe there didn't need to be a reason. Maybe he just made a mistake.

A slight twinge of guilt pulled at him with the knowledge that his actions, mistake or no, had saved a young woman's life. Or maybe just prolonged it, but that was beside the point. More logic parried the thought. Carbon would have undoubtedly found some other sucker to help, and he would still be comfortably sitting at home with a Coke and the remote, his Mustang parked in the garage, alive and well.

He released a sigh, fidgeting in the seat.

"Can't sleep?"

Caught off guard, Shane was surprised to see Jesse watching him from the driver's seat, his eyes glowing an unnatural blue from the dim lights of the instrument panel.

"No," he responded, his tone tight.

"We should arrive in about two hours, just before sunup."

Shane said nothing, staring out the window at the dark sky. Not a star was visible, all hidden past a layer of clouds. A minute earlier he had been ready to berate the man with a tirade of questions and suggestions, yet now he couldn't think of anything to say. What had gone wrong?

When he glanced back at Jesse, he found a warm smile directed toward him.

"What are you smiling about?" Shane snapped. The anger was still there.

Shaking his head, Jesse laughed quietly. "It's just amazing. You're a pretty special guy."

"What?" he returned sharply. What was this guy's problem?

"How many people would willingly risk their lives to save a complete stranger? I mean, not only did you hop into a suspicious talking car, but Dr. Rayford didn't exactly extend a red-carpet welcome. You didn't even give us up when you were tortured."

The adulation was annoying. "It was more like survival at that point." Shane wasn't sure why he felt so driven to argue with the man, but he decided not to hold back. "I'm not sure if I would do it all over again."

But Jesse merely shrugged. "You did it the first time, and that's what counts. Can't change the past."

"Too bad," he muttered.

The blonde cowboy remained unperturbed. "You can drop out whenever you want. Go to the cops, FBI, whatever. You're not a prisoner."

Hats off, this is what bothered him the most. He knew it was free choice that kept him here, and that he would bear the blame for any mistakes. But how could he possibly predict the future? "Look," his tone was tight, but he tried to keep it low to not wake Elise, "I didn't ask for any of this. My life is... gone. I don't even know if I'll be alive this time tomorrow. And I could be in prison. Do you know what that's like for ex-cops?"

"And you're wondering why." Jesse held his gaze pointedly. He continued softly, "Was it worth it? What is your goal?"

"What does it matter to you, anyway?" he retorted. "As long as I do what you want, right?"

"Shane, I appreciate what you've already done no matter what you choose to do next. You're right, I am grateful for your help and I enjoy your company. But I do not need your assistance." Jesse paused as if allowing his words to sink in.

So now he was useless as well. "I don't have to put up with this."

Jesse leaned toward him, "No. You're absolutely right. You don't have to. But don't you want to find out what's really going on? Nothing that's worth doing is ever easy. Dad and I consider you family if you stay, and Carbon already likes you. But it's your life. Your choice. Please choose wisely."

That gave him momentary pause. "So I'm just supposed to take it? Shrug it off like nothing?"

"Of course not," Jesse laughed. "There's nothing wrong with anger. In fact, if you weren't angry over all this, I might wonder what was wrong with you."

Funny, Shane thought, he had indeed been wondering that about his new friend.

"It's what you do with the anger that matters. Which is why my question yesterday is so important."

"What are you, like Gandhi or something?" While he couldn't fault Jesse's words, he was a little reluctant to take advice from a man only a few years his senior. To his credit though, the man did seem to be a genius.

"Nope." Jesse was still smiling, "Don't worry. It's going to all work out for the best. And I can promise you, if you come with me, it will not ever be boring."

He had no doubts about that.

"Or safe."

That caught Shane's attention a little more.

"The truth is all we're after. And Elise's life." Jesse nudged him in the side, "Come on, surfer dude. It's excitement! Living life on the edge!"

Okay, so if he was completely honest, that did appeal to him. But he never expected the cost to be so high, and the rewards to seem so small. Glancing again at the darkness outside, Shane found his anger assuaged. Not gone, there had been no miraculous vanishing act, but it was lessened somewhat by the hope that this might all work out. Jesse's positive outlook really was contagious.

"Now try to get some sleep. In the morning we'll meet with Dr. Batiste and things will look a whole lot clearer."

"You know," Shane leaned back against the seat. "You could make a good lawyer."

"And you'd make a good Batman."

Wondering if he heard wrong, Shane shot Jesse an inquisitive glance, "Why is that?"

"Well, you don't have any superpowers. And you're kind of confused as to how to save the world. But you have an awesome car on your side, and your heart's in the right place."

"Uh, thanks. I think." He wasn't sure how to respond to that. "Good night."

"Good morning."

"Whatever." With no more brainpower to argue, Shane stretched out as best he could and was asleep in a matter of minutes.

Chapter 18

Elise was awakened by the sound of thunder. A grey haze surrounded the car, light misting rain visible in every direction.

Blinking the drowsiness from her eyes, she quickly deduced that Carbon wasn't moving, Jesse was no longer present, and Shane was awake and watching her quietly.

"How are you feeling?" he asked.

She felt exposed, somehow violated by waking up in another person's presence. Sleep was a private matter, in her mind, and she enjoyed time to herself to get her day started. Not that anything was usual or routine about this particular day.

With a stiff nod, she mumbled some sort of reply and glanced around Carbon's cab awkwardly.

Shane answered the obvious question before she could ask, "Jesse went out about fifteen minutes ago. Said he needed some time alone."

Looking at the gloomy weather, Elise only wondered what would possess anyone to leave a dry, warm car for such a soggy and miserable climate. But then again, her brother was proving to be far from normal.

As she stared out the window, the reflection staring back gave her pause. Given, her face looked different framed by short black hair, but her eyes were more alarming. The girl staring back at her had hazel eyes, more brown than green. Which was fine, except her eyes had always been green.

She squinted, trying to get a better glimpse, but that only made her eyes smaller in the hazy image. Brilliant idea. Maybe the reflection was just playing tricks on her.

"Hey Shane," she was embarrassed to ask, but she needed to know. "What color are my eyes?"

"Um..." he responded from the front, turning around slowly. He gave her a suspicious look before analyzing her face. It was hard not to look away.

"Brown," he answered. "Why?"

Elise looked back to the reflection, momentarily panicked. "Carbon?" she asked.

"Hey wait," Shane had remembered. "I thought you had green eyes."

"Me too," Elise's voice was shaky. She could see fine.

"It is a side effect," Carbon informed her. "I thought it would take longer to progress to this stage. Your irises will continue turning darker until they are black."

Elise stared at her reflection, unable to reconcile the horrible thought. "Black?" she asked fearfully. "I'll look evil!"

"You look fine," Shane offered. "The brown matches your new hair, and no one will recognize you now."

She returned the comment with a sullen glare. Black was not brown. "How long?"

"How long for what?" Shane said.

"How long until they turn black?" Elise was surprised at how whiny and panicky her voice came out.

"It is impossible to predict precisely," Carbon responded.

That wasn't reassuring. "Try!"

The car was silent for a moment. "Why do you wish to know?"

"Carbon!" Elise exclaimed. "Just tell me!"

"People tend to like to know things when it concerns them, Carbon. Just guess, will you?" Shane came to her defense, though Elise didn't feel much gratitude.

"Four to five days," Carbon said. "But they will continuously grow darker until then."

Elise only swallowed and tried to accept the news. She could wear sunglasses. It wouldn't be the end of the world. She was still alive. But inside she mourned the loss of her beautiful eyes.

It wasn't long before a yellow figure emerged out of the trees. At first she was alarmed, but figured not many thugs ran around in brightly colored rain jackets. Her brother, however, seemed just the type.

After a brief battle with his poncho, Jesse half-fell into the driver's seat, shaking his wet hair with an exclamation.

"Man!" he ran his hands down a wet arm. "It was really raining there. Nothing like Seattle weather."

"You are wet," Carbon pointed out the obvious. "After you dry off, you should treat the leather seats. They can be damaged by exposure to water."

Jesse laughed it off, patting the dashboard affectionately. "Don't worry, Carbon. A little water never hurt anybody."

"That is not accurate. There are many instances when water has caused considerable damage and even loss of ..."

"Okay, okay," Jesse cut her off. "Sorry. I'll clean the seats later." He rolled his eyes and looked back at Elise, "How are you this morning?"

Elise worked to squelch her smile from Carbon's indignation as the horror of her eyes returned.

"Yeah," Jesse said with a sympathetic smile. "Sorry about that. It is an unfortunate side effect. How are you feeling, though? A little better?"

Running a mental check list, Elise found that she was in fact feeling better. Stronger. "Yeah, a little." She wasn't willing to give up sympathy points entirely. From past experience, she knew things could slide downhill fast. "Where did you go?"

Her brother winked at her and turned back to the steering wheel. Carbon's engine growled to life, earning a pleased smile from both men and frustration from Elise.

"Just sorting things out. It helps to step away sometimes, get a new perspective." Jesse put Carbon in gear and they began moving, her headlights not illuminating much in the dark rain.

The silence stretched about a minute before Shane broke it. "Where exactly are we going?"

Jesse shook his head. "Always wanting to know things, deputy. Don't you like surprises?"

"Not really."

At this, Jesse only grinned. "Too bad."

From the backseat, Elise sighed and stared outside at the bleak scenery. It was getting lighter, though probably not enough that anyone could easily identify Carbon.

Fear tried to rise up again, and she only hoped Jesse's destination held her cure. And that they found it soon.

Chapter 19

The drive didn't last long, and after parking Carbon in a thick patch of wilderness, Jesse grabbed a backpack and motioned for them to follow. Obediently, Shane and Elise got out of the dry car and into the damp morning.

Retrieving a folder from his pack, Jesse shuffled through some papers before sounding a triumphant, "Aha!"

He held an orange envelope out to Elise, and one to Shane. "These should get you by. Bus passes, a little bit of cash, and a cell phone if we ever get separated. Each of our numbers is already programmed, as well as a number for Carbon."

Elise pushed the gracious wad of cash and bus pass into her pocket. The cell phone was a touch screen smart phone. This was a considerable upgrade from Carbon's other phones, and she explored it briefly before stuffing it in the other pocket. Nice.

With a yawn, she stretched her sore muscles, noting that she had begun to feel worse ever since Jesse returned.

"Elise."

She glanced up as Jesse said her name, and he was looking at her with great concern. "Yes?" she answered.

"Try to stay close to me, and always keep your cell phone on and near you. It's very important."

His face was dead serious, and Elise tried to downplay his graveness with a shrug. "Sure."

"As your DNA continues to mutate and bond with Rayford's new... instructions," he seemed unhappy with the term, "your body will emit a certain frequency that he will be able to trace. These cell phones have been altered to give out another signal that will confuse or block this frequency."

"So," her mind fumbled with the reasoning. "This is because of the freerider thing, right?" She recalled Rayford's explanation of genetic experiments and an extra chemical or something built into her DNA. She also recalled that Jesse had never denied Rayford's accusations that her dad intentionally did this to her.

Jesse regarded her evenly. Maybe he didn't want to tell her the whole story. "What he injected into you is changing you DNA by reactivating segments of your genes that have been 'turned off' in a sense, for ten years. For that time, they were harmlessly replicating the instructions, but sitting dormant. Even now, Rayford is probably working on more powerful ways to communicate with these signal emitting devices."

"It's complicated," he explained with furrowed brows. "I don't have time to explain it all now, but it is in Carbon's archives. For now, just stay close to me. And always have that phone with you and turned on." He didn't even try to smile, though he did look honestly concerned.

"Okay," she agreed, not really understanding. Trust, isn't that what he had said? Plus, it couldn't be that hard. It's not like she was planning to go anywhere by herself, alone in a strange city with the FBI and Rayford looking for her.

"Good." Jesse seemed relieved, patting her again on the top of the head. Must be an older brother thing.

Shane's face held a zillion questions, but he said nothing.

"If you ever do get separated," Carbon added, "call me as soon as you can."

"Now," Jesse rubbed his hands together. "Let's get moving. It's about a mile to the nearest bus stop, and the sun's coming up fast."

"I guess it's still too much to ask where we're going?" Shane didn't look very hopeful.

"Of course," Jesse shrugged his backpack on and started walking.

With an unhappy expression, the ex-deputy looked between Jesse and Carbon before cooperatively falling into step.

Elise was not so quick to begin, turning back to the big black car. It represented a degree of safety that she was leaving behind. She knew Carbon was both armed and willing to defend her. Jesse was at least as loyal, but he was only one person. Carbon was like a whole army.

But the other two were not waiting, and with a final sigh Elise hurried to catch up. Despite the cool morning, she found herself sweating after the first half-mile. Jesse was carrying on with a genetics lesson, talking about twenty-three chromosomes and humanity's unique genome. It got more complicated, but as Elise tried to understand, she found her mind slipping into an unresponsive state. Truth be told, it wasn't that interesting, and she wasn't making any sense of it anyway.

Shane didn't look much better, his eyes glazed over with boredom as he walked. Once he shot her a helpless glance. Given his life's story, he hadn't gone much further in school than she had, and did not seem to take to learning very well.

After enduring another fifteen minutes of molecular biology, Elise was elated to find the small sign and bench that indicated a bus stop. Clearing off a small area from standing water, she sat and rested her weary feet. They may have only walked a mile, but she felt like she had run a marathon.

Jesse, however, was not winded in the least. He was continuing, "And that's the amazing part of the genetic code. It's so complex and refined, the likes of which can't be manipulated or modeled with our best super computers."

"Thrilling," Shane remarked dryly, leaning against the bus stop sign. "When is the bus supposed to get here?"

"Six minutes," Jesse replied, unaffected by their apparent disinterest in his lecture. "Give or take." He sat down beside Elise, taking in her exhausted condition. "How are you holding up?"

She tried to smile, "Fine. Just a little tired."

He was quiet for a moment. "Remember when I said this was going to be hard?"

Elise affirmed with a nod, but honestly, she hadn't thought of it that much. She just clung to the hope that things would be improving shortly.

"Never, never, never give up," he imitated the voice of Winston Churchill, but his eyes were not light. "No matter what."

"Got it," she huffed, wishing her lungs would catch up already. "Never give up, trust and rest. Stay close. Got it."

Jesse punched her lightly in the shoulder. "See? You're a genius. Now, if you want to learn more about the composition of ge...."

"No," Shane interrupted firmly. "Please, no. I can't take any more."

"Fine," Jesse gave an exaggerated sigh. "Suit yourself."

They sat in silence for the three short minutes until the lumbering bus appeared on the horizon. It was a far cry from the sleek sports car they had left behind. Elise reluctantly fished for the pass in her pocket. She was almost excited to see where they were headed.

And despite the fatigue cloaking her body and mind, she felt a new twinge in her heart for the first time. Hope. This just might work.

* * * *

Dr. Juan Batiste paced the classroom's worn floor, deep in thought. His theory of genetics was open to anyone who would listen. Currently three graduate students studied under his supervision, each of them a bright young mind who embraced his theories with analytical passion.

Unfortunately, his theories were often the butt of other professors' jokes and his students suffered accordingly. But such is the cost of true scientific pursuit. Popular fads and political correctness play no role.

He checked his watch before observing his small undergraduate class trickle in one student at a time. None looked too eager to be in class that morning.

With a smile, Dr. Batiste adjusted his glasses and opened his binder of lecture notes. This day held a promising surprise, of that he was sure. His old friend Samuel seemed to be on the move again, and he looked forward to meeting the man he had promised to send to make things right.

Tirelessly Juan had defended his dear friend's cause, from composing scientific papers on the credibility and ingenuity of Mathis' theories to editorials and speeches about his innocence and promise to bring justice. The proof was all there, from Samuel's emails to the undeniable mathematical truths in his computations and remaining research.

And unbeknownst to all except Samuel and himself, a key part of his formula was stored securely in Dr. Batiste's safe. He knew it would be needed soon and had placed it carefully in his briefcase, never to leave his side.

Carbon had called him three times in the past few days, a clear sign. Glancing at his case to check on the compound's safety, Dr. Batiste gave his watch a final check and cleared his throat. Yes, it would be an exciting day to be sure.

Chapter 20

The bus' brakes hissed as the door slid open.

"All aboard," came the dull call from the aging driver.

They showed their passes and slipped into the crowd of people. Jesse was first and sat next to a black clad teenager leaving Elise to slide into the next row of paired seats, unhappily noting that she was stuck beside Shane. At least she got the window seat.

With another hiss the bus pulled away, and Elise took to staring at the traffic as they passed. There were enough questions in her mind to keep her guessing for a long time, so in defense of limited minutes and hours she resolved to not consider any questions at all.

Shane was busy playing with his new smart phone, and Elise noted the awkward silence of the bus. All these people, mostly students, stuck together in one space and no one spoke. It must be some kind of unofficial rule or something. Silence on the bus.

Jesse didn't catch the wordless memo. He was already chatting with the stony-faced Goth next to him. The guy didn't look a day over fourteen, with stringy black hair, silver piercings, and black baggy clothes. The only white on his shirt was a skull with a sword going through it.

Elise couldn't help her embarrassment as her brother continued to talk with the kid, some of the other passengers turning to glare at the unsanctioned noise.

Beside her Shane shifted slightly, replacing the phone in his pocket. "He sure is a talkative one."

"Yeah," Elise gave a stiff nod, instantly defensive of her brother and worried about new glares that might be redirected in her direction.

"What about you?" he inquired innocently. "You haven't said much at all. Guess that part's not genetic."

She met his gaze briefly, but turned her eyes back toward the passing city, painfully aware of their new creepy coloring. The Goth kid would be proud. "I haven't felt well." So what if it was a lame excuse, it was true. She didn't have to feel comfortable with people she barely knew if she didn't want to.

"I've noticed. This isn't all over that kiss, is it?"

She spun her head around, speechless.

"You should lift your ban on talking to me, that wasn't my fault anyway. You saved our butts."

"This has nothing to do with … that," she sputtered, her cheeks no doubt turning a bright red. She had tried hard to forget that moment, and discussing on the bus was far past her comfort level.

He eyed her calmly, and it infuriated her. "Well, if it makes you feel better, there are no hard feelings."

Somehow that didn't make her feel any better at all.

"Look, I don't expect anything from you. I just want to know what you're thinking so we can figure out what's going on. Communication," he gave her a look that was strikingly similar to Dr. Phil, "is key."

"As it is," he continued, "if anyone was watching, they would probably conclude that I did kidnap you. So try not to look so … kidnapped."

Elise swallowed, aware that her mouth had gone dry and unhappily aware of how close he was. Would it not be reasonable to assume that dealing with one of your rescuers would be easier than facing death and sickness? And yet, here she was. Frozen by fear of simply talking to a man who had done nothing but help her.

The problem was not with him. Had he been a jerk or rude she would simply dismiss him. She had dealt with those people her whole life. They are tolerated and ignored with relative comfort, posing no threat to the emotions. But here she was totally stuck. Ashamed at being indebted to a nice person that she had no real reason not to like.

No, the problem was that there were sparks. Which led to fire, and Elise felt justified in concluding that she had already burned enough in her life.

"Hey," he ran his hand up and down in front of her face. "You zoning out there? Hello?"

"Sorry," she stammered, wishing she could melt away into the plastic seat. "Yes. I agree. I'll try not to look kidnapped."

He squinted at her and raised his eyebrows. "You still look kidnapped. Like I might bite your head off or something."

"Sorry," she frowned, racking her brain for how to look safe and happy when she felt exposed and embarrassed. She offered a plastic smile.

"Mmmm," he scrutinized her face closely. "That's not going to cut it. You just need to relax. Here, I have an idea. So there's these three guys, right? And they walk into a bar."

"Oh, no," she groaned, dropping her head against the seat in front of her. "Not a bad joke. I can't take it."

"Who said it was going to be bad?"

Elise looked up at him. "You really think this is going to help?"

"Duh." Apparently he needed no convincing of his own plan. "It's already working, you look more relaxed. Now, like I was saying…"

Elise tried to tune him out as he continued through not one or two, but three corny jokes, fighting to hang on to both her dignity and misery. Making matters worse, every person on the bus, excluding Jesse and the Goth, seemed to be watching as he relayed each horrible joke with animated movements and Shakespearean voice inflection.

"Are you done?" she asked when he finally lapsed into silence.

"Yeah," he sighed contentedly. "Pretty good, right?"

Having lost both her battles, Elise couldn't suppress a small smile. "Terrible. Don't quit your day job."

"Too late," he said with a grin. "And it did help. Look, you're actually smiling."

She ducked her head down and looked back out the window. "Yeah, well. It probably won't last."

"Ah, an optimist to the end."

"Next stop is ours," Jesse turned to face them, motioning toward the black-haired kid. "This is Mike. He's practically a genius, studying physics at the university before his fifteenth birthday."

Mike glanced at them shyly, and Elise tried to offer a warm smile. "Hey, Mike. That's pretty cool."

"No kidding," Shane added. "I wish I had half your brain."

Breaking his stony image, Mike gave an impish grin. "It's not that hard, really."

"Such modesty," Jesse shook his head. "It's been a pleasure, Mike. See you around?"

The kid nodded, "Sure."

The bus screeched to a halt, and Elise trailed the two guys out into the cloudy day. Before her sprawled a well-maintained campus. A grassy lawn stretched into the distance with brick buildings lined up on either side. College. A place she might never have the chance to visit.

Jesse stood in front of her and made a sweeping motion with his arm. "This," he admonished, "is where it gets interesting. Bonnie and Shane? You still in?"

Elise had forgotten her new name, but laughed with the memory of street racing Bonnie and Clyde.

"What's so funny?" Jesse asked.

"Nothing." She forced a straight face. "Nothing. I'm still in."

"She probably just got one of my jokes. They were pretty awesome. Sorry you missed it, buddy." Shane patted Jesse's shoulder in condolence.

"What was there to get?" she asked innocently. "You're the lucky one, Jesse."

Her brother just shook his head in amusement and turned to walk away. "Sometimes I wonder..."

They passed many a college student, laden down with books and computers, scurrying here and there, and several larger groups either enjoying a coffee or just hanging out. They were laughing and carefree, and even the more stressful expressions were grounded in an appearance of normalcy and routine life.

The scene was calming, and Elise wished she was part of the reassuring day to day schedule. She didn't even know about the next five minutes.

Jesse never let up his pace, zipping around people and objects as he power walked deeper into the university. They arrived at an elegant brick building with a sign 'McKinnley Hall'.

"The genetics building," her brother announced, pausing by the entrance steps for them to catch up. "Dr. Batiste teaches in here, and if we made it on time," he checked a watch that wasn't there, "then he should be in room 202."

Elise tried not to huff as she followed him into the building, giving the elevator a longing stare as they walked past for the stairwell. She hoped there would be chairs in this classroom.

As they neared the door to room 202, Jesse motioned for them to be silent. A deep baritone voice could be heard from behind the wall, a thick Spanish accent muffling most of the words. Batiste sounded like a Spanish name, so Elise assumed they had come to the right place.

Jesse pushed the door open quietly and slipped in, Elise on his heels. The room was well lit with fluorescent lights and shaped like a half-moon with steppes down towards the center. Rows of desks followed the contour of the floor, and dozens of half-asleep students glanced up at their arrival.

Behind a podium, a stocky man with dark features froze in midsentence, finger pointing at the PowerPoint slide projected on the wall. Dressed in a tweed suit, he looked every part of the nutty professor, missing only thick plastic glasses.

More students glanced up at them, trying to discern why the lecture had stopped.

Dr. Batiste moved his arm to point at Jesse instead. "This is the man," he said loudly. "The one I have told you about all along. He knows things that I can't even fathom. He comes to fix what is broken."

The class as a whole turned and stared at them in confusion. Their faces ranged from complete boredom to shocked amazement.

"Class is dismissed," Dr. Batiste said curtly.

It took the students a moment to recover from the unexpected, but most of them snapped out of it and rose in a loud clamor, headed for the doorway.

Jesse made his way to the front of the classroom, and Elise tried to remain near him and not get sucked into the flood of bodies moving in the opposite direction. Dr. Batiste looked overcome to even be in his presence, and Elise was worried the burly man might cry.

"Alex," he grasped the blonde man's shoulder with affection. "You look just like him, all grown up now. It's good to see you again."

Returning the gesture, Jesse stepped back. "Same here, doctor. Same here."

Dr. Batiste's eyes moved to Shane, finally resting on Elise. His face contorted into a deep sorrow, an inexpressible sympathy. "Irene," he whispered softly. "I would recognize you anywhere. Your father left something for me to show you."

"For me?" She thought this was just about a formula.

He nodded, the mournful expression never leaving his face. She shifted uncomfortably, glancing at Jesse who wore the same look of grief. Did she miss something?

But looking at Shane, it was apparent that she wasn't the only one. His expression was guarded and empty, but she could tell he was lost.

The professor motioned at her to follow. "Come with me."

She looked back at Jesse for confirmation, and he nodded. Half-afraid and half-intrigued, she fell in step as Dr. Batiste led her out of the classroom and into the hallway. He glanced back at her, "This matter is for you privately."

He led her into a lab, similar to Dr. Rayford's in everything but size. It was much smaller. Dr. Batiste sat himself in front of one of the computers near the wall and typed in a password.

"Your father entrusted me with certain tasks, all of which I have completed or continued faithfully. This file he instructed me to show you when the time came, and that time is now."

Typing in several more codes, he inserted a small flash drive into the computer and opened a folder. He highlighted a file titled *Redemption*.

"I trust you can find the classroom again. Come when you are ready. We will either be there or in the hallway outside."

He studied her face for a moment, a resolved and determined flame burning in his eyes. "All is not lost. There is always hope."

With that, he turned and disappeared through the door.

Heart racing, Elise wondered what he could possibly mean. She sat down at the computer, but her finger paused over the Enter button. Something whispered that it would be better not to know, that she should just leave.

What are you looking for? Jesse's question echoed in her mind.

Truth. She had come to find out the truth.

In one swift movement, she clicked the button and a video file opened. Her father's kind face – a bit younger than the previous videos – looked at her without smiling. Instead there were tears running down his cheeks.

"Elise, this message is difficult for me to deliver. Choosing to hide you in the foster system was not easy, and leaving you was... horrible." He brought up his hands, finger locked together with a gold wedding band gleaming in the light. Pressing his knuckles against his mouth, he paused to collect himself.

"Someday you will know exactly what happened. What I can tell you now is that the threat to your life is real, and there are many who would happily exchange your future and your freedom in the name of scientific advancement or for fear of such."

He shook his head sadly. "The problem in your DNA is complicated. Right now, the bottom line is that your life is in great danger unless we get this issue sorted out soon."

"Don't be afraid," he wore a kind smile spoke with great conviction. "I have a plan, and it is going to work. Radical, yes. Even strange. But perfect.

"For this plan to work, it is vital that you listen to everything Alex says. He knows what's going on, and he has a crucial role to play."

Dr. Mathis' face froze like he didn't want to continue, but he pushed through anyway. "The next part I need to tell you is important, but difficult to explain."

What wasn't difficult to explain? Elise wanted to ask.

"DNA is information. It functions as the instruction manual for your body to build cells. Your genes define you, and your traits are decided by code passed down from your family tree. However, your genes – your DNA – is different. It was enhanced to allow a wide berth of capabilities not possible with normal DNA. Superhuman strength, for example. Increased cognitive abilities.

"Something happened, though. SynMOs. That's what we call them. Longhand is Synthetic Molecular Organisms. They're nanites. They were experimental, a project spearheaded by some of my colleagues. I warned you to stay away from them, because of their potential to destabilize your DNA and destroy it altogether. And you did for a time. You see," he scrunched his face, deep in thought. "These enhancements were fully under your control. Any use of these abilities went directly from your brain and then through your neural network with no outside interference. It was a stable system, and you were free, independent. That's how it was designed to work.

"Keep in mind that this project was and is a fiercely guarded secret. Jealousy got the best of one of my colleagues, and as he disagreed with the premise of my work, he came up with a plan of his own."

Rayford. Elise swallowed and gripped the desk tighter.

"But he couldn't take anything without your consent. You were close to invincible, and he knew it. But he was crafty, and somehow he enticed you to introduce some SynMOs into your bloodstream, even though I had warned you, and told you not to do this," he choked up, another tear escaping. Elise felt her heart contract, though she wasn't sure what emotion was behind the response. "You see, you thought it was safe, that you could handle a few SynMOs. But there's never just one. They're self-replicating, designed like bacteria. And they attach to your very DNA."

He took a deep breath and continued, "Bottom line: the written code of your DNA was corrupted, your body no longer capable of replicating and building your cells correctly. Afterward, I tried to control the damage, but almost lost you." His voice broke off with emotion, and a tear escaped before he brushed it aside. "I stabilized your system by shutting off, so to speak, the enhancements and restoring your body functions to normal."

The distraught man in the video, this father she reluctantly remembered, cleared his throat. Elise fought the urge to hide from what he said next. But she stayed, her eyes glued to the screen. In the depths of her heart, she felt a chasm widen. Her father. But all she knew was this empty hole.

He went on, "Not only did the SynMOs alter your DNA, they allowed for an outside force to override you, to set up a foreign control system. So there was always a danger because now someone else could manipulate your abilities, with nothing to stop them. And the SynMOs had become a part of your DNA, impossible to remove except for apoptosis: programmed cell death. At that point, everything that is you would be gone, replaced with these nanites."

Elise blinked, her internal temperature dropping several degrees.

"Anyway, my colleague had more up his sleeve as well. We were forced to run, and the rest is history. There is no way to restore your DNA to what it was. The system has changed. However, like I said, there is a plan. And it is more beautiful than the first. But just as you had to agree – even momentarily – with Rayford's idea, you must choose to accept this cure. I have not, will not, and shall never override your free will.

"I have set before you two options, and I will not interfere with your choice. You see here life and death; the way it's supposed to be versus a twisted version that will destroy you. I beg you to choose life. All Rayford has to offer is poison, no matter how he makes it sound. If you have not already, you will soon see for yourself the wickedness of his schemes. Please be careful."

Elise ground her jaw and bit her lip as a determined look covered her father's features again. "Do what Alex and Carbon say. I love you."

The screen became black and the program closed itself. Elise tried to steady her thoughts, overwhelmed by the download. Too much to consider.

This was her fault?

Numbly she left the computer and headed out the door and down the hallway, almost walking right past Jesse, Shane, and the professor.

"Hey," Jesse caught her arm, and she focused on his face, still in a daze. "Where are you going?"

She didn't really have a plan, didn't really have many coherent thoughts, to be honest. What had her dad meant by this message? She was broken? If she was so perfect before, why would she fall for schemes of Rayford? And he was bad, sure. But wicked? Was her father trying to scare her?

And what did he mean, it was her choice? What kind of choice was that? Life and death?

"Are you okay?" Jesse was looking at her with concern.

Her dad hadn't apologized. This was his fault, wasn't it? He used her like some sort of experiment, how could she possibly be held accountable? And for what? A bad decision she made at age six? How was that fair? And why couldn't she remember any of this? How had she decided her father trustworthy again? No answer came to mind.

She pulled her arm away. "I'm fine."

Dr. Batiste regarded her with compassion. "There is hope. Don't give up."

Looking into his earnest brown eyes, she wanted to believe him. But her mind couldn't differentiate between the words of Rayford or her father, or discern who was truthful. Her father was much nicer, to be sure, but was that adequate grounds to discount Rayford's side or the FBI?

"It's the past, Elise," Jesse said quietly. "You can't change it. Learn from it, yes. But letting it consume you is painful and unnecessary."

The past. Her dad said her genetics were different. So Rayford's story about in vitro fertilization was correct. He hadn't been lying. Her father really did use her as an experiment.

If her dad hadn't come back for her, she would still be safe in Mesa Springs, living life as normal. No one asked her if she wanted to be special or super or whatever. And if they were looking for someone strong enough or smart enough, clearly they had failed. She already messed it up once, how could she hope to live up to that standard of perfection?

Crumbling, Elise turned to leave. She needed to clear her head. She didn't want to be stuck with Rayford, but her dad didn't look much better. What was the difference, being his experiment or Rayford's?

Bitter tears filled her eyes unbidden as Jesse called after her. Maybe she would come back, but she couldn't take him right now. He just did whatever Dad said.

A hand grabbed her arm, and she spun around to find herself face to face with Shane. "What happened?" he asked, not letting go.

He probably thought she was pathetic too. She was just the weak messed up one that everyone kept rescuing. This was not her idea of freedom. With a surprising amount of strength, she jerked her arm free again. "Let me go," she warned before turning and walking away briskly.

Her heart cried out from somewhere that she needed to turn around, that the people who loved her were back there. But wiping the tears away, she kept walking. She could always return later, and she needed room to breathe. If she truly was free, she should be able to leave if she wanted.

The phone in her pocket buzzed and she silenced it with a quick move. She would talk to Carbon only when she felt ready. And that wasn't now.

* * * *

Shane watched helplessly as Elise stormed away. Jesse had walked up beside him and was standing without a word.

"What happened?" he demanded.

"She is free to go if she wants."

"Where is she going?"

Jesse's expression was like a heavy weight, but he said nothing.

"And you're going to just let her leave?" Shane was incredulous. This was the second time they let her walk off. He couldn't imagine what she had learned to make her upset enough to up and leave, and any possible scenarios didn't seem very good.

"We are not giving up. We have to respect her free will and hope she comes around. Until then, we can only proceed with the plan. Otherwise she really will be lost."

"But..." Shane tried to protest, but no logical arguments came.

Last time Jesse had been correct in letting her leave, and Carbon had to be somewhere nearby. They must have a plan. If there was one thing he was sure of, it was the insane commitment this family seemed to have for one another.

Dr. Batiste put a hand on his shoulder and looked him squarely in the eyes. "What she just learned was difficult, but necessary. She'll be okay."

"And if Rayford gets her?"

Jesse spoke up, "Then we will get her back."

Chapter 21

Stewart donned a pair of sunglasses as he got off the charter bus. Seattle was surprisingly sunny at this moment.

It wasn't hard to figure out where to go. Most people involved in the Mathis case had at least rudimentary knowledge of the laboratory where he had worked and purportedly stolen information from, as well as the affiliated Ceeling University.

Getting his bearings would be easy enough, and it wouldn't take long to figure out what kind of force he was up against. From there, he could piece together whatever information he had.

He wondered if Carbon was here personally, or even Dr. Mathis. Unlikely, considering what a hot spot this was.

But nothing would surprise him now.

* * * *

Shane followed Dr. Batiste and Jesse into another lab, the one used for Batiste's research. He wondered if he had done the right thing. Perhaps he should have followed Elise and tried to talk her into coming back, but she probably would only be angry, and if Rayford could locate her... He really didn't want to meet that man again. Especially unarmed.

Dr. Batiste had retrieved a silver canister like an elongated soda can from some sort of safe. He presented it to Jesse, who refused.

"Professor, if you would," Jesse rolled up his sleeve and offered his arm.

Batiste looked shocked. "Señor, no. I can't. If anything, you should ... No. How can I?"

"Trust me," Jesse kept his arm outstretched. "This is necessary."

They exchanged stares until the professor brought a hand to his mouth in horror. With a nod, Jesse seemed to dismiss the other man's protests.

Dr. Batiste entered a code into the top of the canister and it popped open with a hiss. Shane was a little disappointed that no steam came out like in the movies, but the clear liquid in the syringe appeared sufficiently high-tech.

Watching the professor insert it into Jesse's arm, however, was almost too much for him. He had never liked needles.

He looked away, hoping no shots were in his future. But just as the professor mumbled something about being finished, an electrical current shot through the room and almost knocked Shane off his feet.

He fought for his balance and grabbed the nearest table, trying to find the source of the burst. Dr. Batiste was still standing, although the man next to him was no longer recognizable. Jesse had been enveloped by lightning, his skin glowing and his hair standing out with electricity. Shielding his eyes, Shane couldn't help but look away. He could feel the heat from here.

As suddenly as it had come, the brilliance receded, leaving a dim glow over Jesse's skin, his eyes burning like flames of fire. Silently, he walked past Shane and Dr. Batiste and out of the lab.

Shane got up to follow, but his responses were sluggish and his mind was still in shock. His phone buzzed from his pocket, and he flipped it open to read a text message, dazed.

It was from Carbon, one word only.

"Stay."

* * * *

Elise walked out of the building and she did not slow or turn around until her feet had carried her off the campus entirely. Wet streaks were on her cheeks, but she ignored them, wondering what the point was anymore. She thought she knew, but now she realized she had no clue. She had been operating in blind faith. Rest and trust, Jesse had said.

How naïve was she? To assume that everything would work out, that he and this mysterious father only had her best interests at heart. Stupid, stupid. Now she was stuck, alone and broken. But that was better than staying with the ones who not only broke her, but held her responsible. Weren't fathers supposed to protect their children?!

She stumbled into a coffee shop a few blocks down, realizing how thirsty she was. Retrieving some of Jesse's money, she ordered a water bottle and a coffee. Her appetite was gone, however, with this horrible realization of guilt and blame sinking in her stomach. She was six! A child! She wanted to scream that this wasn't her fault, that she was fine without them.

But the guy behind the counter and several other customers were already giving her strange looks, so she stoically got her drinks and sat in the back corner.

Carbon's cell phone rang again, but tempted as she was to answer it, she was far too upset. Instead she sat it on the table, watching it light up and vibrate on the smooth surface. Her father put her in this impossible situation. They were forcing her to make a high-stakes decision, and for what? Scientific observation? No one asked her if she wanted to be involved, to have her life stolen away, inevitably fixed as 'different'.

She tried to sip her coffee calmly, but she was too upset, and she had to set it next to the phone because her hands were shaking. Getting sick again.

What a fool. Completely dependent on Jesse's drugs just to get through the day. If that wasn't control, she didn't know what was.

A feeling of betrayal seized her, and as the phone continued its incessant ringing, she slapped it off the table, pleased as it crashed onto the floor, its battery falling out. They acted like they were helping her? To do what? Fix her father's failed experiment? Try to save his reputation?

Another tear escaped, and she wiped it away in fury. First he made her with this problem, and now she was so weak that she needed them just to survive. Her heart was so desperate, so hopeful for a father that cared that she was willing to overlook the obvious misgivings in logic and trust blindly.

Sick. This whole thing was demented.

But she was still alive, and her father stressed that she had free will, even if he violated it himself. After some deep breaths, things would look clearer and she could come up with a plan. Carbon could track her with the phone, so she would need to move on from this present location. Maybe she could hide out in the city or the countryside, use her new ID to get a low profile job. She could probably make a decent living, even live a normal life.

Who was she kidding? If she didn't get a cure, she wouldn't even live past a few weeks. She was trapped. Was this her father's idea of freedom? A free will but no viable options except the one he wanted? He had said these 'nanites' wouldn't let go except if her cells died. What was that supposed to mean?

The thought of tiny microorganisms filling her body made her shudder. She couldn't stand to think about it.

Elise watched in her periphery as a well-dressed grey haired woman, maybe mid-fifties, headed toward her position. Her eyes were glued to the coffee cup, trying not to draw the attention of any gawking observers. She didn't need or want their sympathy.

To her surprise, however, the woman sat down across from her and lowered her face to make eye contact. The lady's eyes were clear blue, intelligent and composed. "Are you okay?"

"Yeah," Elise sniffled, trying not to squirm under the woman's gaze.

"You don't look okay," she observed, leaning back in her chair. "You look like a lost little girl."

More tears came up involuntarily, and Elise hated them. She wasn't going to fall for this nice act again.

"Kay Summers," the woman reached a hand across the table. Elise didn't move, and the woman retracted her hand slowly. "I know who you are, Elise. I'm here to help you."

Chapter 22

Restless in Dr. Batiste's office, Shane sat awaiting Jesse's return. He had no way to comprehend what had just happened. Batiste had left to teach another class, and with Carbon's last command to stay, he was stuck alone with his shock.

Just like that! Inject a man who starts glowing like a fluorescent light bulb then go on with life as normal. Whatever was happening, it was beginning to freak him out a little.

His cell phone buzzed again in his pocket, and this time he found a call from Carbon. He slid the touchscreen to answer. "What the heck is going on here?"

"Hello, Shane. You need to follow my instructions. Two FBI agents are trying to locate Dr. Batiste, and they will arrive in his office within minutes. Turn left and head down the stairs at the end of the hallway."

FBI. Prison. Jumping to his feet, Shane quickly obeyed. Besides students milling around, he saw nothing suspicious. But he wasn't about to second-guess Carbon with his life at stake.

At the bottom of the stairwell, her smooth tone came over the phone again. "They are in the elevators. It is safe to proceed."

"And go where?" he snapped, nerves on end and patience in short supply.

"B&D's Coffee Shop. Elise is there, and she is in trouble."

* * * *

"You didn't think there might be more at stake?"

Elise blinked, unwilling to easily believe any of this. Dr. Summers had recounted a different version of events from Jesse and her father, and Elise could feel her defenses slipping.

The woman's logic was sound. Did she really believe that her brother and father would risk everything just for her? That they would readily risk their lives and fortune for no other reason than her value as a person?

This explanation was clear. She could find no flaw in reasoning, and inside she felt the cold creeping back.

Her life was valuable, yes. She had been an illegal extension of a government project, courtesy of her father. He wanted to finish the experiment he had started, to prove Rayford wrong and use the leverage to clear his name. This was all a ploy to redeem his name in the scientific community.

Dr. Summers guessed that those helping him – and it seemed that she did not know that Alex Mathis was involved at all – were just looking for the billions of dollars in this technology, not to mention prestige and power.

But that was the end of it. Same old reasons. Same old cold, calculating logic.

Elise fought it. But deep down, she felt the pull of reality. She had been living a daydream, believing she was important because her dad and brother loved her. Like a real family.

There were no angry tears now. She had cried enough today. But her jumbled feelings were overshadowed by a bone-chilling numbness.

Lifting her eyes to meet Dr. Summers, she found the woman surveying her quietly. Maybe her dad was wrong, but that didn't mean she wanted to become the government's experiment either. If only she could access those 'higher functions' everyone kept talking about.

Her dad's voice echoed in her mind. *There is no way to restore the DNA to what it was.* And yet he and Jesse had a plan. Even if he was being honest, that didn't mean he was right. Another scientist could have found a different option.

"What are you proposing?" Elise asked. At this moment, her only desire was to slip away unnoticed into the shadows.

"If you agree, there are those who would like to see this project continued. The outcomes could be amazing. The cure for cancer, AIDS… it's practically limitless." Dr. Summers' otherwise guarded eyes flashed with excitement. "And for you, there is some risk, yes. But we know of your condition. You won't live for long without some sort of treatment."

"You have a treatment?" The cynicism in her tone was unmistakable.

Dr. Summers nodded her head. "Your father was not the only expert in this area. For ten years scientists have been continuing this research. We have developed a number of options, but one in particular that I believe is foolproof."

"Doubt it."

Elise jerked her eyes around to find who had spoken. Shane was ten feet behind Dr. Summers and closing the gap quickly. He slipped a cell phone in his pocket before stopping by their table.

"What are you doing here?" Elise demanded, angry she had been followed.

His face was serious. "We need to get out of here. Now."

"I'm fine," she snapped. "I don't need any help." Her brother might be intentionally misleading her, but this guy had no idea what was going on. He was a pawn, just like her.

Shane stepped forward and grabbed her arm despite her protests. "No, you're not fine. We need to leave."

"Get your hands off of her," Dr. Summers commanded authoritatively. "Don't assume I came alone."

Glancing around, Elise saw several bulky looking men beginning to shuffle around in the front of the shop. She looked back in Shane's face, the fear there confirming he had seen them as well.

Dr. Summers smoothed her grey hair into place. "Now you, Mr. Lawson, can explain to these gentlemen how you were leaving. They can escort you out, or the police can." Her expression was stony, "It's actually quite a generous offer. Kidnapping is a serious offense, as well as aggravated assault with a firearm and acts of terrorism."

Shane released her arm, scanning the room.

"Very good," Dr. Summer smiled. "I promise we'll take good care of Elise. If we see you again, there will be no second chances."

The three thugs were gathered by the counter, less than twenty feet away and clear across the exit path. But when Elise glanced back at Shane, his eyes seemed to focus on something past the shop's window.

He smiled and leaned towards the older woman. "That's very kind, Doctor. But you see," he met her gaze evenly, "I didn't come alone either."

In a millisecond of a stare down neither one blinked.

"Fire! Fire!" a woman screamed from the front of the shop.

An alarm went off, its shrill shriek striking fear inside. The piercing noise caused Elise to duck in pain and cover her ears to no avail. The lights cut off in the next second, and the store was submerged into black obscurity.

There was general panic from the people inside, and through the shouting Elise heard sounds of rushing feet towards the exit in the front.

"Freeze!" A gruff voice called.

Elise felt herself dragged backwards. She struggled as hands pushed her to the ground.

"It's me!" Shane whispered tersely in her ear. "Ready to run?"

She was furious, ready for nothing more than to be left alone. But it was clearly too late for that.

Two deep voices were yelling nearby, and Dr. Summers shouted something back. A flash of light streaked across her vision, and an explosion from the back of the building slammed her forward in the darkness.

"Now!" Shane yelled, half dragging her down the aisle past the stunned men and into the light of day. Tires screeched as Carbon slammed to a halt in front of them, her passenger door flying open.

Elise was all but thrown into the driver seat, Shane jumping in beside her.

"Go, go!" he yelled, but Carbon's tires were already smoking as she gunned her engine, shooting them down the street.

Pulling herself around, Elise fought to focus. Out the back window she saw chaos as smoke billowed out of the coffee shop. People were screaming in front, some staring in shock.

But there wasn't a long opportunity to take in the frenzied scene as Carbon weaved dangerously through traffic on the crowded street.

"Go!" Shane shouted again. "That car's following us!"

Elise's eyes found the dark blue sedan that had already fallen in quick pursuit.

"Yes," Carbon added, no hurry in her voice. "There are two vehicles trailing us. Please fasten your seat belts, and brace yourselves."

"What are you doing?!" Elise yelled, torn between rage and gratitude. "What was that?!"

Shane didn't look at her, too busy studying the cars behind them. "That was a rescue, Elise." His voice was calm, and she wondered what his problem was. "Carbon, pull up a map of the surrounding area."

A terrain satellite map immediately appeared on the screen, complete with current traffic.

"Awesome," Shane chuckled, playing with the zoom.

Elise wanted to punch him. There was absolutely nothing about this situation that was awesome. "What's your plan, cowboy?" she snapped, fearfully watching the obstacles they were dodging and the cars they were evading.

"He does not have a plan," Carbon informed her.

"Yes, I do." He mapped out a route with his finger, "How's that?"

It was less than a second before Carbon responded. "The aqueducts."

"Noticed them when we arrived. Will it work?"

"If we cannot lose them in town, it is a viable second choice."

Shane flashed Elise a triumphant grin, swallowing it slightly at her sullen glare. He checked out the back window again. "What have we got as far as defensive measures? Tacks?"

"I can drop a spike strip, but it will also damage other vehicles and our pursuers are far enough behind to steer around them."

"But it will slow them down, right?"

"It is not an efficient use of the tools available."

- 111 -

"What about the guns? I saw them that night with Rayford."

"It is nearly impossible to incapacitate their tires from this position."

"They're gaining," Elise pointed out the window. "Fast."

"Uh-oh," Shane remarked. She spun to see where he was looking. Two patrol cars were now joining the pursuit, lights flashing and sirens wailing.

"Brilliant," Elise muttered angrily, dropping her head against the seat. Why couldn't they just have let her handle things?

"Do not worry, Elise," Carbon reassured her. "I have a plan."

The car lurched, involuntary screams escaping from both she and Shane as Carbon flung herself one hundred and eighty degrees to face the other direction. The engine revved loudly as their speed barely diminished, Elise smacking the side door as they straightened out.

The two pursuing vehicles were now on an imminent collision course with Carbon, and they both jerked to the outside. Elise gasped as they barreled through with a margin of several inches. Loud noises punctuated the area, and she looked back to see one car on its hood, the other smashed into a parked garbage truck.

"You killed them!" she yelled.

"No, they will both survive."

Elise growled in frustration, feeling utterly helpless.

"The cops!" Shane yelled, but Carbon was a step ahead. Executing a sharp spin, they pirouetted into an empty row of parallel parking, the two cruisers flying past with squealing brakes.

But their reaction times were nothing compared to Carbon, whose momentum had never ceased. Flinging back into the center of the road, they came up behind the two cars. Several gunshots fired from Carbon's front end, leaving the police vehicles' rims lighting up with sparks as bare metal fought against pavement.

With a final squeal, Carbon yanked to the right, drifting across the pavement like a figure skater over ice. An alley appeared in the front windshield, and another roar from Carbon's engine shot them into the darkness.

The noises faded into the background as they continued accelerating, performing several more flying turns until they were headed on an empty street away from the city.

Elise felt sick, sinking down into the seat with her eyes closed. The world was spinning way too fast. It seemed like an eternal ten minutes before Carbon slowed to a final halt, the sound of splashing water giving Elise pause.

Silence enveloped her, and she dared to open her eyes. Carbon had already shut off her engine, and Elise found herself facing sides of a concrete tube. A steady river of water flowed behind them, light visible several hundred feet down the tunnel.

Releasing a long-held breath, Elise thought she might cry with relief.

"Yeah!" Shane yelled beside her, punching the air with his fist. "Carbon, I love you!"

"Shut up!" Elise screamed, more savage sounding than she intended. "Are you crazy? We almost died!"

He fell silent, studying her for a moment. "Aren't you happy? You just got rescued!"

She glared at him. "You don't get it. I was fine. That lady was just talking to me."

He snorted. "Sure. With three body guards, just in case."

"Yeah," she exclaimed. "In case you or someone else showed up to kidnap me again!"

"Kidnap?" his voice dropped in disbelief. "Come on, you don't believe that old lady, do you?"

"You," she spoke the word like poison, "don't even know what she said."

"I do," he was quick on the defense. "Carbon was listening, and she told me most of what *Dr. Summers*," he emphasized the name, perhaps to prove that he was paying attention, "said."

"And just what did she say?" Elise spat back bitterly.

"That your father was using you as an experiment, that he didn't care about you, and that all he wanted was money. Blah, blah, blah."

Elise felt fury rise up like a torrent. "It was a little more than that. You probably just didn't understand."

"Oh, I understood. That lady was playing you like…"

"Excuse me," Carbon's smooth voice interrupted. "But this is fruitless."

They both fell silent, staring at each other like hardened generals across a battle line.

Shane's face softened and he broke eye contact. "Carbon's right. I don't want to fight. I was trying to help you."

Elise tried to stifle her anger as easily, but it just melted into another heap of conflicting emotions. She glanced around the cab, a critical detail occurring to her for the first time. "Where's Jesse?"

Shane shrugged. "Beats me. Last time I saw him, he was glowing like a Christmas decoration."

Not sure what to make of that, Elise paused. "A what?"

But Carbon interjected, "Jesse's body conducted a high level of energy because of the compound injected into his system. He had the appearance of 'glowing', but it receded within a few minutes."

Elise's eyes widened. "What happened?"

"Dr. Batiste's formula operated exactly as planned. Jesse is fine."

She tried to digest the info, but found no resolution. "Where is he?"

"He is with Dr. Rayford."

"What?!" Elise and Shane exclaimed in unison.

"Relax," Carbon instructed them. "He will meet us when he is ready."

"Is he building the cure?" Shane asked.

"Yes. But there are still many stages left."

Stages? How hard could it be to throw some chemicals together? But Elise shoved her thoughts aside, reaching for the door handle instead. She had already been weak without Jesse's drugs, and the exhilarating car ride was over the top.

The handle, however, gave no response.

"Please do not exit the vehicle," Carbon intoned.

Irrational panic seized her. "Why?"

"It is dangerous."

Elise paused, carefully surveying the damp concrete tunnel around them. Nothing seemed particularly hazardous. The water was shallow – only a few inches – and running slowly. The ground and sides appeared a little slippery, but nothing life threatening.

"Come on, Carbon. It's not that bad."

But the car gave no response.

"We're just supposed to sit here?"

"Yes. If you are hungry or thirsty, there are supplies in the back seat."

Elise groaned in frustration, unhappy with where she was and who she was with. Dr. Summers was nice enough, and with recent events, it was reasonable to assume she would be prepared before approaching her. Those 'thugs' might have been undercover cops.

"What did that old lady want?"

Annoyed at having to share her thoughts with someone else, Elise rolled her eyes towards Shane and answered sharply. "That old lady has a name. Said she worked for the government on the same project as my dad."

"Government project?" Shane furrowed his brows in thought. "This genetic stuff, she said it was a secret project or something?"

"Yeah, something," Elise was noncommittal. She had no desire to share information with the idiot who had just prevented her from learning more.

But Shane didn't react to her lack of cooperation. He looked like a bloodhound that had locked onto a scent.

"Carbon," he turned to the dash. "Is this true?"

"Yes. Dr. Summers worked with Dr. Rayford under your father's direction."

"I mean about the government project. Elise's dad worked for the government?"

"That information is classified."

"Ah," Shane let out a long breath. "That means yes." He turned to Elise, "What did she tell you?"

Elise shrugged. "Not much."

But he was not to be put off by her coldness. "When I got there, she was saying that she had another cure. Is that possible?"

Carbon must have figured out the question was aimed at her. "No. There is only one way to build the cure."

"Maybe they discovered the same cure," Shane tried, tapping his fingers as if keeping up with the mental effort.

"Impossible," Carbon continued. "Jesse is the only person who can make the cure. The other scientists involved have neither an accurate picture of Elise's condition, nor the knowledge and tools necessary to counter the problem."

"And you're certain about this?" Shane asked.

An innocent enough inquiry, but definitely not a good one to aim at Carbon. There was no response.

"Okay, okay," he waved his hands apologetically. "I get it."

Maybe Shane was easily convinced, but Elise was the one whose life hung in the balance. "But you can't really know that, can you?"

"Yes, I can." Carbon replied.

Elise found herself defensive of these scientists whose credentials and abilities were dismissed so lightly. "But they worked on the project as well. And what about the main question? Why? If Jesse has the only solution, why doesn't he tell them? And if they want to help, can they? I mean, if my Dad knew how to make the 'cure', why didn't he tell these people in the beginning?"

She glared at Shane, but he wasn't the one who had an answer.

"Those are excellent questions. There is a fundamental disagreement between your father and the other scientists on the project."

"Aha!" Shane exclaimed triumphantly. "I knew it. There is a government project."

Carbon ignored his outburst. "Dr. Mathis was in charge, and he enforced procedures and policies in line with his theories and understanding of the science. They have continued, in his absence, to take things in a different direction. He has already shown them the correct methods toward building a cure or continuing the research at all, but they reject his advice."

"What if he's wrong?" Elise spat out, unable to hide the obvious chink in Carbon's explanation.

"He is not."

"So, this whole thing hinges upon the belief that my dad is smarter than everyone else."

"Your father is a genius," Carbon said, as if that was reason enough.

Elise snorted. "Sure. Rayford seems to be a genius too."

"An evil one," Shane piped up.

Elise really couldn't argue with that one. The man was insane. But if her father used her as an experiment in the first place, what made him so much better?

"I would believe Carbon," Shane offered his two cents, which Elise wished he would keep to himself. "After all, your dad built her. And only a genius could do that."

She rolled her eyes. No one was more impressed with this car than Shane, and she felt a twinge of pride that it was loyal to her. Resting back against the seat, she listened to the running water. She would stay on her guard, but maybe Jesse could offer some more answers.

He seemed earnest about helping her, and Carbon's existence alone combated Dr. Summers' explanation that her dad was in it for the money. If he could build this car, he already had enough money. And Carbon's technology had to be worth billions.

Her limbs seemed to melt into the soft leather, and as fatigue and general sickness washed over her, Elise hoped her dad was right. If only they could get that cure sooner rather than later.

Chapter 23

Alan Stewart sat at a coffee shop, fingers tapping the top of his worn guitar case. It was a good disguise, and he thanked his mom for those years of guitar lessons as a kid. Complete with fake dreadlocks and loosely worn clothing, he could strum and sing as a traveling hippie. So far, no one had even passed a glance in his direction.

The beat-up case contained more than just his guitar, and his tattered backpack held extra gear he thought he might need.

He had already gotten an accurate lay of the land. The building once used for experimentation was set up as a pharmaceutical lab, complete with receptionists and a waiting room. But there was no reason to believe the mirage.

Undercover agents were on every corner. At least two snipers set up. Police patrols passed by with unusual frequency, and without a doubt there would be heavily armed guards inside. Several people in lab coats had come and gone, and while some were probably legit, most carried the look of well-trained federal agents. He didn't recognize anyone personally, with the exception of the two men waiting in the shadows behind the building.

It was hard to get a good look at them, but he would bet anything they were two of the thugs who ambushed them in Colorado. And their operating in apparent conjunction with federal agents and police made the situation worriedly complex.

Two women had entered the building, and he briefly wondered if one was Carbon. But he considered it unlikely.

Stewart was more concerned with the one woman he had recognized.

She was a good tail, and nearly impossible to catch following someone. But Stewart had taught her. And he didn't teach her everything.

* * * *

"Ow," Elise gasped, clutching her ribs. It felt like a knife had been pressed through, and her lungs were pierced with pain. She had noticed a slow increase of aches throughout her body, but they were becoming excruciating. Another pain seared a line across her left eyebrow and around the back of her head.

She hissed through her teeth, trying to take her mind off the torment. When would Jesse get back?

"Are you okay?" Shane was eyeing her worriedly.

Beginning with a nod, the head motion turned from vertical to horizontal as she realized the futility of lying. What was the point? If she didn't start feeling better soon, she would probably begin screaming.

Stifling a sob, she couldn't manage any coherent speech without breaking down. Physically she was on an edge, and she was powerless.

"Where's Jesse?" Shane asked Carbon.

"He is approaching."

Elise squinted at the bright end of the tunnel, but could see nothing. She sat nearly motionless to decrease the pain level. Carbon had provided entertainment in the way of television in the center console, but Elise was losing the ability to focus even on the movie. The pain was crippling. Even worse, she found herself fearing for the future.

What if something happened to Jesse? What if he couldn't make the cure, and she was forced to suffer agony for weeks as her body slowly destroyed itself? The thought was horrible and only made the pain worse, so she tried not to consider the future at all. If she could just make it through the next minute…

She had closed her eyes, focusing on thoughts of Nia and the Madills' peaceful shop, when Shane nudged her.

"There's Jesse," he said quietly.

A glance down the tunnel confirmed it, the blonde man making his way cautiously through the water. Or not so cautiously.

She stared further to find him walking just above the water. It must be an optical illusion, or maybe the water wasn't very deep there. Nevertheless, she and Shane both watched with bated breath as Jesse made his way to the car, exchanging shocked glances as he drew nearer and it became evident he was indeed walking over the water, not in it.

He approached the driver door and knocked on the window with a smile. The door opened, but Elise could think of nothing to say. She couldn't even remember what had been hurting so much.

"What's wrong with you guys? Looks like you've seen a ghost. It's just me," he reassured them.

Shane was still gaping, honest and complete astonishment his only expression. Jesse looked between them, and Elise realized something had changed. She didn't know what it was, but it was disconcerting.

"You just… how did you…" she stammered, wincing as the pain shot back through her head.

"Electrical fields and energy. You'll understand someday." His blue eyes scrutinized her for a moment before he regarded her with compassion. "Will you let me help?"

Elise froze, her hand halfway to her forehead. "Help?"

"Your body has deteriorated further, as I'm sure you've noticed. But I can help you, if you'll let me."

"What, you mean with more of the compound? Another shot?"

He shook his head. "No. Just trust me. Will you let me help?" he repeated his question.

Eyeing him suspiciously, Elise found herself relaxing somewhat. This was her brother, and he wanted to help her. "Okay," she agreed, though her voice sounded small, and it was by no means her most resolute declaration.

Jesse smiled and reached toward her, placing both hands on her head. A strange warmth emanated down from his touch and flooded her aching cells with relief. He muttered something, but she wasn't paying attention, enjoying the mesmerizing peace in her warring members.

"There."

When she opened her eyes, she found Jesse standing back and watching her with satisfaction.

"That's it?!" she exclaimed, moving her neck to make sure the pain was gone. "How did you do that?"

He laughed, "Pretty good trick. No?"

Shane was having trouble computing, "You found the cure?"

"No," Jesse shook his head. "But I know how to get it. This doesn't fix the problem, just the immediate symptoms."

Elise was ready to rejoice now, the agony of her flesh having been healed. "Thanks!" She was beaming, unable to stop a silly giggle from rising up. It was like some kind of high. Lightness without reason. What had he done?

"You're welcome," he responded with a smile. "Now, I have a plan to draw Rayford out into the open. Force his hand, so to speak."

"Force him to do what?" Shane asked. "And how did you do that?"

Jesse's smile broadened. "Let's just say I had help. As for Rayford; we need the remedy, and he's going to help us build it."

Chapter 24

Elise wished she carried Jesse's confidence. If she was toting a hypothetical bag of luggage, it would be filled with doubt, fear, shame and absolute confusion. Certainly resolve and surety would not be among her possessions.

But she felt ninety percent better, and her gut instinct led her to trust her brother, not creepy Dr. Rayford.

Walking back to the campus seemed like a very bad idea, but she had to trust that Jesse knew what he was doing. And since he could walk on water and take away physical pain, maybe he would be able to use some magical power to keep the cops from finding them.

Shane was annoyingly happy and resolved, and she made a concerted effort not to let her disgust at his cheerfulness show. She barely trusted her dad and Jesse. How this man managed to follow them so unreservedly and without proof made no sense at all.

They stuck to sidewalks through the main part of town, headed again for the University.

Elise quickened her pace to catch her brother. "Hey, Jesse."

"Mm-hm?"

"Aren't the police looking for Shane and I now? And you? Carbon said you met with Dr. Rayford. Why? What happened?"

"Whew," in an exaggerated motion, he wiped imaginary sweat from his brow. "That was a lot of questions. I'll do my best."

She made a face, but didn't rescind any of the questions.

"Carbon is the only one wanted right now. She blacked out the security cameras in the coffee shop, so there is no video footage of you or Shane inside. Only Dr. Summers' story and other eyewitness accounts. But Carbon is very thorough in covering her tracks. Don't worry about it. And yes, I met with Dr. Rayford."

Jesse's voice dropped off, his demeanor now somber.

"And...?" Shane asked from behind. "What happened?"

Jesse heaved a sigh. "It was necessary." Blue eyes met Elise's gaze with an unreadable expression.

"Dr. Batiste showed me a video from Dad," she changed the subject, not sure of why. This suddenly seemed important. "He said my DNA is... different." She felt awkward saying it. Like a mutant or comic book superhero. "That as a child, I had certain abilities."

Jesse nodded in validation, but offered no explanation.

"Why can't I remember any of this?"

"The memories are there. You simply can't access them. It was unavoidable when Dad severed the ties between the enhancements and your vital functioning parts of DNA. Think of destroying both a receiver and a transmitter... no way to send the information, no way to receive it either."

Elise didn't understand all of that, but she got the main point. "He also said my DNA could never be what it was, but he has a plan. Will I ever remember?"

Jesse stopped and put a hand on her shoulder. "Yes. But probably not at once. The process of healing your body will be long and hard, but the end result will be even better than the original system."

She recalled him saying that once before, but the thought of the difficulties facing her brought up Dr. Summers' argument. "What if I just want to be normal?" she asked as they began walking again. "Don't you think it was unfair to just expect me to do all this? To suffer?" Surprised at the bitterness in her own voice, Elise was almost afraid to see Jesse's reaction.

"Fair? Wait to make a judgment on that one. Dad would never expect more of you than is possible. Yes, it will be difficult. It is also wonderful."

That was not exactly a satisfactory answer, but Elise allowed her mind to chew on the ideas instead of simply arguing. She did enjoy the thought of having special powers or whatever. But she would like to be able to decide for herself whether or not the costs outweighed the benefits. In all honesty, however, it was truly a moot point.

"I'm lost," Shane shared.

"It's not that hard," Jesse turned and glanced at him. "Just follow behind me. You don't even have to navigate the sidewalk."

Shane frowned, "Very funny. I mean lost in a mental sense."

"Oh," Jesse nodded as if he understood. "Can't help you there. The stress just gets to some people."

"You're as bad as Carbon. You programmed her like that on purpose, didn't you?"

Jesse only shrugged noncommittally.

"I thought so. Now don't distract me. Elise's DNA was purposefully modified, and she had superhuman abilities until ... something happened."

Jesse looked pained again.

Shane voiced the inevitable, "What happened?"

Falling back a step, Elise tuned her ears closely for the answer. Although after what her dad said, she wasn't sure she wanted to know and more details.

His words echoed in her mind. *He could do nothing without your consent.*

Had she betrayed her family?

"Tiny organisms, SynMOs, were introduced into Elise's body. They're destructive, to say the least. Once infected, they're impossible to get rid of. Synthetic Molecular Organisms, if you want the full name. Once the DNA strand is corrupted, they cut off normally automated mechanisms and insert their own control."

He glanced back at Elise, "They effectively hijacked your mind and cellular functions, rerouting data and information through their own signal network. And so you cannot consciously control any of the enhancements you once had, or even remember what it was to have them."

"What enhancements?" Elise piped up. This question had bugged her before.

"All of them," Jesse said quietly. "All of them."

With a deep sigh, he focused ahead and continued. "You can survive like this, but it is an extremely dangerous state. Not only is your body functioning minimally, but there remains the constant risk that someone from the outside could take control."

"Of her body?" Shane asked, incredulous.

Jesse nodded and turned sad eyes to her. "There is only one cure. That is why Dr. Rayford is so dangerous. Though the original SynMOs corrupted your DNA and began incorrect replication, Dad managed to shut off their signal emitting capabilities. But Rayford has now infected you with new SynMOs, a more advanced type that has no off-switch. Not even with his own control mechanisms."

Elise dropped eye contact, ashamed.

"Wow," Shane breathed, staring at his feet as they walked along. "That dude is bad."

With a small chuckle, Jesse agreed. "Yes. He is a bad dude."

"So," he was still connecting dots. "Rayford wants Elise to have access to her super abilities?"

The word 'super' made her cringe. If there was one word that described the opposite of how she felt, that was it.

"Partly," Jesse answered. "But he plans to also reverse engineer Dad's genetic technology to replicate. The power that he would hold is incredible. That's why he's so motivated."

"What about the charges against Dad?" Elise blurted. "Fraud, treason... those are pretty serious."

"When your DNA was compromised, Dad retreated to study and fix what had happened. It took him several weeks to develop a way to counter Rayford's SynMOs and to keep him from finding you. Rayford, always proactive, spent his time constructing a story that he thought would force Dad to hand over his research or better – you – in exchange for a clean record."

"Blackmail," Shane muttered.

"Precisely."

"But everyone believed Rayford!" Elise exclaimed. "Why didn't Dad just go public with what Rayford had done and prove his innocence?"

"Dad's research was top-secret. Very few knew about it, and even fewer know now. He could not make anything public. Even his government contact suggested running underground. And our priority was to keep you from Rayford."

Elise allowed herself to fall further behind. She didn't want to hear anymore. The problems here weren't her Dad's fault, they were hers. Had she really given Rayford her consent? She was only six! But then again, if this story was accurate, she had probably already been at Einstein's level of genius.

She glanced up to find Jesse walking beside her.

"What's wrong?" he asked.

That lit the fuse. How could he possibly ask what was wrong? He knew better than her! Refusing to speak, Elise felt her throat grow thick as she tried to squelch the rising tears.

Jesse spoke, "It is true, what Dad said on the video. But it is also true what he has said all along. What Carbon has said. What I told you on the hike?"

Her memory was jogged easily again, but even remembrance of the words stung like fire against the obvious pain of a greater truth.

"It's my fault?" she whispered, fighting to control her voice.

He didn't answer, but the silence was enough.

"What happened?" The fear was worse not knowing. Maybe she had a good reason.

"You were deceived," he said simply. "A full account exists in Carbon's records, but there's no need for that now."

Maybe it was too horrible for him to say.

"Whatever happened, whatever happens, cannot erase this truth. You are a beloved daughter and sister, and you are worth it."

She glanced up at his face, which was beaming with a peculiar look of joy.

"Dad loves you, I love you. We're going to get through this."

Stifling her embarrassingly emotional reaction, she stiffened at his brief hug.

"Just keep following me and listening to Carbon. You hang out with us long enough, and you'll never forget that."

She sniffled and dropped her eyes to the ground, "Thanks."

"You are welcome," Jesse pronounced the words pointedly before resuming his quick pace toward the university.

Elise fell silent. Headed back into danger, she tried once more to keep Jesse's words from drifting away.

Love. She wasn't sure what the term even meant, but this felt like a small taste. Her dad and brother were committed to her. They were still fighting to fix her, even though she was to blame for the failure.

Shuddering with the thought of what her betrayal might have actually been, Elise began counting her footsteps.

Worth it. She was worth it.

Worth what?

* * * *

"So," Richardson leaned over his chair, facing Juan Batiste. "Good doctor. Why are we having this conversation now?"

The dark featured man met his eyes squarely, never giving an inch. He would be a formidable opponent in the intellectual realm, but moreover, the man's intensity was honest. It intrigued Richardson greatly. Deep conviction was hard to come by these days.

"Okay. Let me begin." Richardson lowered himself into the chair he had been standing behind. "You were a close friend of Dr. Mathis, a fact you do not dispute," he flicked his eyes up to make sure the man had not changed his position. He had not.

"You have persisted advocating all of Dr. Mathis' theories and predictions, even though many of them have been disproven and even dismissed by the greater scientific community. More troubling, however, is your... shall we say, your advocacy of a pro-Mathis 'revival' in your words, where one particular man selected by Mathis will come and 'fix what is broken'. Care to elaborate?"

"I have always spoken publicly," Dr. Batiste enunciated clearly, his eyes never flinching. "My positions have not changed."

"I see." Richardson leaned back, pausing to collect his thoughts. "Have you had any contact with Mathis since his disappearance ten years ago?"

"His emails were sent to me, yes. But they were also sent to every person on the FBI force tasked with finding him and every scientist in the genetics department."

"Apart from that."

"Dr. Mathis charged me with the task of preparing this community for when he comes back."

"He is coming here?"

"Not as you are thinking. But the message he told me to deliver, that he is sending the man he chooses to fix what is broken, is true."

Richardson squinted. This man was undeniably savvy and well-spoken, but it was a bit like deciphering riddles. "Who is this man?"

"The only one who can fix what is broken."

"You can't be more specific?"

Dr. Batiste shook his head. "No. There is no more information to give."

"So that's it? That's all you have for us?"

Silence.

Richardson stood to leave. "I know where to find you if I have any questions. Sorry about the detainment, but until this is sorted out, you aren't going anywhere. We will do our best to make you comfortable."

"You asked me earlier about a substance Dr. Mathis gave to me. You were right, he did leave something in my care."

"Where is it?"

"The container is in my office."

Richardson smiled. Success at last.

"The container is empty."

His face slipped to a frown. "What?"

"I gave it to the man who was sent."

"He's here? Wait… what was in there?"

"Watch the security footage from my office. It was all the proof I needed. Dr. Mathis instructed me to give this substance to the man he sent, and that it would be clear whether he was the one or not."

"And…?"

"Watch the footage," Batiste said softly. "But know this. What Samuel gave me to tell and to give is nothing compared to what this man will do. Water to fire."

Struggling to hold the man's gaze, Richardson realized he understood nothing Batiste had said. He may belong in a nuthouse, but something about the man fascinated him.

"I'll see you later, Doctor," he excused himself.

That provided enough leads for now. Besides, he couldn't stand many more discreetly hidden puzzles. It was time to deal in facts.

Chapter 25

Shane Lawson sat quietly, tracing the beads of condensation populating the outside of his cup of Coke. He counted it fortunate that glowing and possessing super-human abilities, Jesse still appreciated food.

He couldn't pretend to have understood the exchange between brother and sister, but he did pick up on Elise's admission of guilt. It was a point he did not wish to push further, and what he was struggling to explain was Jesse's reaction.

Was this guy for real? Shane couldn't imagine a brother or father so devoted, and logically, he knew it was probably a smokescreen for another agenda. According to Dr. Summers, that was exactly what was going on. Manipulation of a young woman's feelings to entice her cooperation.

Heading back to the University was not a smart move. But it was exactly the sort of thing that Jesse was prone to. Illogical, and certainly not the sign of a diabolical scheming maniac. Okay, maybe a maniac. A kind, philosophical, hardworking, ingenious maniac.

Stuffing a delicious amount of hamburger in his mouth, Shane found Jesse's blue eyes watching him in amusement.

"Whatcha thinking?"

Shane returned his gaze evenly. Maybe he could read minds.

But Elise interrupted the ensuing silence. "Nothing. He's not thinking anything."

He shot her a sideways glance. For whatever reason, he did not seem to be on her favorite person list.

"Come on, let's be fair," Jesse chided her. "Clearly he is thinking. He's a man. That hamburger is the focus right now."

See? A mind reader for sure.

"Clearly," Elise sighed.

Swallowing his bite, he slurped some Coke before collecting his thoughts for a proper response. "Actually, I was wondering why we're headed back to campus. Isn't that where people will be looking for us? They already know Elise and I are here. We are kind of wanted, remember?"

Jesse wasn't fazed. "Don't worry. They won't get you if you're with me."

"And how's that, exactly? Are you going to zap them or something?"

"With his mind, no doubt," Elise quipped sarcastically.

"Hey, you didn't see him glowing."

She shrugged and fingered the remaining fries on her plate. If she wasn't planning on eating those…

"Batiste had several grad students. They may provide valuable help."

"To get in Rayford's lab?" Shane asked.

Jesse folded his hands in front of him. "There are several things that have to happen first. Rayford has a monopoly on most of the genetics department. When Dad left, he all but took over. Batiste held off his small corner, though most of the students – and staff – consider him to be a loon."

The waitress returned with Jesse's change. He thanked her, and after she left with a generous tip, stood beside the table.

"I'm running to the restroom. Meet you guys outside?"

Shane shrugged. As long as no cops were outside, that was fine.

Elise pushed her chair back quickly and darted for the door. Was his very presence poison?

With a low groan, he followed her trail through the door. She was pacing in front of the store, her eyes carefully avoiding him.

In two long strides, he stepped behind her and grabbed an arm.

"Elise. Stop. You're making me nervous running around like that."

She jerked her arm away, "Sorry." It didn't sound very sincere.

"Look, what's wrong with you? What did I do?"

She glanced out at passing traffic, lips sealed.

"This isn't still about that closet, is it?"

No response.

He sighed in frustration. Apparently there was no forgiveness, even though it had hardly been his fault.

The door chimed as Jesse stepped out into daylight. "Ready?" he asked.

Shane looked between the two of them, Elise still gazing defiantly at the road.

He sighed, "Yeah. Lead the way."

* * * *

Elise couldn't figure it out. On every TV they passed, it seemed hers and Shane's pictures were flashed around with the same story of kidnapped and kidnapper. Not to slight their disguises, but surely by now someone would have recognized them. At least one of Rayford's people. If Dr. Summers had found her so easily, then they already knew what she and Shane both looked like now. So why hadn't they updated the photos or searched the city brick by brick?

The University was only a block away, and while they blended well with the college crowd, she still worried. More troubling, where was Rayford? What could Jesse possibly have told him that he wouldn't try to find them here? Why would he give up?

Granted, her relationship with Dr. Rayford was brief, but he didn't strike her as the type to give up and call it quits. Ever.

Quickening her step, she pulled even with Jesse. "Where are we going?"

"The way is steep, the path narrow, and thorns line every side. But if you follow me closely, you'll get there and find out how beautiful it is."

Times like this she wondered if he was insane. Perhaps he fancied himself an insightful philosopher who held not only scientific keys to knowledge, but the whole universe as well. She studied his face to see if he was kidding.

If he was, there was no indication.

"Um," she tried to come up with a suitable response. "But *where* are we going?"

"Back to Dad. But first, I must face his accusers. There are things that need to be set straight."

Again, there wasn't a hint of jesting or playfulness.

"I'm serious," she pushed. "Stop talking like that."

He shortened his step and turned to look at her. "I'm serious as well. Just follow me."

What was wrong with innocent questions? Wasn't it fair to know what was going on?

Falling back again, she couldn't help noticing the frustrating similarities in her brother and Carbon. Either he programmed her, or she modeled her own behavior off of his.

Fair as it may be, this 'you don't get any information until I deem it necessary' attitude was continuously testing her patience. On some sensitive subjects, maybe that was good. If Carbon had tried to explain about her DNA earlier, she couldn't even imagine how she would have reacted. Some things are best taken in small doses.

But just knowing where they were headed was pretty basic. A troubling thought occurred to her. Jesse said to 'rest and trust', but he didn't trust her at all. Maybe he suspected she had second thoughts about this whole thing. That if he told her everything, she would go back to Rayford.

She jumped at a touch on her shoulder.

"Easy."

It was only Shane, who had quickly withdrawn his hand. "You're falling behind. Jesse's way up there."

She followed his gaze to where her brother was walking way ahead of them. How had he gotten there so fast? Why didn't he wait up?

But he never so much as glanced back in their direction, and so Elise angrily jogged to close the distance gap. Students were everywhere, and it wouldn't take much to lose a person in the randomly flowing crowds.

Annoyance was all too readily available, so she refrained from expressing anything.

They entered the lobby of Dr. Batiste's building, but instead of heading upstairs to the offices, Jesse led them down several hallways and into a lounge room of sorts.

Grad Student Lounge, a small sign read on the door.

There were several couches, an oblong table with a dozen or so chairs, and whiteboards lining the walls. A redheaded girl sat in front of a laptop, one hand clenching a bunch of hair in concentration. She didn't so much as blink at their arrival, although a blonde man seated on a couch gave them each a thorough stare. He looked about thirty and was reading through a stack of papers.

Apparently they were not suspicious, for he returned to his reading and the girl never bothered to look. Jesse walked in without hesitation, materializing a dry erase marker from somewhere and starting to write on the board.

Elise stood past the doorway awkwardly, unsure of what to do. Shane made a direct line for the nearest couch, sighing in satisfaction as he swung his feet off the floor and stretched out.

Mad because he appeared so comfortable and because she was generally angry at everything, Elise picked out a comfy chair of her own. The silence was deafening, and she wished someone would speak. But the only noises were the occasional shuffling of paper, the redhead's deft keyboard strokes, and Jesse's marker squeaking as he wrote nonstop.

Trying to get comfortable, Elise conceded that her feet hurt quite a bit from their long walk. She hadn't relaxed enough to take off her tennis shoes, but she tried her best to rest. It was no great sacrifice; there was simply nothing else to do.

Time passed indefinitely and she had almost fallen asleep when the absence of background noise drew her attention. The chatter of the computer's keyboard was gone as well as the shifting paper, leaving only the squeaking. Yet no one shifted, and no footsteps had receded out the small room.

Opening one eye, Elise surveyed the room. The redheaded girl was no longer focused on her computer. She sat rigid, staring straight ahead.

Opening the other eye, Elise sat up slowly to follow the girl's gaze. Blue marker writing was scrawled over the whiteboard walls, the far side completely covered. Jesse was now writing on the next board over.

The girl's expression was mystified. She gazed between Jesse and what he had already written, biting her lower lip.

Her red hair hung just past her shoulders, and though she wore no makeup, she was clearly an attractive woman. Early twenties, Elise guessed.

Shane was out cold on the couch – mercifully not snoring – and though the redhead continued her scrutiny of Jesse's work, it was a male voice that spoke.

"Excuse me," the blonde man had piled his papers on the table and was also watching Jesse with a curious expression.

Dressed in a suit, Elise couldn't tell if he was a professor or a student.

"I don't believe we've met. Are you new?"

Her mouth went dry. If he found out they weren't students, he could call the cops or ….

"No," Jesse responded solemnly, continuing to write.

The man squinted his eyes as they darted back to what Jesse had been writing. "Who are you studying under?"

"Dr. Mathis."

Blinking rapidly, the inquisitor stood and walked to examine the board more closely. "This was his theory."

"Is," Jesse corrected.

The redhead was clearly not getting any work done at this point, and with wide green eyes she closed her computer and pushed it away.

"Who?" she asked.

"Dr. Mathis," Jesse answered again, finally setting down his marker to face the two.

"You studied under him?" The man seemed uncertain.

The girl's expression shifted from puzzlement to shock. "Dr. Samuel Mathis?"

"Yes."

Way to be subtle, Jesse. Even Shane was awakening, glancing around in confusion.

"That's impossible."

He shrugged, "No."

Elise tried to decipher the words on the board, but it was no use. Chemical equations, mathematical markings and diagramed genetic structures were littered around a vocabulary she couldn't begin to understand.

"I've seen this research before. But no one has been able to follow the reasoning. The math is impossible." The man was stroking his chin thoughtfully. "But you seem to have taken a new perspective on the problem."

"What you need to understand is the fundamental basis of Dr. Mathis' thinking. Consider this protein…" Jesse pointed to one of his scribbles.

"You modified the Adenine?" The girl jumped over to where the men were beholding the white board.

"No," Jesse frowned, looking at her. "The basic elements cannot be altered. But if you add a new element, as long as it has compatible characteristics and can be received, the possibilities are limitless."

Elise sighed in frustration as the three began a stimulating conversation about structural DNA nanotechnology and something about genetic information and electronic signals. Shane had relaxed again on his couch, clearly disinterested in the 'smart people' talk.

While she wanted to understand, Elise was so lost that she gave up trying to follow altogether. It was no use. And how exactly this 'showing off' or whatever Jesse called it was going to help build the cure, she had no idea.

Closing her eyes, she tried to drift off to sleep once more.

* * * *

It was now or never.

Stewart swung in behind Agent Kerry in the darkness and pressed his pistol to her back. "Don't move," he warned. He relieved her of her own weapon, tucking it into his waistband.

"What do you think you're doing?" she hissed.

"Be quiet," he instructed. "Now, I would prefer not to cuff you, are you going to cooperate?"

She turned her head sideways enough to glare out of the corner of her eye.

"No?" Stewart sighed, pulling out a plastic restraint.

"Wait," Liz whispered. "I will."

"Will what?" he asked sharply.

The words must have been like pulling teeth to her. She had always hated failure. "I will cooperate."

"Good," he said. "Now walk."

He kept the gun trained on her. "Carefully," he said.

Stewart had predicted and prepared himself, yet his reactions were too slow to hold on to the gun in his hand as she kicked it away. It clattered to the pavement noisily. Her other leg came around to his stomach, but he managed to whirled out of reach. She wasted no time leaping for the gun, and he lunged after her, slamming them both to the rough ground with a solid tackle.

A hard blow landed on his shoulder as they skidded on the pavement. He knew they had landed a few feet shy of the gun.

Liz aimed another fierce kick at his face. Stewart effectively parried the motion with his fist, but she had gained the advantage. With a deft roll to the right, she had the gun and was pointing it at him. But he had already leapt to his feet and pulled her gun from his waist. Just like a Texas gunfight.

"Drop it!" she commanded.

Sighing in annoyance, Stewart brushed pieces of gravel off his shirt. "Thanks a lot, Liz."

"Don't play games," she warned. "I will shoot you."

"Oh, I know," he said with a smile. "But not with that gun."

Her expression dropped slightly, but she was clearly considering that he was bluffing.

"Go ahead." He stared at her, and neither of them moved. They had been through a lot together, and he doubted she would shoot him in cold blood. Nevertheless, he wasn't sure. Which is why he had unloaded his pistol.

"You work with Mathis," she accused him, still holding the gun. "All this time."

"No," he regarded her steadily. "I do not. I never have."

"Why should I believe you?"

It was a fair question, but Stewart had one of his own. "Who are you working for?"

The dark alley left little light to illuminate her expression, but her tone was tight. "I think you already know that."

He raised his eyebrows, not that she could see them.

"I know you've been working with Carbon. What did she say? What are you doing here?"

"You're the one holding the empty gun, Liz. What are you doing here, following me around?"

Stewart heard the click of the hammer falling. No bullet. Looks like she was willing to shoot him after all.

He shot her a look of disgust. "Told you. Now, you can keep the gun if you want, I consider it a fair trade. We need to talk, and I think we should find some place a little more private."

Chapter 26

A gentle tapping on her shoulder snapped Elise to consciousness.

"Wha...?" she shot up with a start, sure she would be surrounded either by several policemen or Rayford himself.

"Whoa," a sweet voice intoned. "Easy."

It was the redhead. Elise glanced around the otherwise empty room. "Where is everyone?"

The girl smiled. Her face was soft and dimpled, her green eyes emanating a light of intelligence, but also kindness. "They stepped outside." Seeing Elise's concern, she reassured her, "They'll be right back, don't worry."

"I'm Lucy," the redhead extended a hand towards her. "It's nice to meet you."

Elise accepted the surprisingly strong hand, "Bonnie."

Lucy beamed. "Your eyes are so beautiful!"

Blinking, Elise wondered if she had heard correctly. "Excuse me?"

"Your eyes!" Lucy repeated. "They're so dark and mysterious," she grinned mischievously. "I'm a little jealous."

"Uh, thanks." Elise couldn't think of much to say, noting that Lucy possessed eyes like sparkling emeralds and couldn't possibly be jealous of her new inky pupils.

"I can't believe what Jesse told me today. All my life I've ..."

"Jesse?" Elise interrupted, fear grabbing her as she realized she was alone with this girl, and had no idea if she could be trusted or not. She swallowed and fought to calm her voice. "Where did he go?"

"I don't know," Lucy answered. "Probably just went to the classroom next door or to stretch their legs. The restroom is right down the hall."

Elise kept her composure, but had to check. It could be a trick. She walked over to the door and swung it open. The hallway was dimly lit, most of the doors dark underneath. But she heard voices, and sure enough Jesse was propped up like a cowboy against the wall. Shane was pacing nearby, but the third man was nowhere to be found. Jesse noticed her and waved. Feeling foolish, Elise gave a halfhearted wave back and closed the door.

Lucy was staring at her in confusion. "Everything's okay?"

She laughed and hoped it sounded natural, "Yeah. Hard to keep track of them."

"No problem," Lucy forgave easily.

Drained by the rush, Elise dropped herself back onto a couch. "What time is it?"

"Late," Lucy smiled ominously. "Only grad students are awake at this hour." She pulled out a cell phone to specify, "Three forty-six in the morning. Still glad you asked?"

Elise gave a slight smile back. "What are you studying?"

"Applied Structural DNA nanotechnology. I'm trying to combine biomolecular nanotechnology with genetics. The human DNA helix is the best model, in my opinion. This is the stuff of the future." Lucy's face beamed with excitement, and Elise tried to feign some interest.

"That's very... cool sounding."

"Yeah," Lucy bounced to sit down beside her. "It is. Most people say it's impossible to master the whole field, but I have a great teacher. I hope you guys get the chance to meet him."

"Who?"

"Dr. Juan Batiste. Some say he's crazy, but they've never really looked at his theories."

Elise supposed it wasn't that coincidental. He did teach here after all. Obviously Jesse hadn't told her of their earlier encounter or his history with Batiste. Maybe he didn't fully trust them.

"Jesse said he studied under Dr. Mathis?" Lucy asked, watching her closely. "Dr. Mathis and Dr. Batiste were good friends. I'm sure you've heard of him."

Elise nodded, "Of course." A change of subject was in order, "How about you? What got you interested in this field?"

She knew it was the question to end all questions and would probably subject her to a long winded answer, but it was better if she let Lucy do all of the talking.

* * * *

"Is there something on your mind?" Jesse drawled from his relaxed position.

"What?" Shane paused from his pacing long enough to glance up.

"You look a little preoccupied."

"I'm just tired of being cooped up all the time." To prove this point, Shane returned to his well-worn path past the drinking fountain and back again.

"That's it?" Jesse cocked an eyebrow.

A sudden creak broke the silence, and they both glanced over the see Elise's head pop out of the lounge. Jesse smiled and waved, and she receded back into the room with a slight acknowledgment.

Shane felt anger rise up involuntarily.

"Ah," Jesse said softly.

Shane speared him with a sharp look, "Ah, what? What did that mean?"

"Why don't you tell me?"

It had truly been eating him up for a while now. Try as he might to erase or ignore it, his frustration was only building.

"You know," Jesse continued. "Guys can have emotions, too. You don't have to let Elise do all the crying."

"Crying?" Shane was defensive. He snorted in derision. "That's not what I was thinking."

"Aha. So there was something on your mind."

Shane gave his at ease friend a sullen glare. "When are you going to get around to building that cure?"

But Jesse only laughed, completely missing the change of topic. "So it wasn't crying, I'm a little disappointed. What does that leave?"

"You're not going to let this go, are you?"

Jesse looked at him pointedly, "Are you?"

Setting his jaw, Shane blew air through his nose in irritation. "I'm trying."

"Maybe it's time to try a new tactic. Tell Dr. Jesse your problems." The shaggy blond man gave him a serious expression.

"You're not a doctor."

"Would you know if I was?" Jesse asked. "Come on, Shane. Why not tell me? If you're in prison or dead soon, it really won't matter."

"Oh, great," Shane shot him another glare. "Way to help."

Jesse shrugged. "I try."

The silence stretched several moments before Shane caved in. It really didn't matter. "I just don't get it!" he burst.

Jesse looked at him stoically.

"She's your sister. You would think after risking my life not once, but twice," he paused to let the full weight sink in. "And all that I've been through, she could at least be a little grateful. But no! She'd be happier if I was dead! What is wrong with her?!"

Jesse remained completely calm. "Why does this upset you?"

"Because!" Shane exclaimed. He couldn't put it into clear words, it was so obvious.

"Did you do it for her?" Jesse asked.

The question gave him momentary pause. What did it matter? He had risked, and was currently risking, his life in the pursuit of saving hers. Of course it was for her.

"Well, I'm not doing it for me," Shane returned sullenly.

"You're sure?" Upon Shane's seething gaze, Jesse put up his hands. "Let's just consider that you did this all for her. Completely. She's sick, and besides that, she simply doesn't care. You go to prison, and never hear from her again. How would you feel?"

This was a dumb exercise in logic. "Mad," Shane answered honestly. "If someone gave up their whole life for me, I would be at least a little appreciative."

"Okay. But what if you weren't appreciative? What if you never had the chance to show your gratitude to that person?"

"Then I wouldn't be a very nice guy."

"But what about the other guy? The one who risked everything to save you – even ungrateful, mean you."

Shane paused. "He was foolish."

"Because there was nothing in it for him?"

"Yes!" That sounded selfish. "No, but…"

"Maybe that guy thought you were worth it. Even though he got nothing back, nothing at all. If you had the chance to give something back to the guy – even gratitude – was he doing it out of love, because he thought you were worth saving, or was he doing it because it was 'right' and because he knew you would be grateful?"

"What?" Shane rubbed his forehead. "It's not that complex. You're making it all … complicated."

Jesse stepped closer, interrupting Shane's forward momentum. "If you are giving of yourself, there is no need of anything in return."

"Yeah, whatever," Shane muttered, looking away. "What if I don't want to give?"

"Then don't. But don't resent Elise for not giving back. How is that any different?"

"I don't know," he was already tired from the debate. "Don't you need to get back to your science friends?"

Jesse grinned. "Science friends? Science is really just observation, so that's a pretty broad category. But yeah. We just need to hang out until tomorrow. The night is getting pretty late."

"Morning."

"Exactly. And yes," Jesse punched him lightly in the shoulder, headed back towards the student lounge. "I am working on building a cure. Patience is a virtue."

"Sometimes," Shane muttered. "Or so I hear."

Chapter 27

Elise yawned widely. If she didn't get some sleep soon, she didn't think she could stand up much longer. Jesse and Shane had returned a few minutes ago and were talking with Lucy.

She hadn't been paying much attention when a fifth figure entered the room.

"Hi, it's nice to meet you," a deep voice intoned.

Jesse smiled and shook hands with a dark-haired man about Lucy's age. Another grad student probably.

"Josh," he introduced himself, turning to shake Shane's hand next. "And you would be…?"

Elise blinked, surprised to find the man's strong features waiting for her response.

"I, uh," she righted herself on the couch, accepting his firm handshake. "Bonnie."

He offered a charming smile, spotless white teeth shining through.

"Sorry for bothering you so late," Lucy was apologizing. "I hope you weren't sleeping."

"Not at all," he reassured her. "I was just finishing up some students' papers. It comes with the territory." Turning to the scrawled writing on the dry erase boards, he paused long enough to take it in.

"This is only the beginning," Jesse said. "Dr. Batiste has been right all along."

Josh seemed impressed, and let out a low whistle. "Just wait till we see him tomorrow. I want to see his face."

Jesse's eyes flickered with brief sadness, but he seemed to move on. "Thanks for putting us up for the night."

"Oh, no problem," Josh said, still studying the board. "My roommate graduated last semester, and I have an empty couch anyway. I'll be glad for the company."

Lucy shot an excited look at Elise. "You'll be staying with me. It's not big, but I have enough room."

Josh clapped his hands together. "I bet you guys are dead tired. I can't wait to hear your whole story tomorrow, but for now I'll just take Lucy's word for it. Come on," he motioned out the door.

Lucy grabbed her belongings. "Josh lives on the floor above me, so we're going to the same place."

Elise sent a worried glance in Jesse's direction, but he only smiled.

Shane looked like a zombie, and as she fell in step behind him, Elise hoped these two students were trustworthy. One thing was for sure, she didn't have much of a choice.

* * * *

Alan Stewart observed the younger agent pacing in the small room. Liz was smart, that was one thing he was sure of. Who she actually worked for was another problem. She said that she worked for the FBI and had been sent to make sure he didn't interfere with their investigation. But that didn't make enough sense to him. Something was missing.

He had taken the battery out of her cell phone and tossed it into a sewage drain. Still, it was possible someone could trace them to this empty building. He remained on guard.

Sitting to think, Stewart decided it was time to return to the lab. If Liz was tied to a chair, it would probably be at least twelve hours before she engineered some sort of escape. That would provide him enough time to figure out who she was working for.

* * * *

Elise was exhausted, but sleep would not come. She tossed and turned, consumed by a desperate annoyance as the sheets tangled around her in the darkness.

In the pit of her stomach was the unmistakable churnings of fear. If they were butterflies, they would be on steroids. She could find no distinctive reason to be afraid. Not that there wasn't a plethora of options available, but because her mind wasn't really playing any role in this emotional storm.

An empty hole seemed to devour any hope that had been in her soul, and try as she could, she couldn't even see out from this cloud of torment. Disquieted. Every part of her.

Right now she longed to be safely tucked in bed at Mesa Springs, but even that would be an illusion. She could no longer plead ignorance, and so the impossible equation of her situation loomed before her like a haunting, hopeless puzzle.

"Ah!" she yelled softly, kicking the sweaty sheets to the side in anger. She didn't know what was needed, but she couldn't take much more of this. Tears of frustration welled up, and the best she could manage was to get up and pace the tiny living room. Lucy was no doubt sound asleep in her room, and Elise didn't want to wake her. The girl was nice, and had no idea what she had just been dragged into.

Grabbing her phone, Elise quietly slipped outside into the hallway. Anywhere was better than here. She would be careful, but just needed to stretch her legs and get her head on straight again. Whichever way that was.

Not a soul was in sight, and Elise found herself almost whimpering. This was ridiculous. Everything was going to work out, her Dad and Jesse were going to help, and fretting was useless anyway. But she wasn't buying any of it. She had just rounded the corner to the stairway, when a movement caught her eye.

A shadowy figure was at the top of the stairs, growing larger as it headed down towards her. Gasping involuntarily, she flattened back against the wall.

"Elise?" Jesse's soft voice called. "It's just me."

Elise felt she might melt with relief, though her legs were wobbly enough already. The adrenaline rush left her tired bones wearier still. "What are you doing here?" she asked breathlessly, not sure if she had the strength to move.

"Carbon woke me up," he stopped on the bottom step. "She was worried about you."

Tears that had come with exhaustion spilled over. Her mind was filled with incessant chattering; incoherent thoughts and worries jumbled in a mess of confusion and despair.

"Hey," Jesse wrapped her in another of his bear hugs. "It's okay. Shh."

Normally Elise would have been embarrassed beyond belief to cry like this in front of anyone, much less her long lost brother. But she simply had no strength left to resist.

Jesse held her patiently as her cries continued, "Peace. You're not going through this alone. It's okay."

Something deep inside Elise seized at his gentle words, and she broke away to cover her mouth to muffle the deeper sobs.

"Come here." With a hand on her shoulder, Jesse led her to the bottom step and helped her down before sitting beside her.

"I'm sorry," Elise got out between broken cries, not sure what she was apologizing for. Existing, maybe.

"For what?"

But she could only cover her mouth again and try to stifle the sound. He waited without a word, and when she could speak she choked out, "I just can't do it. I can't take it." Another sob interrupted before she could continue, "I believe you, I really do, but I just can't …"

"It's okay," Jesse comforted her. "You don't have to do anything. Certainly not to earn my love or Dad's. No matter what you do, we're going to try our best to fix this and get you back. You can't change that. We understand that you're sick, and that the SynMOs are already in your bloodstream, playing on the weaknesses of your condition and weakening your body further. All you need to do is rest. And trust me."

He placed a finger under her chin, forcing her to meet his gaze. "I am going to fix this. Rayford will not win. He is a genius, yes. But Dad and I have a plan even he couldn't begin to imagine."

Even in the dim stairwell, Jesse's blue eyes pierced her with a strange sincerity. And she noticed streaks of tears running down his face as well.

"But that's just it!" she blurted. "I can't do it! I don't know how to 'trust and rest', or, or anything!"

"That's perfect!" Jesse beamed. "Trusting and resting are not anything you can do. You can't do it. That's the whole point. We have spent a long time learning the science, studying your genes and engineering this remedy. At no level do we expect you to understand it! And that's perfect. That's how it was meant to be."

Elise sniffed, and did her best to wipe away her tears. "But …" There was a point here, but she couldn't find it. Then the guilt hit her. "Dr. Summers already knows who I am. I blew it. And now they know what Shane looks like too."

But Jesse wasn't fazed. "Don't worry about it. Carbon and I are monitoring everything. You and Shane will have to lie low, but as long as you're with myself or Carbon, you will be fine. I can tell you – scientifically, of course – that the only thing you need to do right now is rest. Your body is tired, your mind is exhausted, and you need sleep."

"But," she wasn't satisfied. "Even with Rayford, and the SynMOs or whatever. All those years ago, it was my fault. If I hadn't messed up, none of this would have happened."

"Elise, please listen. Dad and I forgave you. There is absolutely nothing to be ashamed of or worried about. We are not holding that, or anything else, against you. We love you. And even if you ran away and went back to Rayford, that wouldn't change." He nudged her playfully in the ribs, "You already know how crazy Carbon is. She'll never give up. And she never sleeps. So you have nothing to worry about."

Elise gave a pitiful laugh. Carbon was insane. "Wait, you and Dad built Carbon, right?"

"Mm-hm."

"So you guys control her?"

Jesse laughed. "Ah, not exactly. Actually, not at all. Dad and Mom built her around when I was born. Not the car, but the computer. She's pretty unique. Built from DNA. She truly has a mind of her own. We only integrated her with the car a few years ago, as we were hatching the plan to save you."

"Oh," Elise fell silent, trying to comprehend that Carbon was a DNA-based computer. It kind of made sense. But right now, fatigue covered her mind and body like a blanket, and deep thoughts were strictly off limits.

Jesse stood, "Come on, I'll walk you back to your room."

Elise allowed her brother to lead her down the hallway, fighting to keep her eyes from closing all the way.

"We'll let you sleep in. You need it."

She nodded and slid the key Lucy had given her into the lock.

"Just call us when you wake up. Carbon will probably inform me anyway." He squeezed her shoulder gently. "Good night, Elise. I love you."

"Good night," she yawned, wondering how many feet away the couch was. "Thanks."

"Anytime," he said as he turned to leave. "You're always welcome."

The door opened easily, and with a heavy body and a calm mind, Elise dropped onto the couch and was asleep in minutes.

Chapter 28

Elise slept soundly for the first time in days. She woke up to soft light glowing behind Lucy's pink and white curtains, and with a luxurious stretch, she lay still for a while longer, enjoying the peace and quiet.

When she finally felt ready to face the day, she found a note from Lucy waiting on the countertop.

> *Bonnie,*
> *I hope you slept well. Anything you find, you can eat. (Good luck!) Hope to see you soon!*
> *Lucy*

Glancing around, Elise saw the girl's point. However, after some scrounging, she found pop tarts in the pantry and an apple in the fridge. Water from the tap was refreshing enough, and Elise was content to sit at Lucy's small table and again enjoy the stillness.

The microwave clock said it was ten forty-three, and after changing into clothes Lucy had been kind enough to lend, Elise texted Jesse. Whatever he had planned for this day, she hoped it didn't involve much walking. Her feet were more than a little sore.

A knock came at the door in less than five minutes.

Cautious, Elise checked the peephole to make sure it wasn't Rayford. But there was no need, as her brother was the only one to be found. Elise tried not to laugh; with slacks and a button down – no doubt Josh had lent clothes as well – he looked like a young quirky professor.

"What are you laughing at?" he asked as she opened the door.

"Nothing," she smiled. "Where's everybody else?"

"Lucy had a class to teach, and Josh took Shane to the gym." Jesse rolled his eyes, "I'm not sure we'll ever see him again. He was so happy."

That figured. "Do you think it's all right to leave my stuff here?"

"Yeah, Lucy said we could get it later. Besides, we might be here another night."

With a nod, Elise retrieved her key and carefully locked the door. "What did you tell them? I wasn't exactly paying attention last night."

"Lucy and Josh?"

Elise nodded.

"The truth."

At Elise's shocked expression, he explained further.

"There is a time for everything. I told them I had studied under Dr. Mathis and that I was continuing his research. We came here to meet with Dr. Batiste, and to finish Dr. Mathis' research. We got in late last night, and didn't have time to make adequate sleeping arrangements."

"That's it?" Elise asked, incredulous. "What about Shane and I? Who do they think we are? Students?"

Jesse looked thoughtful. "I didn't tell them anything. I left that up to their assumptions."

"Great," Elise sighed. "I can't fake this genetics stuff. I haven't even finished high school chemistry!"

"Even fools are considered wise if they stay silent."

"Hey!" she complained.

"I'm just kidding," Jesse laughed. "I'm sure it will be fine. Just follow my lead, and it'll work out. Say you're studying under me. That's not totally inaccurate."

"And what about Rayford?"

"What about him?"

"You met with him, and he knows Shane and I are here. Is he looking for us?"

Jesse didn't hesitate, "Certainly. But he doesn't know you guys are here with me. When he comes onto campus, Carbon will tell me so you and Shane can fade into the background. I have to deal with him, because I need him to build the remedy."

"I thought you just needed his lab!"

"That too."

Elise was skeptical. "But even if you get him to do... whatever it is, he could still find us."

"He won't."

Elise shot him a frustrated glare, "Jesse!"

"Okay. Even if he finds you guys, he won't be able to touch you with me nearby."

"What, do you have superpowers too?" she asked sarcastically.

But Jesse's grin was confident, "Something like that."

That gave her momentary pause, but she couldn't fall behind because Jesse shortened his stride to match.

They had already reached McKinnley Hall, the genetics building, and Jesse opened the door for her.

In the foyer they were met by a nervous looking Lucy, "Have you guys seen Dr. Batiste?"

Elise shook her head, but Jesse remained silent.

"He wasn't in his office this morning, and he even missed his first class. He never misses class." Her concerned eyes flicked between them and the front desk. "I couldn't reach him on the phone, and he hasn't responded to any emails since yesterday morning. I guess I'll have to cancel his other class."

"Don't," Jesse instructed her. "I will teach it."

Confusion clouded Lucy's green eyes, but as she stared at him, her eyes widened as if receiving a revelation. "You know what happened to him."

Jesse regarded her with sad eyes. "Yes. I think we should talk outside."

Lucy was speechless, but followed them to a stone table beneath a large tree. An angry chipmunk muttered some furious phrases and scurried off the table's surface. They sat down just as Josh's voice rang out, "There you guys are! We've been searching all over."

"You could've called," Lucy answered quietly, but her mind was clearly elsewhere.

"What's wrong with you?" Josh asked, Shane walking up behind him. "And where's Dr. Batiste? I can't find him anywhere."

"Have a seat," Jesse invited them. "That's what we we're about to discuss."

Josh looked mystified, but sat silently next to Lucy. The only remaining space was beside Elise, and while Shane looked uncomfortable, he sat down and folded his hands on the table.

Elise felt a twinge of guilt run through her. She was aware she hadn't been very friendly, and wished she could apologize in some way. But instead she studied the table's rough-hewn surface, waiting for Jesse's explanation.

Jesse looked solemnly between all of them. "I met with Dr. Batiste late yesterday morning."

Lucy opened her mouth as if to speak, but closed it again just as quickly.

"Yesterday afternoon, the FBI detained him. He is still in their custody, though it is difficult to say where. They probably had him moved to a remote location. I doubt we'll hear from him again soon."

Lucy's and Josh's mouths fell wide open in shock. The redhead found her voice first, "What? How is this possible?"

"Ever since Dr. Mathis disappeared, Juan alone has defended his innocence. Now they are seeking to silence him."

"The FBI?" Lucy protested. "But he hasn't done anything illegal!"

Jesse offered no answer.

Josh narrowed his eyes. "Stephen told me that you had studied under Dr. Mathis. You weren't kidding, were you?"

Jesse shook his head.

The black-haired grad student let out a deep breath, "Oh my…"

"Who's Stephen?" Elise interrupted.

"He's Batiste's other grad student. There are three of us," Lucy explained. "I think you met him last night. He left before we did."

"Oh," Elise remembered the blonde man.

"I thought he just heard you wrong," Josh was muttering. "That you had studied Dr. Mathis' material."

"I told you," Lucy said.

"I know, but…" Josh didn't seem willing to accept it, even now. He looked up, dark eyes searching each one of their faces. "What's going on?"

Elise felt Shane tense beside her, but Jesse's face couldn't have been calmer. "I came to fix what is broken."

Batiste's two grad students blinked, and blinked again. Elise thought they couldn't have looked any more shocked, but apparently there's always the possibility.

"You're…" Lucy began, drawing her hand to her mouth. "That's what he meant."

"What?" Josh demanded.

"Dr. Batiste. He sent me a strange email yesterday, but I thought nothing of it. It was an equation, and he spoke of Mathis' work increasing, and his own decreasing."

"And that didn't give you any hints?" Josh appeared quite annoyed.

"I didn't know!" Lucy defended herself. "You know Batiste, always speaking in riddles and things. How could I know?"

"The time has come," Jesse inserted. "For Dr. Mathis' research to be completed. You can help me, or not. But I am here to explain what he left unanswered, and to fix the broken code."

"That's impossible," Josh reasoned, shaking his head. "Impossible. I've looked at Mathis' work time and again. There is no solution."

"I will show you the solution," Jesse said firmly. "I will teach Batiste's next class, and I will go through the data as long as you wish to remain."

Josh still looked skeptical, but he gave a small grin anyway. "You're crazy."

"What about Dr. Batiste?" Lucy asked, her green eyes filled with concern. Elise felt guilty as her own heart clenched with envy. Why couldn't she be beautiful and smart like this girl?

Jesse answered somberly, "There's nothing we can do for him now, but finish what he has devoted his whole life to."

Lucy dropped her gaze to the table and fell silent. Elise wanted to give the girl a hug, mad at herself for being jealous. How petty could she be?

"The class is not until one-thirty, so that leaves about an hour and a half," Jesse glanced at his phone. "In the meantime, you guys should go about business as normal. Be careful. If they already have Dr. Batiste, his grad students may be next on their list of concern."

Lucy visibly swallowed, and Josh looked uncomfortable. "What about the police?" he asked.

Jesse shrugged. "They probably know nothing."

"If it wasn't for your work on the board last night, I would never believe you," Josh declared, standing to leave. "I'll be at that class. I have my own in fifteen minutes, so I've got to run."

Jesse nodded as the grad student walked away, but Elise's gaze was on Lucy. The girl had frozen in place, staring at nothing.

"You okay?" Shane asked her.

She looked up slowly. "No. But I have office hours. If I'm not there, students will wonder. What do I say about Batiste?"

"The truth," Jesse answered. "You can't find him, and you can't get in contact with him."

"Okay," she hesitated. "You know, I've waited a long time for this. I always believed Dr. Batiste, but ... I never really thought it would ever happen."

Jesse gave her a warm smile. "You're a bright girl, Lucy. Dr. Batiste is very proud, I'm sure."

She seemed to get something from his gaze. "If you can really do this..." she trailed off, excitement creeping in her tone. "I can't wait until that class."

Grabbing her bag, she jumped off the table and waved. "See you later!"

"Wow," Shane remarked. "She's enthusiastic."

Jesse nodded in agreement. "Remarkably so. Batiste said she is his best student."

"How did you know that?" Elise asked. "About Batiste and the FBI?"

"Carbon," he answered.

"So you've known all along. As soon as it happened," she realized out loud.

"Yes. And right now, turn your heads to me and keep talking. Our friend Dr. Rayford is approaching."

A cold terror filled her, but she obeyed and tried her best to act natural.

Jesse wasn't having any trouble. "How was the gym?" he casually asked Shane.

"Uh ..." Shane's eyes darted back and forth. "Great. It was really nice. Josh didn't have to do that."

"Yeah," Jesse agreed. "He's a nice guy. Smart, too." Stretching his arms, Jesse didn't look the least bit concerned. "So, I figure we've got an hour to grab some lunch, and then it could be a while until we eat again."

"What is your plan?" Shane asked.

Elise dipped her head to try to keep from looking up, black strands of hair falling across her vision. The temptation was terrible. Was Rayford looking at them? What if he knew she was here?

"Plan?" Jesse looked surprised. "You know better than that. I don't need a plan."

"Of course not," Shane sighed in resignation.

But Jesse was chuckling. "I'm kidding. The plan is to teach Dad's theory at Batiste's class. He actually has quite a following here among the students. The faculty may not be so happy, particularly Rayford, but I welcome debate."

Elise felt her face whiten, "He's going to be there?"

"Might be," Jesse answered. "I wouldn't be surprised. But there will be plenty of students, so you will blend in fine."

Elise swallowed. That was a little too close for comfort.

They fell silent, and Elise listened to her heart pounding. Nothing had happened, so Rayford must be gone. Or getting reinforcements.

Jesse stood with another stretch. "We're in the clear. Ready for lunch?"

Elise wasn't so willing to move, but managed to coax her legs out from under the table. She felt all wobbly again, exhausted by the fear.

Shane stood by, uncharacteristically silent. Jesse hummed a little tune and started walking, and Elise forced herself to snap out of it and get moving. The further she was from Dr. Rayford, the better.

* * * *

Alan Stewart dropped the binoculars back around his neck and pushed his earpiece further in. Something was going down at the back of the pharmaceutical lab, and he doubted it was related to the phony business front. And he was less than pleased to see the black haired man from the airport leading a group of men into a white Denali.

They pulled away, and Stewart made a mental note of the license plate number. He would look that up when he got to a computer. Maybe Liz's clearance would come in handy.

Only if they hadn't noticed her absence yet, a scenario he considered likely. She was working alone and wouldn't report in unless something significant happened.

The men didn't say much before they drove away, and the audio equipment Stewart brought along couldn't pick up their conversation anyway. He needed to get closer.

He had ditched the hippie disguise for now, dressed instead as a tourist. If he could get Liz to go along as his wife, the act would be more believable, but he had to work with what was available.

Scanning the entrances to the building, Stewart concluded there was no way in without being discovered. But inside that building would be answers.

Chapter 29

The food court was packed with people. Mostly students, bustling every which way or furiously working over a laptop or book. A few were gathered at tables, socializing.

Jesse had claimed a corner booth while she and Shane got their food, and he jumped into the fray as they sat down. Elise wasn't even hungry, but she had ordered a salad with chicken to keep her strength up.

She glanced across the table at Shane, who wore the same stony mask as earlier. She could hardly believe this was the same guy cracking jokes on the bus.

Pushing her salad around, she tried to bring back an appetite. But it wasn't working. The silence was too much.

"Hey," she tried to cheer him up. "We're all still here, right?"

He glanced up, but didn't smile, his face pained and solemn.

Elise felt her cheeks flush, recalling all too clearly how she had been less than welcoming. She glanced over to the counter where Jesse was in line. "I'm sorry," she said, looking back down at the unappetizing salad. "I appreciate what you did, with Dr. Summers. I wasn't thinking."

He was watching her with an unreadable expression.

"So I'm sorry," Elise tried again, forcing herself to make eye contact. It wasn't easy. "If you hadn't come, I would probably be with Rayford right now."

Shane's face softened, but his eyes remained guarded. Still he didn't say anything.

Setting her fork down, Elise couldn't take the silence. "Say something," she pleaded.

"I don't know what to say." His expression didn't change much, but she could've sworn a small smile was creeping in.

"You? Come on, you always have something to say."

He raised his eyebrows, "Is that so?"

"Yes. And now you're being weird. So stop."

"Well," he cocked his head to the side. "I have been hanging out with him."

Elise followed the direction of his eyes to find Jesse walking up. "You have a point."

"What's this you're talking about?" Jesse placed his tray on the table. "Hey, man. I get the window seat."

Shane lifted a hand in innocence and got out so Jesse could slide all the way into the booth. It was like he was five years old.

"Now what were you two going on about?" Jesse asked.

"The weather," Elise offered quickly. "It's been sunny today."

Jesse looked suspiciously between them, unconvinced. "Sure. What's the forecast for tomorrow?"

"Rain," Shane answered, clearing his throat.

"Lucky guess," Jesse said, picking up his hamburger. "This is Seattle."

"We'll see," Shane returned, but besides Jesse no one seemed to be in much of a mood to eat.

Elise nibbled on a few bites of salad, mostly just picking out the chicken. "What's going to happen to Dr. Batiste?" she asked. The question had been bothering her, and she seriously hoped another person wasn't going to suffer for her sake.

Jesse sighed. "I don't know. Carbon was tracking him, but they took his cell phone and moved him out of the area."

"So they're close," Shane commented, looking less afraid and more resigned. He closed his eyes and pushed away his untouched plate. "Let's say you build the remedy, give it to Elise, and everything works out. What then?"

"It is of no benefit to worry about that yet. I believe when we get there, everything will be clear." Jesse's tone was serious.

Shane breathed in sharply and stood up. "I'm going for a walk. I'll meet you at the genetics building."

He didn't wait for a reply, walking off down the hallway.

Jesse watched him leave, but didn't make a move. Elise pushed her plate back and jumped up in pursuit. She had no idea what she was going to say, or why she was even trying, but she followed nonetheless. "Shane!' she called, jogging to catch up.

The effort left her breathless, but he eventually turned around. "What are you doing?" he asked, his voice tight.

"Wait, I just want to…"

"Look," he held her gaze. "This is not your fault. There's nothing you can do."

"That's not true," she argued, surprised to find this fire within her.

He stepped back, regarding her with that same odd expression. "Don't leave Jesse," he finally spoke, turning to leave again.

Elise made her step match. "No. I'm following you." What was wrong with her?

He stopped and grabbed her shoulders, "Don't. Stay with Jesse. Please."

Freezing, she searched his eyes. But that same crazy resolve cemented within her. "Not if you're leaving."

"I'm not leaving," he said. "Just going for a walk."

"Then wait for us," she stubbornly retorted. "Something's wrong."

"I just need to be alone," he was almost pleading, releasing her.

"No," she stepped forward. "I'm coming with you."

"Ah," he cried in frustration, raking his hands through his hair. "I can't do this."

"What?" she asked, surprised to remember herself saying the same thing to Jesse not so long ago.

Students poured past them through the hallway. Shane turned and kept walking, and though her resolve wavered slightly, she caught up to him.

"No!" he cried again in frustration, picking her up and placing her closer to Jesse. "Stop!" he whispered forcefully, and from the fierce look in his eyes, she guessed he was close to losing his composure. Normally she would have been terrified, but apparently not today.

Taking one step closer, she leaned her head against his chest and wrapped her arms around him. His whole body shuddered, and she repeated Jesse's words softly. "It's going to be okay."

For an eternal second, nothing moved. She could hear the shuffling and chattering of those passing by, and didn't even care that they were probably staring. She released him and looked up into eyes that were wet with unshed tears.

Shane caught her hands and stepped back. "Go back to Jesse. I will meet you at the classroom."

Her courage melted slightly, and though his touch was like fire, she regretted it when he dropped her hands.

"I'm not leaving," he said, swallowing hard. "Please."

Tears came to her own eyes, but she blinked them back. She couldn't even understand why she was still standing here, but acknowledged with a nod.

Shane held her gaze a moment before glancing down the hallway to where Jesse was sitting. "At the classroom," he reaffirmed, turning to leave.

Shaking her head, Elise wiped away the tears and headed back for Jesse. She couldn't believe she had just done that.

Her brother was waiting at an empty table, all the trays cleared off. "Ready?" he asked.

Elise offered a small smile, "Yeah. Where are we headed?"

"To Dr. Batiste's office, and then the classroom. We still have forty-five minutes."

Nodding, Elise fought the desire to turn around and check to see if Shane had come back. He would meet them at the classroom, she scolded herself. Why was she so worried?

Chapter 30

Stepping into Batiste's office, Elise felt like she was entering a war zone. Papers were haphazardly strewn around, and it was clear unauthorized guests had been here.

"What were they looking for?" she asked Jesse.

"This," he responded from somewhere underneath a desk. He held up a syringe filled with a clear liquid. Elise recognized it instantly.

She shrank back, and when Jesse stood up again he held up his hands. "It's your choice. Here," he offered her the syringe to hold, as if closer analysis would convince her. "You won't have the same reaction as me. In fact, you might not feel anything at all. Even if you do, it will feel like a bath from the inside out. This compound will prepare your DNA for the final remedy."

"I have to take it?"

Jesse nodded. "Or Dad wouldn't have gone to such great lengths to hide it with Batiste."

Seeing her stricken expression, he reassured her, "Don't worry. You won't have the same reaction. Look," he tried to illustrate with his hands. "Batiste's shot prepares your body to receive new information. Your cells have been built according to the DNA's instructions. This doesn't alter your DNA, but it begins cleansing the cells and tissues from the nanites."

She eyed it suspiciously. "Cleansing my cells?"

"In a matter of speaking. It begins breaking down the connection of sensors between the SynMOs. It prepares the body for the remedy. Buries the old, so to speak, so that your cells can be made anew."

Elise didn't see much sense in that, but had already decided to trust Jesse. "Ok. But you, why did you take it?"

He held up a finger. "The cure for your situation is impossible, from Rayford's perspective. Your DNA is irreparably corrupted, the coding for your higher functions – the enhancements – lost. Not only can you not access them, he knows that no new link through the SynMOs to them can be forged without accelerating genetic decay. What he doesn't know, is that while that link is indeed broken, your DNA itself can be reprogrammed."

Forget about total comprehension. Elise overlooked his answers that only raised more questions and moved on to the basics. "Which your cure can do? Reprogram my DNA?" It sounded so fake, so impossible, she could hardly believe it.

A bittersweet expression crossed Jesse's face. "Yes," he said simply.

Swallowing her doubts, Elise considered that she had already jumped in. Her faith, at least for now, was with Jesse, and if she trusted him to build the remedy, she could trust him now.

"Okay," she squeaked, offering her arm for the shot.

Jesse accepted the syringe back from her, and helped roll up her sleeve. "I am going to have to go away soon, but I will come back. I will have finished the cure, and will be able to send the help you're going to need. That's a promise."

What was that supposed to mean? Elise almost opened her eyes, barely noticing the shot because of her confusion. A sense of relief flooded her body, like a powerful relaxant. But instead of feeling tired, her bones seemed to zip with energy.

"Whew!" she exclaimed, feeling giddy. "That was … not so bad!"

Jesse smiled, "I told you. Now," he pointed to his wrist, despite the lack of watch. "We need to hurry to not be late for class."

* * * *

Shane Lawson wandered amongst the trees in confusion. There was a small park beside the University, and nature trails were generally calming for him. But not today.

Emotions were not something he enjoyed, and usually he didn't have to deal with them. Fear in particular seemed inescapable. The stress had been wearing him thin, and he honestly didn't know how much more he could stand.

No matter what happened, it seemed, his future was either to flee to another country and live in hiding, or go to prison. And death. There was always that option.

Jesse's questions had forced him to reconsider his basic assumptions for existing, and the closer he examined his motives, the less he liked what he saw.

He had helped Carbon because he was angry over his Mustang and her offer sounded like fun. Rescue a girl, get in, get out, not so bad. But that was hardly the whole story.

His best option was to go to the cops, tell them everything and hope for a light sentence. He could most likely get off with only a few years if he turned in Elise. But what if he was wrong?

If the police had Elise, Rayford would find a way to get his hands on her and they would probably drug her to death. Death that was already certain unless she was Rayford's puppet or if Jesse could make his cure.

The twisted logic made him furious. There was no win. This was a lose-lose-lose situation. How could Jesse be so at peace with it? True, the blonde man wasn't wanted… yet. And making himself a direct enemy of Rayford – on top of being his archenemy's son – wasn't a smart move. But somehow that didn't bother Jesse. He was calm, kind and thoughtful even with his life on the line.

There had to be something major he was missing. Jesse wasn't sharing all of the information.

Shane checked his phone for the time. He needed to head over in fifteen minutes. It was the best option. He hadn't found any great hope for the future, but then he remembered Dr. Mathis' promise of a new Mustang.

Such a silly thing, facing death or worse. And yet his mood lightened considerably. Maybe they wouldn't all die. Maybe they could run away and hide with Dr. Mathis. Surely he had a sweet compound hidden somewhere.

Content to have improved his outlook slightly, Shane headed back towards the campus. With Carbon on their side, they might have a chance.

He was almost out of the woods when a voice materialized behind him.

"Good to see you again, Sheriff."

Shane spun around in horror. A tall man with black hair and blue eyes was smiling, a gun held casually at his waist.

That guy was supposed to be dead.

"Surprised?" the man asked, his smile widening into hateful eyes.

Shane tried to react quickly, but he was completely caught off guard. "You… how did you live?"

But he only laughed, and two more men appeared from the trees.

"I hate to disappoint you, but don't worry." The black-haired man stepped toward him until his breath was hot on Shane's face, "I'll explain everything in time."

He backed off as the other men moved closer. "Don't try anything," he said casually. "I could shoot you right now with no problem."

"Easy," Shane put his hands up. Once he went with these guys there would be no hope. Maybe he could grab the gun …

But he gasped as another man jabbed him hard in the ribs. "Let's not make a scene."

Shane felt the slight prick of a needle as the world blurred into obscurity. Worst option, his mind informed him. This was the worst option.

Chapter 31

Lucy tapped a pencil on the table, staring at Jesse's equation. "That's impossible. You can't construct a mechanism to organize those proteins. It's too complex. Way too complex. Even if the DNA could be altered, how could the cell replicate something like that?"

"It's all in the signals," Jesse explained. "No, a normal cell could not even begin to cope with these instructions, much less carry them. But if a specialized receptor and an enhanced information package were added to the original DNA upon formation of the zygote, each cell could then be built to the enhanced specifications. Every succeeding cell would then have with a copy of the modified DNA and the receptor. It does work."

A student towards the front looked pensive. "It was rumored that Dr. Mathis did his own experiments. That they disproved his own theory. Is that true?"

"His theory has never been disproven," Jesse responded patiently. "If you add extraneous information and interference into the equation, it is no longer fair to judge the science without changes the standards as well."

"So," a girl was toying with a strand of hair. "If this was tested on an animal, the scientist would be able to control tissue growth, development rate, and even movements from... some sort of signal emitting device. Something to send specific instructions to the receptor in the DNA."

Another student was quick to interject, "There's nothing that complex. No computer can handle that much information."

"Originally the system should be self-contained," Jesse answered. "The neural passageways would be structured to perfect specifications for all the commands. Basic systems would run automatically from the DNA, and conscious control of any enhancements would be determined by free will."

The same student raised his hand and spoke again. "But if the DNA copied itself incorrectly – even once – wouldn't the whole thing unravel?"

"Yes."

There was brief silence at Jesse's admittance. Elise wasn't quite grasping the significance, but she could tell the group considered this a fatal error.

"Then it isn't possible," the girl was still playing with her hair. It must help her think. "If that is the end of Dr. Mathis' theory, it is erroneous."

"You are correct. That isn't even close to the end of his theory." Jesse's face shone with enthusiasm. "With the breakdown of the original neural network, some sort of computational device would then be needed to restore communication, assist the cells with correct replication, and stabilize the receptor in the DNA. But it would have to work in conjunction with the person's free will."

He stepped back and examined their blank stares. "Not a computer in the sense you're thinking," Jesse said as he turned to draw a brief diagram on the board. "You would need a DNA-based computer developed from compatible DNA."

Several of the faces were stunned, a few people laughed. Lucy leaned forward, her face intense. "That type of nanotechnology isn't developed yet. It's completely theoretical. Furthermore, that would be like constructing an organism; it wouldn't really be a computer, would it?"

Jesse shrugged. "It would be carbon-based, so you tell me. But it is possible."

That did grab Elise's attention. Carbon-based. Carbon. There was a connection here, she knew it.

"So there is a working model somewhere?" It was the same student who had asked about the experiments.

But Jesse dodged the question and shifted topics. "Be careful of theories that can revoke or override conscious control. They are not science in the strictest sense, and the ethical violations nullify the point of such experiments in the first place. You cannot ever ignore a person's will. The body will eventually self-destruct."

Lucy blinked, and Stephen shifted beside her. He raised his hand and spoke, "Let's say the technology does exist. How would you use a DNA-based computer to assist in managing the zillions of DNA strand replications and *not* override a person's free will?"

"Because the program is designed to only operate in conjunction with the person's brain and the signals it emits. It would resurrect, in a way, the original neural network, and become fully integrated. Conscious cooperation would be required with every new action."

"Forgive me for asking the obvious, but where does this get you? Some Captain America type superhero?" A male student toward the back stared at them skeptically.

"Far better," Jesse replied.

"So all the applications would be military, correct?" the student demanded.

"No. What's your name?" Jesse asked.

"Matt." The young man answered curtly, as if he wasn't sure giving out a name was a good idea.

"Okay, Matt. You're asking some really good questions. Let me turn it around. What do you think the implications of such research might be?"

Matt fell silent and dropped his gaze. The rest of the room was hushed for a moment.

Stephen raised his hand again, "So your model works, but a corrupt strand of code either mutates or is intentionally introduced and begins replicating. How would you then have a DNA-based computer handy to fix the problem, and how would it even be compatible?"

"Good question," Jesse said. "Once the system is damaged with any error, the signal network and neural control would break down instantly. Even if you had a refined DNA-based computer, it would no longer compatible. Now there is no way to find the mistake, and no way to stabilize the receptors."

He stood behind the podium and paused. Elise found that his gaze had wandered to her, but he blinked and looked away before continuing. "A perfect strand of DNA – with no corrupted code and a functional uplink to the computer – would have to be introduced into the bloodstream. From there, it would spread and give a new start. A new network of signals, this time stabilized from the outside. Except that now the possibilities would be endless."

Stephen seemed to grow more incredulous. "And how would you propose to build something like that?"

Jesse gave them a serious look and didn't respond.

"Class is over," one student declared, standing to leave. The statement began a rush toward the two exits.

Elise waited for the stampede to end before moving towards the front of the room.

Jesse was in a discussion with Lucy, Stephen, and a man she didn't recognize, but he excused himself and walked over to her. "Are you okay?"

"No," she admitted wearily, sinking into a chair. Truly her head was beginning to ache and her body felt like jell-o. "Where's Shane?"

He wrinkled his brow. "I don't know. He texted Carbon before class started. Said he needed some time, he would meet us later."

Elise dropped her gaze. Maybe he was upset with her. She felt her cheeks flush involuntarily with embarrassment. She shouldn't have chased him down earlier.

Then again, he hated school. He might have been avoiding the whole idea of sitting in a classroom while one person taught.

"Come on," Jesse motioned to her. "One more meeting, this time with grad students. Then we can grab dinner?"

She nodded, grateful her stomach was at least not aching and her appetite was intact. "Sounds good."

Jesse patted her on the shoulder. "Boring, I know. But I have to explain what Dad's theory is, what is really going on, so these people will know. You will need their help in the future."

Elise had been staring at the desk, but the last statement gave her pause to think. But when she opened her mouth to ask, Stephen had already drawn Jesse away with a question of his own. The future?

What future?

* * * *

Stewart had watched the men return within the hour carrying an unconscious male between them. It took him a minute to recognize the man's facial features at such distance, the blonde hair throwing him off at first.

Deputy Lawson. These people had taken him into custody, and by all indications the police were not involved. The FBI, on the other hand, seemed to have a rather large hand in it all. Stewart grimaced with the thought of the Bureau cooperating with thugs. To steal a package from their own team.

The contents of the shiny briefcase were still a mystery to him, but he had a plan.

"Hey Liz," he greeted her. She had managed to loosen some of her bonds, but was still in the chair. "Brought you some rations," he set down a bag of fast food as he untied her.

"Don't expect any thanks," she snapped.

"You're going to be helping me," he informed her. "And if you don't, I will see to it that the Bureau thinks you've been willfully helping me all along."

She narrowed her eyes, undoubtedly analyzing the validity of his threat. He could deliver on the promise, and she knew it.

"What do you want?" she asked, not touching the food.

"We're going to the university library, and you're going to provide the access codes to the FBI database."

"They'll be all over the library in minutes," she retorted.

"No, they won't. They'll assume you were doing some research."

"What research?" she demanded.

Stewart studied her face. She could be bluffing. Maybe she worked for the black-haired thug. "In Colorado, you tipped off those guys at the airport."

"I did not!" she responded hotly. "They shot Guerrez. I would never help them."

"Who else knew we found the briefcase? You were gone shortly before we left, and conveniently never found that recording device I sent you after."

Her chin jutted out defiantly. He had struck a nerve here.

"I work for the FBI. I would never betray the trust, like you. Who told you where those recording devices were, hm? Carbon. You are working with her. We were always one step behind in the investigation because you were purposefully keeping us there."

She was glowering at him, and though he was sufficiently surprised at her accusations, he kept his cool. He worked best alone, and was happily in control of the present situation. Unhappily, he remained decidedly perplexed about what was true and what wasn't.

Stewart shook his head. "How do you think the gunmen found us?"

She didn't answer.

"Who did you report to?"

No response.

"Liz," he met her furious dark brown eyes calmly. "You need to level with me."

"You first," she never missed a beat.

He let out a short breath in anger. She was so stubborn. It made her a good agent, but a formidable adversary.

"How about you see for yourself? Your friends from the airport seem to be working with the FBI here. They took Lawson into custody in the old Mathis Lab, and I'll just bet that silver briefcase is inside."

Liz flexed her jaw, but fell silent again.

"Look, neither one of us really knows what's going on." Stewart had decided to make a gamble. If he was wrong, it could lend to valuable information and he still had a chance of survival. "I don't work for Carbon. Yes, she did contact me. I was compromised by the situation, and the information she offered was invaluable. She was right about the briefcase in Colorado, and she warned me of others trying to take possession of it.

"I'm not saying she or Mathis is correct or right, but more is going on here than we've been led to believe. I am going to investigate further, because I want to know what really happened. And I will bring the perpetrator to justice. Now, you can join me or not, but you are going to help me access these files. If you're not convinced, you will be free to leave."

She studied him closely, and he studied her back. The art of trying to read minds, determine intentions and know loyalties. It wasn't a science.

Offering her wrists to be unshackled, Liz nodded. "I'll go to the library."

Chapter 32

Wondering about the future, but mostly fighting off a crushing boredom, Elise sat and listened as Jesse talked with students and professors about Dad's theories.

She hadn't quite figured out why this was important, or why it had to be done before he built the remedy, but she hadn't had the opportunity to ask yet. Maybe the students' help was needed to gather the materials.

Amazing to her was the fact that people gathered around to hear Jesse speak. They all seemed enamored with his scientific knowledge and his explanation of Dad's work. She didn't understand much of the lingo, but she picked up on Jesse's not so discreet antagonism toward most of the professors. He had thrown one of the textbooks on the floor in anger – to more than Elise's surprise – declaring that the miserable excuse for a scientist who had written it had twisted everything into nonsense.

Things had gone downhill from there. Apparently, some of those present had been grad students of the textbook's author – none other than Rayford himself. An argument had ensued, and Jesse firmly stood his ground. The audience was divided, with Lucy and some of Dr. Batiste's other students were ardent in their defense of Jesse's theory.

Rayford's two grad students – a black haired girl named Meredith and a middle aged doctor named Tim – were steaming mad, their faces glowering.

Meredith was speaking, and clearly it was a struggle to keep her voice calm. "This university and its affiliates around the globe have been working for ten years developing this model. The science is more than good, it's revolutionary. And Dr. Rayford worked side by side with Mathis when he was developing his theories; I think he'd know what he was talking about."

"You can never follow this model to finality; it's impossible," Jesse countered. "Restoring perfect replication is beyond feasibility. Once the first mutation occurs, the DNA cannot replicate without multiple, fatal errors."

"As you yourself have implied, difficulty does not equate to impossibility." Meredith took a defiant posture. We've been working on this for a long time, and we are getting very close."

"Besides," Tim rearranged the spectacles on his nose. "Dr. Mathis already has the complete code. He had it all written out. If he hadn't burned down the lab, we wouldn't have wasted years figure out the perfect sequence. Plus, if you claim to believe Dr. Batiste, he has said all along that Dr. Mathis would find a way to reveal to full code. To 'fix what was broken', as he called it. That proves it is possible."

Jesse shook his head in disbelief. "Dr. Rayford never could understand the complete sequence of DNA. It was theoretical exercise, trying to demonstrate the complexity of such a system. A single error will destroy the entire signal network, and then the system must be changed altogether. You can't simply patch up the individual cells."

"What are you suggesting?" Meredith asked, though all the students were watching for an answer in rapt attention. Even Elise began to forget her tiredness, the room was so tense.

Jesse calmly eyed the group, ending with a small smile for Elise. He bent over to retrieve the book he had thrown, "This correctly sequenced code, with all its instructions that build perfect cells – overcoming disease, weakness, even mortality – adds up to nothing. It requires a system with no errors, no mistakes."

He set the book down on a desk, pushing it aside. "Let's say we have an organism with enhanced DNA that has a built-in receptor. It allows the owner's cells to access the advanced genetic coding and build enhanced cells. Essentially, it allows higher-level functions. Superpowers. But, there is an error; a foreign substance is introduced into the body."

Elise thought of the nanites. SynMOS, her dad had called them.

"It would be unrealistic to assume any of this technology could be developed in a vacuum. It is security sensitive and highly sought after, so there will be those trying to steal or destroy the research. So, let's say the system has been polluted and the cells are searching for the signal needed to transcribe the DNA and build the correct proteins. They can no longer even understand the input.

"To stabilize the system, the receptor is shut down. The cell reverts to basic DNA replication."

"A fail-safe?" Lucy asked, pensive.

"For basic survival, yes. But this is a dangerous situation. What next?" Jesse asked.

Meredith raised her hand half-way, "The system is ruined. You could try to reintroduce the perfect coding, but at this point, the DNA will already have replicated the corrupt code many times."

Jesse nodded, "That is the limitation of this system. Finality. The system needs to be living, breathing and able to absorb and adapt to change."

"So you keep working, and develop a resistant strand of coding. If it's perfect, it will have more fail-safes to deal with any problems," Tim suggested.

"But there is an infinite amount of possible failures, how could you predict even a few of them?" Jesse asked.

There was no reply, just puzzled and blank faces.

"Back to my illustration," Jesse said. "The system is broken. With the receptors shut off, the code will only degenerate further. But it can be redeemed. Made new."

Meredith laughed. "And you say we have impossible plans?"

But Jesse only regarded her evenly. "For you, it would be impossible. But Dr. Mathis found a way."

She returned his gaze coldly. "And what would that be?"

"Simplify," Jesse answered. "A perfect model can be introduced to override the system."

"Now," Jesse was continuing, "the cells no longer need to conform to the DNA's original instructions, because now another law is at work."

"The law of irrationality," Tim offered mockingly.

"Yes!" Jesse exclaimed. "That's just it. The cells cannot transcribe these complex codes, and now they no longer need to. The new neural network will stabilize the receptors and allow limitless possibilities."

"How would you build something so complex?" Lucy asked.

"It isn't easy," Jesse admitted. "It's essentially a DNA-based computer that takes over the communications with the receptor. It can now conduct repairs from the inside out."

Lucy simply blinked and stared at him. "You're talking about complex nanotechnology that doesn't exist yet."

"It does exist," Jesse persisted. "Dr. Mathis built a working model. But there is a catch; to be introduced into a corrupted system, it first requires a perfect model of what the DNA was to reactivate the receptors without destabilization. There needs to be an uncorrupted system that gives the converter, this DNA-based computer, the opportunity to recognize and correct for the corrupt data. To fulfill the old instructions, and then to be able to operate beyond them, since they already exist in the old system."

Elise glanced around the room. Everyone had fallen silent. The grad students were all staring with open mouths, as if they couldn't believe what was heard.

Meredith finally found her tongue. "You're crazy. This is absurd, and it has nothing to do with Dr. Mathis' science. Why would he design a complex system, only to completely override it?"

"Because there's something greater," Jesse explained. "The old system is limited. This has an infinite number of possibilities. They never end."

"Everything is limited!" Tim exclaimed. "I'm with Meredith. If Dr. Mathis plans to fix his system, he's not going to replace it."

"You have to listen to him!" Lucy blurted out. "Can't you see? He's the guy Dr. Batiste was talking about! He studied under Dr. Mathis, and now he was sent here to show us how to fix the system. Can't you see it?"

"There's nothing to see," Meredith stared in disbelief. "Come on, Lucy. Use your brain. There are way too many impossibilities, and besides that, it doesn't make any sense. Dr. Batiste lost his mind a while ago. Don't follow him blindly."

"Blindly?" Lucy returned. "If you can't even…"

But Jesse silenced her, raising his hand. "They will not see, because they don't want to," he turned back towards the group. "But I promise you this. Those of you who cling to this old theory, you will never progress anywhere. I was sent here by Dr. Mathis to explain to you the correct approach. But you will not listen, and you will be as lost as your faulty science."

Tim stood in indignation. "If Dr. Mathis wanted to fix anything, why didn't he come himself? A simple demonstration of this technology would suffice. But we just have to take your word for it? You don't have any formal education, no one had even heard of you before yesterday."

"This 'education' is your problem," Jesse said. "You are so narrow-minded, you cannot step aside to consider that what I'm saying is true."

Angry murmurs swelled up from the crowd, and Elise glanced around nervously. Jesse wasn't being very careful, stirring everyone up like this.

He continued, "You though I was coming to prove you right, to prove all these years of research were worth something. But I didn't. I can only tell you what Dr. Mathis has planned, and it is to bring down all this research on its face. The implications are disastrous, and cannot be allowed to come to fruition. Dr. Rayford has fooled you all, and if you choose to look at this theory instead, you will understand that."

At this, multiple people muttered in protest, all speaking at the same time. Tim hushed them and raised his voice, "We can now see that you are insane, perceiving nothing of Dr. Mathis theory, or genetics at all. There is no reason to listen to your babbling any longer. If you were sent by Dr. Mathis, prove it."

"My words speak for me," Jesse held the man's gaze unflinchingly. "If you do not believe me, your ruin is on your own head."

Livid, Tim turned and strode out of the room. Meredith followed suit, after staring at Jesse and Lucy with an icy expression. The dozens of students filling the room were again divided, though many left as well.

Jesse waited until they were gone, and gazed at the remnant with a smile. "Would you like me to explain how this is all possible?"

They nodded, Lucy more enamored than anyone else.

Swallowing from confusion and fear, Elise sank lower into the uncomfortable chair. She hoped Shane would show up soon. If nothing else, to provide another non-geneticist to commiserate with. And having another person on your side wasn't a bad feeling. Where had he gone to anyway?

He would probably show up that night, just in time for food. It seemed to be a priority for him.

In the meantime, she had to survive a few more hours of mental torture and hope she didn't deteriorate physically.

* * * *

When Shane regained consciousness, he found his body surprisingly free of pain, though he was handcuffed to the table in front of him.

An interrogation room. A nice one, to be sure. Either Rayford had his own, or the not dead black-haired guy had turned him over to the cops. Why not just kill him?

The door swung open and in walked a short balding man who clearly hadn't exercised in a while. He was dressed in business attire and holding a manila folder.

"Deputy Lawson," the man greeted him, pulling up a silver chair across the table. It screeched horribly on the tile floor, and the man sat down with purpose. "I'm excited to finally meet you."

Probably the truth, Shane reasoned. "Who are you?" At this point, he couldn't decide if the cops or Rayford would be better. At least with Rayford, it would all be over soon.

"Special Agent Donald Richardson, FBI." Richardson surveyed him with a keen eye.

Shane was being assessed from the inside out, and he knew it. What he didn't know was if this guy was actually FBI.

After a long silence, the agent in question sighed and dropped a hand on the table. "I have two options for you, Mr. Lawson. One, the state will prosecute all pending charges, including but not limited to: kidnapping, attempted homicide, aggravated assault with a firearm, destruction of federal property, resisting arrest, reckless driving, conspiring with a suspected terrorist, and falsifying your identity."

Hardly true, but Shane bit his lip. Probably better to wait for option two, though he doubted it would be much more appealing.

"Two," Richardson gave him a hard stare. "You were a victim of circumstance. A cop placed in a difficult situation, trying to save a life and solve a crime. When you could, you made your way to the officials and told them all that you knew. The criminals will be charged with their crimes, and you will face minor charges that the state recommends be dropped in light of extenuating circumstances."

Shane blinked. "How do I know you work for the FBI?"

The man laughed and slapped a shiny badge on the table. "Believe it. Remember Agent Alan Stewart?"

The grouchy man who needed a break. Who could forget?

"Elizabeth Kerry?"

The suspicious lady who talked on the phone in back closets.

"You worked with both of them in Iowa, when the girl was taken. In their reports, they listed you as a mildly incompetent but well-meaning deputy who had no idea what was going on. I'm inclined to go with that theory, but you have to offer me something in return."

Mildly incompetent? The FBI thought they were so special, if nothing else, this proved that Richardson worked with them. "What are we talking about?" Shane asked.

"You returning to life as a free man instead of living in prison."

Shane would be lying to say that didn't sound appealing. But that didn't solve the problem of Rayford.

"In return, we expect the truth. Everything that happened, from start to finish."

He looked into the older man's steely grey eyes. An image of a green-eyed teenager came to mind. He saw Jesse's tanned and gentle face, the man's brotherly advice and kindness speaking strange peace to his soul. The shiny image of Carbon, her silky but curt voice telling him how things would go down.

It was hardly his fault he had been captured. He had no intentions of betraying Elise, Jesse, or Carbon, but was it worth life in prison? He probably wouldn't survive very long once the other inmates learned he was an ex-cop.

Besides, it was about time someone told the FBI the truth. About Rayford, first of all. Surely the state could find enough evidence to indict the man.

"Mr. Lawson?" Richardson was watching him. "What happened that night you jumped in your car and drove to Montana?"

Shane held the man's gaze. "I received a phone call."

Chapter 33

Elise sunk warily into Carbon's soft seats. She was more than grateful to be done with lectures for the day.

Following their last 'meeting', she and Jesse had caught a bus to a remote stop where they got off and walked a few minutes before Carbon showed up.

Now she was grateful to be off her feet, and off hard plastic chairs. College was not designed for comfort.

"You okay?" Jesse asked. "I was thinking of Chinese for dinner."

"Sure," Elise answered, her eyes closed. Her head was aching, but that's not what was bothering her. "Did Shane ever talk to you?"

"No. I haven't heard from him. Carbon?"

"I have not," the car replied. "His last text was sent at twelve twenty-eight PM."

"Wait," a light bulb went off in Elise's head. "You can track him with the phone. Where is he?"

"I cannot locate the signal from his cell phone."

"Why not?" Elise asked with a start.

"If the battery has been removed, Carbon can't access the phone," Jesse explained quietly.

Elise glanced at him in horror, and his expression was solemn. "What does that mean?"

"It is impossible to tell," Carbon answered. "He either removed the battery or someone else did. It is highly unlikely, though possible, that the battery failed. My last analysis indicated the phone was functioning properly and was fully charged overnight."

"Where was his last known location?" Jesse asked.

"The text was sent from the park outside McKinnley Hall. The phone's signal disappeared shortly thereafter."

"The text was from his phone, but someone else could have sent it," Jesse pointed out. "There's no way to find out. Carbon, monitor all frequencies, especially police, for any word of him. And if you can access any of Rayford's communications, that would be good to check."

Elise felt numb with the implications. Shane may have been in trouble, and they did nothing.

"Police bands reveal nothing. I can no longer monitor Dr. Rayford's or his associates' conversations. They have brought in signal jamming equipment

- 167 -

and set up secure routing of all internet and phone communications. It is taking me some time to break the code."

"Keep trying," Jesse said. "We still don't know what's going on, so monitor everything you can."

"I have been and will continue to do so."

"I know. Good job, Carbon. Elise?" Jesse was looking at her with concern.

She jerked her attention back, her mind already running through possibilities. Shane had intentionally left and just wanted space, or the police had found him, or worse ... Rayford. "Yeah?"

"We can't do anything else for him now. He's going to be on his own unless he contacts us."

Elise nodded, running fingers through her black hair. "I know."

"Carbon, find us a good Chinese place. Preferably secluded." With a sigh, he glanced over at her. "We still need to eat, and I have some things to explain to you. Okay?"

"Yeah," she muttered, trying to rein in her fears. Jesse was right, there was nothing they could do. Carbon would undoubtedly do her best to locate him. Shane had been stressed before he left, he probably would return later that night or in the morning.

And if she was about to get some answers, even in her tired state she was eager to know more. Shane would be fine.

At least that's what she told herself.

* * * *

"Dad doesn't want you to be confused."

Jesse had folded his hands and sat them on the table, watching her as he spoke. Confused she was, and not only over the genetics thing.

They had gone into a small Chinese restaurant and after ordering, Jesse had launched right into an explanation. Too bad Shane wasn't here, he would be happy to hear this. Or maybe it was better he was gone.

"There are enemies here who would use you for their purposes, ultimately to your destruction. Rayford is the chief, but he is not alone. Many people, even in the FBI and government, agree with his ideas. Remember," he looked at her solemnly, "you always have a choice."

Elise was tempted to rebut him, but she sat back and decided to listen instead.

"Like I've said, things will happen that you don't understand. I have to be arrested and turn myself over to the FBI."

"What?" Elise spat the question out with a stream of water, letting go of her straw too quickly. "Arrested?" What was he thinking?

"It's the way in," he said simply. "These things must happen. But first, let me explain."

Their waiter appeared again with a warm smile, setting two bowls of soup on the table.

Jesse motioned for her to go ahead and eat. He took a deep breath and launched into what Elise presumed to be a long-winded explanation. "I have to go back to Dad."

She nearly dropped her spoon, struggling to voice one of the myriad of questions that instantly filled her.

"Believe me, everything I have been doing and that I am about to do is exactly what Dad wanted. You haven't met him face to face yet, but you kind of know who he is because of what I do."

None of this made sense to Elise, and she wondered why he was talking about the future when she needed an explanation of the past.

"I have to go back, because I will need your new genetic information to recalibrate Carbon's biosensors. She will come back and help you, but it may be a while until you see me again."

Jesse looked at her sadly, and Elise understood what he was saying. First, Carbon would provide the stabilizing link he had discussed with the students. She had already put it together, but now it was clear. Second and more alarmingly, he was going to leave her here by herself. "Why can't I come with you?"

"You will. Just not now."

She studied his face, a sense of loss already growing within her. And fear.

"It's part of building the cure," he explained. "You have to believe me. You cannot find Dad unless you accept what I am going to give you."

Accept it? "The cure?" Elise blinked.

Jesse nodded, "I have to build it inside Rayford's lab, but don't worry. It's all going to work out."

His efforts to reassure her only worked partly, and she pushed her bowl aside, appetite gone.

"In fact, part of why Rayford is so scared is because after you have the cure in your body, you will be his undoing."

"What do you mean?" Elise asked, cold.

"When I send Carbon back, she will remind you of everything you need to know. You will do greater things than I have." He grinned with the thought, then frowned upon noticing her stricken expression. "Really, it is for your good that I am leaving. And I will come back."

"What am I supposed to do in the meantime?" Elise cried out. All her hopes rested on building the cure, and going to her father. Not being abandoned again.

Jesse's face grew dark, "Carbon will help you, and you're going to need her for more than just genetic stability."

"What does that mean?" Elise didn't bother to use her inside voice. She needed to know.

"There's much more to be done. Rayford has built quite an empire for himself, but your very DNA, the link with Carbon... you will expose what he's doing. And it goes much deeper, much farther back than you know."

Elise was overwhelmed. "I can't..." she stuttered, flustered that he would think she could and would do this. "I'm not even a scientist. I haven't graduated from high school yet!"

Jesse only smiled. "I know. Carbon will help you. But first things first. I did promise you an explanation. Keep in mind this is a very shortened version."

He cleared his throat, and Elise tried to focus on what he said. Her mind was already slipping away with fears of the future. She was going to be left alone again.

"Elise?" Jesse snapped his fingers in front of her face. "I think you need to eat something."

"No, I'm fine," she protested. "Just talk."

He eyed her with concern, but dove right in. "Pretend this is a strand of DNA. Information, written in a code with precise sequencing of four nucleobases: instructions for building new cells and programming their functions. Now, in an ordinary person, this DNA is self-contained, it's hard wired, pre-programmed and all packaged like a huge encyclopedia that your body uses to build cells and function. Your cells are replicated – along with these instructions – many times, though eventually errors occur and the code is corrupted, until something vital fails and the body ceases to function.

"DNA is the limit of the human body. It's our makeup, it defines who we are and who will become. Your DNA is different. Built into your DNA – from the time of conception – when that first strand of your DNA was fused together into what uniquely makes you you, was an extra compound. Rayford called it Compound X, but it was more accurately known as Compound C, a carbon-based information package that operated as a receptor. A receptor to translate the complex information packages hidden in your genes so the cell could conform to the higher level instructions."

Elise squinted with the strain of keeping up. "Wait," she held up a hand and pressed her other palm into her face. "The receiver, Compound X or C or whatever, took information from....?"

"Your DNA. Your genes are just the compilation of your DNA."

"Where did the information come from?" Proud she had at least followed that much, she rubbed her forehead and determined to keep up.

"Your genetics are uniquely you, with traits passed from both Mom and Dad."

Elise decided to let it go. She waved a hand dismissively. "What was the point of all this? The compound and my genes. The whole thing."

"No limits," he explained, clear blue eyes sincere and appreciative. "And seamless integration. The receptor acted like a processing system and greatly accelerated translation. Moreover, electronic impulses from your brain could communicate with this receptor, and it in turn communicated with the DNA and organized the proteins into working parts. Normal functions, like growth and tissue formation, ran automatically off of your base DNA."

He was smiling with the thought, amazed by the construction of it all.

Elise was not comprehending everything. "So there were normal functions and then..."

He finished the sentence for her, "...higher functions. Enhancements, Dad called them. Incredible strength. An intuition that makes ESP look like child's play. Intelligence."

This was weird. If not for past events, unbearable pain, and a talking car, she would have laughed every one of Jesse's words off as ridiculous.

Wishing for that intelligence now, Elise swallowed several spoonfuls of won-ton soup. In that time, Jesse downed his entire bowl and was washing it down with water as she pushed away her uneaten remainder.

Jesse never missed a beat and jumped back on his earlier train of thought. "Rayford designed a system based on his own compound and synthetic calculators that could manipulate DNA information. No one knew of his efforts, because Dad had given him free run of the labs and never interfered with his work. He wanted the respect of his employees, and gave them the same benefit.

"In order for Rayford's system to work, he had to change the genetic code and alter your very DNA. The hard part was finding a delivery system. Just slipping you a drug or chemical would be difficult if not impossible, and your immune system would quickly find and destroy the threat anyway."

Jesse heaved a sigh, "No. He was smarter than that."

Elise remembered her father's video. "I had to give consent?" she asked, not quite in accusation but her defenses were rising.

"Of course. But that was also difficult."

"What do you mean? Dr. Rayford tricked me?"

Jesse looked pensive. "No, not really. He lied to you, yes. But Dad had already told you the truth."

That ticked her off. "What truth?"

Her brother remained silent.

Further enraged, she clenched her hands into fists and dropped them on the table. "Why is everyone so secretive about it?"

"It's not a secret. It's in Carbon's logs."

"Well, she wouldn't share any of those with me," Elise snapped in exasperation.

"You have to ask direct questions," he explained patiently, but it was more annoying to Elise.

Direct questions that had to be perfectly phrased and prepared ahead of time. These standards were ridiculous, but she knew better than to complain. She needed to focus on the main point here. "Okay. What happened when I lost these powers and Rayford lied to me?"

Jesse opened his mouth but she interrupted, "The real answer. Concrete. Not some philosophical stuff."

She thought his lips turned up into a small laugh, but it turned so quickly into a grimace she couldn't be sure. "Rayford had his own ideas about DNA and how to manipulate genes. Control must be kept outside of the individual, for they could never be trusted to obey or do what they were supposed to. So, he designed his own system. There were fatal flaws, one being that he couldn't create anything stable with an artificial link like that. As similar as DNA is to computers, the human body is not just a machine. Mind, will, and emotions all play a part. The body would self-destruct if outside commands conflicted with what the body was doing. It just wouldn't work.

"So he developed a new tactic. It was relatively easy to develop a way to 'hijack' the system Dad had designed. If he could get you to give that initial consent, it was all he needed and he was in."

Elise interrupted. "What exactly did he tell me? What happened?"

"Remember you were very intelligent despite your young age, and Rayford came into the lab one day when you were alone. He showed you two beautiful silver bracelets, told you they had been specially made for you."

How criminal was that? Elise wondered as a vague memory stirred. Sparking silver bands, crisscrossed and emblazoned with elegant curves and patterns.

"These bracelets were kept in the lab, they were part of an experimental delivery system. But Dad had forbidden you to touch them, and you had

- 172 -

always stayed away. He told you they would kill you, and that was enough deterrent.

"Dr. Rayford presented you with a new perspective. The bracelets wouldn't kill you, but instead would only make you more powerful. The system was limited, as it was. If you introduced more information, you would then be able to figure things out for yourself instead of depending on Dad and the original code of your DNA."

"So... he said the bracelets would make me more powerful?"

Jesse shook his head. "Kind of. But not the bracelets alone. They were composed of a special alloy that conducts a signal very similar to the one inside your cells. Like any current, you just need to find the right frequency and modulation. Remember they were a delivery system. They disrupted the signal enough to give the SynMOs a chance to infiltrate your cell walls."

The nanites. "And I... put them on?" Elise asked.

"Rayford convinced you to try them for a moment, but that was enough," Jesse answered. "Once the circle was complete around your wrists, they were much more like shackles than bracelets."

Elise only eyed him skeptically, but the waiter brought the rest of their food with a smile and a small bow. She began pushing the food around with her fork, struggling to think.

"I think that's enough genetic engineering for now."

She looked up to find her genius geneticist brother with a piece of chicken impaled on a chopstick, grinning. He didn't look the part.

Brain as fried as her egg roll, Elise agreed. She could ponder more later. If there was a later.

They chatted about the school campus, Lucy, and Carbon's obsession with a clean interior until Elise had all but forgotten her microbiology lesson. Shaking his mop of blonde hair, Jesse stood after they had paid for the meal.

"The plan for tomorrow..." he paused for suspense. "Drumroll, please."

Elise chided him with a menacing look. She wouldn't stoop that low.

He acquiesced with a tolerant sigh. "Rest, and trust me."

"That's it?" she asked, too tired to be more annoyed.

Jesse pushed his chair in and offered her an arm. "That's it, little sister. Now... your chariot awaits you."

Puzzled and emotionally sapped, Elise accepted and let him lead her to Carbon. Rest and trust.

On top of all she had just leaned, it didn't make any sense at all.

Chapter 34

Elise perched herself on Lucy's couch, her mind struggling to find the logic in Jesse's plan. If it could be considered a plan. She hadn't slept well, finding no good reason to relax and rest. It was a mixed blessing. Her fears over the far future were swallowed by concerns for immediate survival. Honestly, she would prefer not to think about either.

Jesse had left with Stephen to finalize arrangements for that night. There was some sort of conference/social event for the entire science department, and Jesse was the main speaker. How he had pulled that off, she had no idea, but it seemed stupid. Confronting Rayford openly was the opposite of helpful.

I'm going to be arrested.

Why on Earth did Jesse think that was the best plan? For all they know, that could've happened to Shane, and they still hadn't heard from him.

Lucy was finishing getting dressed, and they were supposed to go buy something suitable for Elise to wear to the event. That too was stupid in her mind. Wouldn't it be safer to stay away?

But she tried not to think about it, especially because apart from Jesse and Carbon, she had no real plan for survival, no one else to turn to.

Shane had left. Or maybe worse. So what? He was just a random stranger anyway, he couldn't help her.

"Ready?" Lucy asked, purse and keys in hand.

Elise forced a smile, "Yeah."

Undoubtedly Carbon would be trailing them somewhere nearby, so she wasn't worried for her immediate safety. But she was worried about the future. Whatever Jesse had done was barely masking the sickness now, all she could do was grit her teeth and bear it. The game was getting old, and Elise dearly hoped that Jesse's plan worked, and that it worked tonight.

* * * *

The sun had yet to set, but Elise was already growing more worried about the night's events. Lucy had helped her pick out an elegant black dress, and combined with the makeup the older girl had applied, Elise had to admit she looked nothing like herself. Nia wouldn't even be able to recognize her.

Lucy had been excited, though the strain could be seen on her face as well. Jesse's speech, she was convinced, would be revolutionary to the field of genetics and maybe even all science. But all revolutionary things held their cost, no matter the benefit.

The establishment usually didn't appreciate revolution.

Elise was frankly more concerned with living and not getting captured, so the enormity of it all was somewhat lost on her. What hadn't escaped her notice was Shane's extended absence.

She got up from her seat in front of the large building where the event would be held. Jesse was with Stephen, and Lucy had gone off to meet someone. Elise had purchased a tiny purse to keep her phone in, and with that constant link to Carbon figured she was safe for now. She kept a wary eye out for Rayford, but all she saw were students milling around, wandering here and there.

Part of her wished Shane would walk up and explain why he had gone missing. Maybe he had needed room to think as he had said, and just wanted to get away for a day. Or maybe something had happened.

Unsettled, Elise walked towards the double glass doors. A tall Hispanic man opened the door for her, and she tried to flash a smile of thanks. It probably came across as a grimace.

Something just wasn't right about all of this, and she tried to steer her thoughts towards the positive as she headed towards the ladies' room.

But it didn't work. Here she was again, alone and waiting for what already seemed like a bad plan. Maybe she should just call Carbon and wait it out in the car.

The restroom had a sitting area in front of it, nicely decorated with a couch and two chairs. An odd little room, but Elise was grateful for the privacy. As much as she tried to deny them, fear and anger were both boiling over, and she wasn't sure if the motivation was selfish or selfless.

She couldn't truly talk to anyone. Even Lucy didn't know what was going on or who she really was. The only person she could talk honestly to was her brother, who was busy, or Shane, who had disappeared.

He had been upset, yet he did say he would be in the classroom. So was he in trouble, or had he left?

Elise hadn't decided which option was worse. If he was in trouble, especially if Rayford had him, they should all be gravely concerned. He may not even be alive.

She shoved the thought aside, fear turning to anger.

On the other hand, he could have removed the battery from his phone and walked away. She hadn't exactly been welcoming, and Jesse was... Jesse. It was fair to think he might simply leave and try to lay low somewhere. Being hunted was scary, and he had no real stake in anything that was going on. He had already helped a lot as a complete stranger, even saving her life. She should be grateful, and leave it at that.

But she wasn't. She was furious.

Surely he would have at least told them he had changed his mind; Jesse had made it clear he could leave whenever he wanted. He hardly seemed the type to just walk away without a word.

Maybe he couldn't face them or maybe he thought she would try to stop him. She blushed remembering her earlier hug. He probably thought she was an emotionally immature teenager and wanted to leave without a scene.

Why did she care? He was nothing to her. A nice guy who helped and then went his own way. It shouldn't matter. She shouldn't care.

She tapped her hands nervously against the wall, forcing herself to be still and rest her forehead.

More important things. She needed to focus on more important things.

Things like, say, survival. Finding out what was really going on. Finding her father.

Standing straight, she set her shoulders and reached for the door. She would find Jesse and find out when he was going to finally conjure up that cure.

Shane didn't matter right now, there was nothing she could do.

Perusing the hallways and the now crowded atrium, however, Elise realized that finding her brother was easier said than done. People stood around munching on finger foods, some in deep discussions, others were chatting lightly. Most were mid-twenties, she guessed, though there was a wide age range. Grad students and professors, maybe even some undergrads.

She could call him on the cell phone, but she might interrupt whatever he was doing. Frustrated, she was about to give up when her eyes caught a glimpse of a figure on the other side of the room.

It couldn't be, she reasoned. Her heart jumped inside, and she took a deep breath. This was ridiculous, it didn't matter.

Making her way through the crowds, Elise could see that the man's back was to her, as if he was trying to not be seen.

But she had seen his face. She was sure.

"Shane?" she asked.

The man didn't turn around or even acknowledge her voice. She momentarily doubted herself, but stepped around to get a better look.

Unless he had a twin who had also dyed his hair, this was definitely him.

"Shane!" she said so he couldn't miss it, moving her face to look him directly in the eye. It was like he was trying not to look at her.

"Oh, hi." He said with an expression like he didn't know who she was. "I'm sorry, I don't remember your name."

Elise squinted at him. "Bonnie," she intoned slowly, trying to catch on to whatever clues she was missing.

He looked relieved. "Well, nice seeing you. Maybe I'll catch you later?"

Why would he appear and then try to get rid of her? Elise glanced over her shoulders. "Did you come by yourself?" she asked. "Where's your date?"

His eyes gave her a dangerous look, but his face was relaxed and his tone was light. "She's around here somewhere. The jealous type. You should leave before she gets back." He made a throat cutting motion with his hand.

Elise understood. With a fake laugh, she conceded the point. "I'll disappear." There was so much she wanted to ask, it was hard to walk away. But she had to go warn Jesse.

As she made her way to the stage, however, a grey-haired professor was approaching the podium. She was pushed into a nearby seat as the crowd hurried in.

"Good evening," his deep voice rumbled. Elise didn't recognize him, but that was true of most people in this room.

"Ladies and gentlemen, I know you've all been waiting for a lecture by a special guest, but we've had some problems."

A murmur rippled through the audience, and Elise's heart nearly stopped beating, her ears pricked for his next sentence.

"Jesse is suffering some effects of food poisoning, and I regret to say his lecture has been cancelled."

Impossible. Elise opened her purse quickly, grabbing her cell phone.

No signal.

This was bad.

"If he feels better," the man continued. "We'll let you know. But until then, I'd like to introduce my friend and colleague Dr. Sidorov."

Elise drowned out the sound of the man's voice. Something had happened.

The police, or maybe Rayford, had followed Shane here, and somehow knew about Jesse.

Somehow? It's not like he tried to keep it a secret, openly claiming to be Dr. Mathis' son.

Elise pushed the anger aside. She needed to get to Carbon, and fast.

Someone had blocked all cell phone signals into this room. They must have had Shane bugged, and he was probably being watched as well.

Which meant her disguise had worked, but it wouldn't take them long to figure out who she was.

Everyone was seated or standing still, listening to the lecture. If she left now, she would be easy to spot.

If she waited, undoubtedly they would have picked her out of the crowd by the time it was over.

Elise saw her opportunity. In the disappointment, a few people had decided to leave. Smiling apologetically at the man next to her, Elise got up and likewise pressed through the crowd, happy to reach the back of the building.

Her eyes scanned the room for anyone watching or following her, but everything appeared in order.

A door.

The main doors would be monitored, but this side door had to lead out to somewhere.

She pushed it open, her heart pounding in her chest. The empty hallway was lit, and she gingerly closed the door after slipping through.

A red exit sign at the other end of the long carpeted stretch gave her hope. She quickened her step, trying to appear nonchalant. Hopefully no one was watching, and she resisted the urge to look into the security cameras at either end of the hall.

Underneath the exit sign was another door, this time leading to an elevator. She pushed the down button and waited. This must be the exit in the back of the building.

The elevator dinged as its door slid open, but Elise thought she heard another noise. A door down the long hallway opened. The same door she just came from.

Her mouth had gone dry, and jumping into the elevator she punched the down button as fast as possible, multiple times just in case.

No one appeared as the doors slid shut, and the machine creaked as it headed down. They might be waiting for her there.

Checking her phone, she fought slippery palms to not drop it. Still no signal.

The elevator chimed and opened to the ground floor, and Elise followed the exit sign out an inconspicuous white door. The cool air whipped around her, and she breathed a sigh of relief.

The night was pitch black, however, and there were no lights on this side of the building. Must be a service entrance.

Picking her way carefully, Elise was glad for the flat bottomed shoes she had chosen. Heels would be impossible.

The cement ended at a square retention pond. As her eyes adjusted to the lighting, she was able to make out wire fencing and power generators.

She walked quickly, trying to distance herself from the building. There were woods beyond the retention pond, and if she made it there she was probably safe. She could wander until her phone had signal again and call Carbon. She could do this.

A door creaked open, and Elise spun to see a man stepping out the same way she had just come. She had been followed.

Quickening her pace, Elise tried to make it toward the trees before the man could see her.

Noises scattered around in the night. The wind blowing leaves, small animals scampering, or people hunting for her?

She whispered a breathless prayer in the darkness, hoping she was far enough that she would be invisible.

Stepping into the woods, she was too frightened to look back and see if the man had followed. She tried to melt into the trees, relieved that the ground beneath her feet was soft with the earlier rain, not brittle and crunchy.

"Bonnie!" a male voice whispered her name with urgency. She froze in fear, though it only took her a moment to recognize who was looking for her.

It was Josh, one of the grad students. They must have heard of what happened to Jesse.

She didn't move until her eyes found him shuffling around in the woods off to her right. He hadn't seen her yet.

Just because he studied under Dr. Batiste didn't mean he was trustworthy. She watched him for a moment longer, calling her name again in hushed tones.

If he wasn't quiet, the man at the door might hear him. Maybe he was working with them.

She glanced at her phone, which still had no signal. If she couldn't contact Carbon, she would be hopelessly lost. Josh might be her only chance to get out of here.

Which was better, lost without knowing a soul or taking a chance with a stranger?

Licking her lips and praying for the right choice, Elise moved forward to stand behind Josh. He was holding some sort of case, and she began to regret it the moment she reached out to tap his back.

"I'm right here," she tried to whisper inaudibly.

"Bonnie!" He looked relieved, like he might give her a hug. But he didn't. "We need to get out of here, they already have Jesse."

"Who?" she asked as fresh panic returned.

"Shhh," Josh put a finger to his lips. "Not here."

He motioned for her to follow, and she prayed she had made the correct decision. She had lost her bearings in the woods, but it seemed he was leading away from the building and the men. A good sign.

But there was nothing to rejoice over yet. Whoever had Jesse, Elise knew well that she couldn't build the cure without him. And there was probably very little she could do to help him.

Chapter 35

"Weakness," Dr. Juan Batiste bit his lower lip, the video crackling once before he continued. "Weakness is not a thing to be despised."

"In genetic coding, the 'weaker' strands are thrown out in favor of the stronger, more durable and better performing genes. We seek to weed out the traits that emulate something like weakness or any general susceptibility to fatigue."

The Hispanic man shook his head, dark brows furrowed deep in thought. "No. We keep trying this, but it is the wrong method. It comes from faulty understanding. No," he shook his head again. "It will never work."

"Weakness," he pointed a finger at the camera, "presents the greatest opportunity for strength."

There was muttering in the background chatter of the recording, but Batiste was not to be hurried.

"No, no, *listen*," he pressed. "Listen and think. Open your minds."

The chatter hushed, and Batiste let out a huff of air as he leaned back on the podium. "Look at my notes."

Papers ruffled, but no image appeared on screen. Guess that wasn't part of the recording.

"Which strand of DNA would you think most capable of supporting 'converter' to handle higher level input translating to increased yield, be they physical strength or mental resilience?"

"You have to pick one," Batiste urged them gently with a smile. "Let's say this was *your* DNA, and it was your life at stake. Which will you bet on?"

More murmuring, more paper shuffling.

Batiste was nodding. "Yes, that's what we tend to think. This strand is more stable, more tightly woven together, and the information more complex and precise, presumably its function more important or vital to the organism's survival. And this is what we've tried to make successful for a long time."

He took a deep breath. "But we had miscalculated. This strand of DNA was utterly resistant to any messages or impulses we sent through the converter from the complex calculator. Sometimes these strong genetics would comply partly, but it was difficult, and the results unstable." He gave a severe look, "In other words, I would be highly uncomfortable if this situation was a reality for myself. No thanks.

"Now, my colleague Dr. Mathis took a different approach. We thought he was crazy, but he focused on the weak, less complex strands of DNA."

Batiste paused again, surveying his audience meaningfully. "The results were breathtaking. What we thought was strength was actually weakness, and what we presumed and wrote off as weakness and failures, was actually strength and the greatest success."

"You see…" the professor continued, but the video cut into static.

Stewart continued staring at the screen, hoping the feed would come back. All the videos were like this. Some scientific talk in the beginning, and before the heart of the lecture, the data was corrupted and wouldn't play anymore.

"There's nothing else here," Agent Kerry said. She was sullen, but had ceased arguing a few videos back.

Stewart was no scientist, and he barely remembered high school biology, but he didn't need a degree to grasp that there was a serious disagreement among those involved with Dr. Mathis' project. The Bureau had only informed them that Project Excalibur was classified research of biologic weaponry.

Dr. Mathis had been suspected of leaking sensitive information to unauthorized persons and embezzling funds from the project. Before he could be caught, he had been tipped off and escaped, destroying the collection of data in anger and stealing the rest. The murder of his wife, disappearance of his children, these were all seen as further crimes and evidences of his foul character.

He was also accused of sharing top secret weaponry and information with other governments, and receiving funds for his traitorous actions. Stewart had seen the paper trail, and it all used to add up.

This is why the FBI was hunting him, and why they were so interested when his daughter reappeared. Wasn't it?

"Stewart," Liz was staring at him, one hand on the computer mouse. "Can I shut this down? There aren't any more videos."

He nodded. She had to be putting this together as well. The charges or treason and embezzling aside, there was a lot more going on in Project Excalibur than they were being told. Dr. Juan Batiste, who had also worked under Mathis in the project, spoke of some form of genetic engineering, and a little bit of extrapolation made Stewart think they were building super soldiers.

"What now?" Liz sat rigid in her chair.

He flicked his eyes to her face. Her dark eyes were pensive, and angry. But he doubted the anger was still directed at him.

"Thanks for your help, Liz. You're free to go."

He got up and turned to leave the library. The next step was to find this Dr. Batiste, who was a professor at the university. Stewart had a long list of questions for the man.

"Wait," Liz jumped up and followed. "What are you going to do?"

"Don't worry about it. Just do your job."

She studied his face, "How can I contact you?"

"I'll contact you. And you should take a different exit. Less suspicious."

Without giving her a chance to reply, he headed towards the main doors. She was a good girl, and a great agent. He wasn't sure exactly how she would handle this, but he was sure of one thing. She wouldn't cause him any more problems for a while.

On the street, Stewart observed the light flow of students. Must be in between classes.

"Agent Stewart?"

He spun around in surprise. A teenage guy was holding out his cell phone.

"Yes?" he answered, suspicious. He had never seen this kid before.

"The phone's for you. It's okay," the kid reassured him. "The lady explained this is FBI business."

Stewart continued glancing between the phone and the boy. What had she done to make a teenager willingly hand over his phone?

"Here," the kid pressed, shaking the phone. "I gotta get to class."

"Thank you," Stewart tried to nod officially, like lifting phones from college students was standard FBI procedure. "We'll make it up to you, I promise."

"Yeah," the kid shrugged, walking away.

Stewart lifted the phone to his ear, "Hello?"

"Agent Stewart."

Surprise, surprise. It was Carbon.

"How did you get that kid's phone?"

"That is Jake McCoy, and he was quite willing to help. He will be reimbursed well."

"A random kid?" Stewart asked. How could she possibly pull that off? Must be a serious hacker. "Look," he focused. "I need to know what's going on. I've been watching ..."

"I have been monitoring your access to videos, I am aware of what you know."

Stewart suppressed a groan of anger. It was alarming that she was already one step ahead of him. "Where can I find Batiste?"

"He has been placed under arrest by the FBI, and is being held in a secure facility."

"Why?" Stewart asked.

"Feared connections with Dr. Mathis and suspected conspiracy. Although that is the official reason, I doubt it is the true cause of his arrest."

He didn't want to agree with her, but he had to admit it was a likely scenario. "What do you want from me?"

"You want to know the truth."

"Is that a question?"

"I would like to meet with you, Agent Stewart. There is a trailhead outside of the city. It is usually empty except for a few day hikers. I will send the location to this phone and meet you in the parking lot. Good bye."

As usual, she ended the conversation abruptly. Slightly ticked at this rude tactic, Stewart pocketed the kid – Jake's – cell phone. She hadn't even given him a time to meet.

That meant he should head there now, at least to scope out the area. She was already monitoring him closely, and he was in too deep to pull out now.

Besides, he really did want to know the truth.

* * * *

Shane backed towards the wall. The boring lecture was finally over, and he had been chatting with a nice girl from Brooklyn who had been highly disappointed to miss this 'Jesse's' speech. She was a student of genetics, and although she knew of Dr. Batiste, she rolled her eyes and mentioned his name with disdain. He learned through her that a fair amount of the students here had come not to learn, but to laugh at and dispute whatever Jesse said.

Another guy walked up to them, his suit a little too big. "Hey, I've seen you before."

Shane blinked, "You have?" If not for the people surely watching him and the bug they placed on him, he would have tried to escape decades ago. As it was, he was an involuntary informant of the FBI. At least Elise got away.

"Yeah," the guy said, snapping his fingers. "You were with Jesse. Do you know what happened?"

"What?" Shane glanced from the guy to Lauren, the girl he had been chatting with. "I think you've confused me with someone else. I don't know him personally, although I do know *of* him." He tried to smile, but they didn't look convinced.

"No," the kid pressed. "I'm sure of it. And there was a girl, she had black hair?"

"You *know* him?" Lauren asked.

"I've heard this food poisoning story is fake," the kid said, looking at Shane for confirmation.

"Look," Shane explained. "I don't know what you're talking about."

"There are police cars outside," the boy continued. "And black SUVs. The government's involved."

Lauren's face lit up with excitement. "Oh my gosh! Then it's true. He *is* Dr. Mathis' son!"

Shane didn't know where this was going, but he didn't like it. If the FBI was still monitoring him, where did they go? If they really did arrest Jesse, maybe they were too busy to be concerned with him.

A cell phone rang loudly from Lauren's purse, and she retrieved it in surprise. "I thought I silenced this…" she murmured. "Hello?"

Shane met the eyes of the kid who was still watching him like a hawk. What did he want?

"It's for you," Lauren handed him the phone, a confused look shadowing her face.

The kid's eyes widened, and Shane tried to mirror the look, motioning at himself innocently. "I have no idea," he tried to explain, not that it would help. "Hello?" he said into the phone.

"I have disrupted the FBI's signal jamming device. They cannot monitor you now, except that one agent has been watching you from the South door. Make your move to the north exit, I have distracted the man for now. Hurry."

Shane tried to digest the information quickly. Carbon was to the point, as always.

"Be right back," he looked at the two with a smile as he left. "This is important."

"Hey, my phone!" Lauren protested.

"I told you!" Shane heard the kid whisper loudly as he walked away. If they followed, that wasn't his problem.

"What next?" he asked.

"They have taken Jesse to a private room to speak with a number of professors and board members. He is on the fourth floor in McKinnley Hall in the conference room."

"Wait," he said as he pushed through the crowds to the south door. "What am I supposed to do?"

"Go there."

The line went dead, and Shane looked in disgust at the phone in his hands. Not only was it pink, but it was encrusted with sparkling pink and white gems.

So they had taken Jesse somewhere 'private'. He was a little sore at Carbon, as the car had not prevented his kidnapping or tried to rescue him from FBI custody. Nevertheless, he supposed it best to figure out what was going on.

He hadn't given the FBI much to go on, and he wondered what exactly they were doing. If they weren't working with Rayford, they were probably in the dark about his nefarious schemes.

With a curious thought, he remembered that he was still bugged, unless Carbon had disabled that. His best guess was that she wanted the FBI to hear what went on in that conference room.

Chapter 36

Elise sat across from Josh at a small diner, her hands fighting to not tremble around her cup of tea.

"There are cops all over the place," he said. "The campus looks like a war zone. What happened?"

"I don't know," Elise answered. "What happened to Jesse?"

"They just took him," Josh shook his head in disbelief. "Myself, Lucy, and Stephen, we were all with him, just talking about what he would say in the presentation. Some guys came in suits, said they were FBI and that they needed to talk to Jesse. Stephen tried to stop them, but Jesse told him to not to. He went with them willingly."

He said he had to be arrested. But surely he was kidding, that seemed like such a bad idea.

"What?" Josh asked, as if he could read her mind.

"Nothing, I just…"

"Just what?"

But Elise couldn't bring herself to speak. She didn't want to talk about it to anybody, and wasn't sure how much to trust to Josh.

"Look," he said gently. "I know from Jesse and Dr. Batiste that there's more going on here than revolutionizing science in the theoretical."

Elise stared at him. In the theoretical?

He glanced around as if to make sure no one was watching. "I know what I've been told, but I want to hear it from you. Are you Irene Mathis?"

She felt her heart seize. Jesse told them? Josh was waiting expectantly for an answer, studying her. She had never been a good liar. Her face undoubtedly proclaimed the truth of his statement.

"It's true?" he asked again.

Denying it at this point wasn't going to help. "Yes," she answered meekly. "I think so."

"You *think* so?" he asked in surprise. "How can you not be sure?"

"It's … complicated," she explained, not wishing to share any more of the story. "Look, I don't really know what's going on here. But I need to get back to Jesse."

With a slow nod, Josh seemed to agree. "Okay. I'll help you get back there."

"First, look at this." He pulled the small briefcase onto the table, snapping it open. Inside was a metal case, the locks already undone.

"Here," he handed it to her. "Jesse was going to use this at the presentation, and I think it belongs to you."

She hesitantly accepted the case, setting it in the space in front of her. "Jesse had this?"

Josh nodded, "I took it and ran before the cops could confiscate it. Or me." He smiled bashfully.

Taking a deep breath, Elise flipped the case open, gasping when she saw the contents. Two shimmering silver bracelets, each one intertwined with beautiful silver bands crisscrossing elegantly. They were beautiful.

"Pretty, huh?" Josh said. "I figured they must be important to be in a case like that. Maybe a family heirloom?"

Elise stared at the bracelets, "Jesse had these?"

Again Josh nodded, his dark eyes looking concerned. "Is something wrong?"

But his voice was obscured by a barrage of thoughts and emotions. Jesse told her to avoid these. Why would he have them?

Tucked underneath one was a handwritten note, and Elise gingerly pushed the bracelet aside to retrieve the paper. What had Jesse said about them again? Some alternative signal network. A way to go beyond the bounds of her own DNA.

"For emergencies only," the note read.

Emergencies? Had Jesse foreseen that the FBI would find him?

Maybe he couldn't make the cure, maybe she had to put these on to survive in the meantime. Just touching the smooth silver brought a strange calm over her fingers. Maybe the signal was working. After all these years, though. How could they still work?

"What are they?" Josh asked, peeking around the open box. "A gift?"

"I don't know," Elise responded, dumfounded.

"Well, I'm sure Jesse meant for you to have them." He set some money on the table. "For now, let's get you back to him. Maybe then we'll figure out what's going on."

She should keep them, but ask Jesse when she saw him.

What if she couldn't get to him?

Carbon. Elise checked her phone, but it still said no signal. That was weird.

Josh was waiting patiently, and Elise forced herself to close the box and stand. "I'm coming," she said. "Thanks for the tea."

"No problem," he smiled. "Let's hope we can find your brother."

* * * *

"Well, you sure have been creating a stir amongst the students here, Mr…"

"Jesse. Just Jesse."

The grey haired man nodded, stroking his moustache. Mrs. Allen would be impressed, Shane thought as he stood watching from the back of the room. He was glad for the suit and tie the FBI had dressed him in, as he was able to slip in easily with a few other people and sit in the back.

"Ah, yes," the man continued. "There are even rumors circulating that you are Alexander Mathis. And yet you do not claim this name?"

"If you knew Dr. Mathis, you would know me. All I told your students, everything I taught, was his theory. You should know that."

"So you *are* Samuel's son?"

"Yes," Jesse replied simply. "Dr. Batiste told you I was coming. My dad is going to fix what was broken."

The man gave him a condescending look, "I wasn't aware that anything was broken. What are you talking about?"

Dr. Rayford was indeed present, and though Shane had tried to shrink unobtrusively into the corner, he was pretty confident that the scientist had noticed him. However, Rayford was not paying him any attention, fully engrossed with his colleagues in their interrogation of Jesse.

"My dad's theory and his research you have distorted and twisted. I have spoken with the students, I know what you are teaching them. You say that he supported Dr. Rayford's theory of genetic manipulation, even that he developed it. That he eventually wanted DNA to be perfected and honed by eugenics, building a stronger race by trampling the weak."

"That's absurd," Dr. Rayford snapped. "I worked with Samuel most of my life. This *is* his theory."

Angry murmurs from the crowd followed.

"You've seen the figures," Jesse said. "I worked through the equations with your students, I know they've shown you."

"Dr. Mathis took an unacceptable fall from grace, for which none of us can be held responsible," the man with the moustache said. "This … science, if you can call it that, is not in line with any of his other theories. If he really sent you, where is he now? Why don't you prove it?"

Dr. Rayford spoke calmly, "We all know the stories, even if Dr. Batiste was insane. If you really are who you claim to be, your DNA should tell us the whole story. Give us a sample, and we'll run some tests."

"No," Jesse replied firmly. His face was tight with anger. "You all claim to be teaching my dad's theories, yet you have no idea what he taught. What you

- 189 -

discount as disputed hypothesis is in the flesh fact. If you can't understand that, you don't need any further sign. The code *you*," his eyes turned to Rayford, "corrupted will be repaired, and my dad's work will be finished."

Rayford shrank back slightly, but recovered and stepped forward. "Are you admitting that he performed illegal experiments? Even tested on animals, the results were clear. There is no solution. Certainly not through *his* theories. To think that a strand of enhanced DNA could be stabilized from the inside... it's just impossible."

A woman from the back spoke, "I have seen this gentleman's theories on paper. My students were quite impressed, and with good reason."

"Dr. Bates," another scientist replied. "You are not familiar with Dr. Mathis' original theories. Compounded with this... it truly is absurd."

"Are you questioning my expertise?" she demanded.

The man relented, "No. But we should give the matter further study."

Rayford's eyes rested on Shane briefly, and he felt a chill creep in. "Who is this?" the scientist demanded.

All eyes glanced over to where he was sitting. Shane swallowed hard, looking to Jesse.

Dr. Summers was also present, and she feigned surprise, drawing near for a closer inspection. "Wait!" she called. "I recognize him. From TV." She looked at Shane with wide eyes.

Others in the room began to shift uncomfortably, recognition dawning on many faces.

"He kidnapped that girl!" a white haired man exclaimed.

Shane shook his head vehemently to deny the accusations. He tried to keep panic from taking over, hoping Jesse would do something.

"What's the meaning of this?" the man at the podium demanded.

Jesse stood at the front of the room, completely confident. "There is much you don't know. That girl is Irene Mathis, my sister. If you would open your eyes and ears, maybe you would understand. She was not kidnapped, though she is indeed very sick, and I'm sure you would like to know why."

"This man is insane!" Rayford shot up from his chair. "We need to call the police!"

"Have I offered any resistance?" Jesse held up his hands. "Hear me out, and then decide."

"I want to hear him," Dr. Bates spoke up. "Let the man speak."

"Dr. Williams," Summers addressed the moustached man at the podium. "I object. We need the police here."

An angry murmur swelled up from the crowd, and Shane was afraid the group of scientists was near rioting.

"Hear me out first," Jesse said quietly.

Dr. Williams nodded reluctant approval, motioning to the crowd to be silent. "There are easily enough of us that these two will not leave until we've been satisfied." His booming voice held an ominous threat, and Shane hoped his intentions were friendlier than the icy gaze he directed toward each of them in turn.

Jesse took a deep breath. "My dad pioneered the field of integrated bio-nanotechnology, culminating in a working model of enhanced DNA that could be added as the zygote formed. Using a carbon-based receptor, he broke the code of neural communications and found a way to place condensed instructions for higher functioning cells inside the DNA.

Murmurs of anger and disbelief swirled around the room.

Jesse continued unhindered. "Part of the genetic code, this allowed for a person to access any wide array of features, such as incredible strength, enhanced ability to regenerate and heal, rapid processing in the mind, and the ability to fight off virtually any disease.

"Such a discovery has many potential uses, most of which are not benign. As such, this research was highly secretive and classified above top secret. My dad's good friend and colleague, Dr. Rayford, grew suspicious and discovered the project. In an attempt to supplant the research and steal the technology for his own means, he fatally corrupted the system."

Shane glanced at Rayford, whose face had turned an indignant shade of purple. He maintained his silence, but his fuming reaction was not hidden.

"Dad was able to stabilize the base DNA, but the modified strands that controlled the higher functions had unraveled. There was no choice but to destroy the receiver so it would not transmit the damaged data and kill the individual, my sister. If corrupted, the biofeedback loop would begin to trigger apoptosis. Worse, Irene was now susceptible to being taken and used by Rayford or anyone else."

Too many big words. Shane wondered about apoptosis but focused instead on the point. What did he mean, *used* by Rayford or anyone else?

Judging by the shifting around the room, many of the scientists had already formed rebuttals and were chomping at the bit to interrupt. The mustached man at the podium set them at rest with another stern look.

Jesse's eyes were brimming with emotion as he continued, "The steps my dad used shut down the other portions of her brain, but the link was still open to her DNA. The signal was shut off, so to speak, but it was possible to reactivate the receiver and even reprogram it. Damaged, using any new link would make her very sick and eventually kill her, but with the right technology, someone could now access those 'enhancements' from the outside.

"Facing the loss of his daughter and exposure of his security sensitive work, Dad fled with his family, myself included. Rayford took the opportunity to frame him, shifting the attention and sliding under the radar. And he has begun restoring the DNA subplant, the biologic receiver, artificially. That is why Irene is sick."

The room was hushed, each person stunned by disbelief and shock.

"But Dr. Batiste was right. I am going to fix what was broken, and I am going to restore Irene's DNA. I am the only one who can."

Rayford found his tongue. "Impossible! This man is crazy! We all know what happened, the evidence is clear!"

More angry tones rushed forward from the group.

"Calm down, doctor," Dr. Williams was clearly struggling to keep control of the situation. He turned to Jesse, "Can you prove your story?"

"I already have."

"And why is Irene," he rolled the name off his tongue as if he was unconvinced, "still so sick? Why haven't you 'fixed' her yet?"

But Jesse offered no reply, falling silent.

"Excuse me," Dr. Summers interrupted. "But we should at least call the police to detain this man while we discuss this. Even if he's telling the truth, we should contact the authorities. He can prove himself later."

There were several nods around the table, and Shane realized he was holding his breath.

"Dr. Batiste was right," Jesse spoke boldly. "You will not listen, and you are blinded by the thought of your own brilliance."

Nice, Jesse. The man sure knew how to make friends.

Two big guys had moved to stand next to Shane, and as he glanced around the room that was murmuring angrily, he realized he wasn't going anywhere unless Jesse could become mighty convincing.

But as they fell into arguments with scientific jargon lost on Shane, he only hoped for the man to come up with a plan for once. Then there was always Carbon.

Chapter 37

Stewart observed the empty lot with trepidation. He had taken a taxi to get out here, and doubtless the driver had unvoiced questions as to his passenger's remote destination. He asked the man drop him off a mile away, saying that it was as far as he could pay fare for. He doubted the driver bought his explanation, but it was of little consequence.

What mattered now was that he had arrived at an empty parking lot without a soul in sight. If that woman had sent him on a wild goose chase…

But he seriously doubted it. He would bet she was already here.

He wondered what she would look like, if Lawson's description could be trusted.

Not that it made a difference. There didn't appear to be anyone out here. She was likely already well entrenched, well-armed, and not alone. Hiding was probably against his best interest. He was already playing into her hands.

He walked out into the empty parking lot with his arms raised in surrender. "I'm alone!" he called out. "I just want to talk."

A high pitched whine grew closer, the only man-made noise in this harbor of nature. Then a rumbling. What was coming, a train or a jet?

Keeping a wary eye out in all directions, Stewart braced himself and waited.

It wasn't long before the nose of a black Dodge Challenger appeared down the road, headed his way.

The same car. What was it about that car? He would have thought Carbon to be smarter than that.

As it pulled up beside him, he couldn't see well through the tinted windows, but he had glimpsed a woman matching Lawson's description in the driver's seat.

Jake's phone rang from his pocket, and Stewart hoped it was Carbon and not the kid's mom. He wasn't disappointed.

"Why not just get out and talk to me?" he asked, irritated.

"I cannot," Carbon replied. "Though you are welcome to get inside and talk to me."

Stewart was instantly suspicious, trying to stare through the passenger window to see the lady inside. "Why? Is it not safe out here?"

"It is safe, Agent."

"Then what's the problem?" He walked around to the front of the car to look through the windshield, careful to not stand in a place too easy to be run over.

And he was indeed surprised when the woman behind the steering wheel vanished.

"Because I am not in the car as you are thinking," Carbon replied. "I am the car."

* * * *

From the passenger seat of Josh's Porsche – which, while not Carbon, Elise could find no reason to complain about – the situation did not look good.

Police cars surrounded the University, though traffic was not completely blocked off.

"Over there," Elise pointed to where a sedan was attempting to drive onto campus.

But the car stopped as a policeman leaned down to talk to the driver with a flashlight, checking out the passengers.

"Oh, no," Elise groaned. "We'll never make it. How do we even find him?"

Josh was shaking his head, "I don't know. But with this many cars here, they probably still have him somewhere nearby."

"We can't get past all these, unless…" she trailed off.

The thoughts had been plaguing her for the entire drive. The bracelets would reconnect her to the enhancements, even if briefly. Jesse said they were dangerous, but if he had left them for her, maybe he meant just using them a little wouldn't hurt. Besides, they were only bracelets. She could always take them off.

Again she checked her phone for a signal, but there was none. Surely Carbon could have found a way to get through by now. Unless…

Maybe something had happened to her too.

Opening the box in her lap again, Elise fingered the bracelets. The same calm spread over her hands.

"What are you thinking?" Josh asked, glancing over at her as he was driving.

Elise sighed. "I think maybe these trinkets will help us find Jesse."

Josh seemed skeptical. "How?"

"I'm not sure," Elise admitted. "I guess I have to put them on to find out."

"May I?" Josh asked, reaching into the box.

Elise nodded, and he slid one onto his wrist. "Well, they fit."

She gave a tiny laugh, appreciating his attempt to make her feel better. "They look very nice on you."

He returned the smile, pulling the bracelet off and handing it to her. "Thanks. But I think they belong to you."

See? Even Josh could put them on and off with no effect. Maybe they didn't work anymore.

There was only one way to find out.

With a final glance at her phone to confirm no signal, Elise picked up a bracelet and slid it onto her wrist. The cool metal felt nice against her skin, but that was it. No sparks, no magic, nothing.

She shook her wrist, watching the bracelet jingle loosely.

"Maybe one on each arm?" Josh offered.

Elise shrugged, trying not to let the disappointment show. The other one slid on just as easily, the cool metal brushing against her like any other bracelet.

"I guess..." she began, but a strange tingling gave her pause. Did she imagine that?

Searing pain shot into her wrists as the silver rings clamped onto her skin.

Elise would have screamed, but her mouth was inexorably shut. The sensation was like fire, brutally hot, burning through her entire body, spreading from her wrists. Drenched in excruciating agony, she had no other thoughts as her mind spun mercifully into a black unconsciousness.

Chapter 38

Shane was growing weary of this game. These people were not going to be convinced by Jesse, even though the woman professor, Dr. Bates, had taken to his defense several times. And he could barely understand what they were talking about.

If they had called the police, the authorities should be flooding the room any minute.

Jesse had remained mostly calm, but didn't shy from heated debate. He told it like he saw it. Which was a trait Shane could admire, but he would really like to put some distance between them and this room right now.

On his own, that was impossible. He had two big guys on either side, and the room was filled with angry people. There was no escape.

If he did meet the FBI again, it wouldn't be pretty. He had managed to convince them he was more of a victim than a perpetrator – and the slight degree of truth made it an easy story to sell – and that he was willing to help. But a bluff only works once.

He wondered what had happened to Elise. If Carbon had broken though the communication barrier, then she was probably fine. That was Carbon's priority, after all. People like himself were sent to meetings with Rayford and the police.

The noise at the front increased, and Shane fell into a defensive posture without thinking. Several guys moved to grab Jesse, but to Shane's disbelief and shock, their hands slid off as if he was butter.

"Hey!" one of them cried in frustration, trying harder to grab an arm or any part of Jesse. But it was to no avail.

The men beside Shane were momentarily distracted, and he wasn't about to waste this opportunity. Ducking quickly, he spun a one-eighty and pushed through the back door. The plan worked, though the two men stumbled in some form of pursuit.

Jesse had already walked out the first exit, and as Shane caught up to the blonde cowboy, the building's lights shut off suddenly.

He grinned. Carbon was watching, of course. Why had he doubted?

"The stairs," Jesse whispered, one hand on his shoulder to guide him.

Shane didn't need much encouragement, and in his opinion their pace could have been a little quicker. But they made it down the stairs and out the building without anyone trying to stop them. As they were about fifty feet away, several cop cars pulled up by the building, sirens screaming.

"Good timing," Shane murmured to Jesse, keeping his walk brisk.

"Carbon," Jesse whispered back in explanation.

Shane gave a small laugh of victory, but paused when Jesse didn't join in the celebration. "What's wrong?"

Jesse shook his head, and even in the dark Shane could see the tightness of worry on his face.

Elise. Something must have happened to her.

Shane felt guilty. If he hadn't been in that building, no one would have been able to recognize her. Cooperating with the FBI had seemed like his only chance of escape. He tried to not reveal her identity, but of course they could see through his act.

"What happened?" Shane needed to know.

Jesse stopped walking and closed his eyes painfully. "I'm sorry," he said after a minute. "I need some time."

With a sincere look at Shane, Jesse again started walking across the dark campus.

Trailing a bit behind, Shane considered all the options. The police, Rayford... It must be the latter. And even if it was the former, it would only be a matter of time. His capture by Hitchens and ending up with the FBI had convinced him of that. They must be working together.

They were already off campus walking down a random street when Jesse finally stopped to let Shane catch up.

"Elise was captured," he said pointedly. "But it's worse than that."

Worse? "I'm listening," Shane said.

* * * *

When Elise awoke, she was staring at a group of people she had never seen before. Doctors and nurses, standing over her like she was in surgery.

Doing a mental check, Elise noted that her body worked. She wasn't in surgery and she wasn't injured.

What had happened? Who brought her here?

Josh. He probably took her to a hospital after...

The bracelets. Elise jolted fully awake, lifting an arm to see that they were in fact clamped to her wrists.

But she didn't really need to check to know they were there. She could feel them. She could feel vibrations deep inside her body, as if her cells were waking up. Or as if they were being lulled to sleep by another force.

It was power, she knew it.

"How are you feeling?" a doctor asked. She could barely make out their faces, as they were all wearing full scrubs and mouth coverings.

"Fine," she answered, noting that the sickness that had been plaguing her body seemed to have left. It wasn't a feeling of wellness that filled her now, though, it was a tightly wound energy. She was almost trembling.

"A little shaky," she added.

"Shaky?" the doctor asked, motioning to another similarly dressed figure. "In what way?"

"Just… a little trembly inside." She didn't know how to describe it. "Where am I?"

"Don't worry about that right now," the doctor reassured her. "You're safe. We're going to take care of you."

Where was Jesse? Where was Josh? If she was in a hospital, she needed to get out before they figured out who she was and called the police.

She dropped her legs over the side of the bed, pulling out the IV in her arm.

"Hold it!" the doctor called, several of them moving to restrain her. But she shrugged their hands off easily, surprised at her own strength. It was working. The bracelets were working.

The doctors backed off, stepping out of her path.

"Elise!" the same man called.

"Just let her go," another one said quietly.

They knew her name. Her real name. No, her fake name. Her real fake name. The one she had thought was hers for ten years.

She was even more surprised when Dr. Summers met her at the door. "Hello, Elise. How are you feeling?"

She blinked rapidly as a download of information and memories flowed into her mind. "Where's Josh?" she demanded. How had he gotten her to Dr. Summers?

"Who?" the older woman asked, her grey hair pulled into the same tight bun.

Elise studied her. She didn't know who to trust.

"Dear, the hospital gave us a call. I don't know what happened before then."

Glancing around, Elise saw that she was not in a hospital, but a smaller clinic type building. When she looked back at Dr. Summers, she found the woman staring at the bracelets with a strange expression.

Suddenly she was overtaken with regret. These bracelets were from Rayford, she should never have put them on. She needed to get out of here and find Jesse or Carbon.

"It's okay, Elise," Dr. Summers tried to calm her. "We're going to help you."

It was not okay. Jesse's words came back to her plain as day. *They're more like shackles.* She would not be able to take them off. She could feel them painfully tight around her wrist, tiny needle like obtrusions biting into her skin. Just thinking about pulling them off brought pain.

Dr. Summers was backing away from her. "You can't leave now. We can help you."

"Where am I?" Elise demanded, her heart sinking with dread. She could feel it. Deep inside, in every part of her. A coldness that wasn't there before.

"You're in the lab. It's okay," Dr. Summers repeated. "You've been stabilized. Now please, cooperate so we don't have to drug you or take extreme measures."

Some of the doctors had also stepped out into the hallway, all of them staring at her.

Elise felt horribly trapped.

"You've been given a tremendous gift," Summers was almost pleading. "Please, be reasonable."

"Where's my brother?"

Dr. Summers blinked. "Who?"

Elise was furious, and the woman cowered before her. "You know who! Stop lying! Where's Jesse?"

But no one answered.

She had to find him. Taking off down the hallway, Elise sprinted away from them. She had no idea where to start looking, but not here.

She rounded a corner where two armed guards blocked her path. Without thinking, she found herself hurtling at them through the air. She downed one with a kick to the face while her upper torso spun into the other's chest. She felt the wind knock out of him as he fell backwards, and it was only seconds before she was holding both of their guns over unconscious bodies.

Tossing the weapons down the hallway, she took off again, shocked at her own actions. The hallway ended in a waiting room of sorts, but a much worse surprise was waiting there.

She fell flat on her face, breathing hard. But she couldn't move a muscle. Gasping for air, she was relieved when she could roll over and stand up.

"Hello again."

Elise stared up into the face of Dr. Geoffrey Rayford.

"You," she hissed.

"Yes, it's me." He seemed amused, not threatened.

Her head ached and her lungs couldn't get enough air. The exertion had been too much.

"Yes, I know," Rayford commiserated. "You have to work up your strength slowly, get used to the new abilities. Your body must develop evenly."

Elise fought for air, unable to voice the retorts that came to mind.

"You will learn. That was impressive, though. You have a lot of potential."

"I won't work with you," Elise managed to get out between gasps.

"Yes, you will. For now, you will probably lose consciousness soon. Don't fight it, my girl. It's really a special gift you've been given. We'll take good care of you."

Rayford continued speaking, but as the dizziness overtook her, she couldn't resist and tumbled again to the floor, her panicked thoughts overcome by blackness.

Chapter 39

Shane sat at the wooden picnic table, shocked.

He supposed he shouldn't be so shocked, after all he had been through. What *wouldn't* seem natural after all this?

He thought he had understood the basic nature of the situation, no matter how elementary his grasp on the science, but it kept taking turns toward impossibility. There were bracelets, apparently, that were composed of a certain alloy which conducted a particular signal that allowed for Rayford's control mechanisms to work.

Electroporation, Jesse had explained. Dr. Rayford had mastered and refined the technology of high voltage electrical discharge that made cell walls 'leaky' and thus vulnerable to new genetic material. Jesse's face had been dark as he explained the dangers of such a device. Elise's cell walls could become irreversibly damaged.

The exact result of this was lost on Shane, but he could tell by the gravity in Jesse's tone that it would be disastrous.

He further explained that the SynMOs which had been damaging her system were now being actually incorporated into all of her cells. Nanobiosensors not only provided Rayford all the feedback he wanted to study Elise's DNA, but he would be able to manipulate her genetic code through the converter.

Shane tried to swallow the scientific jargon, understanding enough to grasp the implications.

There was a way to fix it, Jesse said firmly. But he wouldn't go into details.

They had reached a small park, which was vacant this time of night except for several homeless men sleeping off to the side. Jesse had disappeared, emotionally overcome.

The blonde man had become completely distraught. When he returned about twenty minutes later, his face was tight with worry and he was drenched in sweat.

"Jesse," Shane stepped off the picnic table. "You can still fix this, right?" He had never seen him like this, Jesse had always been relaxed and confident.

"Jesse?" Shane asked again.

Tormented blue eyes locked onto his own, and grief seemed to leap through the connection. Shane blinked back tears, surprised at the emotion.

"Very soon now," Jesse finally answered.

"Then why …?" Shane gestured towards him. "What's going on?"

"This is why I came here, you know. If there was any other way to build the cure …" his voice trailed off.

Shane bit back his impatience, "What are you saying?"

Jesse paced briefly and looked back up at him. "Carbon is key in all of this. When I leave, she's going to help. And for Elise, she's part of the solution. This is only the beginning."

Now was not the time for coded messages and cryptic language. But something in Jesse's mannerism made Shane hold his tongue.

"I'll be back, just stay and keep an eye out if anyone comes."

Watching Jesse walk back into the dark woods, Shane sat back down at the picnic table. An eerie feeling of dread overshadowed the night, and as he tried to rationalize his fears, he wondered what could possibly happen next.

* * * *

"You're lying."

"No."

"This is ridiculous." Stewart leaned back in the comfortable leather seat, arms crossed. "Absolutely ridiculous."

But it did make sense. All the holes he had been poking through in the official explanations of the Mathis case lined up with this car's theory. And cars weren't supposed to have theories, or talk. Or make people think they were other people.

"You know how valuable your technology is," Stewart pointed out.

"Yes," Carbon replied. "I am the only one who can stabilize Elise's DNA after Jesse repairs it."

"No," Stewart tried to explain. For a supercomputer, this car seemed a little on the dense and naïve side. "Because if word got out, people will be hunting for you. Because your technology is very valuable, and people would pay a lot of money."

"I do not see how this is relevant."

"It doesn't make sense!" Stewart exclaimed. "Dr. Mathis has *this* kind of technology? Why would he waste time embezzling funds?"

"I already informed you that those charges are false. As are the charges of fraud and treason."

He had to concede the point. Her explanation made much more sense than the other. They thought they had concrete evidence against him, but with closer inspection of Dr. Rayford, Stewart suspected that it would fall apart.

"There are other videos, Agent Stewart. Would you like to watch them?"

This car was a boatload of information. He had come to the right place. "Yes, I would."

* * * *

Dr. Rayford stood above her, pacing the floor. "Don't you see, my dear?"

They were in a small, bare room where she had been awakened thirty minutes ago surrounded by white-coats. Initially they had been pleasant, but their attitudes had worsened as she resisted their brainwashing.

Dr. Summers and another woman had left after further efforts to convince Elise to cooperate, and now she was alone with Rayford. She was fighting, but the effort was draining her. That and a tormenting guilt.

"Don't you realize?" Rayford was saying, concern in his voice. "Why do you think your father came for you now? It's been ten years!"

He looked at her sadly, "No, he acted because we forced his hand. He would've left you in obscurity, where no one even knew you existed. He couldn't fix you, so he hid you. But once we finished refining the technology in these bracelets," he motioned at the ornate silver bands on her wrists. "Now he's curious."

"He knows that we are close to understanding this technology and even passing it. We've found the solution for what he thought couldn't be fixed. And he knew we would be looking for you. So, he got there first."

She glared at him, but her mind was fuzzy. She couldn't tell if it was Rayford's control or the constant barrage of lies, but it was almost impossible to focus on anything, to remember anything Jesse or Carbon had said.

"Really, Elise. We want to help you. It's your father you should be worried about."

Fatigue swept over her, and she closed her eyes to get away from the mental stress. Her resolve was slipping, but there was nothing she could do.

"How about we make a deal?" Rayford sat down beside her on the cot. "I know you can still be reasonable. If your father comes to rescue you, you are free to go. But until then, you cooperate with us."

At Elise's immediately sharp glare, the scientist stood and rubbed his hands together. "It's an offer. This doesn't have to be a prison. We just want to run some tests, and develop these gifts you have. They are really incredible, most people would love to be in your shoes. Consider it. Otherwise we'll be forced to continue to keep you under lock and key."

With a look of compassion, he smiled wistfully and headed out the door.

Elise despised the man. He should have been an actor, with his convincing routine of being a nice person. She knew how he could change.

Nevertheless, her resistance didn't seem to be helping anything. Maybe if she got some of these people to trust her, she could eventually escape. Maybe she could utilize the bracelets, since she was stuck with them for now.

Jesse hadn't come yet, Dr. Rayford was right. For all she knew, he was already in prison – or worse. He said not to listen to Rayford, but surely he didn't mean she should sit here and do nothing.

She couldn't get out of here like this, fighting was only wearing her down.

Stifling a tormented cry, Elise dropped her head on the mattress and allowed a tear to slide down her cheek.

* * * *

When Jesse returned, the moonlight revealed an even deeper strain on his face.

Shane was quiet for a few minutes, not sure what to say. And against his better wishes, he was fighting off a heavy sleep dragging his eyes shut.

"Stay awake," Jesse urged him. "Can't you keep watch?"

"Look, its early morning. I haven't slept in… a long time. What am I watching for anyway?"

Jesse swallowed hard. "The police are coming."

Shane jerked around at Jesse's voice, computing what he just said. "Excuse me?"

"I'm not running."

Shane was incredulous. "How do they even know where we are?"

"We were followed," Jesse said simply. "And they are almost here."

* * * *

Elise had no concept of how much time had passed.

"They're not coming," Dr. Rayford told her. He had gone but returned again, just when her exhausted mind was drifting into a black sleep.

"Your brother and your father, they can't do anything now. Those bracelets can never be removed. The nanites I gave you have already bonded to your cells, and the new connection has been established. The process is irreversible. They know that."

Rayford studied her, but she refused to give him a reaction. It wouldn't take much imagination to see the deep hurt inside, and she hated that it was so obvious.

"You actually believe they're coming for *you*," he said with a sneer. "Come, come, child. That's absurd! How did they brainwash you so quickly? Where was your dad these past ten years? Hmm? He didn't save you then, and he won't now."

He turned with a sigh, "Yes, you will see. They haven't come yet, and with good reason. It's hopeless. And this building is protected by police and FBI."

She continued studying the floor, wishing with all her might she could disappear and go anywhere away from this evil man. How had she ever thought he was good? Not that her father was either. It was true, he wasn't here.

No one had come for her. Not Jesse, not Carbon, not Shane. No one.

She was alone.

And it was her fault for putting these cursed bracelets on. She should have known better, should have seen this coming.

But why had Jesse left her? Why didn't he or Carbon warn her?

He did. A small voice mocked her inside.

Memories of her life before. Many foster families, most she had tried to forget. Hurtful words, loveless homes... this is what she remembered as childhood. Why had her dad left her? He could have kept her.

"Come here, Elise," Rayford called.

Fire shot through her muscles as Elise refused to move. Gasping, she was horrified when her legs began to obey. Against her will, her own legs carried her – albeit unsteadily – over to where he was standing.

"Excellent," he smiled. "Why are you fighting this? You can't win. You'll see in time, this is what you were meant for. You chose it."

Her mind and will tried to fight, but the efforts were useless. Her thoughts were already foggy.

"You may rest now, regain your strength. You'll need it tomorrow."

Dr. Rayford disappeared through the simple door, and Elise sagged back onto her cot-like bed. She had never known such pain existed.

* * * *

"It's the way in," Jesse explained simply, though his tone suggested it might not be so simple. "I will find Elise, get the bracelets off, and then start building the remedy."

"That's absurd!" Shane explained, dumbfounded. His friend had made some crazy plans before, but this was way over the top. "They won't let you *near* her."

Jesse held his gaze evenly. "The police are only minutes away."

Shane looked out into the darkness wildly, trying to calm his racing thoughts. "What am I going to do?"

"You'll probably leave."

Shane's eyes flashed in anger. "And just what is that supposed to mean?"

Jesse placed a heavy hand on his shoulder, "You're my friend, Shane. And that won't change."

"This is ridiculous," Shane stepped back and paced, raking his hands through his hair. The wail of many sirens reached his ears. They were very close.

"I'll see you again when I've finished," Jesse offered a faint smile.

Flashing lights were now visible through the trees. "Look, I can't go to jail," Shane backed away, his courage nowhere to be found. Where was that line between bravery and stupidity?

Jesse had turned his attention to the approaching patrol cars, his hands held up in surrender.

This was stupid.

Shane backed a step further and ran for the trees.

* * * *

Elise's exhaustion never left, though she had hardly moved.

Rest. There was no rest. Her body was tingling with fire, yet her skin was cold and clammy.

The wracking pain washed over her in waves, her insides trembling with dread for the next. Yet she could scarcely react, she could do nothing to relieve her body of the pain. If she tried to move, nothing happened.

Finally, a lull. Elise tried to catch her breath, but her lungs refused to draw in more air. Steeling herself for the next assault, she whimpered with the horror of this nightmare.

A wave of powerful emotion swept over her, and it took a minute to identify. Her first instinct was to deny it as her own, shove it somewhere obscure. Someplace dark, where no one could see the ugly truth in her soul.

Hatred.

Not dislike, not simple anger, no. This had developed over time, and threatened to overcome her.

Pure hatred.

It wrapped itself around her soul, choking out any remaining shreds of compassion.

She hated Dr. Rayford. Despised him for doing this to her.

Who? Her mind taunted. *Who is responsible for this?*

No. She resisted, trying to turn her thoughts away.

She didn't have to be this. This wasn't her. She didn't want to be bitter and hate-filled, an echo of the object of her hatred.

No hate. No, her mind pleaded, despising the emotion while it wrapped tighter around her heart.

She should be able to take it, suck it up. Lots of people had it worse.

Who cares? Her mind screamed. Who's helping you now? No one!

Some tried, but they failed too.

Loneliness had its fangs in deep, sunk to the bone. Its tendrils were deeply embedded in her soul and she had no idea how to remove them, or if she could. Did she want to?

Why? Her soul ached from this torment. *Why?*

Her best efforts were not enough. Why?

She didn't want to face this. Couldn't face this. The torment was too great. *Who* was responsible again?

No! Her mind slammed the door on the question. It didn't matter.

Her father. *Daddy.* Her own thoughts mocked her. The one who should have protected you. He fed you to the wolves.

No! He is the only hope out! If he wasn't really going to help, then she might as well cooperate with Rayford. What was the difference? The problem wasn't her dad, was it? It was someone closer.

Herself. She was weak, and couldn't do anything right. She had messed up twice putting these bracelets on, it was a trend.

No, deep down she couldn't blame the others for leaving, or for keeping their distance.

And she was mad because it wasn't fair.

Her brother was a genius. He had done everything well, and no doubt her father loved him for it. He was hard not to like. But that left her all alone.

The failure. The one who was abandoned to be raised by the state, by a cold system. A girl with no identity, no family.

The hatred only deepened.

How could she have known? Who asked her if she wanted to be an experiment? It wasn't fair! She didn't deserve this any more than the next person.

"Why?" she wailed.

In anguish, Elise tried to sit up again. The shame and guilt were weighing her down, overshadowed by bitterness.

But as another wrack of pain filled her body, it was all she could do to hang on.

Chapter 40

Richardson surveyed the shaggy blond man in front of him. In no way did he appear much of a threat. To the contrary, he could've been dropped right off of the hippie train, especially if he sported some tie-dye and dreadlocks.

The police had apprehended him without a fight at some obscure little park outside the city. An eyewitness had called in a tip, and it didn't take long to find him with the entire force already mobilized.

He sighed, "Well, son. Looks like you're in a lot of trouble."

The man stared at him with intense blue eyes, but his expression was mild and he didn't open his mouth.

"Should I call you Jesse? Or Alex?"

He watched the man's reaction, but there was nothing to discern. "You are Samuel Mathis' son, are you not?"

Still the man remained silent.

"Understandably you are pleading the fifth," Richardson leaned forward, motioning with his hands to get his point across. "But this is not the time. If you have something to say, say it now. Do you know what they want me to do with you?"

No response.

"They say you are a dangerous terrorist, leaving you virtually no rights. Not to a trial, not to a jury. Nothing. Do you get it?"

"I understand," the man spoke clearly.

"Good," Richardson leaned back. "Because if they have their way, you will become their next little science experiment. That being considered, I'm all ears. I believe in justice, and your story seems to hold merit. Convince me."

But again, the man maintained a withdrawn expression, offering no explanation.

"Darn it, man!" Richardson exclaimed. "I've heard of all your stories, and you seem to be quite an orator."

Silence.

"Let me get this straight," he tried again. "You say Rayford is the one who destroyed your Dad's work and research, that he poisoned your sister, that he framed your Dad, and even now is pursuing science with disastrous implications and must be stopped."

The man only eyed him with a heavy look.

"You are Alexander Mathis, aren't you? Dr. Samuel Mathis' son?" he repeated the question.

"Yes."

Clearly the man was not in a talkative mood. For his sake, that wasn't good.

A fierce pounding came on the door. Richardson glanced back to his prisoner, who showed no reaction.

"Sir!" one of his agent's voice came loudly from the other room. "Time is running out!"

Drawing a long sigh, Richardson stood. "Last chance, kid."

No chance, apparently. The man never uttered a word.

"Okay, okay," Richardson complained, opening the door carefully. "I hear you."

"Did he confess?" the excited agent asked.

Not sure why, Richardson felt his shoulders sag as he responded reluctantly. "No. He won't talk."

"Then the claims against him must stand. If he won't fight them…"

Richardson glared at the younger man, "I know, agent. Stay with him."

Hawthorne obeyed quickly, leaving him to face his toughest audience: Dr. Rayford and the other members of Excalibur. They had come to the station to after learning this man had been taken into custody. How they got that information was a good question, but it really didn't matter anymore.

"Richardson," Rayford rose to greet him. "How did it go?"

Staring into the respected geneticist's face, Richardson wondered how this got so twisted. He should have retired a long time ago. "I can't find anything to fault the man."

Dr. Summers gasped, "But sir, he's been stirring up the students and causing riots right and left. And his threats, those cannot be ignored. We're talking mass destruction. Who knows what he has planned!"

Another scientist rose, "Agent, this man claimed he would personally destroy our colleague, and all of our work. He is a terrorist, inciting people with false words! He knows too much and threatens to undo everything we've accomplished here."

"Did he deny the claims?" Rayford asked quietly. Gathering the answer from Richardson's silence, he frowned further and continued, "If he can't offer any explanation, we already have records of what he's been 'teaching'. We're risking total exposure. The least we can do is ascertain how much he knows. Many lives are in the balance."

"He has not broken any law," Richardson pointed out. "I need proof to detain someone as a terrorist."

"We have more than enough proof!" Dr. Summers protested. "If he is the son of Dr. Mathis, he may know dangerous information. That cannot be ignored. Worse, he was flinging death threats right and left! The man is insane. And dangerous."

"And legally, he doesn't exist," a woman pointed out from the back corner. "He won't allow tests to identify him as Alexander Mathis, and records of this 'Jesse' are nowhere to be found. Fingerprints turn up nothing, and he doesn't even have a last name. He might not even be American."

Dr. Rayford's eyes narrowed. "He may indeed be working with Dr. Mathis, gathering intelligence to report to another country. He admits that he has been with his father all this time. We need to know everything he knows. The law demands it."

Richardson kept his eyes on everyone in the room, weighing his options. There weren't very many.

"This is the technology that Dr. Mathis was trying to keep from us, selling out to the Chinese or whomever," Dr. Summers' eyes flashed. "He knew the possibilities were limitless. Not only does this man need to be eliminated as a threat, but he must be studied to learn more of this genetic mutation. The military implications threaten national security. This isn't a light matter, agent. The fate of our country is at stake here. We might not get another chance."

"I know my job, *doctor*," Richardson informed her curtly.

"And Elise, or Irene," Dr. Rayford brought up. "Her life is certainly in danger. We know he had something to do with her situation. He probably has critical information, and may be the only person who knows what's been done to her. She'll die if we don't do something, and fast."

Maintaining her silence for several seconds, Dr. Summers spoke again. "There's not much margin here. We need to act now."

The weight of condemning a potentially innocent man crushed Richardson, but his hands were tied. "It will be officially recorded as against my recommendation."

With a stiff nod, he authorized another agent to retrieve the accused terrorist with Hawthorne. "Report your findings directly to Director LaSalle. I'm clearing out my desk."

Dr. Rayford took his hand solemnly. "Sir, you serve your nation well. Such decisions are necessarily difficult, but you just saved many lives."

"Yeah," Richardson shrugged off the hand. Pushing past them out of the room, he headed to relive an old habit.

He had kicked smoking when he retired, but now he felt ready to go through a whole pack. Shuddering as the door slammed behind him, Agent

Richardson made a beeline for the nearest convenient store. Hopefully Stewart was up to something, but one rogue agent against the entire force was a far-fetched chance.

He never should have left retirement.

Chapter 41

The moon continued to cast eerie shadows through the forest, but Shane didn't dare walk any closer to the road. It would be daylight in a few hours, whatever that would accomplish.

He wasn't sure what to do next, and he was frustrated by his lack of options. Part of him screamed to get the heck out of Dodge, leave while the going's good. But it wasn't good, and he was still headed back to that cursed lab.

Jesse's plan was to get arrested, which left Shane where exactly?

Releasing a long breath through clenched teeth, Shane drudged on. He had his cell phone, but couldn't bring himself to call Carbon. She would call first, he had decided.

So far, he was wrong.

Would the police hand Jesse over to Rayford? The man hadn't committed any crime, for goodness sakes. How did they even get a warrant?

A cheerful ring assaulted his ears. Finally.

"Hello, Carbon," he answered the phone.

"What are your intentions?" her smooth voice asked.

He let out a deranged chuckle. As if he knew. He felt guilty for deserting Jesse, but what could he do when the man practically leapt into the backseat of a police cruiser?

"Shane?" Carbon broke the silence.

"Yes, I heard you. I don't know."

"If you are willing, I could use your help."

"Do I have to get arrested too?" he retorted sarcastically.

"Shane, I cannot offer you more information. There *is* a plan," Carbon reminded him.

"I keep hearing that." Maybe Jesse was right. He had displayed some impressive abilities, so making the cure might not even be that hard. Then why had the man been so upset before his capture?

"Do you doubt that we can succeed? Why are you worried?"

Shane grimaced, "No deep questions right now, Carbon."

She conceded easily. "Fine. Are you in?"

Shane released a heavy sigh. Jesse had certainly acted like he was walking to his death, but he had also assured him that this would all work out.

"Yes. I'm in."

* * * *

Elise struggled upright as alarm bells sounded within the building. At first she thought she was dreaming, but the shrill warning was too realistic.

Blinking against the pain, she realized that she had actually managed to sleep.

Her body was feeling better, but a heaviness pulled her down even as she slid off of the cot. The piercing whine didn't let up; the panic it inspired not even rational.

Was this some sort of drill? Was this a fire, and they might leave her here to die?

The door burst open as two armed guards flew in, several more running past in the hallway.

"She's here," one yelled into his radio. The other man slammed the door shut, securing the lock. "Watch her!" he shouted to the other, bracing his weight against the door.

The other man looked at her through nervous brown eyes. "Nothing funny!" He had his machine gun trained on her, apparently not aware that she could barely move.

Elise put her hands up, fighting to calm her racing heart. "Easy," she tried to calm the man, wondering why he was so scared.

Their radios cackled a harsh message that she couldn't understand, but they only looked more strained.

"What's going on?" Elise asked, noticing the odd tingling that was returning to her senses. She stared into the barrel of the man's gun, noticing the curving grooves inside the metal.

"Shh!" The guard hushed her, pointing his gun more ominously.

The power was back. She could feel it.

Another cackle from the radio. *"Nearing your position, watch out! Delta three, authorized."*

The man wrestled her into a headlock, pointing the gun at her and holding her like a human shield. Elise gasped for air and her body responded purely on instinct.

Swatting the gun away, she jerked it out of the man's grasp and brought the butt sharply against his head. He collapsed, and she spun quickly with the weapon aimed at the other guard.

He turned in surprise, but he wasn't alone in his reaction. What had she just done?

A loud commotion sounded outside the door, gunshots ricocheting down the hallway.

"What's going on?" Elise demanded, adrenaline and that trembling power racing through her veins.

The remaining guard began to open his mouth when the door vibrated behind him. With a horrid tearing noise, the entire frame was ripped out of the wall and thrown aside.

A reverberating crash echoed through the building and shook the foundation at her feet as the door and frame were tossed aside. "Jesse?" Elise gasped, shocked to see her brother standing where the doorway had been.

His face was terrifying, and he turned his fierce gaze to the guard. His blue eyes burned with an unnatural fury.

"Step aside," he commanded. The astonished man complied quickly, dropping his weapon on the ground.

Elise could barely reconcile the figure before her as her brother, and she found herself cowering towards the back of the room.

He looked directly at her. She tried but couldn't break away from the intensity of his eyes. Solemn and burdened, he was regarding her with something like compassion. "Elise," he took a step towards her.

"Stop!" Rayford shrieked, running up behind Jesse. "Elise, don't listen to him! Did you feel that power? That strength? That's what your Dad tried to steal! He only wants to use you like a puppet. Don't give in!"

Jesse didn't even bother looking at the doctor, who stayed safely out of arms' reach. Elise found herself unable to glace away. Rayford. How did Jesse get here?

Dr. Rayford was right, she could feel the power. The strength, and *she* could control it. She lifted the huge gun, which felt weightless in her hand, aware that she could crush the metal if she wanted.

"Elise, come here," Jesse softly beckoned.

Elise shook her head, trying to clear the thoughts. A strong instinct urged her to attack him, to destroy him. Fear consumed her restraint. She had betrayed her family. They would torment and humiliate her if she went with them. They would control her, destroy her.

Jesse reached out and touched her. The heavy gun dropped from her hands.

"Help," she managed to croak as the power fled her in an instant. She collapsed to the ground, painful fire falling over her like a blanket.

Jesse caught her as she fell into him, every part of her body screaming.

With his touch the torment receded, the only pain remaining in her wrists as the bracelets' needle sharp edges dug deep into her flesh. Jesse looked her in the eyes as the others in the room stood back, no one daring to move.

Elise was too exhausted to speak, overcome with the trauma of war in her body. She couldn't stand on her own.

"What are you doing?" Rayford shouted in confusion.

But he gave no answer, gently picking up Elise's left arm and studying the bracelet twisted into her wrist.

"You can't do anything now," Rayford scoffed. "The nanites have bonded to her cells, the code has been changed. Even if you could remove the bracelets, it wouldn't do any good."

"Elise," Jesse regarded her with concern. "You have to trust me. This is going to hurt."

Elise swallowed, her dry throat like a pincushion. It couldn't be worse than what she just went through. She managed a small nod.

"Don't touch her!" Rayford warned, but even to Elise's strained vision he was staying a good ten feet away from them. The doctor must be scared of her brother.

Jesse gave her a smile, but there was something deeper in his eyes. "We're going to cut this experiment short."

He let her down to the floor, and she managed to sit upright against the wall. Her legs ached, every muscle in them trembling. She wouldn't be going anywhere on her own.

"What are you doing?" Rayford demanded again, and again Jesse ignored him. Facing her, Jesse picked up her arms in his hands.

"Remember." He smiled at her tenderly.

She struggled to hold his gaze, tears forming in her eyes.

"Ok, Carbon," Jesse said under his breath.

Elise screamed as an electrical current jolted through her wrists, the needle sharp incisors ripping out suddenly.

The bracelets clattered to the floor as they fell off. The pain was over as quickly as it started, and Elise blinked to focus as a wave of white washed over her vision.

Jesse snatched up the silver bands, deftly sliding one onto each of his wrists.

Before she could comprehend what had happened, her brother clutched his arms to his chest and fell to the floor with a heavy thud. He lay there, motionless.

"Jesse?" she stammered. She struggled to reach him, sharp pain still flooding her body.

There was a gasp from someone in the room, and Elise glanced up to see Rayford beholding the scene in bewilderment. "What the...?" he muttered.

Horrified, Elise crawled close enough to see that Jesse was still breathing. The bracelets had latched onto his wrists as they had hers. As she felt for a pulse, warm blood trickled down her hand from the bracelets' wounds.

"Security," Dr. Rayford snapped at one of the men. "Take the girl back to her room."

"No," Elise whimpered. What had he done? She would have fought as a guard scooped her up, but her muscles wouldn't respond. All strength had been sapped from her body. Her vision was blurring, and she struggled to hang on to consciousness.

What had Jesse done?

Chapter 42

Shane sat at a table outside a coffee shop. Carbon had instructed him vaguely to wait somewhere near the lab, so he had selected the closest outdoor cafe to set up shop.

Shop included a newspaper and sunglasses as a disguise, which seemed to be working quite well. But he had to admit the jitters were hard to shake. Was Jesse's plan even working? How could he spend hours in hostile territory building a chemical compound, and especially while being in custody?

Since Carbon was helping, and Jesse did have 'abilities', he supposed anything was possible. But it still made him nervous.

Part of him worried over what was next. They were so close to achieving their goal, what would happen then? Would they finally get to meet the elusive Dr. Mathis? But success seemed too dismal to spend much time in that line of thinking.

His phone vibrated on the metal table. Finally.

"It's about time," he answered.

Carbon ignored the comment, "I have sent help to you. The man has your earwig, and will assist you in recovering Elise."

"Wait. You just recruited a random guy?"

"I recruited you."

"That's not... It's not the same," he sputtered. "Where did you find this guy?"

"Do not worry about him, just focus on your task. I wish you the best."

"Hey, wait! Carbon?"

But the phone call had ended. Shane growled in frustration. Why did she always do that? She didn't even tell him when this unidentified 'help' was coming, or what his 'task' was.

Ruffling his newspaper, he brought it back up to his face, pretending to read.

Why was he doing this again? He had already been captured once this week, that was enough.

No, he knew why. There were several reasons, but the main one was a sick girl who needed his help.

He remembered her embrace, wondered why he cared. What was it that made people do ridiculous things for one another, even when they were almost strangers?

There was no answer, but as he continued to pretend to read his paper, he found himself busy pushing aside thoughts of failure, death and capture. No, everything was going to work out fine. It had to.

* * * *

Dr. Rayford leaned over his computer screen, amazed at the results of his tests. An hour ago he had been livid, but now he wasn't sure what to think.

This was indeed Alexander Mathis, Dr. Samuel Mathis' eldest and only son. His genetics were the perfect example of all of Dr. Mathis' theories. Theories that Rayford thought had been proven wrong with Elise.

The cells each had functioning receptors for signal; stable data ports built right into the malleable DNA. Well, they had been functioning. Up until this young man decided to put those bracelets on.

It was smart, in a way. The only means of preventing anyone from putting them back onto Elise was to put them on another. Rayford had no idea how he got them off of her to start with. Some sort of signal interference, he supposed.

Whatever it was, it clearly didn't work very well, because the bracelets were now thoroughly embedded into Jesse's body. The signal that had been there was completely blocked by the signal emitted by the bracelets, Rayford's efficient SynMOs already spreading through every organ and tissue in his body. Whatever 'higher functions' the eldest Mathis child had been using, they were long gone. Erased.

Samuel must have miscalculated somewhere. Now Rayford not only had Irene Mathis, he had Alex as well. He didn't want to underestimate his admittedly brilliant former colleague, but there was no reason not to proceed. A little more research and he could figure out exactly what was going on in the young man's body, and what he was trying to accomplish.

In the meantime, he had made absolutely certain that the man would not be escaping again anytime soon. Rayford couldn't help trying to rationalize both Samuel's motives and possible plan. Far be it from him to underestimate the man again, but the more he uncovered, the more he was convinced of one fact.

His old friend had made a serious mistake.

* * * *

Shane jumped as his newspaper was snatched away.

"You've been reading the same page for ten minutes, Lawson," a gruff voice informed him. "And those sunglasses aren't much of a disguise."

Surprised, Shane blinked at the tall strawberry blonde man in front of him. *This* is who Carbon brought?

"You?" Shane asked, incredulous.

"Who were you expecting?" The FBI agent reached into his pocket. "Here. That's from Carbon."

Shane recovered from his shock enough to accept the tiny earwig. "You, uh... you met Carbon?"

The man grunted and took a seat across from him. "Yeah. She's pretty special."

Why would Carbon recruit an FBI agent?

"This is what we're going to do," the man began.

"Wait," Shane interrupted. "Can I have a name?"

The man tossed him a look of disgust. "Alan. Now, we're going to sneak in there and find Ms. Perry. Or Mathis, whatever. Elise. You will take her out of the building and get lost. I'm doing some recon; I want to catch these people red-handed. You will stay out of my way, got it?"

Shane swallowed, trying to ignore his new partner's antagonism. "What about Jesse?"

"Who?"

"Jesse..." Shane repeated slowly, not to be misunderstood. "Carbon didn't tell you about him?"

Alan regarded him with doubt.

"Elise's brother?"

The man's face relaxed. "Ah, yes. Alexander Mathis. Yeah, Carbon said he was building the cure. She said he would come out when he was done. Our job is to get Elise. Or rather *your* job. I'll help you first, and then disappear."

Shane studied the FBI agent's expression, "Shouldn't you be in there with them, being FBI and all? How can I trust you?"

Alan grimaced. "You can't, Lawson. You can't trust anybody here."

That was really reassuring. "Thanks. I look forward to storming the fort with you."

"Good." The agent was curt.

Shane sighed, not quite comfortable with circumstances. But Elise was in there, Jesse was somewhere, and Carbon had to know what she was doing. "How much time before we go in?"

The agent checked his watch. "Forty minutes. Until then, read your paper."

He pushed the newspaper back in Shane's face. "But I suggest turning the page."

"Thanks. They don't teach deputies to do that, you know. Must be an FBI thing."

Alan just looked at him.

With a shrug, Shane pointedly turned the newspaper to the next section.

"I'll be back," Alan promised before turning to head into the coffee shop.

For better or for worse. Forty minutes.

Chapter 43

In the central operating room, Dr. Rayford was putting the finishing touches on a new compound. After some research, he had decided on several things. First, he needed to get the bracelets off of Alex and back onto Elise. Time was running out for the girl, and if she didn't get them back on soon, the DNA could destabilize. Second, he wanted to learn exactly what was going on in Alex's body and how Samuel had managed to build such a perfect specimen. Last and most importantly, he couldn't reach any conclusions as to why Dr. Mathis had sent his son here, and the man's troubling lack of resistance worried him deeply. As such, it was far too dangerous to keep Alex alive.

Fortunately, all three of these objectives lined up, and this little compound he had devised should solve the problem.

"Kay," Dr. Rayford walked up behind the older woman and put a hand on her shoulder. "Why don't you go fetch some lunch?"

She looked up from her microscope, glancing between him and the unconscious man lying on the operating table. "Now? But I just..."

"Don't worry," Rayford interrupted. "I can handle things here, and you need a break. There are guards outside if I need them and constant surveillance. We're about to jump into a very long day, so take a moment to rest. And bring me something?"

Dr. Summers knew better than to ask him to clarify again, so with a final glance at their 'patient', she peeled off her plastic gloves and stepped out of the room.

Releasing his breath, Rayford retrieved a small glass bottle from the refrigerated storage. Pulling a small amount of its contents through a needle, he tapped the syringe twice with his finger. Everything was difficult now, his prosthetic limb unable to mimic the precise motions of his missing hand. Anger flared up anew, and he fought to keep a level head.

The son of his enemy lay motionless, though even unconscious he looked to be in pain. Satisfaction swept over Rayford as he realized what he had. Dr. Mathis' experiments were undoubtedly limited to his children, his ever precious theory demanding such. Such science had its advantages. It also had its limits.

And now, every piece of data Samuel had destroyed, every recognition the favored scientist had stolen, they would all be returned to Rayford. Certainly, there was work to be done, extracting DNA and playing with the signals. But he was a patient man.

Dr. Rayford quickly inserted the clear liquid into Alex's arm. Moments later, he was staring into the clear blue eyes of Samuel Mathis' son. They were no longer glowing that unnatural color, but that was because his DNA was now reduced to a *normal* human. No more help from Daddy.

"Good morning, son," Dr. Rayford smiled, working to appear civil. "You've gotten yourself into some trouble." He gestured towards the silver bracelets entwined into flesh.

Alex didn't take his gaze off of Rayford, and the intensity the man's countenance it bothered him.

The grey-haired scientist leaned closer. "What are you doing? What do you think you are accomplishing here?"

The man gave no reply.

Just like his father. Dr. Rayford was instantly seized with hatred. He pushed harder, "I suppose you came back to save your sister." Upon Alex's expression, Rayford knew he had hit gold. "Come on, you must know how futile that is. Look at her!"

His eyes blazed with indignation, with conviction. "What is there to save? This should be more like damage control. I mean, you wouldn't want your name on that. One sample of that DNA and your father's work is ruined."

Alex's face remained the same.

"What? Even now, you think you have some sort of plan. Some sort of way out." The handsome grey head shook solemnly, "I actually expected more resistance. Disappointing."

He glanced at Alex, who again did nothing but return the glance with the mildest expression. It was like some kind of disease infecting all of them. First Samuel, then his children. Fools.

"She can *never* access those functions again, don't you get it? You may have gotten the bracelets off for now, but her DNA is completely bonded with the nanites. You cannot bypass that. She *chose* to give me control."

The man's blue eyes flashed. Finally, a response.

"Elise made a grave mistake, yes," Alex said through clenched teeth. "But you *stole* from her. Life and health, family, her amazing abilities. You worked with Dad, he was your friend. How could you do that?"

"Your father," Rayford lashed out, his eyes burning with fury. "Is an insolent, stubborn and proud man. He didn't deserve all of that. Why was it always *his* way? He always had to be right. His theory was faulty, and I went to the only means I could in order to prove that. He didn't listen. He never did."

"That's not true," Alex argued. "He listened and even tried to help you understand his work. But you were too jealous and focused on yourself. A big project, major funding, secrecy ... and you were left out. It was more than you could take."

"Shut up!" Rayford raged. His whole body stiffened, and his lip curled into an ugly sneer. "Samuel's theory – and as I see now, his practical science – is broken and useless." Tapping Alex's wrist, he let his finger rest on the visible vein. "This has everything I need to prove that. It is a waste, but the world will be better off in the end."

Resigned and accepting, the blond man stifled another spasm of pain and closed his eyes. If only escaping reality was that easy.

"As for your sister," Rayford continued, "Irene has already made her choice, but don't worry, I'll take good care of her. She's quite valuable."

"You have no idea," Alex returned evenly.

"Oh, yes. But I do," Rayford quipped in his British accent. "We'll do things legally, finishing what Samuel could not. And you will need to be out of the picture. I've seen what you're capable of, and I know you're capable of much more. As you've probably noticed, whatever 'link' your father had established cannot penetrate my interference. And as your power is completely dependent on that link, you can't do anything at the moment."

The man's face contorted with the agony of his cells beginning to die from the inside out. Internal organs would be shutting down about now, heart failure in the next hour or so.

"So your DNA proved your dad's theory, that he could internally stabilize the perfect system." The scientist threw his head back and laughed. "But what a great system, no? Run a little interference, and it all comes crashing down."

"My dad has the only working theory, and you know it."

"However you want to look at it. Doesn't matter anyway." Standing, Rayford shook his head. "Why don't you try to ask for help, see if your dad can reach you now. And where is he, by the way? Why doesn't he come rescue you?"

Walking over to his array of chemicals on the marble countertop, Rayford retrieved a fresh needle and syringe filled with his newest compound. Time was ticking down for the young son of his old colleague. But advancement to the human race was just around the corner.

"Don't worrying about answering, son. It may take time, but I will decipher every piece of information hidden in these genes of yours."

Truly, Samuel must have no idea how advanced Rayford's technology had become. What was begun shortly after World War Two was about to reach its final stage. No need to wait any longer.

He set a bar stool beside the table where Alex was strapped down and sat slowly, purposefully. Every time he looked at the resolved face, it only served to infuriate him further. And they had called *him* arrogant? Is this how you treat someone who holds your life in their hands?

Grabbing the younger man's forearm, he stabbed the needle violently into soft skin, pleased at the wincing response and pain that flashed across the calm face. Drawing the needle back, Rayford confirmed that he was in a vein.

"Giving up your life for nothing." He smirked and grasped Alex's arm tighter, "Clearly your father didn't even care to save you. And for what?"

Rayford watched with growing confidence as he pushed the dark compound into the man's bloodstream. He would remember this moment, and the world would someday realize its importance. It was almost over.

"Your father was a fool and cared nothing for his children. Your death will at least be used to better science. Remember that when you start to doubt if it was worth it."

Chapter 44

Alan motioned for Shane to follow him around the corner.

Carbon's voice crackled in his ear, "We may lose communication in the building, so listen carefully. There are several men at each entrance. The front is heavily guarded with four plainclothes agents outside, another FBI agent just beyond the door, and two uniformed policemen."

They both paused, listening for her instructions.

"The rear entrance is locked, but I will be able to remotely unlock it. Fortunately, these systems are electronic and I have gained access."

Shane glanced up at Alan, again having to work to squelch his doubts.

"There are two men watching the rear entrance outside, and two uniformed policemen inside the door. I will distract the police officers, but you will need to find a way past the two outside."

Alan raised his eyebrows with an amused look. Hopefully that meant that the FBI agent had an ingenious plan already worked out.

"Once inside," Carbon continued, "You will need to head left. I will unlock the doors you need to go through, so move quickly but pay attention. Elise is isolated in a small room, and she may be unconscious."

Shane found his mind wandering. How could he be distracted at a time like this?

"Bring her out the way you came in. If we reestablish contact, I will give you further instructions. If not, proceed to a safe location to wait for Jesse."

She made it sound so simple. Somehow Shane doubted the execution would be black and white.

"In five minutes I will distract the policemen. Good luck."

Alan turned to him. "All right, deputy. I have an idea. Think Star Wars."

"What?" Shane asked.

Pulling handcuffs out of his pocket, Alan smiled. "Presumably, they don't know I'm not on this case right now. And being FBI, they should know how to keep quiet."

Shane groaned. Why did he always have to be a prisoner? Real or fake, he didn't want to be arrested. He peeked around the corner. The two men were each off to a side, barely visible in the building's shadow.

"Can't we just take them out?" he asked.

"We're buying time, Lawson. That would definitely give us more attention than we need. And I'm not going to attack two FBI agents."

Sure, because this guy wasn't considered a dangerous criminal yet. Shane had nothing left to lose.

"We have three minutes," Alan reminded him. "Turn around."

With a hard glare, Shane did as he was told. He hoped the cold metal on his wrists was not a foreshadowing of how this day would end.

"I could get in so much trouble for this," Alan muttered as he led Shane towards the entrance.

"You?" Shane snorted. Sympathy was in short supply. Why was he doing this again?

As they drew closer, Alan dug his fingernails into Shane's arms.

"Ouch!" he complained. What was this guy's problem?

"You're supposed to have been arrested. Don't look comfortable."

That wasn't difficult.

The two men stepped out of the shadows as they approached, hands hovering over their weapons. Shane recognized one from Rayford's mansion. Moe or Curly, he didn't remember.

"Agent Stewart," Alan flashed his badge at them. His voice was gruff. "This is under the radar, don't mention it to anyone." He glowered at them menacingly. "Be careful. They're planning something, so don't be obvious. We're drawing them in."

The two men nodded, looking pleased.

"'Bout time someone brought you in," one of them grinned at Shane.

"Pay attention," Alan snapped, shoving Shane through the door. "No squawking. Our communications are being monitored."

The men acknowledged Alan's order and stepped back into the shadows. That wasn't too bad.

Once in the hallway, Alan continued to push him along. The police officers were nowhere to be found, so Carbon must have done her job.

"You can take these off now," Shane whispered.

Alan tossed him a severe look, and Shane momentarily panicked. What if Carbon had been wrong to trust this man?

With a small laugh, Alan retrieved the key and quickly removed the cuffs. Who could be joking at a time like this?

But the FBI agent's face straightened instantly. "Let's go."

Shane took off, following him at a jog.

"If you can hear me," Carbon's voice crackled with static. "You are headed in the correct direction. Take the fifth door on your left, and ..."

But the rest was garbled beyond recognition.

Nevertheless, a strange calmness flooded Shane, his focus on listening for which doors' locks whirred open as they passed.

This compound was surprisingly similar to Rayford's lab in Colorado, though less high-tech.

He and Alan slowed to a casual walk as they passed a group of white coated scientists. No one tossed them any special glances, and Shane breathed an inward sigh of relief.

"It's a shame," one of them was saying. "He had even more potential than his sister."

Shane's ears perked, and he exchanged a troubled glance with Alan.

"I think we can learn more this way," another voice argued, but the conversation was muffled as the group rounded the corner they had just come from.

This way? How did they know about Jesse?

Alan put a finger to his lips, motioning for silence. Shane made an effort to step lighter, shadowing the FBI agent as he pushed his way into a room the group had come from.

The lights were off, but the many computer monitors cast a blue hue around the room. It was filled with test tubes, beakers, and other stuff Shane would consider normal for a lab.

However, it also contained monitors that looked like they belonged in a hospital. Another quick glance around confirmed that the bluish light wasn't mainly from the computers. A large rectangular window looked into another room where a person was strapped to an operating table in the center.

Shane stepped closer, blinking in shock.

"Who's that?" Alan whispered, stepping up behind him.

But Shane couldn't answer, he simply stared in horror. It wasn't possible.

"That's her brother, isn't it?" Alan asked quietly.

When Shane didn't respond, the man placed a hand on his shoulder. "I'm sorry," he offered.

Shane brushed off the hand as he moved past the initial shock. "We don't know that he's dead," he darted over to one of the monitors, each displaying a constant flat line. Heart rate, blood pressure… they were all zero.

Voices sounded nearby, and a door opened into the room where Jesse lay. Dr. Rayford walked in with several other people.

Alan shoved Shane down beneath the window and dropped to the floor beside him. "We need to get out of here."

Rayford's crisp British voice was muffled, but Shane could still make out the words. "We did everything we could, but we could not stabilize his system. His cells rejected the SynMOs." His voice lifted slightly in pitch, "At least the bracelets detached easily."

"Look, doctor." It was the voice of that old lady in the café and the classroom. "A sample of his blood. It's really strange; it appears separated and dehydrated."

There was a muted muttering, tinny clanking of metal and glass, and the whir of several machines.

Someone sighed, and Dr. Rayford spoke again. "Take him over to Room Twenty, we can't risk any more decay setting in. Kay, over here. Look at the count of nanites…"

But Shane didn't listen to the rest of Rayford's sentence. He was dead. Jesse had failed.

Shane's thoughts were jerked back as Alan shook him.

"Get a hold of yourself," the man said sternly. "You can grieve later. We need to get Elise."

Elise. Was she even alive?

Alan grabbed his shoulder painfully. "Lawson. Pull yourself together."

He could still hear Rayford's voice. The scientist sounded excited.

"Now," Alan whispered urgently, pulling him across the room and through the door. "We have to find Elise."

Something finally clicked in Shane, and Alan's tense face came into focus. They needed to get out of here.

Alan noticed the change. "Good. Follow me, I think I know where to find her."

He followed behind, strangely detached and numb.

Find Elise, get out. He clung to the task. It was all that mattered now.

* * * *

Elise glanced up, her body melting from fatigue and pain. She had been locked back in a small room and received no word from Jesse or anyone else.

Indefinite time had passed, and though she never lost consciousness, she came close several times. She was stuck in a nightmarish hell, and could barely discern what had actually happened or what she had imagined.

But the bloody marks on her wrists wouldn't let her forget. Why had Jesse put the bracelets on? Why didn't he just carry her out of there?

She would have cried, but she was numb with the horror. Horror that wouldn't go away.

When she heard the door swing open, she didn't even look up. Rayford had probably come to torment her further.

"Elise."

She jerked her head up. Shane was standing in the doorway, another man behind him.

"Hurry," the other man urged, glancing back and forth down the hallway.

"Can you walk?" Shane asked.

"I don't know," she said honestly, attempting to get up off the cot. Her bare feet hit the cold floor like pins and needles, and she clenched her teeth.

"No," Shane answered his own question. "I'll carry you."

"Hurry," the other man pressed again, stepping back out of her line of vision. All she could see was the pistol he held ready.

Shane picked her up gently, and she noticed his vacant expression. "What's wrong?" she asked, terrified for her brother. "Where's Jesse?"

"He said he'd find us later." Shane refused to meet her eyes. He turned to the other man, "Let's go."

The man nodded, "You first. I'll cover you until you're out of the building."

Soon they were jogging down hallways, headed for the rear exit. Elise clung onto Shane's neck as she was bounced around. Why wasn't Jesse here? What was he waiting for?

"Freeze!" A female voice commanded, and Elise turned her head to see a dark skinned woman pointing a gun at them.

Shane's friend had his gun pointed at her as well. "No, Liz. Don't."

The woman's eyes flashed between the members of their small group. "*She's* here?"

"Trust me," the man was saying. "I have all the proof we need."

She didn't look completely convinced, but brought her gun down slightly. "Proof of what?"

"We've been set up. The whole team. I know what's really going on. Trust me."

"You better be right," Liz warned.

"You know me," the man returned. "Now help us get her out of here, and I'll show you all the proof you need."

She stared at him hard in the face before lowering her gun. "There are two guards that way. Follow me."

Shane looked skeptical, but the other man followed without hesitation.

Elise's heart was pounding, and she was frustrated she couldn't even walk. Hanging on to Shane was hard enough, her muscles as weak as jell-o.

"Wait here," Liz instructed them. "Two policemen are at the door, I'll distract them."

"Hey guys," she called, walking towards them. "I've got something you need to check out over here. Hurry! I'll watch the door."

Elise heard the patter of feet moving the opposite way.

"Now," the other man whispered. "I've got the two outside."

Craning her neck, Elise strained to see as Shane carried her out the door.

"Get out of here," the man admonished. Not that Shane needed urging, already sprinting away from the building.

"Hey!" another voice cried, a man emerging from the shadows with a drawn gun. "Stop!"

Elise glanced back as Shane ran, watching as their accomplice struck the man at the base of the neck with his gun, quickly aiming at another figure that had likewise emerged.

The scene disappeared from view as Shane turned down the street. He was breathing heavily, and slowed to a fast walk.

"What happened?" Elise asked.

But he still wouldn't look at her, his eyes scanning the street instead. "We need a taxi," he said breathlessly. "Try to flag one."

Elise did as she was told, a cold fear gripping her. The warm sunlight was a welcome shock after the cold lab, but it brought no comfort.

A yellow taxi pulled over, and Shane smiled at the driver. "Thanks, buddy. Can't carry her much further."

The man looked questioning, but said nothing as Elise tried to smile as well. "Where to?"

"Uh," Shane stammered. "The Motel 6."

"There is no Motel 6," the man returned flatly.

"Oh. Must have the wrong name then." Shane snapped his fingers, "What's it called?"

"Motel Placid?" the man offered. "It's on Eighth, just outside town."

"That's it," Shane smiled again. "Thanks."

The man shrugged and pulled into traffic.

Shane's pleasant expression dropped quickly as he turned to stare out the window. He took several deep breaths and closed his eyes.

"Shane?" Elise asked quietly, trying to fight the rising panic. "What happened?"

He swallowed hard and finally turned to look at her. "Nothing," he said, but his eyes betrayed him.

"Jesse?" she asked worriedly, her heart catching in her throat.

Ignored her question, Shane picked up her arm to survey the bloody wounds on her wrist. "What happened here?"

Elise's eyes filled with tears at the memory. "The bracelets... Jesse took them off." She looked up sharply. "What was he doing?"

But Shane looked overcome. Shaking his head, he closed his eyes again.

Something terrible had happened. Jesse had put those bracelets on himself. Why?

Elise felt her mind slipping back toward unconsciousness, pressed by a tremendous weight of sorrow. Leaning against the door of the taxi, she felt a wet tear slide down her face.

The pain in her wrists didn't register; the agony in her soul was beyond bearing.

Please, please, her mind pleaded. Please let her brother make it.

He knew what he was doing, she reminded herself. He knew what he was doing, and she had to trust him.

* * * *

"It's not possible," Agent Kerry breathed. "I can't believe it."

"Believe it," Stewart said roughly. "They just killed this man with no trial, nothing. I doubt anyone was even notified."

"You're sure he was Alexander Mathis?"

Stewart nodded. "Liz, this project is illegal. I'm going to bring it down."

She blinked, trying to digest all her boss and friend had just told her. His tale fit alarmingly into place with events, and she couldn't deny the confirmation that what he said was indeed truth. But he was talking about a major conspiracy like it could be brought down easily. "How do you intend to do that?"

He motioned around him. "This place has all the evidence we could ever need, I can't believe no one has found it."

She stared at him. "Found it? Alan! The FBI is working *with* this project! We're guarding it!"

"We need to expose this." His gaze was intense, and she knew there was no persuading him otherwise.

"Okay," she whispered again, reminding herself to keep quiet. "But you need to get out of here now. They will find out any minute, and when they come looking…"

"Shhh!" he hushed her, listening.

They were hiding in a dark room filled with filing cabinets, and rapid footsteps pounded from the hallway outside.

"I'm going to take some pictures," he stated matter-of-factly, pulling his cell phone out of his pocket.

Liz exchanged glances with him. He was not to be stopped. "Fine. But I'm coming with you. You'll never make it on your own."

He looked like he was going to argue, but didn't. "We need photos of the body. You know this place better than I."

Agent Kerry nodded, and she drew her gun. "Follow me."

Chapter 45

When Elise awoke on the soft bed, she was momentarily disoriented. Time, place, events … she couldn't remember what happened.

But with the next breath, the memories all came flooding back.

She must have passed out in the taxi. Jerking upright, she instantly regretted the action.

Tiny pricks of light clouded her vision, and she almost passed out again.

When she managed to gather herself, she glanced around the dark hotel room. The sun was setting outside, and she wondered how much time had passed.

Her heart stopped. Where was Jesse? He should have met them by now.

Shane was sitting at the small table by the TV set, his head down.

Elise swallowed, trying to moisten her throat to speak. "Shane," she croaked at first, trying again when he didn't budge. "Shane!"

Still no response. Elise dragged herself off the bed and stumbled over to him. Her muscles ached, but they seemed to work again.

"Shane," she repeated, shaking his shoulders. "Wake up."

He stirred slowly, picking up his head enough to look at her. "Sit down," he said quietly.

She lifted her chin in rebellion, "No. I'm fine. Just tell me what happened."

He eyed her in silence, defeat clear in his face. Finally he spoke, "You should sit down."

"Is he dead?" she blurted.

Shane didn't answer, he only looked away.

Every ounce of blood drained from Elise's face, and she felt her body sway backwards. No. This wasn't possible. He said he knew how to get the cure. That he was going to fix this.

It was her fault. She could have avoided this.

Her chest forgot how to contract. Breathing no longer was possible. What was he doing? He said he knew what he was doing.

"What happened?" she whispered, numbly sitting down on the bed behind her.

Shane shook his head, "I don't know. He said he was going on to build the cure. He told me to go in three hours later and get you out."

"And he was supposed to meet us later?"

"Yes."

"He said he knew what he was doing," Elise said quietly, as if to rationalize her faith in him. "Are you sure?"

"Elise," Shane looked at her firmly. "I saw him myself. They had him hooked up to these monitors. There was no heartbeat, no pulse. And they were talking about it."

Her weakened body began to tremble. It couldn't be true.

She felt like the wind had been knocked out of her. Without Jesse, there was no hope of building the cure. The pain was relieved with the bracelets gone, but she could still feel the dizziness, the sickness creeping over all of her.

Why would he do this? He had to know what would happen when he put those bracelets on. He had to have a plan.

But if he was dead, it was over.

Where was her father? Watching from a distance? Anger filled her. Had his precious science been wrong?

"Where's Carbon?" Elise asked in desperation. She would know what to do.

Shane stared off into the distance. "I don't know. I haven't been able to reach her. Not even on the cell phone."

Elise couldn't process it. This was the worst case scenario, she hadn't considered it an option. Jesse had been so confident.

"We shouldn't stay here long," Shane stated matter-of-factly. "Rayford will come looking."

Like it mattered. Die now or later, it wasn't much of a choice. What was the point?

"No," she answered, surprised at her own resistance. "No, we stay here. Jesse said to wait."

"He's *dead*," Shane said angrily. "We need to get out of here."

"You leave," she retorted, her eyes flashing. "I don't have anywhere to go."

Her fury only burned for a moment, and she turned away to wipe a tear off her cheek. She couldn't be healed without her brother. She didn't want to. He was the only family she really had.

She heard the chair slide back as Shane stood. "I need some fresh air. I'll be back."

As the door shut, Elise collapsed on the bed. Curling into the fetal position, she hugged her knees tightly.

Jesse was dead.

Nothing left to hope for, Elise surrendered to the sorrow and wept bitterly.

* * * *

Agent Kerry released a slow breath. This was truly unbelievable.

A lie this big would cause major waves when it crumbled. Which meant they were in serious danger.

"Stewart," she whispered urgently. "We need to get out of here. Now."

He was finishing taking photos of the body they had pulled out of a cold box in the facility's mortuary. "Ok," he returned his phone to his pocket.

Liz took a final look at the motionless form on the metal shelf. They had moved him quickly into the morgue and would be stepping up efforts to find the girl.

How on earth did this project exist without rules or oversight? Who knew about it? This was calculated murder at best, in the middle of a government experiment. Not the middle, at the heart of it all.

She shuddered with the thought. It was sick.

Stewart pushed the tray back into the cold box and closed the door quietly. The look on his face was of utter disgust, and he shook his head as he walked past her. "You're right, they'll probably be back soon."

But when he tried the lock, it didn't budge. Instead the door opened, swinging in from the other side. Dr. Rayford met them with a stern glare. "Agents? Am I interrupting?"

"No," Stewart replied, hand resting over his sidearm. Rayford flicked a glance down and back up to show he wasn't worried.

"Do tell," the scientist pressed, three guards standing behind him.

"You first," the agent jutted his chin in defiance and fixed unflinching eyes on Rayford. "Dead body, no trial... Care to fill in the blanks?"

"I see. Let's put it this way. Interfering with a federal investigation, willfully disobeying orders... I think I understand now."

Liz held her tongue. She could think of nothing to say that would help their situation.

"I'll be back, *agent*," Dr. Rayford stressed. "You would do well to remember your place."

With that, the scientist stormed out the open door and a guard swung it shut in his wake.

Stewart launched himself to intercept the handle before the lock clicked and whirred into a permanent position. Too late, he brought himself upright and gave the metal grip several violent jerks.

"Boss," Liz tried to calm him. "Let it go. We'll find another way."

His morose expression dripped water onto her small flame of hope.

"There is only one other way out of this, Liz."

She had never before seen him admit defeat. "There's a lot we don't know. Don't be stupid."

Stewart's lack of response was worse than any rebuttal. He ran a troubled hand through his hair. "I guess we have twenty minutes to find a miraculous escape."

"Let's not waste it," Liz tossed him a severe look.

Holding her gaze a second longer, he shook his head and went to work.

Twenty minutes was not a lot of time. Liz prayed it would be enough.

Chapter 46

Shane Lawson was walking beside the road in broad daylight.

And he didn't really care.

Sure, some part of him cautioned against it, especially when a police cruiser passed his position. How had he come so far? Three weeks ago and that ignorant man driving by would have been him.

Happy, carefree and ignorant.

He had believed Jesse could pull it off. Worse, the man had become a friend. He fought the pain with hate. This wasn't *his* fault. Now he was stuck alone, still hunted by Rayford and the FBI.

Oh, yeah. He got the girl, but she was dying. His throat closed with emotion seeing her so distraught over her brother's news. She knew what it meant.

Part of him had wanted to comfort her, to hold her close. But he couldn't bring himself to. He was already attached enough.

How could this get any worse?

Kicking a stone off the sidewalk, he swallowed his emotion as best he could. If there was a positive side here, he was struggling to find it.

Maybe he shouldn't go back. Just keep walking.

Find a place somewhere, live as a hermit. At least he wouldn't be in prison.

He didn't want to leave Elise all alone to die, but if she wouldn't leave there was nothing he could do.

* * * *

"No way out, no cell phone signal," Stewart sighed deeply. "We don't have many options."

"Not after you confronted him like that." Liz had been shocked that he would act so foolishly, and was becoming increasingly angry.

"Someone needed to," Stewart said solemnly. "When they come back, they're going to take us somewhere, and I doubt they want a scene."

"Too late for that. Why did you tell Rayford we were onto him?" Her bos could be impetuous, but that was just stupid. "We could have talked our w out."

"Unlikely," Her boss dismissed her, scrutinizing the room for a way out.

She resigned herself to likewise, swallowing the many comments that came to mind. Arguing wouldn't help them now.

"Liz," Stewart pointed upwards. "The vents."

Glancing up at the vent cover by the ceiling, she sighed. "Even if I stopped eating completely, I could never fit in there. And there's no hope for you."

He eyed it further, but moved on in his search. "Help me with this," he leaned against a heavy desk and grunted. "We can at least buy some time by keeping them out."

She saw his point, but as they heaved against the massive desk, she was sure everyone in the city heard the horrendous screeching of metal against the tile floor.

"What was that?" Stewart stopped suddenly, perking up like he was hearing something.

"That," Liz puffed, leaning against the now stopped desk after the exertion, "was an awful noise."

"No, shh." He held up a finger to silence her.

Liz froze, listening. "I don't hear anything."

She strained her ears against the silence, neither one of them moving. Suddenly a thunderous boom exploded, fiery beams of light searing through the cracks of the cold chamber.

Bomb! Liz's mind screamed in warning, and she jumped under the desk, shielding her face and upper torso.

Her vision was temporarily blinded by the brightness, and her ears rang from the sound. She heard the muffled noise of something sliding, a hissing, and a metallic ring. Drawing her service pistol, she prayed for her sight to return quickly.

All fell silent again, and her eyes began to focus on dim outlines. The underside of the desk, then the wall. With a deep breath, she crawled out from her hiding place and stole a glance around the desk.

"Liz?" Stewart called quietly. He had jumped to the side, and was struggling to stand by the wall.

"Over here," she returned, blinking as she began to see in color again.

Footsteps pounded outside, drawing closer.

"What happened?" she asked urgently, still holding her gun at the ready. Muffled voices could be heard by the door.

"I don't know," Stewart ran his hands over his eyes, clearly suffering similar effects. "But we're about to have company."

Liz fingered the smooth steel in her hand. If these were fellow agents, she couldn't justify shooting. Cursing under her breath, she returned the gun to its holster.

The door swung open, two armed guards entering first. Glaring at the two men, Liz wasn't the least bit surprised when Dr. Rayford marched in with several other white-coats.

"Where is she?" he snapped, eyes flashing.

"Who?" Stewart asked innocently, earning him a kick in the stomach from one of the guards. He doubled over, but the other guard restrained Liz from interfering.

"Hey!" she yelled. "What's going on here? He's FBI! Back off!"

"We know who he is, agent. It's quite suspicious that you would be consorting with him, we'll have our own questions for you. Take him," the scientist motioned to another two guards that came through the door.

"This isn't legal!" Liz shouted.

Agent Stewart stood stiffly as he was handcuffed. When he was led past Dr. Rayford, he jerked back enough to meet the scientist eye to eye. "You will pay for this."

Rayford met Stewart's hard gaze without flinching, and Liz found herself shrinking back from the evil malevolence emanating from the man's mild expression.

A nod to the two guards was sufficient for them to pull Stewart through the door.

"Where are you taking him?" Liz demanded, determined not to let the wild beating of her heart have control.

"Elizabeth Kerry, isn't it?" Dr. Rayford faced her now, ignoring her question.

"What are you doing here?" She fought to keep her knees strong, wondering how things had gone so wrong.

He broke into a small smile, and Liz was astonished at the transformation. Wicked to friendly. "I should better ask you what *you* are doing back here. This is *my* lab. You are only assigned to guard the front half of this building, and track down the man you allowed in."

Two more guards stepped towards her as Rayford beckoned them with his hand.

Liz refused to shrink back, but it was another battle. Concern for her boss consumed her thoughts. They would probably torture and kill him. And her. Looking into Rayford's maniacal eyes, she realized he would stop at nothing to get what he wanted.

Stewart said he had figured everything out, but he hadn't told her much yet. Even if they tried to get information out of her, it wouldn't work.

Gathering her courage, she stepped forward. "I want to speak to Agent Hawkins."

But Dr. Rayford only seemed amused. He regarded her as if deciding how much she knew, how dangerous she was. She returned his gaze brazenly, though inside she was melting with the knowledge that she might not make it out alive.

"You're welcome to speak to Hawkins," Rayford seemed to reach a decision. "Guards, put her in a holding room."

They moved to grab her, but she spun out of their reach. Gun drawn, she aimed it at Rayford's face. "Don't touch me."

Each of the guards had their hands covering their own weapons, but she didn't have her reputation for nothing.

"On the ground," she snapped. "Now!"

"Don't do it!" Rayford commanded them. "She won't shoot."

He smirked at her smugly. She wondered where he got his confidence from, considering that he had just kidnapped her partner and was likely going to kill her. The trigger felt light under her finger.

"Leave her here. She doesn't know anything." With a final glance, Rayford spun around and headed out the door. The guards followed, eyes watching her closely.

The door clicked shut, many locks again sliding into place.

Liz cursed and slid to the floor, overwhelmed. She had to get out of here. She had to find Stewart before it was too late.

Chapter 47

FBI Agent Elizabeth Kerry paced the floor, desperate for a way out of this room. Five minutes since Rayford left. Seven minutes since they took Agent Stewart. He was onto something, and now the world might never know.

She stilled her breath, listening. A knocking sound was coming from somewhere. The room was dim, but as she looked past the empty examining table, all she saw was the row of doors into the freezer. Why did a lab need its own morgue?

Chilled again, she turned back toward the wall she was feeling out for an exit.

Bang!

Liz spun around at the loud noise, stumbling backwards as a screeching noise followed and another light blinded her.

Blinking against the darkness, she struggled to see.

A glowing figure resolved in her vision, and she fell completely backwards. She was hallucinating. She had lost it.

Closing her eyes, she reached helplessly for sanity. For reality.

But when she opened them again, the figure was leaning over her offering a hand to help her up.

Liz had never experienced such terror in her whole life. This was the man who had been dead. Whose body they had just taken pictures of.

His blue eyes seemed to be fire, his skin glowing a strange hue. And he was smiling.

"It's okay, Agent Kerry. I know who you are, and I'll get you out of here. Come with me."

* * * *

"Dr. Rayford," a voice boomed, and the distinguished doctor spun around.

He nearly dropped to the floor in shock. Dr. Summers had been standing behind him, but a thud indicated that she had passed out.

"What...?" he whispered in disbelief, eyes wide. No words, no thoughts would come to him.

Alexander Mathis stood before him, blue eyes blazing in unnatural fury. "You made a mistake, doctor."

He held out his hands, and Rayford's eyes fell to the fresh wounds circling both wrists. "It's over, Rayford. The thing you feared most will be your undoing. Irene isn't yours anymore. I could destroy you now, but Dad doesn't work like that."

Dr. Rayford remained speechless. This man was dead. Completely dead. For hours.

"I left a sample of my blood in your lab. Run some tests, figure out the science. My remedy will undo everything you have done. Far from proving your theories, Irene will be the one to expose you and your lies.

"I will be back to finish this work, but while you wait, let me offer a piece of advice." The blond man leaned close, his face glowering. "Stay away from my sister."

He lingered a minute before backing away. With his next step, Alex turned and walked through the wall.

Dr. Rayford was fighting a losing battle to maintain his composure. Clutching his chest, he fell back against the wall and slid down to the floor.

Impossible. This was impossible.

* * * *

"Where are you going, stranger?"

Shane spun around, prepared for a fight. A man was behind him on the sidewalk, motioning if they could walk together.

Blinking, Shane wondered what cruel twist of events caused this man to come alongside him. He looked like a businessman, wearing a black suit with a professional looking blue tie. The tie reflected his eye color, and his blonde hair was cropped short. He could've been Jesse's twin, but something was definitely different about him.

That and Jesse was dead.

"What can I do for you?" Shane asked curtly. If this was some trick of Rayford's, he wanted no part of it.

The man's expression was placid; a far cry from his late friend's outgoing nature. "May I walk beside you for a while?"

Shane released a heavy sigh, "Fine." Not in a conversational mood, he turned and headed down the sidewalk.

Cars flew past them, the busy four-lane road never slowing down.

"Nice day for a walk," the man remarked.

Shane said nothing. No, it was a horrible day for anything.

The man let the silence stretch on for a few minutes, but apparently couldn't take it anymore. "Are you headed home?"

As if. "Look, what do you want?" Shane stopped abruptly and glared at the man. He really did look strikingly like Jesse.

"Maybe we can help each other," the man offered.

"Doubt it," Shane muttered. "Just answer my question."

The man surveyed him pensively, and Shane couldn't meet his gaze. Was he going crazy? It was unbelievable how much this guy resembled Jesse.

"I think you should turn around," the man said. He reached a hand into his coat pocket, and Shane was instantly wary. "No gun," the man laughed. "Look," he held out a syringe filled with red liquid. "It's finished. Shane, I built the remedy."

Shane had no response. He looked up from the vial to the man's face. This wasn't possible.

"I changed my appearance a little," the man said matter-of-factly, replacing the syringe into his pocket. "But it's still me. Look," he rolled back his jacket sleeves, and Shane saw red blood that had already seeped through the white shirt underneath. Each wrist had a ring around it, exactly like the marks Elise bore.

No way. Shane shook his head in disbelief. "Jesse's dead. I saw the body."

The man cocked his head and gave him a strange expression. "Didn't you listen to the lectures by my dad? The ones from Dr. Batiste? They said all this had to happen. It was the only way to remedy the situation."

Shane couldn't comprehend what was being insinuated. That Jesse was dead, and was now not dead? His ears picked up a distant whining, and he recognized the sound immediately.

"The only way to overcome the nanites in Elise is to kill the cells so they let go, and then Carbon's signal can destroy them. But Elise's cells cannot link with Carbon until the nanites are destroyed. Catch twenty-two. Unless..." the man grinned, and Shane couldn't help recognizing the mischievous twinkle in his eyes. "Unless someone with a link to Carbon and compatible DNA introduces the nanites into his own body. Instead of simply destroying the nanites outright, Carbon stopped sending any data, fooling the nanites into attaching to all of the cells. Without the stabilizing link to Carbon, the cells – and the organism – began to die. Rayford thought the nanites were working, that they could overwrite the coding and change the system like he did with Elise."

Carbon had pulled up alongside them at an idle. Jesse paused in his explanation to open the door and hop inside.

"Hello, Shane," she greeted him.

"Hey," he replied meekly, lost in thought and astonishment. But he climbed in as well, glad to see the car and overwhelmed with the reality that Jesse's story was true.

"Dr. Rayford was wrong," Jesse gave him a pointed look as Carbon pulled out with a u-turn. "My DNA is resistant to his nanites, even though they firmly attached and acted as a poison. My cells ceased functioning, for all medical purposes I was dead. But inside my body, Carbon reactivated the link. She is highly complex, far more than Rayford's computer controlled nanites, and she observed exactly how the nanites worked. My DNA remained uncorrupted even though the cells died. She 'restarted', if you will the replication process. This time, however, she included codes that could defeat and neutralize any nanites."

Shane could feel his heart beating faster. "Okay," he didn't completely follow, but got the gist of it. "So...?"

"So... my DNA now contains the information necessary to destroy the nanites in Elise. Because my cells died rather than submit to the nanites' altered code, they allowed Carbon to reactivate them and with her help, to fight against the nanites. My blood now provides the template for Elise's body to begin fighting off the nanites. They've already died to the nanites effects, and they will show Elise's how to do the same. To cut them off, so to speak. Through this, Carbon can restore the signal network in Elise. Not to what it was, because she has lost the conscious ability to independently manipulate the higher functions. But through the link to Carbon, she can access an unlimited number of possibilities that my dad and I can program."

Shane missed most of that, but he didn't care. Jesse was alive. "Why couldn't you tell me all this *before* I thought you were dead?"

"I couldn't risk Rayford figuring out what I was up to. My plan depended on his ignorance. He played right into my hands."

They pulled into the motel parking lot, and Shane was at a loss for words.

Jesse patted his shoulder before stepping out. "I said I knew what I was doing."

* * * *

Elise hugged herself tightly. Her body was freezing cold, yet burning hot. Nothing she did would relieve the pain. She had already cried through the agony, but she had no more tears. It was evident at this point that Shane wasn't coming back, and it seemed her destiny to die alone in this room.

Honestly, she didn't care. She would do anything to make it stop. To make the torment stop.

When she heard the specific noises of Carbon's engine and then Jesse's voice, she was convinced she had lost it. Her eyes were dimming, and she couldn't tell if they were open or shut. She couldn't see anything.

Something warm touched her shoulder, and she recoiled.

"*Elise*," a voice whispered. She fought to open her eyes, but all she saw were faint shadows.

Maybe there was a prick in her arm, but maybe it was just another spark of pain.

"Elise," the voice said, clearer this time. "It's Jesse. Can you hear me?"

Again she tried to see, and this time a figure emerged from the dark surroundings. She blinked several times, the ache in her head weighing down her thoughts. The man's face above her looked like Jesse. Less hair, but the same face.

"Jesse?" Her speech was slurred.

"Shh," he soothed. "Just rest. I've given you the remedy. It will take some time, but that's okay. Just rest for now. Your body is already beginning to heal."

Rest. Closing her burning eyes, Elise was willing to comply, even if this was a hallucination.

"I have to go with Carbon. We have to get to Dad quickly, to give him this information. You won't see me again for a while, but in a few days I will reactivate the link with Carbon. I can't do it from here, that's why I have to leave."

Elise tried to hang on to his words, but her mind was spent. Her body was spent.

Slipping into a black sleep, Elise hung on to one word.

Rest.

Chapter 48

Elise cracked one eye open, reluctant to leave her blissful state of sleep. She surveyed the room, squinting against the sunlight streaming in through two large glass windows.

Tucked between warm sheets, Elise merely closed her eye again. This wasn't the motel room, it was much nicer. Jesse must have moved them.

Stretching, she rolled over and opened both eyes. Her body no longer ached. In fact, she felt better than she had since Rayford's Colorado house. She even stretched out her toes and fingers, delighted to find all soreness and fatigue gone.

How long had she slept?

Sliding her legs to the edge of the bed, she sat up with a yawn and another generous stretch. There was a note on her bed-stand, and she deduced that she was now in a hotel by the logo on the pad of paper. The note was from Shane, and he said to call him when she was awake.

So he hadn't left.

She tried to remember what Jesse had told her, but she couldn't recall anything. Only that she had been commanded to rest, and that he had given her the remedy.

With a smile, she rejoiced that he was alive. Shane must have been tricked by Rayford.

On the floor was her suitcase from Mrs. Allen, and after enjoying a long shower, Elise was grateful for the clean clothes and overall feeling of freshness.

The preceding day seemed like a distant memory.

Flipping open her cell phone, she opted to text Shane instead.

Awake. Where r u?

She also sent Carbon a quick message, surprised when there was no instant response.

Shane replied quickly.

In lobby, 1st floor. U feel good enough to come down?

Elise responded that she was on her way, still surprised that Carbon hadn't responded.

Walking out into the hallway, she shuddered at the memory of Rayford's controlling her like a puppet. How grateful she was to walk on her own, where she wanted, and without pain.

In the elevator, she couldn't help grinning. She felt like a new person, inside and out. She was free. And no longer dying. Her whole life was in front of her.

Several other people joined her in the elevator, giving her space like she was an alien specimen. But she didn't even care, she was so overjoyed.

Shane was easy to find, sitting in a loveseat reading the newspaper.

"Hey," she greeted him with a smile. The lightness of her tone surprised even her.

He looked up from the paper and set it aside. Surveying her quietly for a moment, he finally stood with a smile. "You look much better. Are you hungry?"

A brief investigation turned up that she was indeed starving. But the joy of living overcame her. She bounded over and wrapped him in an exuberant hug, standing on her tiptoes. She squeezed him tightly, the amazement of it all exploding. "Thank you," she said, unable to suppress the smile that now covered her face. She broke into a laugh, "I'm not going to die."

Tears blurred her vision, but they had nothing to do with sorrow. It was a revelation. The sickness in her body was gone, the overshadowing aura of death dissipated.

"No, you're not going to die," Shane laughed gently, returning her hug. "Jesse did it. That crazy brother of yours…"

Elise wiped the tears from her eyes, joy still exploding within. She felt like she was about to burst. Not today, no dying today. No more being Rayford's slave.

"Come on," Shane guided her out of the room. "Jesse said to feed you when you woke up. You've been out for thirty-six hours, you know?"

She had no idea, but neither did she care. Elise followed him out of the lobby. They were in a city, but it was a lot smaller than Seattle. "Where are we?" she asked, basking in the sun's light, in the cool breeze on her face.

"Elise," Shane caught her arm before she stepped in front of traffic, pointing to the crosswalk. "It's not time to cross just yet."

She admittedly wasn't paying any attention; she felt like she was walking on clouds.

Shane looked at her like she was crazy. "You sure you're okay?"

"Positive," she swallowed her grin somewhat, but it wasn't effective.

He just shook his head. "Can't have you hit by a car after all of that. Come on, the restaurant is right here."

True to his word, the little diner was nestled in a shopping center directly across from the hotel. After ordering a generous meal, Elise leaned back in the booth, satisfied.

"Where's Jesse?" she asked. He was probably off with Carbon somewhere.

Shane folded his hands on the table. "He told you. You don't remember?"

"No, I don't remember much of anything."

"Hm. Why don't you eat something first, and then I'll bring you up to speed?"

Elise shrugged, relief still running through her veins. When was the last time she felt so alive?

The food came, and she ate voraciously. Shane had explained that the remedy had been working in her body while she slept, repairing damage. The use of energy, combined with the length of time she had been unconscious, left her more than hungry. He advised her to eat slowly, though she could hardly imagine being sick again.

Their waitress, an older woman with a kind smile, said nothing but observed her young guest's appetite with raised eyebrows.

When she had left, Elise sighed contentedly, her stomach full.

"I'll start with the good news," Shane said.

"Sounds good to me," Elise responded, slightly worried at the prospect of bad news. But what could possibly outweigh the fact that she had been healed?

"Jesse and Carbon agreed, the remedy works. Your body is healing, though the complete process apparently takes some time. Jesse destroyed the bracelets, so you won't have to worry about them again. Also, Rayford seems to be on the retreat for now, or at least too scared to come after you."

Elise lifted an eyebrow. "Scared? What did Jesse do?"

Shane studied his hands, as if the answer was difficult to come up with. "Uh, quite a bit actually. It's a little difficult to believe. Remember when I told you he was dead? That I saw him?"

She nodded.

"Well, he was dead. That was part of his plan. Something to do with building the cure inside his body. Because of the link to Carbon, he kind of came back to life." Shane looked like he was still unsure even as he told her the story, "He had the marks on his wrists from the bracelets, and he sure seemed like Jesse. And Carbon was with him. They brought us here, a small city about a hundred miles out from Seattle."

Elise wasn't sure she had heard him correctly. "He was dead? Jesse?"

"Yeah, he explained the whole thing to me. It was complicated, so I'm sorry if I don't tell it right. But important things..." Shane waved his hand in the air. "The cure worked, though Jesse left with Carbon to go back to your father. He said they had to hurry. He needed to reconfigure parts of Carbon so that he can initiate your link with her. In a few days, you should be able to tell."

"What?" Elise blinked. "How?"

"I have no idea," Shane said apologetically. "But once this link is in place, she can communicate with your cells and even your mind. This is what Jesse told me."

Elise was struggling to put it all together. "So we're just waiting for ... for what?"

"The link to be activated. He said not to leave here until that happened."

"Oh." She sat back, trying to comprehend everything.

"After the link is active, Rayford will be able to find your location. Jesse said he won't be able to take over again, but the authorities will know where we are." Shane narrowed his eyes before finishing. "It will be a while until Jesse comes back, he said he needed to stay with his father. He also said that if we get arrested, not to be worried, that when the right time came, they would break us out."

Elise tried to respond, but the syllables that came out weren't intelligible. Her thoughts were jumbled. "Prison?" she finally managed.

With a solemn nod, Shane met her eyes. "You'll probably get some form of juvy, some rehabilitation. Jesse said to trust him. This is the part of the plan to set everything right."

Trying to mask the rising fear, Elise broke his gaze. Her happiness over being alive was suddenly drained. She had survived to go to prison?

"Elise," Shane leaned forward. "Your brother *died* for you. I'm having trouble accepting all of this, but I saw it myself. He knows what he's doing. Whatever happens, I believe him."

Elise wished Jesse could've been here to say everything in person. Why couldn't she have gone with him to her father?

The disappointment was a heavy weight, and Elise was glad she had eaten before. Shane left to pay the bill, and when he returned, Elise had not managed to recover a great deal.

"Why didn't Carbon respond to my text?" she asked.

Shane blinked. "What?"

Elise repeated her question, and he nodded in understanding.

"Communication silence. Until the link is active, Jesse said it was too risky. We have to lay low until then."

Upon her blank expression, Shane reached into his pocket and handed her a folded piece of paper. "He left a letter for you."

It was typed, but Jesse had signed his name and drawn a large smiley face.

Shane slid back into the seat opposite her. "Read. It will help explain things."

Dropping her gaze to the paper, Elise's pulse quickened.   She scanned the page quickly.

Irene:

I already miss you dearly, but you will soon realize why I had to leave. If I did not go back to Dad, I could not send Carbon to help. You know her as a protector, and that she is. She also stabilizes your DNA, and if necessary, provides you with the complex instructions and ability to operate a vast number of higher functions. My DNA allowed a direct connection so she can override and begin to repair the damage done in your body by the SynMOs. They will eventually be destroyed and their effects nullified. The old has gone, the new has come!

She can also communicate with you, so don't be too surprised. But remember that right now, you have many SynMO-infected cells, and Rayford can communicate with you in the same way. You have to learn to differentiate between the two.

Most times you will think they are your own thoughts. Sometimes they will be, lots of times they won't be. You will know when the link is activated. Try to remember what Carbon's voice sounds like so you can pick it out in the days to come.

Your thoughts will gradually learn to align with Carbon's. Your body – and your mind – will overall feel better as you listen to her instructions and learn from her instead of Rayford or your SynMO infected cells. It's not easy, especially at first. Following Carbon's instructions and disobeying Rayford's will make you feel violently ill, it will seem like your body is at war and your mind is a battlefield.

As I said, the link had to be established with Carbon, but that couldn't happen until I made the remedy and administered it to you.

These higher functions are for an express purpose. Your life is not useless! When you and Carbon are a team, you'll get to find out why you have these abilities, what exactly they are, and how you should use them. And believe me, it will be fun.

Missing you already but excited about the incredible new adventure! Remember Dad and I are always in communication with Carbon, so it's like we'll never truly be apart again.

Love you!

Jesse

Shane interrupted before the download could sink in. "We should prepare now for when the link is activated. We won't have much time, but there's a chance we can slip away and avoid being caught."

She looked up at him. "How? If they can locate me through the link, they'll catch up eventually."

He shrugged. "True. But the less time spent in prison, the better. I'm game to try running as long as it works."

Elise stared at him. Living on the run was not an experience she enjoyed. But he had a point, prison was not where she wanted to be either.

"Why are you doing this?" she asked. "They can track me, not you. If you disappear now, they'll probably never find you."

Shane didn't respond right away, staring out the window instead.

"Elise," he finally spoke. "I just watched a man come back from the dead." An incredulous smile crossed his face. "He was crazy enough to do anything to save his sister, and works with a talking car. I have nothing to go back to. I intend to find out what's going on, and do everything I can to stop Dr. Rayford and the people he works with. And..." but he trailed off.

Elise didn't know what to say. At this moment, she couldn't think very far into the future.

"I made a promise to your brother," Shane said, standing. "Now let's go. We need to walk or something. I've been sitting around for a day and a half."

He offered a hand, and she stared at it. What promise? But as the feeling of life and wholeness washed over her again, she closed her eyes and took a deep breath.

One step at a time, never looking too far ahead, never accepting vain regrets. Her grandmother's catchy song echoed in her mind.

Looking up at Shane, she accepted his hand with a small smile.

Chapter 49

"Hang on," Shane breathed, throwing the little car into a higher gear. They had jacked the tiny Geo from a gas station when its owner had stepped out.

Elise felt guilty, but they had no choice. The police were hot on their tail.

Only yesterday had the link with Carbon been restored, and it was becoming evident that it wouldn't be long until they were captured. Barring an extreme miracle, there was no way they could keep this up.

She could feel the link. It was odd, another conscience gently brushing against hers. She recognized Carbon's voice and welcomed the reassurance it gave her. She couldn't hear anything clearly, but Jesse's letter said as she learned to focus on the link more and more, she would be able to directly communicate with Carbon in her mind.

And that her 'higher functions' could be activated as the strength of the link grew. It was exciting, but right now her thoughts were diverted by the chase at hand.

Shane threw the little car around a corner before trying to drive calmly and blend with traffic.

"I think we lost them," he said, glancing in the rearview mirror.

Elise breathed a sigh of relief, but it was short-lived.

Sirens erupted behind them, the flashing lights bringing fear. If they kept this up, she worried that people would end up dead. Likely both she and Shane.

Another police car was coming towards them from the other direction.

"Shane," Elise said quietly. "I think we should…"

"I know," he responded, downshifting the Geo. "It's okay."

But she could see the fear in his face, for it was mirrored in her own soul. "Jesse said to trust him." She closed her eyes, blocking out the chaotic scene outside. The Geo came to a stop in the middle of an intersection, completely blocked off by the police. "Carbon says it's okay, to surrender to them. She'll come back for us."

When she opened her eyes, Shane was studying her.

Police yelled commands from outside, some officers pointing guns at them, barricaded behind their cars.

"Okay," he said slowly. "I guess I'll see you on the other side."

She looked into his brown eyes, and they were filled with compassion. He stroked her cheek gently with his thumb, leaned forward, and kissed her.

She nearly cried from his tenderness mixed with the terror in her heart. With a reassuring smile, he opened the door of the car and got out with his hands up in surrender.

There was nothing left to do. Opening her own door, she did likewise, offering no resistance as she was handcuffed and led into a patrol car.

A single thought impressed strongly on her mind, a strange peace and yielding in her soul.

I am here.

The voice was Carbon's, but she knew that it represented more than that. Her brother and father were waiting for her, working to make sure she would see them again.

And she would see them one day, of that she was certain.

Epilogue:
2 years later, in a federal prison

"What's that you're holding?"

"Nothing," Mole said slyly as he drew the object secretively toward his body, obscuring it from Shane's view. "Nothing you'd be interested in, anyway."

Shane shrugged and started walking away. "Well, I guess you're probably right. I'll just go back and…" he spun around sharply and grabbed the object – though it was still clutched tightly in Mole's large grasp.

"Aha!" he exclaimed triumphantly. "Not interesting, my butt."

"Hey!" the round man protested, successfully wresting his hand and prize back from Shane's arm. But the damage was done, his secret was over.

"You know you're going to share that, right? No one ever sends me anything."

Mole snorted. "Share? With you? Pfft."

"I mean, "The Cow that Jumped the Moon"? Has a more interesting film come out lately? I can't miss it."

"Yeah, well. Like you said, no one sends you anything anyway. At least it's something besides the old reruns on that garbage TV. Seriously, if I have to watch 'The Watsons' one more time, I'm going to…"

Mole was interrupted mid-sentence by two guards who appeared at the door. Shane just shook his head and smiled at his friend.

"It's for you, Lawson. You've got a call."

Officer DeSoto gave him a half friendly expression, but the other, a new military sort only stared warily and at attention. The regular staff, for the most part, had warmed up to Lawson because of his good behavior and cooperation, some respecting his background as a cop and the uncertain circumstances of his presence here. And of course, his basically charming nature.

"Okay," Shane sighed and held out his wrists to be cuffed. Who would be calling him now? His family had cut off contact with him, except his sister who had been sneaking calls and letters until they transferred him. His parents, especially his mom, couldn't understand why he wouldn't just give up Mathis and clear his own name. His silence in their mind was evidence of guilt, and they didn't want their remaining child to be influenced by his criminal status.

It hurt, and he couldn't deny it. They had spent a year trying to get him released, trying to convince him to talk, but the emotional stress was too much, and they had given up before the beginning of his second year in incarceration. He couldn't blame them, but the sadness remained. The fact that they didn't trust him or believe his word was the worst. Except his sister Emily, of course. He smiled with the thought. Maybe she found the new number and devised a way to call. She was almost eighteen now, anyway.

Officer DeSoto opened the door to the telephone station, and the other guard pushed him in.

"At ease, soldier," Lawson gave a slight salute. The man didn't even blink. Maybe he used to be one of those fuzzy-hat wearing guards in England. No expression.

DeSoto rolled his eyes, "You have five minutes, Lawson."

"Hello?" he answered.

"Lawson, this is Carbon. Do not worry, and do not look alarmed. This call is not being recorded. I have provided an alternative conversation with your sister that is being received by the prison's system."

Shane blinked, and tried to look normal. But inside, his heart was racing. Jesse said they would come back. "Emily! Good to hear from you. How's Mom?"

"You have been allowed no contact with Elise and I know you are unaware of the specifics of her condition. She has been in several centers for rehabilitation and treatment. They are convinced she will speak, given enough time and a degree of brain-washing."

Shane smiled. That girl was one tough cookie. "And how's Dad?"

"Things are being set in motion within the government, and the time to act is now. Elise's caretakers have become more desperate, and they have decided to bring her to your holding center. I have contacted her, and she has convinced them she wants to talk to you about what happened. They have told her they will allow a private conversation, and are planning on listening in to ascertain details about Dr. Mathis."

"Well, that's good news. How about yourself?" He fumbled, distracted by Carbon's information download. Three more minutes. "How's school?"

"There is an agent working for us who will provide you with a key to the manual lock. I will remotely open any other necessary doors. You will find what you need in your food rations tonight. I will lead Elise into your cell, and you will both escape through the supply landing area."

Landing area? Lawson had no idea where he was. Everyone in this prison was flown in blind.

"Jump. I will provide everything you need to escape."

Jump? "That's great, Emily. Really great."

"That is all, Lawson. I am looking forward to seeing you again."

"Yeah, me too." He no longer needed to lie. "I miss you."

"Good-bye."

* * * *

That evening, dinner couldn't come fast enough. He worked hard to act natural around Mole, but his friend prodded him anyway.

"Hey, who was it who called you? You're all jittery and…"

"I am not!" Shane protested.

"Mm-hm. Sure, buddy."

"It's just," he paused, noting something metallic in his mashed potatoes. He slipped it under his tongue. "It was my sister again."

Mole regarded him somberly for a moment, glancing up and down. The man's chubby face was playful, but Shane knew there was real sympathy underneath. "Aw, man. You're all emotional and stuff."

Shane glared at him, noting that it was actually difficult to keep this key under his tongue and talk at the same time. He forced tears into his eyes, a much easier task given that the emotional strain was real.

He pushed his plate away and put his plastic utensil down. "Here, you can finish it. I'm not hungry."

That brought a certain light into his big friend's eyes. "Hey, man. No prob. Just take it easy. Maybe I'll even share my movie."

Nodding with a small smile, Shane tried to keep from pacing. What was Carbon going to do? When did he need to be ready? Would it really hurt the car to be more specific?

He stood and returned to his hard bed after stretching. *Don't look nervous*, he kept reminding himself.

It wasn't long before Mole had finished both plates and they had been collected. The other man was humming to himself contentedly in the other corner as Lawson fought to lay still. And then the moment finally came.

The door swung open without a sound. Mole didn't even bother turning around, reasonably expecting a guard.

Elise appeared in the doorway, her gaze flicking briefly around the room. Her eyes were shadowed by deep black circles, and her once again sandy blonde hair was shoulder length and flat. She wore a black prisoner outfit and her pale face was nothing but stoic, her expression empty. But she was there.

He jumped up, spitting the key into his hand. Carbon had said the supply landing. It had been over two years since he had seen her, and he was shocked at the transformation. She was no longer a scared little girl. Scared, maybe. But no longer a child. Even stressed and worn out, she was even more beautiful than he remembered.

Mole chose that moment to turn around, staring in shock, mouth hanging open. Elise jumped inside the cell as if receiving invisible direction, and the door swung shut.

"A guard is coming," her voice was strained, fear evident on her face.

Glancing around, Shane shoved her into the corner behind the door. "Shhh."

His cellmate looked back and forth between he and Elise in bewilderment. But understanding dawned quickly, and he rolled off like a champ.

"Like I was saying buddy, if you just stop thinking about it, it won't be so hard. And if I catch you with my movie," Mole's brown eyes bulged out of his face as he held a chubby finger in Shane's face.

He lifted his hands with a coy smile, observing the guard walk past the small window without notice. "Hey, you know me. I would never…"

"Yeah, right." The large man snorted. But the guard was now out of earshot. They had five minutes before he made another pass.

"Hey, I'm…" but Shane didn't really know what to say. He had no time, and the big guy had been a friend like no other.

Mole raised his eyebrows and looked from Shane to Elise and back. "There's no way outta here, you know. You're crazy."

"I'll say you tried to stop me," Shane offered.

Mole smiled, "Get lost, buddy. I'll hold down the fort."

"We need to go," Elise said quickly.

Shane gave his friend a final glance. His gratitude was wordless, but it was enough. The door swung open again, and he followed Elise through it.

"This way." She took off sprinting, sliding to a halt at a door with a combination of manual and digital locks. He placed the key in her outstretched hand, noting the earwig in her ear as she brushed back a strand of stray hair. The locks disengaged simultaneously, and she handed the key back to him as they slipped through and it shut again. They were in a small, dark cement corridor with an odd smell. Almost like bad sushi. Where were they?

"Carbon says there are two more doors. She will open them." Elise informed him breathlessly as she took off again.

He fell in suit, and sure enough, another heavy looking steel door opened just enough for them to squeeze through before it shut again. The next hallway was bigger, and… wetter. And something else. The sound of thunder.

But they were running without a chance to think about what was coming next. Only Carbon's instructions.

The last door was lighter looking, and while he heard the lock slide back, Elise motioned to him that it needed to be pushed on manually. It wasn't as light as it appeared, but with both of them heaving it did move enough. They didn't bother to close it; their surroundings were enough to distract anyone.

The cement continued out a few hundred feet, with solid guardrails on both sides. It was like a wide driveway that ended in nothing. But the sound of thunder was explained. Stormy skies above were darker than night, and rain fell hard, stinging his skin. But the roar was deeper. It was the ocean.

An angry, dark grey ocean with massive swells and crashing white water. And it was quite a distance beneath the ledge.

Elise shrank back, clutching the railing. It was a safe guess that she hadn't been aware of their surroundings either.

He stood between her and the ocean, breaking her stricken gaze away from the waves. "Hey," he took her face in his hands. "You can do this."

Shouts erupted from the tunnels.

She let go of the side rail and turned toward the raging water. He likewise faced the stormy seas, pulling her to himself before stepping to the edge of the cement. They had come this far. "Carbon has a plan," he said into her ear. "She said to jump."

Elise offered no resistance, but put her hand on top of his.

"We have to trust her," he whispered.

"I know," she nodded, her soft hair brushing against his face.

Shane honestly had no real desire to take the leap of faith. But as voices closed in on them, he swallowed his doubts and fears.

Closing his eyes, he pulled Elise closer and jumped.